The Composer's Legacy

Michael DeStefano

Vinny,

Wow! Where does the time go? I'm so very proud of you for your success in family and vocation. I wish you many more years to come.

Veteran of the Class of '79

Mike "D"

PAGE PUBLISHING, INC.
New York, NY

First originally published by Page Publishing, Inc. 2017

ISBN 978-1-64082-621-2 (Paperback)
ISBN 978-1-64082-623-6 (Hardcover)
ISBN 978-1-64082-622-9 (Digital)

Printed in the United States of America

To listen to the novel's soundtrack (composed by the author) or to order additional copies of this book, visit:

Website: www.LibrettiPress.com/books
Twitter: @AuthorComposer

Edited by: Melissa Manes
                www.scriptionis.com

Cover design: Joshua Jadon
                www.joshuajadon.com

For my parents, Donna and Joe

Chapter One

The season's opening concerts were ambitious even for the gifted students of the UC Davis Symphony Orchestra. The noble but lengthy *Seventh Symphony* of Anton Bruckner and the evocative *First Essay for Orchestra* of Samuel Barber kicked off the inaugural concert in elegant style. The Christmas series featured Brahms' lullaby in the guise of his *Second Symphony*, Vincenzo Bellini's *Oboe Concerto*, and the seldom-performed *Triple Concerto* of Johann Sebastian Bach. Despite the hustle and bustle of the season, the late December concert was a complete sellout, a testament to the orchestra's brilliant execution of musical repertoire. With the holidays over and the New Year well underway, rehearsals began in earnest for the upcoming spring concert series. Among the works scheduled were Bruch's *First Violin Concerto* and Beethoven's *Choral Fantasy*.

Ascending the podium was the familiar personage of the assistant dean of music, Dr. David C. Whealy. The assistant dean was a singularly recognizable figure with strong aquiline features, significant height, and closely cropped muttonchops. His salt-and-pepper hair was reminiscent of our sixth president. Always well-groomed and impeccably dressed, he commanded carte blanche in any tailor shop in San Francisco. The dashing college professor with the perceptive gray eyes was the epitome of his art—demanding, articulate, and a musical perfectionist.

The spring concert series was right around the corner and rehearsals were less than stellar. They had been making a hashing of the Bruch all afternoon and judging from their lack of concentration, they hadn't improved much for the ten-minute break he'd offered them. David regarded the open score, picked up his baton, and peered over the conductor's stand at their sullen faces.

"Okay everybody, let's try this again. Three before 175, brass only, please. And this time, let's get it right."

Nothing seemed to be working well in the horn section. The principal horn was Holly Runyon of All-State caliber. David was sure that whatever the problem was, it wasn't her. The second chair was one James Spence, a musician with an over-inflated opinion of himself. He seemed to be churning out notes with no regard for expression. Janet Phelps and Carl Somersby, both fair talents, didn't appear to be on their game today. After a stern warning for them to pay attention to each other, David raised his baton. As he gave the downbeat, he was interrupted by a nervous voice approaching the podium.

"Professor, I have a message from your office. It's marked urgent." The woman reached up to hand David a note. He regarded it with suspicion.

> *A registered letter just arrived for you in today's post. Since it's registered, you will have to go to the campus post office to sign for it. - Peggy*

The assistant dean's secretary had exceptional penmanship, but in this instance, David noticed the handwriting to be uncharacteristically sloppy.

David shook his head in disbelief as he turned to his concertmistress. "Myung-hee, run through the movement again until I get back. This shouldn't take long."

The campus post office located in the Memorial Union building was a short walk from the music building. The brief pause gave him time to rethink the movement he'd been rehearsing all afternoon.

He rounded the corner of the post office, still perturbed at the interruption. As Peggy's messy handwriting implied urgency, and since the addressee took the trouble to register the letter, it had to be important.

David signed for the registered piece of mail, thanked the clerk and scanned the return address. Then he said to no one in particular, "Who the hell is Simon Talbridge?"

It wasn't from the standard Alcott, Briggs, and Clive law firm, but the words *Attorney-at-Law* followed the name. Inside the legal-size envelope was an unusual looking piece of correspondence clipped to a brief cover letter.

Dr. David C. Whealy,

You have been named sole beneficiary to the estate of Mr. James Burton West. Further instructions will be forthcoming in accordance with the wishes of the benefactor.

Short, sweet, and to the point. The letter further instructed David to contact Mr. Talbridge's office at his earliest convenience to schedule an appointment to take care of some paperwork. He looked closely at the office location: Georgetown, Delaware. He didn't have any family on the East Coast. Well, none he knew anything about.

What kind of nonsense is this, he thought. He was quite sure this was all a mistake. His attention was drawn to the odd-looking correspondence enclosed. It was folded in thirds, the upper flap secured with burgundy wax. Stamped into it was the design of a slightly misshapen butterfly. David broke the seal, opened the letter, and marveled at the pristine handwriting that met his gaze.

Dr. David Whealy,

I write to you as a kindred spirit. I must first tell you that I didn't just pick you at random. I've studied your career with great interest and am satisfied you might appreciate my life's work. You have the education and eclectic musical taste to evaluate my output. If the work is but trivial in substance and devoid of musicality, please destroy them. My only interest was to contribute to the canon of humanity in complete anonymity.

It is, indeed, regrettable that I felt unable to set forth these works to the public during my lifetime. You will receive my recorded memoirs, in due course, which will explain my decision regarding this matter.

James Burton West

"So, you've decided to go, huh?" Carla asked.

David had known Dr. Carla Macklin since her posting to the campus of UC Davis nearly ten years now. A virtuoso harpsichordist and harpist, she was also an accomplished pianist, a professor of composition, and a conductor of master classes on the baroque era. She had an impressive array of performance awards and academic honors to her credit, but her main passion was sharing her love of music with her students.

Both musically and intellectually, she was David's peer. Most of their colleagues had learned to keep their distance when they got into a serious musical debate. These discussions usually ended in a draw, so neither of them could lay a decisive claim to the title of champion musicologist. But Carla possessed a more intuitive power of observation than David. When the vanquished party conceded the argument, they did so with *that look*.

"How did you know that?" asked David with a raised eyebrow.

A knowing smile graced her lips. "When you finally make a decision about something important, you only have one cup of coffee with no sweetener and take only one serving of cream."

"Hmm, I didn't know I was that transparent. That couldn't be the only way you knew."

"You're right, it wasn't."

"What was the other?"

"Others, my dear David. *Others*."

"All right, others. Well, are you going to share or not?"

She spun her chair around, threw her leg over the seat, draped her arms over its back, and sat down. She looked into David's eyes as though she were the cat who ate the proverbial canary.

"I've witnessed you depart for the airport on three separate occasions. Invariably, when you go on a trip requiring air travel, you take that silly stress ball with you. Outside of driving, which takes concentration and presumably both hands, it never leaves your office except those exact times when you took a plane somewhere. Today, it's missing."

His curiosity aroused, David folded his arms across his chest, crossed his legs, and leaned up against the doorjamb of the faculty lounge. "Go on," he encouraged.

"All right. When you're absent for the day, you don't care who takes over your classes and rehearsal schedules. But when you're gone for longer periods, you won't leave your students in the hands of just anyone. Since Dr. Cobbett doesn't usually extricate himself from his throne atop Valhalla to assume responsibility for any classes or rehearsals *except yours,* and his name is on the schedule for next week, it stands to reason you plan to meet up with that Delaware lawyer. Am I right?"

David wouldn't stand for anyone to read him so thoroughly. But this was Carla after all. From her, he tolerated such observations, if only to note her peculiar body language as she detailed her detective-like deductions. Seeing her reclined in her chair looking quite pleased with herself, David realized he once again succumbed to the power of her sound argument. Wordless, he turned to leave Carla alone to relish her victory.

♪

Chapter Two

David's flight to the East Coast was uneventful. He went through security at the Sacramento Airport without incident, stopped off at a food kiosk to select a freshly made sandwich, and within forty-five minutes, boarded his flight. Armed with the book on Delaware history he picked up at the library, he found his seat, stowed his carry-on, and settled in for the three-hour flight to his O'Hare connection. His next flight from the adjacent concourse took off on time.

He was on the last chapter of the informative read when the captain's voice broke through to welcome her passengers to the Baltimore area. The last time he was on the East Coast was for a conductor's conference in Maryland a few years back.

It was late afternoon when he picked up a rental car for the last leg of his trip to Georgetown. Loading his baggage in the car, he let his thoughts drift to the only real question on his mind: *What would cause a perfect stranger to bequeath his worldly possessions to someone they didn't know and from the opposite end of the country?* Unable to resolve the question, he started the car and turned on a classical music station so he could relax.

His trip took him past the Naval Academy and Maryland's state capital of Annapolis before he went over the Chesapeake Bay Bridge. Crossing the Kent Narrows Bridge, he was surprised to see so many sailing vessels berthed on such a small island. He continued to follow Route 50 until he found himself over the state line into Delaware. David went through several small towns until he finally got to Route 113, one of three main north-south thoroughfares in the state he'd read about. The Historic Georgetown Circle was less than a mile away, and so was his appointment with destiny.

Musical history was always an interest of David's. He could get into a marathon discussion over the mere mention of the Brahms-Wagner debate or of the Soviet condemnation of Prokofiev and Shostakovich in '36 and '48. But the East Coast and its colonial past were foreign to him, thus, his aerial reading assignment.

David enjoyed the chapter about Georgetown's rich history, which dated back to the time when the Delaware peninsula was part of William Penn's holdings called, the Three Lower Counties on the Delaware. The county seat of Sussex, originally established at the coastal town of Lewes, was moved to Georgetown and named after the politician George Mitchell, who championed the move. Among some of the more unusual bits of trivia regarding the town was its post-election tradition of "burying the hatchet" following statewide and county elections. The Return Day tradition traced its roots as far back as the early 1800s when the town crier would announce the election results two days after an election. It demonstrated that although rivals politically, civility and amity would be observed within the political precincts of the state.

When he reached the Georgetown circle, he couldn't help smile, observing the genuine articles he'd read about. The Sussex County Courthouse sported the elegant colonial styling typical of the period with sturdy red brick walls and a colonnade entrance. Along with other brick structures that surround the grass-laden circle, graced by a stunning three-tier black marble fountain, the atmosphere of the circle was like taking a step back into our colonial history.

David rounded the circle, exited at Route 9, and headed east, arriving at the parking lot of a charming old red brick building that matched the other historical structures. Jutting out from the corner of the building's period façade was a weathered black and gold shingle with the words "Simon Talbridge, Attorney-at-Law" spelled out in Old English font. Even the main entrance held colonial charm with its old-fashioned door knocker situated just above the lever-style handle David reached for.

The interior of the office, however, was quite modern right down to its décor. The receptionist was finishing up a call while updating some information in her files when she noticed David enter.

"May I help you?" Angela Lingo asked as she looked up from her computer terminal.

"Yes, David Whealy to see Mr. Talbridge."

"Oh yes, Mr. Whealy," she said with an unusual accent that he couldn't quite place. "You're right on schedule. I'll let Mr. Talbridge know you're here."

As receptionists go, Angela was considered one of the more pleasant ones in the office. Indeed more human than her boss, Mr. Simon Talbridge, Esquire, graduated *magna cum laude*, and a senior fellow at the Harvard Law Review. He was the personification of self-importance with the standoffish personality to match but feigned a pleasant demeanor as he greeted David.

"Good afternoon, Mr. Whealy. How was your trip?"

"It was a lengthy one, but I endured it all right."

"Have you been to the East Coast before?" Talbridge asked as he guided David through the threshold of his office.

"Once, but it was another business trip."

"I know what you mean. I've been to all fifty states, most of Europe, and several countries throughout Asia…"

The lawyer prattled on for several minutes as though David were genuinely interested. He continued his monologue, while David observed not only Talbridge's swagger but the room in general.

On the center of the desk was a timeworn brown valise with a large buckle secured by a two-inch belt. Talbridge barely acknowledged it as he adjusted his highbrow leather chair. He continued his dissertation without missing a beat. The bookcase behind him with an armada of leather-bound reference books spoke volumes about his character. The bookcase was flanked by his two *I-love-me* walls, one that sported his credentials and the other his accolades. But the bookcase was the centerpiece to his self-importance. David recognized this kind of person immediately. He'd had to deal with people like Simon Talbridge, esquire attorney-at-law all of his life. His immediate boss, the dean, fit that bill perfectly.

The current dean of the Music Department at UC Davis, Dr. William Tipton Cobbett III came into his haughty blue-blooded lifestyle the old-fashioned way; he was born into it. Descended from a long line of aristocracy that dated back to eighteenth-century Sussex, England, his family raised him in an isolated environment with all the standard trappings of his class. He was provided all the privileged pomp and ceremony accorded royalty, and he owned all the peculiar mannerisms commensurate with a man befitting his station. Cobbett possessed a deep baritone voice that lent an air of authority to his words. Despite his diminutive stature, the tonal quality of his speech was enough to command immediate attention, if not respect.

Dr. William Tipton Cobbett III, a virtuoso on the violin as well as the cello, graduated with honors from the world-renowned Eastman School of Music and was the latest recipient of the prestigious Gold Baton Award from the League of American Orchestras. It could easily be said there was little room in Cobbett's ego for further inflation, but David knew how to deflate it. He knew how to deal with people like him and Mr. Simon Talbridge.

David had had enough. "Pardon me for interrupting, but I've had an incredibly exhausting day. Can we expedite this?"

Unable to extol his self-importance, his minuscule smile evaporated, along with his civility. "Very well then," replied an indignant Simon Talbridge. "Let's get down to it, shall we?"

Drawing a packet of legal papers from the center drawer of his mammoth desk, he placed it dead center on the blotter just below the valise. Talbridge stepped back and observed David's grimace as he looked at the thickness of the packet. Both men reached for their chairs and sat. Talbridge lowered his smug face as he reached into his suit pocket for his reading glasses. David smirked at the vain man.

The insufferable attorney began, "I, James Burton West, being of sound mind and body..."

When he finished, Talbridge moved aside the documents from which he was reciting and reached for the valise to remove its contents. He spread the various sundry items across his desk. Contained in the large manila envelope was a checkbook, a savings account passbook, a medium-size portfolio with official-looking papers, another of those unusual pieces of correspondence sealed with a wax stamp, and a single photograph—a picture of West's immediate family.

Also inside, was a set of keys on a keychain similar to the kind hanging on the side of a high school janitor's belt. Each key had a blue label on it – except one. The unique key resembled a novelty item rather than a genuine key. It was larger and considerably older than all the rest, made from a heavy metal. It didn't appear to belong with the other keys. David didn't dwell on it, but he did make a mental note as he assumed possession of the articles Talbridge inserted back into the valise.

After he signed and initialed where Talbridge had highlighted in the legal package, David asked, "Is that it?"

The lawyer's expression became noticeably more confident. A slight reptilian grin played across his lips. "There's a small consultation fee that you may take care of with Miss Lingo." Sensing the role reversal in superiority at David's continued silence, the smug Talbridge added, "As executor of the will, I must inform you that Mr. West's estate tax liability remains outstanding. As the benefactor, you will have to make provisions for its restitution along with my consultation fee."

"Fine."

Talbridge looked quite pleased with himself, unprepared for what awaited him. David moved toward the door to the anteroom where Miss Lingo was no doubt waiting to update *accounts receivable* with a new check from David. As he reached for the knob, he stopped in midmotion and turned his steely-eyed gaze on the unsuspecting Talbridge.

"On second thought, I shall do nothing of the kind. Perhaps you should reacquaint yourself with that dusty old volume on the third shelf, second in from the left, called the Delaware Code. For pursuant to Title 30, Chapter 13, all such income, inheritance, and estate taxes were repealed in 1999." Pausing for effect, he added, "As any competent lawyer would have known."

At that moment, the ironic term *mouthpiece*, as applied to the tongue-tied lawyer, hit David like a dissonant chord. He left the pompous attorney standing in the middle of his office, with his mouth hanging open.

The West home was about five miles from Talbridge's office and within earshot of the Cape May-Lewes Ferry's boat whistle. The short drive would've allowed David to take in the sights, had it not been so late. He chose instead to head toward the Lord De La Warr Bed and Breakfast where he had reservations. He was looking forward to putting an end to this long day, sampling the local cuisine, and enjoying eight hours of uninterrupted shut-eye.

David secured his room and went across the street to the seafood restaurant the manager recommended. The dimly lit room made for a comfortable and relaxing atmosphere to enjoy the house specialty of stuffed blue crab and white wine. Each table had a lit candle and place settings to serve four. The tables were generously spaced to allow each guest plenty of privacy. Right now, that's what David needed. He ordered his meal and removed the latest West correspondence he'd placed in his suit jacket. He broke the seal, removed the letter, and read it.

Dr. Whealy (David),

Please forgive my forwardness. Since beginning my journals, I hadn't considered writing to an individual, so I never addressed them to anyone special. As I started to think to whom I was writing, you became my preferred recipient.

My executor was instructed to use my financial resources to pay for the home's utilities for one year after my death. The home was completely rebuilt in 1995, and with the notable exception of your impending possession, the property has been owned by our family since 1724. Unfortunately, the only remnants of my family's history I can pass along to you are my journals, a signet ring that belonged to the very first owner, and the iron key that you have by now received. It is my sincere hope that I've been able to make a proper accounting of my life and my work in the volumes you now possess.

I also wish you to know that I thoroughly enjoyed your concert this past December. If you're keeping score and are wondering how you can reciprocate a perceived kindness on my part, believe me when I say, you already have.

My warmest regards,
James Burton West

David was stunned as he read the last portion of the letter. Here was a man who David never knew existed. This man made a complete stranger his beneficiary. He also chose to follow David's career anonymously. But worst of all, this man could have introduced himself during the December concert but chose not to. Why? That lone question occupied his thoughts for the remainder of his dinner.

David continued to mull over this latest revelation as he took a short leisurely stroll back to the quaint colonial style lodging. As he headed up the stairs to his room, an object that failed to catch his eye the first time commanded his attention now.

Hung over the fireplace mantle was none other than a portrait of the bed-and-breakfast's namesake, Lord De La Warr. It was a full-size rendering of the original painting done in oils. The eyes of the man from which the State of Delaware gained its name seemed to look at David with a regal bearing. A slight but noticeable smile graced his bearded face giving him a mild countenance. Having seen similar paintings of the Founders done by Gilbert Stuart and Charles Willson Peale, he wondered who might have been the artist. With the image of Delaware's namesake fresh in his mind, he climbed the stairs to head toward his room.

David retired to bed with a child's anticipation of Christmas Day. The passing interest he felt when he first received that lawyer's letter had now blossomed into intense curiosity. He thought about what treasures awaited him in the home of his benefactor, James Burton

West. As he pondered the day's events, the effects of a satisfying meal and a tipple of wine forced his conscious mind to surrender to the exhaustion of his body and the oblivion of sleep.

Chapter Three

As David reached the end of the straight road where it bent left, he could see the Cape Cod-style home of James Burton West. It was situated just over a slight hill and on the outer side of the street's hairpin turn. The weather-beaten driveway curved up to a garage door hidden from street view where a copper-colored Jeep Wrangler was parked. David swung his rental car behind it.

He took in the magnificent view of the coastline as he exited the vehicle. The unbroken line of surf and sand was framed by the ferry's port on the north side and the Cape Henlopen lighthouse standing like a proud sentinel to the south. The fresh salt air was pungent and distinctively noticeable. The waxing sunlight beaming through the sporadic cloud formations in the foreground was a vision to behold. David took a moment to absorb nature's beauty before he turned his attention to the front door.

Locating the house key, he gained entry and followed the foyer's short hallway past the guest bathroom and into a typically furnished great room. Adjacent to the great room was the combination kitchen-dining area and on the left side of the great room was the master bedroom with connecting master bath. A second bedroom was located on the right side of the great room. At first blush, the West home seemed no different than any other home in the neighborhood.

As he stood by the kitchen island surveying the first floor's modest decor, David noticed the striking landscape pencil sketches that populated the walls. The kitchen had the obligatory combination range and microwave, refrigerator, walk-in pantry, and ceiling-size cabinets. The great room was tastefully furnished with a couch, love seat and recliner centered about the coffee table. A massive two-story bay window captured the picturesque Cape of Henlopen.

He walked into the master bedroom and found only the barest of furnishings; a full-size bed, one nightstand with a reading lamp, and a bureau. A few more pencil sketches decorated the sparsely covered walls. Neither the master nor guest bedrooms proved themselves to be out of the ordinary. But something wasn't quite right. That's when he noticed a few creature comforts were missing from this idyllic scene. The most glaring were the lack of entertainment devices. There was no television or stereo. Phone jacks were visible in the kitchen and the bedrooms, but no phones.

The only out-of-place feature was the spiral staircase with ornate handrails of semigloss walnut. It was a portent of what he would find upstairs. The design of the handrails bridged the staircase in a seamless transition with the upper landing and provided the outline for the balcony above. David moved toward the incongruent staircase and noticed a framed embroidery on the wall by the foot of the stairs that contained a familiar quote.

Style, in its finest sense, is the last acquirement of the educated mind.

- Alfred North Whitehead

He couldn't suppress his grin as he read it. Even the sign seemed to belong anywhere but here. But that opinion was about to be shattered when he ascended the stairs to the second floor.

The balcony rail was a huge semicircle making a single fluid line from the bottom of the spiral staircase to the opposite end of the room. The shine of the mahogany hardwood floor reflected any light that touched it. The walls were monopolized with bookshelves. A modestly designed walnut desk with an office chair was placed so as to allow access to the books behind it, yet offered a commanding view of the shoreline and the Cape Henlopen lighthouse through the massive bay window across from the railing. One of the pencil drawings downstairs was of this particular view. On the desk were several journals of varying design. The array of shelving units didn't just hold books, they held something more precious—vinyl records. Row after row of vinyl records. Next to them was a treasure trove of

CDs that would make any disc jockey envious. Incorporated within one of the walls was a doublewide file cabinet made of the same style walnut as the handrails, the bookshelves, and the desk. Encased in another wall were specially sized cutouts for the only entertainment device in the home, a complete stereo receiver with a multi-CD changer and a direct-drive turntable. It was then David took notice of the ceiling to see not only recessed lighting but flush mounted speakers at various locations. He did not see them downstairs, but the same ceiling speaker system was wired throughout the house. Thinking that it would be a long time before this room's treasures could thoroughly be explored and examined, David knew he would need assistance.

Turning his attention to the great bay window across from the balcony, there were two subject pencil sketches that adorned either side of the window. He recognized them as portraits of West's immediate family. They were portraits of a man and a woman on the left side of the window and two young men on the right. The others that decorated the sparsely adorned walls downstairs were of landscapes, the old Lewes lighthouse, an old-style 1940s Army Air Corps Star and Wing, and a montage of some sort.

But the crown jewel of this austere room was the black satin finished Bösendorfer Grand whose central location within the room underscored the importance placed upon it by its owner. Its lid was opened to the lowest prop setting and an opened white leather music folder was perched on the music rack. Flanking the piano on each side was a chair and an ornate hardwood music stand with a lyre head. On the left chair was a violin stand containing a full-size violin with the bow carefully preserved on the seat. Next to the other chair held up by its own stand was a cello, its bow similarly maintained. On each stand was an opened leather bound music folder, one red and one blue.

Contained within each of these three folders was the *pièce de résistance*, the promised music David was anxious to find. Each folder was filled with parts for each instrument, and the parts were written out in the same exacting hand that wrote the correspondence he initially received.

He retrieved the folders from their stands and brought them to the desk for further inspection. With the sun now providing an excellent light source through the window, David leafed through page after page of previously unknown musical gems. On the left side of each folder, he found parts to several chamber works from piano trios to sonatas and other nontraditionally titled works for the three instruments in the room. On the right side were solo and duet pieces for that particular instrument. In each case, the notes that graced the staff paper were in the same telltale hand that scribed the letters David had received. Typical of a thrifty composer, he observed that West had written violin and cello cues on all the piano parts. In all, he counted no less than six piano trios, two sonatas for each instrument, and several duets for violin and cello. But something else lay hidden at the bottom of the right-hand stack of music for the cello and the violin; he discovered the solo part for a full orchestra concerto for each instrument. The question that remained was where the autograph scores to these works could be?

As he gave that query some thought, he reached for the three journals that were situated at the upper left corner of the desk. He opened the cover of the blue leather journal on top to find the following written on the initial page.

Preface
To the Collected Works
of
James Burton West

Hmm, David thought to himself, *now we're getting somewhere.* The next page drew David into the mindset of a previously unknown artist, composer, and man of letters. Awestruck as David began to read, he lowered himself into the chair and became completely lost in the eloquent writing displayed before him.

Why?

This singular question tends to take up far too much time in the minds of philosophers and other luminaries as to what would motivate someone to create a work of art from nothing more than one's own imagination. Perhaps creating a visual or aural work of art is a way of expressing that for which words would be an injustice. Or maybe, in the case of music, give universal understanding in a language accessible to any living creature. For me, I'm able to commit to canvas a detailed rendering in pencil of any subject I see.

Musically, I must work out the argument in my head before I can commit the finished work to paper. I have here made a late start explaining myself in words, for I would have thought the music would speak for itself. If the work is to be considered successful, it should be able to stand on its own merits. But it can only do so if it is performed by gifted musicians and enjoyed by an audience with a discerning ear.

Sketching is a natural escape. But music takes a significant investment of time for me. Time to find the right muse, time to work out each musical argument, time to finally draft the autograph score. Only those works dedicated to my immediate family (for piano, cello, and violin) have parts written for them. All other works are in autograph score only. As I had decided to put my effort toward composition, no separate parts were ever written. You will note the earlier works are of standard fare, traditionally scored, and based on typical compositional patterns, like sonata-allegro form. As evident in my later works, I've departed from that exacting premise. My only guiding principle: the creation of melodies that stir the heart and nourish the soul.

As I considered the variants of musical style and instrumentation for my work, I drew inspiration from the pioneers of important motion picture scores, Max Steiner, Frank Skinner, and Hans J. Salter. These stock music composers created the signature sounds of Warner Bros. and Universal Pictures. All three composers wrote music that became synonymous with their respective motion picture company. Steiner set the standard of excellence at Warner Bros. by marrying suspenseful and patriotic music with storyline simply through his highly original scoring. Skinner and Salter breathed life into the horror film genre of Universal Pictures from the Wolfman to the later Frankenstein franchise films. Even the Sherlock Holmes and the Abbott and Costello series couldn't escape the unique touch of Frank Skinner's lush and enduring scores. It's their innate ability to capture pure emotion and being able to paint horror, mystery and comedy with equal precision through their music that caused me to shy away from more traditional venues of composition. This above all else is the main reason why I only wrote four symphonies...

"What?" David said to an empty house. He then thumbed through the journal in his hand to find an abundance of titles ascribed with opus numbers that reached into the low 200s. Along with the foretold symphonies, he was astounded to discover no less than forty symphonic poems, twenty-plus concertos, several overtures, thirty-four completed string quartets and a broad range of other chamber works of varying sizes and instrumentation.

Now he realized the magnitude of the work ahead of him. He set the journal aside and turned his attention to where West might have secured the works alluded to in this journal and the concertos he discovered in the two folders.

David searched the room with an intense gaze as he scanned the wall of bookshelves, but failed to see where West might have secreted the larger works until his eyes lit upon the inset file cabinet. He wasted no time in heading toward the wood framed drawers that may hold a treasure on the order of the lost books of the Alexandria library; the collected music of a previously unknown composer. The usually unflappable assistant dean was noticeably excited as his hands awkwardly reached for the handles of the uppermost file cabinet door to pull it open.

What greeted his eyes was nothing less than a miracle. From the first written work to his final opus in the bottom drawer of the cabinet was score after score of music written long hand and set on full orchestra score paper. Some smaller pieces were completed on standard-size staff paper and equally filed in what appeared to be catalog order. Sifting through the many scores, David was amazed at the sheer volume of work done by just one man. Of course, the quality would have to be thoroughly examined, but from what he was able to glean from his quick scan of the contents of these precious vaults, a musical treasure had been discovered.

Chapter Four

Audra Bunting returned from lunch to a desk cluttered with paper, a full email inbox, and a headache. The pile of research notes to her latest project was still sitting on her desk, and her short break had done little to revive her interest. After checking the laundry list of emails, she downloaded the important ones to her read file and deleted the spam. She confirmed her attendance at a project meeting, addressed a question about books on local family genealogy, and Marge Tompkins' urgent request to know if the reservations for the upcoming visit by the Smithsonian scholars was arranged. With all the importance attached to this conference, any reasonable person would have felt the pressure, but not Audra. She dispatched each request with the utmost professionalism.

As she completed the last request, she turned her attention to the stack of notes on her desk. Audra was hoping the conference would shed some light on the missing period of the Delaware General Assembly when most of the evidence of their legislative activity was lost. Unfortunately, Audra's headache got much worse, affecting her concentration. Her waning interest caught the attention of Tracy Harrington from the cubicle across from Audra.

"Do you need something for that?"

"No thanks. Lunch was what I needed. That's what I get for eating so late I'm afraid."

"Oh, Marge Tompkins called again about the reservations for the Smithsonian delegation."

"Thanks."

Tracy sensed something in the older woman's voice. "Why is that conference so important?"

Audra stopped organizing her documents and turned toward her singular audience. "There were many documents thought to be lost to us that were either kept by people who didn't know the significance of what they had or were discovered quite by accident. We're putting together a giant jigsaw puzzle with small, nearly identical pieces. And all too often, the puzzle itself remains incomplete because the pieces are forever lost through calamity, negligence, or ignorance."

"What project are you working on?"

"The early activity of the Delaware General Assembly from 1704 to 1739, most of which was thought to be lost due to poor record keeping of the period. Our guests will be demonstrating updated techniques to help us locate and verify these documents."

"Is that what you have there on your desk?"

"I'm not sure yet," Audra admitted. "I received some of this from the Lewes Historical Society, some from the National Archives of College Park, Maryland, and my own research here as well as the Smithsonian in DC."

Tracy was about to ask something else when the phone rang.

"Delaware Public Archives, Audra Bunting speaking. How may I help you?"

"Yes, my name is David Whealy. Do you have a moment to address a question regarding a piece of property in Lewes?"

Audra went from studious lecturer to accommodating service professional. "Regrettably, we're not staffed to do research for the general public. We can, however, offer you a tour of the facility to aid you in your research."

Sounding a bit disappointed, he said, "I'm only asking because I'm not from Delaware. I acquired a property at the south end of Frontage Road here in Lewes that's been in continuous possession of the previous family since 1724. Would the archives have any information about the history of property that predates the country?"

As questions go, Audra received more than her share that required a few hours of research, but this one?

"Perhaps, if you stop by the archives, I might be able to guide you through our facility. It may help you get your research off in the right direction," Audra suggested.

They exchanged contact information and set up an appointment to meet in Dover.

Before David left the West home for the day, he gathered the journals and placed them in the old valise. He also took the three music folders and a sampling of different scores for his colleagues to study and evaluate. He thought about staying the night, but as the day progressed faster than he anticipated, he decided to remain at the Lord De La Warr instead. He finished loading the car when he heard footsteps approaching from behind. He turned to see an attractive older woman.

"May I help you?"

"My name is Beth Grey, Jim's neighbor." She eyed David with a hint of suspicion. "I couldn't help but notice you were here all day, but I didn't see Jim. Is he around?"

He offered his hand. "Nice to meet you, Beth. I'm David Whealy." Not knowing how to soften the blow any better, he looked at her and said in a subdued tone, "I'm sorry to be the bearer of ill tidings, but Mr. West passed away."

"He what?"

"I'm sorry you weren't told, but he passed last month."

"Oh my! Do you know what happened?"

"I don't know all the details myself. I only know it happened last month. Did you know him very well?"

"Jim never really got close to anyone," she said with a trace of sadness in her voice.

David assumed she might have wished for a closer relationship with his benefactor but was unsuccessful. Now, she'll never have the opportunity.

"Is there anything I can do for you?"

"That's very kind of you. I don't wish to impose."

"Helping a person cope with this kind of unexpected news is far from an imposition. I was just finishing up for the day and was considering an early supper at the Second Street Tavern. Would you care to join me? You could share your memories of Jim? That's if I'm not imposing on you."

"You didn't know Jim?"

"I never had the privilege. But I would be most appreciative if you joined me for supper and shared what you knew about him."

"You're very kind." Eyeing David a second longer, she said, "Give me a few minutes to get ready. My house is the tan one across the street."

David took about ten minutes to secure the house in time to meet Beth at her place. As he picked her up, he couldn't help notice that she cut a stunning figure in her pastel summer dress. The trip to the tavern was a blur for David, Beth's physical presence and charming voice detracting him from his driving.

As they arrived at their destination, Beth asked, "How did you find out about this place?"

"From the manager of the bed-and-breakfast where I'm staying."

A waiter quickly greeted Beth and David and escorted them to a table near the tavern's open-air entrance. David held out the chair for a surprised Beth Grey, who wasn't expecting such courtesy. After the two had ordered their meals, he turned to Beth. "I just want to say I appreciate you allowing me to take up your time like this. But before we begin, are you sure you're all right?"

"Your news came as a surprise, but then again, I wasn't that close to Jim myself."

"Then you didn't know him that well either?"

Beth smiled. "I don't know of anyone in the neighborhood whoever had that luxury. From what I'd seen, Jim was a loner."

"What makes you say that?"

"I never saw him with anyone. I don't believe he ever had company over to the house. The only car I ever saw in the driveway was his."

"It looks like my inquiry will take longer than expected."

With a heightened sense of suspicion, she asked, "Are you a cop?"

David smiled broadly. "I'm not a police officer, a reporter, or an insurance agent. I'm just a puzzled college professor from California wondering why a stranger would leave me his estate."

Upon hearing that bit of news, Beth felt more comfortable being with her dapper dinner companion. With a demure look, she said shyly, "I see. I suppose I'd be as curious." She started fidgeting with her silverware, not knowing how to begin.

Gently prompting her, he said, "Perhaps if you told me how you first met."

She thought back to her first encounter with James Burton West as recollection reflected in her eyes.

"I first moved here from the Midwest about four years ago. I'd just finished unloading my clothes from the moving van and was deciding how I was going to tackle the furniture when I saw Jim walking up the road. He was tall, about your height, with long wavy gray hair under a faded yellow ball cap. He wore a light brown polo over knee-high shorts, and he was wearing light brown deck shoes. Jim saw I was in need of assistance, so he offered his help. After we'd loaded the last of my heavy articles, I offered him dinner. He politely refused, claiming a previous appointment. I only ran into him maybe three more times after that."

As Beth finished her last sentence, the waiter arrived with two glasses of wine. The waiter stood by as David swirled the contents in the glass, sniffed, then sipped. Having nodded his satisfaction to the young man, he acknowledged its palatable taste to Beth, who couldn't hold back her smile at this rather formal performance. When the waiter departed, David held up his glass to Beth and asked, "What shall we drink to?"

She thought for just a second. "To absent friends?"

David tilted his head askance and with a raised eyebrow added, "And discovering new ones?"

Beth mimicked his movements, smiling in agreement.

The timing couldn't have been more perfect, for once the toast was complete, their dinner arrived. After an enjoyable meal seasoned with small talk, the conversation soon returned to the subject of the meeting.

"Did you ever have a lengthy conservation with him?"

"Once. It was a day I will always treasure."

"Why is that?"

"Right from the get-go, I could sense that Jim was an intensely private man. As I had previously told you, he had no visitors to the house. I thought Jim was utterly friendless."

David observed Beth trying to hold back her emotions as she delved into what seemed a painful memory. "Are you okay, Beth?"

"I'm all right. I'm just trying to be a faithful reporter. As I said, I only ran into him those few times. He was friendly, soft-spoken, and neighborly. The last time we met was on the beach after the tourists had left for the season. I was taking in the last warm September evening on the sand. I spotted Jim strolling along the surf a few yards in front of me. I asked him to come over to share a beer. Surprisingly, he agreed. He sat next to me, and we engaged in several minutes of innocuous talk. When I asked him if he'd ever been married, he became withdrawn." She paused, trying to shore up the courage to continue.

"What happened?"

"I guess he was trying to decide whether or not to reveal his heart. He said he was married and it was the happiest twenty-three years of his life. He had an adoring wife and two wonderfully talented sons. He went on like that for a while discussing his family in such glowing terms. It was heartwarming. Then his face changed again. He cast down his eyes, and he suddenly stopped talking as though he would have let go completely had he continued. I had the feeling he wished to unpack his heart. But just when I thought he was going to do so, he chose to close up and change the subject. He then apologized. I thought we might've had the beginnings of a true friendship if not something more."

"What made you think otherwise?"

"From that day on, he shied away whenever we saw one another. It was as though he was embarrassed to confide in anyone. I only saw him once after the New Year. I figured he'd gone on one of his long trips."

"I'm sorry things didn't work out for you and Jim. And unfortunately, I must soon be on my way back to Sacramento."

Disappointed, she asked, "When will you be back?"

"Once this semester is done, I plan on returning for the summer. There's still much for me to do and I was just getting my feet wet trying to figure this puzzle out."

"If there's anything I can do to assist, don't hesitate to ask."

"I may take you up on that. Thanks for the insight. And your charming company."

"You're quite welcome," she said with a smile.

Taking his leave of Beth Grey, David returned to the Lord De La Warr. It was another revelation-filled day. But with each new revelation came more questions. After meeting Beth Grey, he wondered how West could rebuff someone of her obvious charm and attraction? What burden did he carry that was too painful to share?

David's mind was awash with everything that had transpired. Unable to stop his wandering mind, he took out his portable music player, popped it into its docking station and turned on some New Age music. His eyes closed as he laid down taking in the sounds wafting in his ears. His right hand squeezed his stress ball intermittently and on the beat. It worked for a while, but it was no use. He couldn't tear his thoughts away from the old valise and the colorful leather music folders sitting on the small table near the window. That did it. He had to explore at least one of the musical pieces and the contents of the valise.

David turned off the player and opened the piano folder. He removed the first work that caught his eye, a trio for violin, cello, and piano where the piano owned the exposition. The chord progression of the first phrase began in second inversion A minor. It moved to second inversion F major, back to the second inversion A minor then ended the cadence on D major. The next phrase went from second inversion A minor to second inversion B-flat major back to second inversion A minor to finally conclude the phrase on the first inversion of D major. After a repeat, the cello entered by an ascending arpeggio from its low C string to take up the theme.

David was completely caught off guard by the obscure strains of West's minor/major oscillation in which the passing tones provided the sweetness and gentle phrasing required to build the theme. The chord progression of the exposition provided the framework for the ensuing theme and variation the work represented.

Now more relaxed, David turned his attention to the old valise. He opened the large buckle and removed the three journals, the key chain with the old iron key, the bank documents, a folder with West's papers, and the single 8x10 photograph. The photo was a testament to West's astute eye for detail in the pencil sketches he produced. The sketches of his family members were a spot-on match with the photo. It was becoming evident to David that this man's visual art was as astounding as was his obvious compositional skill.

The attractive woman in the picture was perhaps an inch shorter than West himself, with penetrating brown eyes, a lovely smile, and long-fingered hands suited to play the piano. The young men were a handsome blend of both parents. The older was strappingly muscular while the younger retained his mother's slim build.

David then reviewed the enclosed bank documents. They showed an alarming sum of money contained in his savings and investment portfolios. The savings passbook showed a regular monthly deposit of a retirement annuity, but his checkbook demonstrated minimal deposits and smaller, infrequent withdrawals.

He finally opened the medium-size portfolio to find a US Air Force Certificate of Retirement, a Certificate of Appreciation from the President of the United States, and a retirement order. But that wasn't all. David found three other documents carefully preserved under West's retirement order that shook him to his core.

They were three certificates of death. And the dates were identical.

Chapter Five

"What do you mean the dates were identical?" asked a very puzzled bank president.

"It doesn't matter what date I input into this new database, it just keeps coming up January first for all the files I attempted to update," said an equally frustrated loan officer.

Walter Kelly tried to offer his upset employee words of consolation. "It's a good thing we didn't move forward with the system upgrade last month. This software obviously has a few design flaws." With a tinge of resignation in his voice, he added, "Forget the new system and update the records using the old one for now until I can get someone from IT to look at it, okay?"

"Sounds good to me."

"I had a feeling we should've run this new system through a few more quality checks before we accepted delivery."

Just as he uttered that statement, a bank teller came around the cubicle. "Mr. Kelly, there's a guy out front who wishes to speak to the bank president."

"Did he leave his name?"

"It's David Whealy."

"All right, show him to the office, and I'll be right with him."

Kelly opened the opaque glass door to his contemporary-style office to find a smartly dressed gentleman seated in the client's chair. He greeted his guest with an outstretched hand and a genuine, outgoing smile.

"Good morning, Mr. Whealy. Walter Kelly."

David rose to his feet to offer his hand. "Thank you for seeing me on such short notice."

"My pleasure. How may I help you?"

"I came into possession of an estate here in Lewes whose holdings are located at this bank." David dug into the valise for the documents. "Here are the check and savings passbooks, investment statements, a copy of the death certificate, and my legal endowment."

Kelly received the paperwork with a businesslike demeanor, reviewing each article carefully. Neither check or savings passbooks had a full name, so he didn't catch who it was that had died until he came across the death certificate.

"Jim's gone? What happened to him?"

"I don't know all the details. The death certificate only cites natural causes."

"But he wasn't even sixty!"

"I'm sorry that you had to find out about Jim in this way," said David with a sense of déjà vu. "Did he have any outstanding accounts?"

Kelly initially sported a questioning look as though this were a joke. But he quickly gathered himself, set down the death certificate, folded his arms and tried to recall what details he could. "No, he didn't. I came to this bank in '94 around the time Jim had applied for a loan to remodel his home. Why he chose to do so, I never understood. He had enough money in his investment portfolio to pay for the remodeling outright."

"How much was the loan?"

Looking back toward the monitor, Kelly pulled up Jim's file. "The exterior remodeling and interior restoration project Jim had planned cost one hundred and twenty thousand dollars. A considerable sum to you and me, but based on the liquid assets he had available at the time, he could easily have afforded to pay the entire amount."

"Is the loan still in force?"

Kelly smiled. "That was the beauty of Jim's ability to plan. The loan was paid for in just eight years."

"You saw him frequently, then?"

"No, not really. Jim wouldn't say much to anyone beyond the usual pleasantries."

"What was it about him that would make you remember him so clearly?"

"Jim made an instant impression on you when you saw him. He was instantly recognizable in his non-descript yellow ball cap. He usually wore a distressed aircrew bomber jacket, jeans, and brown work boots. In the summer, he'd wear solid-colored polo shirts, khaki shorts, and deck shoes with no socks, but he still wore that same yellow ball cap. But what made you notice Jim was his unusual gait."

"Unusual gait?"

"He appeared to walk with a limp that favored his left leg. He kept his left arm motionless by his side while his right arm swung naturally."

"He had a stroke?"

"Not to my knowledge. I've seen him use both his left arm and hand with dexterity, so I don't know what would account for his unusual stride."

"Did he always walk with a limp?"

"I've seen him jogging on the beach from time to time with no ill effect."

"That is odd. Did he sustain an injury that would explain his occasional limp?"

"I don't know. Like I said, I only saw him on an infrequent basis."

"Well, that's a bit of detail for someone you didn't usually see."

"This is a small town, Mr. Whealy. Despite our recent urban sprawl, we take great pride in our knowledge of the community and the needs of its people. We believe this makes for a more client-oriented environment to conduct business in what's considered to be the chilly atmosphere of an impersonal banking system."

"I don't mean to be insulting, Mr. Kelly, but in my experience, I've never known people in the banking industry to take such interest in their client's traits, personal habits, or appearance."

"Does it not make sense to get to know your clients and their goals before you recommend an appropriate financial plan?"

"Touché," David said as he yielded to Kelly's logic. "What were Jim's goals?"

"I wasn't involved with Jim's initial intake, but I did work with him on his future financial planning. Except for his home restoration, Jim seemed to have modest goals."

"What for example?"

"Well, like most clients, he wished to ensure he had enough money to keep the estate going. He also wished to have enough financial resources for periodic unplanned excursions to places in the United States. He had no interest in leaving the country but held several overseas charities in high esteem. To that end, he established several trusts. He also made sure there was funding available to make quarterly anonymous contributions to local charities."

"He didn't have any relatives to whom he could transfer his wealth?"

"Unfortunately, Jim had no extended family. Both his parents were dead. His wife was an only child and both her parents have since passed on as well."

"Jim sounds like an extraordinary man," said David with an expression that reflected sadness.

"We believe our clients to *be* family, Mr. Whealy, as I hope someday you will be," said Kelly. He hit the intercom key for his office manager. "Miss Fenwick, would you be so kind as to perform a review of any accounts outstanding for a Mr. James B. West, please?"

"Right away, Mr. Kelly" was the response at the other end.

"Thank you." Kelly continued to scan his computer for West's investment files. Locating them, he casually stated, "The total assets Jim has in his income fund totals $2.6 million dollars." The statement was so nonchalant it was as though the sum was the usual amount for the average depositor.

"Are you sure?"

"I double-checked the math. There's no mistake. That's the amount," said the bank president. "Jim also had a military annuity that was divided between his investments, his savings, and a portion into his checkbook. It also shows he came into the bank on occasion to withdraw the cash he needed for his unsuspecting charities and his own day-to-day expenses."

"Do you know if he donated to these charities on a regular basis?"

"It doesn't say. Only that he made cash withdrawals."

"How did he pay his bills if he didn't use checks?"

"At the beginning of the year, Jim had automated his payments to the power and gas companies, so he didn't have to worry about paying bills in cash. According to this limited power of attorney, his estate shall continue to pay the utilities for up to one year following his death. Unless you decide to extend or curtail that function?"

Still stunned, David asked, "Where did that staggering amount of money come from? He certainly didn't get it from being in the military."

"Jim had the presence of mind to purchase a one-million-dollar life insurance policy on both he and his wife when they were married in 1970. He also purchased a five-hundred-thousand-dollar policy on each of his children when they were born, so they had firm financial security in their later years. Unfortunately, due to their untimely deaths, he ended up redeeming his policies faster than expected. After settling his family's final expenses, he chose to invest what remained in an income mutual fund with the bank as the fiduciary. As a result, his portfolio had built up over time to its current level owing to his demand that the income generated was reinvested into the principle."

"Sounds like Mr. West had planned very well. A testament to your bank's commitment to your clients."

"Thanks for the kind words, Mr. Whealy. We try."

Miss Fenwick came into the office with the information and a key. "Mr. Kelly, I happened upon this receipt for a safe deposit box," she said matter-of-factly. She turned to David and stretched out her hand to offer him the key. "I believe this is now yours."

With the look of astonishment written on his face, Kelly thought he knew most everything about his clients and about Jim West, but this was indeed a surprise. "I don't recall Jim ever owning a safe deposit box or even asking to access one."

Miss Fenwick glanced at the receipt. "It was taken out and last opened on the same day, April 23, 1975."

"Well then, I think it's high time someone opened it." Turning toward David, he said, "If there are no further questions, Miss Fenwick can take care of you from here."

David got up and shook Kelly's hand. "I appreciate your time and assistance."

"You're welcome," said the bank president as David followed the woman out of Kelly's office.

She escorted David to a secluded room off the left side of the main office to afford him some privacy. The dust of thirty-six years drifted onto the table as he unlocked the lid and opened the oblong metal box. Inside were two cushioned presentation cases that might have contained a bracelet or a choker necklace, but they were military decorations. Both were dark blue with a thin gold ornamentation that ran the entire length of the left side cover with the words "United States of America" embossed in gold at the bottom. He removed one of them to open it.

David's expression reflected the significance of the medal he beheld; a swatch of dark purple ribbon with thin white edges that tapered down to the medal attached to it. The medal had a white shield with two red horizontal stripes and three red stars above them. The shield was flanked on either side by olive branches. It topped the medal whose outline was that of a gold heart with purple inlay. Prominently appliquéd on top of the purple field was the gold profile of America's first president.

David set aside West's Purple Heart for the moment to see what other medal this previously unknown war hero had earned. He opened the duplicate case to find nothing less than the Air Force's highest decoration, second only to the Medal of Honor; the Air Force Cross.

The accompanying citation, contained in a blue cushioned folder with the seal of the United States Air Force embossed on it, told the harrowing story of how James Burton West managed to garner such military accolades. It was typed on cardstock, with the picture of the medal centered in the upper margin with the medal's ribbon colors of red, white, and light blue laid horizontally across the top of the citation. Below the embossed designed was the justification for its award.

CITATION TO ACCOMPANY THE AWARD OF
THE AIR FORCE CROSS

TO

JAMES B. WEST

The President of the United States of America, authorized by Title 10, Section 8742, U.S.C., awards the Air Force Cross to Sergeant James B. West for extraordinary heroism in military operations against an opposing armed force while serving as an AC-130 Loadmaster near the Tan Son Nhut Air Base, in the Republic of South Vietnam on 3 February, 1974. On that proud day, Sergeant West was assigned to prepare the evacuation of 12 members of the American Embassy staff, when his AC-130 aircraft with a crew of seven received a barrage of small arms fire. The aircraft's co-pilot mortally wounded, Sergeant West led a successful counterattack to repel a numerically superior enemy force. With complete disregard for his own safety and at great personal risk to his own life, Sergeant West purposely exposed himself to intense small arms fire on seven separate occasions to secure the safety of the embassy staff and the three remaining aircrew members. On his last attempt, Sergeant West and the severely wounded airmen he was carrying were both hit by small arms fire as they boarded the moving aircraft. In the end, five of seven aircrew and all 12 civilians survived owing to the decisive actions of Sergeant West. Through his extraordinary heroism, superb Airmanship, aggressiveness in the face of the enemy, and in the dedication of his service to his country, Sergeant West reflected the highest credit upon himself and the United States Air Force.

♪

Chapter Six

David opened the bank's front door directly into a quickly developing thunderstorm. The wind was already coming from the southwest at over twenty-five miles per hour, and the driving rain was just beginning. This sort of weather pattern was strange to David, but it was not an uncommon occurrence on the Delmarva Peninsula. The worsening weather and the lateness of the hour, he decided to check out of the Lord De La Warr and move into the home he now owned, since it was furnished and the utilities were on.

Residing there, he figured to make better use of his time, combing the autograph scores of his benefactor. A quick stop at the grocery store near Five Points to pick up a few days' worth of provisions and he'd be settled in for the rest of the evening. Jet lag and the excitement of discovery had taken its toll. All he wanted to do was relax for the balance of the day and process all that he'd learned.

The only thing he needed was company. Wondering if Beth would be inclined to join him, he reached for his cell phone.

"Hello?"

"Hey, Beth, it's David Whealy."

"David! What a pleasant surprise. How goes the research?"

"Quite well actually, considering I knew nothing about Jim a week ago."

"That's wonderful. What are you up to?"

"It's why I called. Since you were so kind to put me on the right track about Jim, I thought I'd return the favor. How would you like to hear what I've uncovered over dinner?"

"I have a few errands to run this afternoon, but I'm curious to know what you've come up with. Sure, I'd like that."

"I've finished my research for the day, so what time would you like to get together?"

"That all depends on where we're going."

"Since I'm in the house, I thought I'd make my own epicurean concoction for you right here."

"You cook, too?"

"I'm not fanciful or anything, but I wouldn't consider myself completely untried in the kitchen. That's if you're game?"

"Now how can a girl refuse such a flattering offer as that? When would you like me to come over?"

"Anytime after six would be fine. I should have everything prepared by then."

"Would you like me to bring anything?"

"No need. Just bring yourself, a curious nature, and a hearty appetite."

"Look forward to it. See you around six."

David put the extra time to good use. He headed upstairs to explore West's extensive CD library to set the appropriate atmosphere. Filling the CD changer with his selections, he inventoried all the ingredients needed for the evening's meal—spicy shrimp fried rice with a light Caesar salad and white wine. Having selected the music and the menu, he freshened up, donned more comfortable attire, and set a match to the three logs he'd set up in the stone fireplace. Diligently working on his culinary task, he found himself chopping the garlic to the percussive rhythm of Saint-Saens, the fourth movement of his *Second Symphony* that had started to issue from the ceiling speakers.

With the evening's preparations complete, David looked around to make sure that everything in the home of James Burton West was as he originally found it. All the journals and the music folders were returned to their respective places so he could share that experience of discovery with Beth. Satisfied that all was as it should be, he came back to the living room and took up residence in the recliner with his feet propped up. Schubert's *Serenade* made its way to his ears as he reached for his stress ball. This was the first opportunity for him to think of his class, the upcoming spring concert series, and that last disastrous rehearsal. His thoughts had strayed toward Carla and that snide look she gave him as he left the faculty lounge that day when an incongruous sound suddenly broke through the music.

It was his ill-named smartphone notifying him that he had a text message. David rolled his eyes up at the ceiling as he forced himself out of the recliner to retrieve his cell and the unwelcomed message it contained. It read, *"Okay, who is she?"* He stared at the short statement in amazement. That text could only have come from one person. Carla.

Rather than reward her guess, he just sent her the curt reply, *"Good night, Carla!"* Her response was swift and just as insolent, *"Have a good time! ttyl. :)"*

David shook his head, smiled, and returned to the recliner for the few remaining minutes before Beth's timely arrival.

The wind and rain had since stopped, but the quick temperature drop created some patchy ground fog that covered the beach. Only the mast of the departing Cape May-Lewes Ferry and the top of the Cape Henlopen light were visible.

The streetlight near Beth's home gave off an eerie glow through the increasingly dense fog. Leaving her home, she couldn't see the driveway across the street, but that didn't stop her from proceeding to her appointment with David and the home of Jim West. Her heels made blunt muffled sounds as they struck the pavement. She reached the door, and it hit her; this would be the first time she had ever been inside Jim's home.

The door chimes ringing out the opening phrase of Beethoven's *Ode to Joy* let David know Beth had arrived. He opened it to find Beth's fog-incased silhouette surrounded by moonlight. She looked like a photo negative of a ghost until she moved inside the threshold to take David's hand in greeting.

She was stunning. Her toned and proportioned body was accentuated by the light of the streetlamp behind her. A tousle of full bodied, shoulder length dirty blond hair cascaded around her face. She wore a stylish sweater and jeans as protection against the chilly evening air.

"Please," he said as he stretched out his hand. "Won't you come in?"

"Thanks for your gracious invitation." She entered a home she had longed to see before now.

"You must be hungry."

"Famished! I had a hectic day at the office, so I missed lunch."

"Oh really? What was it that had you so occupied you didn't eat?"

"I work at a consulting firm," she began. "Our current client is a real estate developer, and it was our initial meeting. Our one-hour appointment went into overtime. We didn't finish up until well after three, so naturally, I'm quite hungry."

"In that case, I'll have dinner ready in about fifteen minutes. Please make yourself at home while the specialty of the house, spicy shrimp fried rice is prepared. Would you prefer a Chardonnay or the Chablis Blanc?"

"Chardonnay sounds perfect, thanks."

"Good choice," he said. He poured two goblets of wine and handed one to his guest.

She held up the glass and offered the words, "Friends well met?"

Reconsidering the toast for a second, he said, "Discoveries."

She nodded her approval and issued her glass toward his. The goblets clinked with the softest of rings. She moved the glass under her nose and swirled and sniffed the contents to appreciate the aroma before she allowed the goblet to touch her lips, never taking her eyes off David. Slowly sipping the delectable fruit of Bacchus, she savored the flavor as it lingered on her tongue before she swallowed it. She telegraphed her satisfaction to him with a gentle smile. She could convey emotion and meaning without uttering a single word. But for David, at least for the evening, she wouldn't be so cryptic. "If dinner is as tasty as the Chardonnay, then this afternoon's fast was worth it." Bringing the subject back to David, she asked, "So you said you're a college professor from California?"

He finished his drinking ritual, set his drink aside, and turned his attention to dinner. "That's right. I'm just a boring old music professor from Sacramento," he said before he segued into dinner

45

conversation. "I'll have your salad up in a moment. Do you like Caesar?"

"Love it!" she said, her eyes focusing on David's hands as they flew from one side of the island to the other. He worked the thick kitchen knife over the head of lettuce with the dexterity of a magician, reducing the medium-size green ball to shreds and fit for a salad in mere seconds. "A musician, huh? You don't strike me as the musical type."

"How do musicians generally strike you?"

Visibly cornered by the question, she adjusted herself in her seat and responded, "Don't musicians typically have a disheveled outward appearance? Outlandish clothing? That sort of thing?"

Turning his head, he stopped mixing the salad, raised an eyebrow, and stared at her. Seeing that was enough for Beth to toss out the stereotype.

"All right, point taken."

David's response was to soften his stare, nod, and return to his culinary duties.

"If you're a musician, what instrument do you play?"

"My primary instrument is the cornet, but I have been known to fool around with the rest of the brass family. I'm a fair to midland talent when it comes to tickling the ivories, and I know just enough about playing the oboe and the violin to be dangerous."

"Wow! You really are a one-man band, aren't you?"

"Not really. When I was younger, I was curious enough about the various instruments to engage the interest of my music teachers. They invited me to study them further, and I accepted the challenge." He added without missing a beat, "That was some thunderstorm this afternoon, wasn't it?" Placing an even distribution of dressing-coated lettuce on each plate, he garnished the salad with some grated cheese and garlic croutons before he served it.

"Oh, that looks perfect, thank you," she said before addressing his question. "I only heard an occasional rumbling just before our office meeting broke up."

"Is the weather always so unpredictable here?"

"Having come from California, you're not used to our sudden changing weather patterns. It must be nice to live where the sun is always shining."

Playing a hunch, he said, "You obviously don't have the same accent the native Delawareans seem to have. Where did you call home before you came here?"

Tapping an inquisitive finger on her chin, she said, "Let's see now. What did I put on my résumé? Oh yes, I remember. I was born in Sedalia, Missouri, but raised in Calumet City. I majored in business at Southern Illinois University and started working in Chicago soon after as an advertising consultant. I tend to call Chicago home even though my second marriage brought me to Lynchburg, Tennessee. I run five miles a day and can press twice my weight. I can speak three languages although my Italian is limited to the more colorful metaphors. My favorite color is blue, I'm a second-degree black belt in Taekwondo, and I can chamber a round and can give a gnat a third eye from 500 yards out in less than three seconds. Now, did I miss anything?"

"Okay, okay, Uncle!" he chuckled. "So how did you end up here in Lewes?"

In a less sarcastic tone, she responded, "My second marriage only lasted a few months before we called it quits, so I tried to move back to Chicago to get my old job back. The company did rehire me, but with the caveat that I fill the position here in Delaware. That was about four years ago now, and about the time I first met Jim."

"And from what you shared with me before, you didn't get to know him as well as you'd have liked, did you?"

"No," she said with some trepidation.

David stopped his preparations long enough to open a drawer to take out the letter he received from Jim and handed it to Beth. "This is what was among the effects I received from the lawyer earlier this week. It was addressed to me from Jim."

"May I?" she asked.

"Please."

She took the old-fashioned correspondence from him and opened it. Beth was just as taken by the eloquent handwriting as

David. Reading the letter, she was now aware of the magnitude of Jim's generosity.

"Did you have an opportunity to read his journals yet?"

"Only briefly. The key I'm having the Delaware Public Archives look into for me."

"What about the signet ring? Did it have any particular significance?"

"Unfortunately, I haven't as yet found the ring. It wasn't among the effects I was provided, nor was it in any place I've looked so far," he said as he continued to fold the veggies in with the sesame oil and shrimp.

Beth fired off three questions in rapid succession. "So what was this concert Jim was talking about? Was he actually in California and did you get to meet him?"

He stopped stirring the mixture a moment as he responded, "The university holds several concerts a year, the December concert being the best-attended one. I had no idea Jim existed until I received that letter from Simon Talbridge, and I was surprised when I read the last paragraph. It was Jim's choice to remain anonymous and I don't know why."

The feeling of empathy enveloped Beth as he revealed the answers to her questions. Instantly, the vision of that day on the beach with Jim sprang to mind. "I'm sorry, David," she said as she considered her words. "I didn't mean to come on so strong."

David folded the sliced jalapeños in with the shrimp and vegetables and now the delicate aroma that filled the kitchen started to pack a spicier punch. "No apologies necessary. Jim seems to have been an enigma to both of us."

"Thank you. And you're right." As she got a whiff of the pleasant aroma, she said, "Oh, that's starting to smell real good! Are you sure you don't moonlight as a maître d' in some posh hotel someplace?"

"Good music and fine food! What else should there be to life, save the possession of an all-consuming love?"

"Hmm. What else indeed," said Beth as a flirtatious expression played on her face.

His only concession to a homemade meal was adding prepackaged sticky rice. He worked the rice into the shrimp and vegetables until it was completely coated. The steam rising from the pan offered a hint of the flavor they were soon going to enjoy. "It's just about ready." Lifting the bottle of wine, he asked, "Would you like a refill?"

"Yes, please."

After he had filled her goblet, David scooped up generous helpings of fried rice for each plate and brought the entrées to the table.

"David, it looks and smells fantastic! Thank you so much!"

"You worked hard all day and fasted for lunch. It was the least I could do."

Finally getting to sit down to enjoy dinner and Beth's stimulating company, he asked her, "What is it about Delaware that made you want to transfer here?"

"I've always been a history buff, especially early American History. Being the first state, Delaware is the perfect place to study the first stirrings of independence and liberty. Wouldn't you say?"

"The history I enjoy is more musical in nature, especially how it transcends linguistic barriers. Humans, animals, and even plants respond to music, which makes it a fascinating field of study." Turning back to his original question, he asked, "But why Delaware? One would have thought the actions at Boston, Philadelphia, and Yorktown more compelling."

"Oh they were," she began. "But have you ever heard of Caesar Rodney and the impact of his singular vote for independence? Or of Delaware's Colonel Allen McLane, who was dispatched by Washington to ensure the arrival of the French fleet in time to secure a Yorktown victory over Cornwallis? Or Representative James Bayard of Delaware whose decisive tie-breaking vote in the House of Representatives on the thirty-sixth ballot gave us a President Thomas Jefferson instead of a President Aaron Burr?"

"No, I can't say that I do."

"I find it frustrating that these noteworthy accomplishments of Delawareans remain unknown in American classrooms today, especially in Delaware classrooms. Our colonial history is more than obscure dates. It's alive with facts waiting for rediscovery."

"Well, I may not be able to shed light on America's colonial history, but I can shed light on our mutual friend."

Beth quickly changed her mindset from presentation to reception. "I'm all ears. Enlighten me!"

David cleared his throat and started his narration as though he were reading from a dossier. "James Burton West, born August 23, 1952 right here in Lewes, graduated from Cape Henlopen High School. Married his high school sweetheart, Isabella Rodriguez, in 1970 and enlisted in the United States Air Force that same year. He did two tours in Vietnam from which he was highly decorated. Jim was also a veteran of the First Gulf War. His military decorations included the Purple Heart and the Air Force Cross."

He paused for a moment before revealing the next bit of information. "Jim tragically lost his entire family on the same day he was to retire from the Air Force in 1993. He took out a loan in 1995 to remodel this house. Then for all intents and purposes, he dropped off the face of the planet, cutting off every human contact. To put it in colloquial terms, he went off the grid."

Beth considered his last statement as though revelation visited her. "No wonder he lived like a hermit!"

"What do you mean?"

Excited by the feeling of being one up on David for the first time since their meeting, she asked, "Don't you see? Between the wars and the loss of his family, Jim must have suffered from some form of post-traumatic stress. The disorder must have made him withdraw socially."

He contemplated her theory a moment, then said, "Psychoanalysis may not be my strong suit, but isn't it true that the most persistent symptom of such a malady would be emotional instability manifested through erratic behavior? Or at the very least atrocious penmanship."

Looking as though her diagnosis was rendered flawed in some way, she said, "Possibly."

"You saw the letter. Did it provide sufficient evidence to prove Jim suffered from such an ailment to the point his handwriting was adversely affected?"

"I guess not," she said as she finished the last of her meal. "David, that was delicious! Thank you for being such a charming host, for dinner, and for opening a larger window into Jim's world for me."

"The meal and the letter were only the beginning," he said. "If you want to understand who Jim was and my response to your theory regarding Jim's mental state, then a more impressive surprise awaits you when you see the rest of the house. Are you ready for the grand tour?"

Feeling apprehensive, but willing to go along, Beth got up to join David. He escorted her from the dining room to the great room, and she was captivated by the drawings on the wall. She had noticed them when she first came into the house, but she didn't pay too close attention to them.

"They're beautiful," she commented. "Jim sure had a discerning eye for art. I've never seen such detailed work before. Where did he buy them?"

"He didn't," responded David.

"Then where did he—"

"He sketched them himself."

Beth looked at David to see if he was joking. The deadpan expression staring back at her left no doubt that he was serious.

"Oh my!" she exclaimed as she scanned all the sketches on the first floor walls.

"I don't believe he would have been able to produce such highly intricate and detailed works had he been afflicted by post-traumatic stress. And his visual art wasn't the only area in which he excelled."

"Oh? What was the other?"

Unable to conceal his amusement as he thought of a similar conversation between himself and Carla not more than a week ago, he said, "Actually, the answer to that question is contained on the second floor, for the secret of Jim's true talent resides there."

Beth's instincts for self-preservation were piqued but only momentarily. Reviewing her brief time with David Whealy, she decided he'd been nothing but an attentive gentleman. Her long history of failed relationships taught her to be on her guard all the time. David was decidedly different. She realized he wouldn't take advantage of her vulnerabilities or emotions.

David softly clutched her forearm and guided her toward the spiral staircase. "Go on ahead and experience the discovery for yourself. I'll be up in a few minutes."

She was still marveling at the pencil sketches of landscapes, beach scenes, and the Air Force collage as he spoke, then she regarded David with a questioning glance. "Are you sure?"

"I want you to discover Jim's world the same way I did—with surprise, amazement, and awe."

"Okay," she said as she moved up the spiral staircase, taking in the framed view of the large bay window that took up two floors. The higher she went, the more she could see the fog bank that covered the beach beyond and how the moonlight glistening over the ocean split the view into two equal parts. Before she got to the top landing, she noticed the portraits of West's family. She stopped for a moment to study the pencil sketches of both Jim and his wife. The intensity of the woman's gaze, even through pencil, held her attention the longest. Then she proceeded to the top. Beth's mouth was agape, silent but expressive, as she scoured the entire layout of the character-filled second floor.

She marveled at the three instruments in the middle of the room as David came up the stairs to stand next to her. "He was a musician?" she asked.

"He was a composer and a highly talented one, too."

"How do you know he wrote music rather than play it?"

"Take a close look at the music contained in the folders on the stands. All the sheet music was written in the same hand as the correspondence I showed you earlier."

Beth crossed the floor to the piano and thumbed through the numerous pieces contained within the folder. Not being at all musically inclined, she understandably didn't recognize the handwriting. "I'll just have to take your word for it."

"Let me guess, you don't read music."

"No, I can't."

"Well then, if my sight-reading skills haven't failed me, allow me to share with you what was in Jim's head as he penned these notes. If you look out the window, you'll see the beach scene Jim sketched downstairs. Of course, the fog will mask most of it, but the moon's reflection on the water between the Lewes ferry and the Henlopen light is appropriately accented by the piece you are about to hear."

David played the exposition of the theme and variation trio he'd analyzed earlier at the Lord De La Warr. The raw emotion that permeated the room captivated Beth as she looked out over the banister. The phrasing was so poignant, so filled with boundless love that she was carried away. David turned to see Beth as she stood there, hands firmly gripping the rails, and looking out into the moonlit Delaware night.

After he stopped playing, he went over to her and said, "Beautiful, isn't it?"

"Yes, she certainly was," she responded with the slightest catch in her voice.

David finally caught on. Beth wasn't looking out the window like he thought. She was staring with intense interest at one of the pencil sketches of James Burton West. She was looking at the near lifelike visage of Jim's wife, Isabella. She was unable to turn her tear-filled eyes away from that lovely, expressive face. Standing there with the music in her head and the image of Isabella West looking back at her, she grasped the depth of West's feelings for his wife and his sons. She understood now. The answer was so clear it hit her like a thunderbolt. A man who poured so much love into his work, both visual and musical, couldn't possibly be lured away from a love so eternal, even death was powerless to extinguish it.

♪

Chapter Seven

Gray brick paved streets with their red brick sidewalks marked the boundary of Old Dover; established by William Penn in 1682. Radiated out for several blocks past that barrier, the streets were paved in red brick. The Old State House building, now a museum, presided over Dover's historic district locally known as the Green.

On the east side of the Old State House was the Legislative Mall, an enormous rectangular patch of green grass bordered on the north and south side by trees. The east and west side of the mall were left open giving an observer from the Old State House a grand view of the current Legislative Hall. Visitors strolling along the mall's herringbone patterned red brick sidewalk would find the policeman's memorial and a full-size replica of the Liberty Bell. Surrounding the mall was the Biggs Museum of American Art, the lieutenant governor's office, the Armory, the capital police headquarters building, the supreme court building, and of course, the center of political life for the State of Delaware, Legislative Hall.

Accessed by the four-lane entrance, the Hall's spire could be seen from Route 13 even at night. During the month of December, the alternating colors of red and green silently announced the coming of the Christmas season, the season of peace. Although peace is a description that rarely defined the conduct of American politics, even for a state the size of Delaware. It was the sight of that spire and the materialization of the majestic building beneath it that informed David he was headed in the right direction. The uniquely shaped architecture of the Delaware Public Archives soon came into view as he turned the corner onto Duke of York Street.

David pulled into the archives parking lot. Audra Bunting was standing just inside the building's cylindrical entrance waiting for him. She had on a maroon smock with the name of the archives embroidered in gold on the left breast pocket. The pink reading glasses she had perched on her head performed double duty as a barrette holding back some of her curly auburn hair. As David came into view, she seemed to recognize him.

"*Dr.* Whealy?" she asked, with emphasis on the doctor.

"As a matter of fact, I am," David confirmed. "How did you—?"

Without hesitation, she rolled off his credentials. "Dr. David C. Whealy, professor and assistant dean of music at UC Davis, virtuoso cornet player as well as several other wind instruments. You're the founder of the jazz group *Hot Brass Five*, winner of three Grammy Awards, and rated best university conductor among your peers for four years running. I saw the documentary about today's great composers and conductors a few years back. Needless to say, I'm a fan and very pleased to meet you."

"I'm flattered you'd remember."

"I've always enjoyed the versatility and range of your music," she offered. "Although I must confess, I hadn't seen any of your concerts in person."

"Well, if you ever find yourself in Sacramento, I'd be more than happy to hold one of our reserved box seats for you and a guest."

"I'd like that a lot," she said appreciatively. "I don't think I'll be making it out to California anytime soon, but if you can promise that a Rossini Opera would be on the program, I would certainly drop whatever I had planned for that!"

Thinking back when UC Davis put on Rossini's charming and funny one-act opera, *Il Senior Bruschino*, but not wishing to disappoint her, he said, "I'll be sure to mention it to our staff."

Directing him through the glass doors of the archives, Audra said, "If you come this way, Dr. Whealy, I'll show you around our facility."

"David, please."

"Very well then," she said smiling at him. "David it is." Nodding her assent to his suggestion, she escorted David to the cloakroom so he could store his overcoat and the valise he brought with him. She also cautioned him against bringing pens inside the facility. He took the pen from his suit pocket and placed it into the valise. Once he had stowed his prohibited items in a locker of the cloakroom, they proceeded through the metal detector and into the central archives.

To the left side of the entrance was a curved information desk with a double door elevator located behind it. At the desk, three staff members were busy going about their various tasks. In the center of the room were several oblong worktables surrounded by low back leather chairs. It must have been a slow day, since there were only five people seated at the various tables.

Immediately to the right was a long bookcase filled with color-coded index binders. They were broken down by resource group, reference books, historical record books, oversized books, maps, card catalogs, and microfilm. Specified binders also allowed the researcher to locate information arranged by probate index, county orphan's court index, chancery and levy court indexes, recorder of wills and deeds, the Tatnall Tombstone collection, and coroner's inquests for each county. The extensive card catalogs were also color coded and separated by county. They covered everything from land records, ship passenger lists, marriages, wills, deaths, burials, births, and baptisms.

Audra concluded the tour with a brief summary. "As you may have surmised, the archives would be an excellent resource for you to conduct your investigation."

"I see I have my work cut out for me," he said with some reservation in his voice.

Chuckling, she added, "Not to worry, David. Although our staff may not be able to assist you in conducting your research directly, they can point you in the right direction."

Taking a second look around, David tried to think what was bothering him about the archives. He was hoping to resolve some of the questions regarding the estate by using the staff's expertise. Unfortunately, it looked like he was going to be responsible for the lion's share of his own research. But there was one small puzzle he had to solve that the archives was ill-equipped to handle—that of the iron key. He supposed if he were going to discover anything about it and how it fit into the mystery of West's estate, he would have to seek out an expert.

"Where would you suggest I begin my investigation?"

"The Sussex County Probate Index or the Sussex County Recorder of Deeds would be a good place to start. You could cross-reference what you find in the card catalogs with either the indexes or the recorded documents in the microfilm room."

Feeling a bit overwhelmed at the prospect of so massive an undertaking, David resigned himself to the long, laborious task ahead of him. This project was going to require commitment. And assistance.

"Well, I appreciate your time and patience in showing me around, Ms. Bunting."

"Audra, please," she said as she walked with David to the cloakroom to retrieve his belongings.

"Very well then," he said appreciatively, "Audra." Before he departed the cloakroom, David began to fish through the valise for something. At first, Audra thought he was searching for his pen since he was told not to bring it inside the archives with him. Locating the item, he retrieved it slowly as he said, "Along with Mr. West's correspondence that told me the age of the property, he mentioned something about a signet ring that I haven't as yet found…and this." He held up the iron key.

At first, Audra did not react with exceptional interest until she focused in on the key's bit.

"That's quite a rare design!"

"What do you think?" he asked as he handed Audra the key.

Wordless, she examined the pockmarked iron artifact. It had some rust spots and dings that showed its age and was shaped like a handcuff key on steroids with an oversized ring at the bottom of a thick cylindrical shaft. But it was the other end that drew her interest. The shaft was hollow and had a trapezoid-shaped bit.

"Do you know of anyone who could tell me something about the origin of this key and what it may have been used for?"

"Perhaps," she admitted, thinking of her meeting with the Smithsonian delegation. "We're hosting a research conference for the formative years of Delaware's General Assembly next month. The curator of the Smithsonian, Dr. Giles Radnor, is scheduled to attend.

He is well versed in pre-revolutionary American history and might be able to shed some light on the origins of your curious artifact. You could stop by with your key and ask him?"

Not ready to surrender that easily, he said, "I have to return to California tomorrow. Would it be too much of an imposition for you to share this key and its circumstances with Dr. Radnor? I plan on coming back during the summer break to complete my research. You could return it then?"

"I'm not supposed to do that, David. I could get into serious trouble," she admitted. "I could lose my job."

"Not if you weren't using the archives' resources to directly aid in that research, correct? Besides, I'll offer you my permission in writing. What do you say?"

Audra considered it for a moment as she looked at the unusual key that rested in the palm of her hand. Even though she'd be placing her job in serious jeopardy, David could tell she couldn't resist the mystery of this piece of actual Delaware history that could unlock a secret held for almost three hundred years. The answer to that mystery just might be worth taking the risk.

♪

Chapter Eight

David's car coursed through a violent thunderstorm as he headed southbound on Highway 1. Making his way past Milford, an electric hand appeared, stretching out its deformed and growing fingers in jarring directions. Seconds later, an enormous vertical column of blinding light issued from the sky slamming into the ground about a mile ahead of him. A concussion wave rocked the car making him swerve onto the shoulder. To take his mind off this cauldron, he turned on the radio. Bach's *Art of Fugue* worked its magic, diverting his attention from the weather to Jim's neighbor, Beth.

Her powerful reaction to his revelations about West exposed how vulnerable she was and how she must have fallen for a man who barely knew she existed. David felt equally sad for both of them. His benefactor was not perceptive enough to figure out that a person like Beth could have fallen in love with him while Beth suffered from her unrequited love for Jim West.

Should he call her before he leaves for California tomorrow? She hardly spoke two words after she broke her intense gaze from the likeness of Isabella West. Neither did she stay long afterward. She seemed lost, preoccupied, and distant.

David looked at the empty driveway in front of Beth's unlit house as he turned into his own. Although it was not quite one o'clock in the afternoon, he figured he accomplished enough on this trip. He wasn't going anywhere for the rest of the day, so he could lounge about in his favorite house pants and robe. William Tipton Cobbett III would have called it a dressing gown. But what you called it didn't matter to David. It was the one and only time he allowed himself to dress down. Once fixed in his minimal attire, he called Beth.

He planned to tell her he was sorry if he said something wrong or did something to upset her last night. That he'd be leaving in the morning for the Baltimore airport. He wanted to tell her he would be home for the rest of the day if she wanted to stop by. He wanted to say these things, but he couldn't. All he got was her voicemail and leaving messages on a machine was not his style. Instead, he decided to call later. David's growling stomach informed him of his next priority—lunch, but first, some music to cook by. Scouring the selections of soft jazz contained in West's impressive library, he found his muse—shakuhachi flutes.

The only items he had left in the pantry were a few spices and a single can of coconut milk. With a package of chicken breasts, some fresh garlic, a stalk of lemongrass and a half-inch piece of ginger in the fridge, he had the ingredients to make some fresh Thai chicken soup. The scent of ginger soon filled the kitchen with its delicate aroma.

Soup was the perfect complement to the sedated timbre of the Japanese flute. When he finished eating, David settled on the recliner slowly squeezing his exercise ball. His consciousness started to drift into contemplation. Thoughts like making sure he had all the available journals of James Burton West packed away. Of perusing West's cataloged works to see what scores he had to bring with him along with the music from the three folders. Placing them in with the checked baggage was not an option.

With his mind focused on the mysteries surrounding the life of James Burton West, he totally ignored the upcoming spring concert series, his classes, and his students. All of these concerns now flooded his brain. With the inspired technique of his concertmistress setting the example, he'd have no problem coaxing a brilliant performance from the rest of the orchestra. The problem was the strength of the individual groups involved with the beginning of the *Choral Fantasy*. It wasn't just the strength of the piano soloist that worried him. If the solo winds and strings couldn't carry the entrance of the theme or the solo voices unequal to the occasion, the entire piece would be an unmitigated disaster.

David was getting concerned about his lectures and lesson plans for the classes he taught. Though Cobbett was the only one he'd consider taking them, this was the first time he left them in Cobbett's hands. Exacerbating the problem of teaching musical performance, he hadn't touched his cornet in over a week, which tended to have a deleterious effect on his embouchure. But even with all these unresolved issues piling up in his head, the thought that gave him the most pleasure was seeing the faces of his students once again.

This year's crop was exceptional, and the most talented that had come through the university in recent memory. There was Myung-hee Chun, the child prodigy from Los Angeles who mastered the violin at the age of five. She even made a recording with the San Francisco Symphony at age ten. Then there was Clayton Forbes. Aside from his superb abilities as flutist and oboist, he was able to lay down arrangements for any musical contingency and in short order, saving the faculty's bacon on several occasions. A cross between Sabine Meyer and Artie Shaw, Florida native Elaine Kirkwood's silky smooth reed could charm a snake right out of its skin. David was also blessed in the field of cellists. He easily had three first chair players in Aaron Godwin, Renatta Johnson, and Robert Caulfield. But David's kindred spirit of the brass section was three-time All-State champion Holly Runyon. Her well-deserved notoriety won her an offer from London Records to record Mozart's four horn concertos.

As David kept drifting between consciousness and a dream state, his thoughts became less cogent. The CD changer had long since passed the mournful Japanese flutes, blew through Smetana's *Ma Vlast*, and was nearly done with the third movement of Prokofiev's *Fifth Symphony* before he even realized it. He was about to slip back into unconsciousness again when the irritable sound from his smartphone announced itself again. *Damn,* he thought, *what does Carla want now?*

It wasn't Carla. The brief text only said, *"Could I come by later?"* It was from Beth.

Relieved that he'd have an opportunity to find out what happened the night before, he responded, *"I'm home. Stop by at your convenience."*

The fourth movement of Brahms' *First Symphony* had begun. It was a work that, in the view of the critics, was an attempt by the composer to copy the famous *Ode to Joy* theme of Beethoven's Ninth. Beethoven's own precursor to the Ninth was the piece David was rehearsing, the *Choral Fantasy*, which was likely the reason he wanted to hear it.

As the low strings of Brahms' counterfeit theme began, they were overlapped by Beethoven's familiar anthem, informing David someone was at the door.

Opening it, he found an attractive, yet distressed Beth Grey. Under her stylish raincoat, she wore a red halter top and a floral skirt that showed off her toned legs. But the stress of her day was plainly written on her face. He suddenly felt underdressed in his casual attire. Beth's reaction informed him she didn't seem to mind.

"Please, come in. You didn't sound like yourself this afternoon?"

"I'm better than I was earlier."

"My goodness, you're shaking like a leaf! I can stoke the fire if you'd like?"

"I'm all right."

Unconvinced, he said, "I'll get the fire going."

"You're not going to believe this."

"What?"

"I was on my way into work this morning when my car's engine seized up. The steering wheel jerked out of my hand, and I lost control." Raising her hands with palms facing each other, she continued, "I came this close to hitting a brick wall!"

"You could've suffered whiplash. Did you at least see a doctor?"

She rubbed her neck as she responded. "Yeah, went to the ER. They said I'd be sore for a few days, but I suffered no serious injury."

"Thank God for that. How did you make it home from the hospital?"

"I was close enough to the office at the time of the incident for one of my coworkers to see my car veer off the road. She came to my aid and took me to the hospital. She stayed with me as the doctor looked me over then she brought me home."

"And your car?"

"I have AAA. My insurance company had it removed, but I'll have to wait on the mechanic's report to find out how long I'll be without it."

David tilted his head in a questioning manner. "Does your insurance cover car rentals?"

"I don't remember if it does or not."

David's eyes grew wide as he snapped his fingers and pointed at Beth. "Can you drive a vehicle with a manual transmission?"

"My dad taught me to drive on his old pickup with three-on-the-tree, so four-on-the-floor shouldn't be that difficult."

Smiling at the levity in her answer, he opened the island drawer and pulled out the key chain with the numbered keys. One of them was a valet key to the Jeep in West's driveway. He removed the key for the Jeep and placed it in Beth's hand. "Would you look after this for me?"

"Oh no, I couldn't."

"Why not? No one will be driving it for the foreseeable future, and I don't need it right now. Take it. Please?"

Beth nodded and forced a smile. "Thanks."

"It's the least I can do after the day you've had. I'll wager you haven't eaten yet either. I still have some soup if you don't mind leftovers."

Detecting the scent of ginger and liking what she smelled, she said, "Sure."

David reserved a curious glance for Beth as he rounded the kitchen island to heat up her soup. She was in the room, but her mind was obviously elsewhere. Her unsettled reaction to the intense love Jim felt for his dead family and her trainwreck of a day was plainly evident in her expression. Beth's inner turmoil finally got the better of her as she assumed a deflated posture with half-opened eyes staring blindly at nothing in particular.

Catching David's movements out of the corner of her eye, she raised her head to face him only to see he was sporting a questioning eyebrow. She tried to play it off with a forced smile, but David saw through the deception. The kind college professor seemed to wield a wrecking ball designed to break through her manufactured barriers. His most effective weapon was the direct approach.

He stood in front of her and looked into her eyes. "Beth, did I do anything to upset you last night?"

Snapping out of her self-induced trance, she reached for David's hand. She gave it a gentle squeeze. "Oh no, David. You have been nothing but a gentleman since the moment I met you."

"But I was the one who thoughtlessly shared my discoveries about Jim without considering your feelings—"

"You didn't know how I felt about Jim."

"I suspected. I was too caught up in the excitement of discovery to take your emotions into account, and because of that, I hurt you. It was unintentional, but it's still my fault."

"David please," she said, squeezing his hand tighter. "Don't blame yourself, okay? You couldn't have known what I was thinking. Besides, I was the one who pressed you to tell me more about Jim. I wanted to know because I was jealous of your access to Jim's world."

"Well, you may not believe it, but I'm the one who should be envious of you."

"Why?"

"You met Jim. You talked with him. Spent time with him. This is something I'll never be able to do. The more I learn about him, the more I regret never having that opportunity."

"I didn't mean to put so much on your shoulders. I'm grateful to you for helping me understand him. That understanding got the better of me. I was overcome by emotion, and it became too much for me." Beth began staring off into space again.

"I shouldn't have put you through all this so soon after telling you of Jim's passing," he said returning her gentle squeeze with a restrained grip. "It was thoughtless of me."

Beth stood up and looked at David with eyes that seem to have exhausted their bank of tears. They stood, looking at each other. Her expression was one of emotional exhaustion. His was a mixture of relief and remorse. He noticed an unmistakable forgiveness reflected in her beautiful pale blue eyes. Without averting her gaze, she edged closer into his personal space to gauge his reaction to her advance. A brief hesitation was all she needed to realize David was not going to push her away. Embracing him fully with her arms wrapped around him, the side of her tear-streaked face nestled through his robe to his bare chest.

"Thank you, David. For everything," she sobbed.

Chapter Nine

The stodgy little man arrived at his office after conducting the last of a week's worth of boorish classes and dry lectures that seemed, somehow, beneath him. Both of his administrative assistants were still out to lunch leaving the outer office deserted. Frowning at the prospect of not obtaining his customary greet and brief by his staff, he checked an empty mailbox to see if there was anything of interest. Glancing at the clock, he noted the time. They were late. He'd have to have a little chat with them about punctuality.

Cobbett entered his office with an arrogance that was uniquely his. He removed his felt bowler and placed it carefully on a hat peg between his brown fedora and his favorite Gatsby cap. His suit may have been a hundred years out-of-date, but he wore it well. This particular handmade suit came direct from a Mayfair haberdashery in London's famed Savile Row. The suit consisted of a single-breasted brown tweed coat with a stiff, upturn-collared shirt and bowtie. The low-rise, two-button waistcoat was adorned with a gold watch fob and the cuffs of his black-and-gray-striped trousers covered a pair of hard-soled oxfords that were buffed to a high gloss shine. It may not have been all the rage in the fashion world, but it was comfortable and suited Cobbett's sense of style and self-importance.

Too late for lunch but too early for afternoon tea, Cobbett decided instead to review the pieces of correspondence on his desk. He took up his letter opener, a diminutive replica of Excalibur, and sliced open the first envelope. The letter was from another academic contemporary from another university who wished to congratulate him on his receipt of the Gold Baton Award. The next few letters were interoffice memos relating to college business, and there was one more. And for him, the most important.

It had all the earmarks of an engraved invitation. Even the lettering on the modest-size envelope was embossed in bold handwritten Old English. His cheeks flushed pink with satisfaction as he read the return address. It was from England. The letter inside was from the managing director of the London Symphony Orchestra who also wished to acknowledge his success.

Looked upon as the epitome of the conductor's art, the Gold Baton is the pinnacle of recognition for a conductor. The recipient of such an accolade would command and receive primary consideration for any conductor's posting they could have wished.

He'd been receiving congratulations from colleagues across the country, but this. This was the only recognition he held in high esteem. The only note he was keen to receive. William Tipton Cobbett III looked to be a hair's breadth away from his ultimate goal; to be named the Principal Conductor of the London Symphony Orchestra.

Cobbett was keenly aware of their stringent criteria for selection. He also knew of the upcoming retirement of the post's current occupant and their active search for a worthy successor.

His immense ego could only interpret this note one way. The managing director was telling him he was on the short list. Pleased that he captured their attention yet worried the remaining concert schedule would hinder that effort, he decided then and there to take whatever steps necessary to solidify his chances of selection.

One of the measures he contemplated would no doubt disappoint the entire music department.

William Tipton Cobbett III was beyond caring at this point.

♪

Chapter Ten

David entered the lecture hall to an outpouring of warm, spontaneous applause. If David were wondering how his substitute handled his lectures for the past week, he now had his answer.

He made a calming motion with his hands and said, "All right, folks, save the enthusiasm."

The students' overwhelming respect for David would've resulted in an immediate cessation of applause, but it took a bit longer to accede to his request.

"Welcome back, Professor!" came a shout from somewhere in the upper seats.

"It's good to be back, Jennifer." With a touch of sarcasm, he added, "Now with your kind permission, I'd like to proceed with today's discussion?" Several muffled giggles followed this exchange.

Never one to chain himself behind the lectern, David centered himself in front of the instructor's table to begin. His oratory was deliberate and lyrical and usually had a mesmerizing effect on his intended recipients. It was a performance Cobbett was never quite able to replicate. He folded his arms and looked down to recall his opening monologue before raising it up again to address the impatient throng. With the slightest hint of mystery, he engaged his opening.

"Someone once said that music hath charms. It's also true that music has the sinister power to reach deep into the dark recesses of our souls to terrify. Case in point. In the summer of 1975, a simple two note baseline motive managed to scare the living crap out of the theater-going public."

This last line elicited unexpected laughter from the assembly. They were plainly shocked at their normally reserved professor's use of straightforward language. David became more animated, using his hands to punctuate his remarks as the discussion progressed.

"Think of the undeniable power that this music contained. Snatching one's imagination in a flash, instantly conveying the whole of a character in the space of two half-stepped notes played in rapid, oscillating succession. The idea isn't original, having been employed as far back as Wagnerian times, but never to the success and irrefutable command of a single composer and with so minimal a theme." Looking around the lecture hall, he asked, "Does anyone know what the theme was and who composed it?"

Hands went up almost immediately. David had briefly touched on this material last year, but he was hoping they remembered enough of that lesson to have come up with the right answer. He picked on one of the new faces in the crowd, "Yes, sir."

"It was the shark theme from *Jaws* by John Williams," the young man responded.

"That's correct, Mr....?"

"Preston Stoddard," the young man said.

"I don't recall ever seeing you in class before, Mr. Stoddard."

"My parents just retired from the Marine Corps, and we just moved back to the States from their last posting in Japan. It was too late for me to enroll in classes at the MCAS where they were stationed, so I waited until I returned to the States."

"Which Marine Corps Air Station was it, Mr. Stoddard? The one at Iwakuni or Futenma?"

"Marine Corps Air Station Iwakuni. MCAS Futenma is on Okinawa," Stoddard emphasized.

"My apologies, Mr. Stoddard. Please pass along to your folks my sincere appreciation for their service to our country. And welcome aboard." David pressed on with the lecture after the tepid applause ceased.

"As Mr. Stoddard indicated, it was, indeed, one of the twentieth century's most influential film composers, John Williams. Music and theatrical performance have been married since the genesis of both art forms. However, at the dawn of moving pictures, music was to play a more dominant role in their production. Several late nineteenth century inventions, such as the kinetoscope and the vitascope ushered in new technologies that were later developed to make the moving picture more accessible to a growing audience. At this time, however, the problems of synchronization made the marriage of sound and film impossible. Live musicians had to be called upon to provide the musical background. So even at this early juncture, music was still considered to be a necessary element for a successful *silent* movie experience."

David moved about the lecture hall as he continued. "The term *silent* movie is, in fact, a misnomer since live music was performed throughout the entire length of a so-called *silent* film. Ironically, when *talkies* first made their appearance in the early 1930s, it was the music that was silenced in favor of the spoken word. When movies like *Dracula* were remade in the early '30s, the only music used was during the opening and ending credits. Does anyone remember the piece used for the opening credits of the 1931 version of *Dracula*?"

He scanned the room, but this time no hands went up.

"No takers, huh? I suppose, in the era of the desensitizing horror flick, Lugosi's tame portrayal isn't exactly a sought after staple for the horror genre enthusiast." Disappointed, he revealed the answer. "As the curtain went up on Bela Lugosi's *Dracula*, it was an abridged version of Tchaikovsky's *Swan Lake* that functioned as the picture's main title. All through the 1930s, Hollywood experimented with film music, using either well-established classical works or recycled stock music to aid in telling the story the director wished to convey. Can anyone identify a composer from this period?"

Again, he received no answer. A brief smile graced his lips.

"Don't worry, most acolytes of the cinema forget that Charlie Chaplin, among his long list of acting and directing credits, composed the music for his 1930s era movies, *City Lights* and *Modern Times*. Composers of the 1930s have never been household names, but that would soon change in Hollywood's golden age of the 1940s.

"It was during this period that stock music composers began to expand on their art form, making their mark on the studio system and the moviegoing public. Can anyone recall any influential composers from the 1940s?"

Disappointed, David shook his head when no hands went up. This era was perhaps the Cambrian explosion for talented and prolific Hollywood composers. Their roles were so crucial to the success of these motion pictures, they were prominently displayed in the opening credits. As a result, their names became synonymous with memorable films, yet no one seemed to understand that. He was about to tick off a list of composers of the period when Preston Stoddard sheepishly raised his hand.

"Yes, Mr. Stoddard?"

"Only three come to mind."

Others in the vast semicircle of students began to laugh at his statement.

"Go ahead, Mr. Stoddard. And those three?"

"Dimitri Tiomkin, Max Steiner, and Bernard Herrmann."

"Excellent, Mr. Stoddard," said David as he looked around at the rest of his audience. "Anyone else?" Remembering West's journal mentioning the grandfather of the modern motion picture soundtrack, he asked, "Who remembers Max Steiner or any film made famous by his music?"

Other hands went up this time.

"Yes, Jennifer?"

"'Tara's Theme' from *Gone with the Wind*!"

"That's correct," David confirmed. "So what was it that set this theme apart from any other film music of that decade?"

"The theme itself was instantly recognizable," Jennifer responded.

"That's right," David said. "Many motion pictures had scores with such catchy themes. In fact, one could recapture the flavor of the movie by singing the tune. But how many of you can walk down the street whistling any theme used to provide the mysterious atmosphere so prevalent in the horror films of that period?" Looking around, he only saw heads shaking. "Yet these successful films were still able to convey the powerful feeling of mystery, horror, or comedy intended by their composers. Once again, this takes us right back to the old Brahms-Wagner argument, does it not?" The audience seemed to grasp the idea.

"So who was right?" asked a student from the right side of the audience. It was Clayton Forbes, the oboist.

"Fancy you ask, Clayton. You're getting a bit ahead of me, but that is the question you all shall ponder for your assignment this week," David responded. He centered himself in front of the instructor's table again. "Pioneers such as Steiner irrevocably placed a musical stamp on films from that decade on. No longer would music be relegated to an afterthought of directors and producers. Music became an integral part of telling a powerful and convincing story. The question that remains is, which form told a more compelling story—the Brahmsian style of music to set the atmosphere or the Wagnerian treatment of musical character assignment?"

The electronic gong soon signaled the end of the period in annoying fashion. It was a sound the students detested whenever David was in the throes of his lectures.

"Don't forget about your assignment on the board, twenty-five pages, by Friday."

Even with this admonition, David still received a round of applause for today's lecture. He gathered his notes as the students began to file out of the lecture hall. All of the students, that is, save one. She sat in the upper seat nearest the exit with her legs crossed and her arms folded with a scowl that could melt steel. If looks could bore holes, David would have resembled swiss cheese. As he approached the seated woman, it became apparent that she wasn't a student, but faculty. He recognized her immediately.

"Okay," he said as Carla sat there, a cynical eye cast his way. "What is it now?"

"You mean you don't know?" she chided.

"Know what?"

She just glared at him.

"Was it the fact I left you all week with Dr. Cobbett, complete with all his eccentricities?"

She didn't answer.

"Was it because I left you to mull over the details of the upcoming concert? The Faculty Solo Showdown?"

She maintained her dead-on stare.

"Oh, I get it. You're upset that I didn't call you during my absence."

"You're damned right! And I thought we were going to meet at the *Dolce* when you got back?" Carla softened her tone to emphasize her next point. "She must have made a hell of an impression."

This last statement took David by surprise. He never knew Carla to have a jealous bone in her body, yet her reaction was one of a jealous lover. He always believed their relationship to be stronger than just colleagues but nothing more than that. Realizing Carla may have thought differently, he softened his tone to offer an apology.

"She was simply the neighb—" His softened tone dissipated. "Wait a minute, how did you know?"

Her now-I-gotcha smirk reappeared with a vengeance. "I didn't *know* until you confirmed it. You expect me to believe you can't tell when someone is preoccupied with a budding relationship?"

"What relationship?"

"Oh, you know. The one you've managed to start during this trip whether you realize it or not. The one that had you so engrossed, you couldn't even send one word back to your favorite adversary and confidant: *me*!"

He tried to reply. "Events moved so fast from the moment I arrived—"

"For the entire week?" she said, cutting him off angrily.

"There was so much happening," he began weakly. "I was still trying to piece things together. A mere phone call would only have led to more questions, and I didn't as yet have the answers."

"You always call me!" she shot back. "You always let me know you arrived safely! You even kept me up to date on what you were doing. At the very least, you always asked about your students. If not within the first couple of days, definitely on our evening! Thursday evening! And you didn't even so much as text me!"

She was right. Thursday evenings had always been reserved for the two of them. They never considered it a date, but that particular night became very special to them both.

A few years back, Carla needed David's assistance with a troubled student. Owing to the delicate complexity of the problem, they decided to do a working supper that Thursday evening. Over time, they had come to make this weekly appointment a regular thing. While the students had their hangouts, the typical haunt for the faculty had always been a particular tavern-style coffee house in Old Sacramento that played soft chamber music as a soothing backdrop. Light meals, gourmet coffee, and music of the baroque period were this popular establishment's board of fare. The place, located east of the Tower Bridge Gateway near the riverfront, was called *Dolce*.

"You're right, Carla. I should've been more considerate. At the very least, I should've let you know I arrived in one piece and that there was much more to this West character than I was led to believe. I never meant to shut you out. Let me make it up to you."

"What would you do to *make it up* to me?"

"How about the infamous seven-course meal at *Gelmetti's*?"

Not wanting to give David so easy an out yet liking the idea of dining at the finest Italian restaurant in all of Sacramento, she turned her head in a questioning fashion and asked, "When?"

"There's always our Thursday evening? Then I could fill you in on my week-long adventure?"

Carla briefly held her stern expression before relaxing into a skeptical smile. "Thursday evening it is, but I'd better get the whole story to the very last detail!"

Chapter Eleven

The department heads gathered outside David's office waiting for the assistant dean to arrive. Peggy had this weekly meeting on the calendar for her boss, but Cobbett had chosen to forgo it last week. Now David had to play catch up.

Four of them arrived within minutes of each other, prompting Peggy to shuttle them into David's office. Though warm and inviting, she had room for just two chairs, her workstation, the file cabinet, and a copy machine. David's office was a bit more austere but much larger and contained a sizeable conference table that could accommodate everyone.

Henry Tanaka, head of the woodwind department, had recently joined the university after the retirement of his predecessor. Lindsay Morgan led the choral department and had been with UC Davis since the Mondavi Center first opened in 2002. Julia Winslow, the string department head and composition professor, Antara Singh, professor of world instruments and non-western music and Carla represented the senior faculty of the music department. The university's keyboard master class instructor and music theory professor, Carla was the last to arrive. She walked in as the others were chatting among themselves.

"Carla, do you know what favor Dr. Whealy was talking about in his email?" Lindsay asked.

Having just left David and the subject not discussed, she said, "No, I have no idea."

Skeptical, Henry asked, "He didn't say anything about it when you saw him this morning?"

Still smarting from David's secretive behavior about his week in Delaware, she looked Henry dead in the eye. "No, he did not." Carla's sour mood quashed any further conversation until the assistant dean's arrival.

David's week-long diversion did nothing to alleviate his anxiety about the concert. His last rehearsal was a disaster. Someone in the second violin section had a loose E string peg, and he had to figure out who it was before the performance. The horn section needed to focus on their listening skills and the principal flutist split his lip. Those were the problems David was aware of. He still had no idea how the solo groups or the chorus were developing for the concert and Lindsay wasn't forthcoming with such information.

David hoped to resolve these issues today, but with a packed schedule, he didn't appear to have the time. First up was the faculty meeting in his office. Following that was the preplanning meeting for the Faculty Solo Showdown, whose elimination round was fast approaching. He needed to discuss the particulars of this year's event with the organizer, student liaison, and concertmistress, Myung-hee Chun. And he would've rather gouged out his eyes than attend his last appointment of the day. It was with Cobbett.

Checking her email this morning, Peggy found a cryptic message from Cobbett, a request for David to meet with him this afternoon. The meeting was scheduled when David was supposed to be leading the rehearsal. Knowing Cobbett's history of tossing wrenches into the machinery at the last minute, he assumed the worst. But coming fresh from an enjoyable lecture, he was in good spirits as he walked into the conference room.

"Good afternoon, everyone," said David, cheerfully. "I trust you had a satisfying lunch?" Scanning the looks on their gathered faces, everyone seemed satisfied, except Carla.

"You're in a chipper mood today," said Lindsay.

"Your week away seems to have agreed with you," Julia added.

Even Henry piped in. "You do seem quite relaxed."

"It was a nice change of pace, I grant you," said David.

Antara didn't say anything. Though her demeanor suggested shyness, she was far from it. Given the proper topic of discussion, she would talk a person's ear off. For now, she seemed content to listen. Carla sat there stewing with her arms and legs crossed.

David moved to the head of the conference table. "Before we get into the agenda, I have a request of all of you. It's not school related, so please feel free to decline if you wish."

Antara straightened her posture, suggesting she was intrigued. Carla, on the other hand, thought if this request wasn't school related, her presence wasn't required.

"As you are no doubt aware, I returned from Delaware this weekend with an unusual inheritance. My benefactor saw fit to bestow his canon of unpublished autograph scores along with his estate. There are many pieces of varying arrangements and complexity, so I was hoping to enlist your aid in reviewing them. There's an unusual reason tied to this request that my benefactor, Mr. James Burton West has asked of me."

David reached into his coat pocket and pulled out the correspondence he received that addressed the disposition of West's music and passed it around for their examination.

He now had everyone's undivided attention, even Carla. David handed her the West correspondence first, hoping to hook Carla into the quest. She knew all about the lawyer's letter, but David hadn't shared this one with her yet. As she opened the letter with the strange wax stamp that resembled an oversized pair of scissors, David went to his desk to retrieve the faculty's assignments.

Splayed out over the surface of his desk in various organized stacks were the West scores he brought with him from Delaware. He'd separated each short pile by musical genre from chamber works to full orchestra pieces. He reserved the works contained in the three music folders for Carla's examination, choosing a select few for himself. The remaining works he divvied up among the other department heads by placing a cover sheet with their names on it, so he could effectively pass them out. Each of his colleagues brought a unique perspective to their approach to music theory and instruction. And David was counting on that diversity to help him evaluate West's musical output. He waited patiently as the letter completed its circuit around the table.

Assuming the eagerness reflected in their faces meant they were all in, he gave each their selected scores. Antara was already skimming through her pile to see how much work awaited her. Judging from the smile that grew larger with the turn of each page, she must have liked what she read. Henry was also moved by something he liked in the exposition of the piece he scanned. His eyes grew into saucers, and he wasn't even done with the first page.

David looked around the table at his deeply absorbed colleagues. "The scores you have in your hands are originals. There are no other copies, so please treat them accordingly. Remember, our priority is the upcoming spring concert. After spring break we have finals then the Faculty Solo Showdown, so we're going to be busy over the next few months."

"When would you want us to get these back to you?" asked Julia.

"I don't expect you'll have much time for a thorough review and what I brought back is only a small fraction of what he composed. I'm not even sure these represent his best work. How about the week before the start of the fall semester?"

Lindsay nodded. "That should give us the summer to do an extensive review. Sounds reasonable to me."

Henry nodded his agreement as did Julia. Antara was still engrossed. Wordless, she bobbed her head in agreement as she turned yet another page.

David turned to Carla. Her face was ashen as if she'd seen a ghost. The piece she read was the music David played for Beth. What Beth heard with her ears, Carla read with her eyes. Along with West's note and its unusual request, she was able to grasp the depth of feeling so prevalent in the opening phrases of this heartfelt piece. Even though Carla didn't have the complete picture, her powers of observation were keen enough to comprehend the meaning of the work. West seemed to be apologizing for something, but what? The name West chose for the work plainly stated as much. It was a piano trio entitled *Reverently Isabella*.

The concertmistress waited for her appointment with David. Since Peggy was finished for the day, she apologized to Myung-hee for leaving her to her own devices until David was done with his current meeting.

Myung-hee was a statuesque young woman. Feeling self-conscious about her height, she felt the need to dress down so as to not attract too much attention. Constantly aware of strange eyes taking in her beauty, she took conscious measures to discourage this unwanted attention. When she dressed to the nines, as she did during concerts, Myung-hee was drop-dead gorgeous and attracted more than her share of suitors. But it was her intimidating, dynamic presence on stage that gave them pause.

She heard the muffled voices from David's office as they grew louder. Then the door opened, and each faculty member filed out with their assignment in their hands. Julia noticed Myung-hee in the seat next to Peggy's desk.

"Oh, hello, Myung-hee. What are you up to today?"

"Hi, Professor Winslow. I have a meeting with Dr. Whealy about this year's Faculty Solo Showdown. Will you be participating this year?"

"Probably not. I'm booked solid for the remainder of the year, but thank you for asking."

"I'm sorry to hear it. You'd have made a strong contestant for the final public concert."

"Thanks for the vote of confidence, my dear. How is the quartet shaping up?"

"Robert had a family emergency, so Renatta stepped up to be our cellist. She's thoroughly familiar with the pieces we've rehearsed, so her substitution shouldn't present a problem."

"What happened to Robert?"

"His mom had a minor fender-bender on the Ventura Freeway the other day. She's still in the hospital but listed in good condition. Robert just left for Oxnard to see her."

"You're on top of it as usual," said Julia. "Tell Robert I'm sorry about his mother and hope she gets back on her feet soon."

"I shall, thank you for your concern."

"You're welcome and thank you, Myung-hee."

No sooner did Julia depart, then Carla appeared from David's office. She looked preoccupied and distant. Myung-hee had seen the music theory professor on many occasions, but today, something was amiss with her. Myung-hee was too apprehensive to ask what it was. She acknowledged the older woman with the dip of her head. Carla passed her without comment.

David stuck his head out of the office door. "Come on in, Myung-hee."

She entered the office and took a seat at the conference table. He returned to his desk and began to sift through it looking for something. While he kept searching, he asked, "Did your quartet manage to select enough pieces to take up the entire hour before the concert?"

She nodded and tapped on the book bag she brought with her. She pulled out the three pieces they were working on, keeping the choices in line with this year's theme of the B composers.

"We've been rehearsing selections from the early Beethoven quartets, the third quartet of Brahms, and the second quartet of Borodin," said Myung-hee.

"I haven't heard either of the Borodin quartets for a while, so it will be a nice change of pace." David continued to dig through his desk drawers. "And how goes the preparations for the Faculty Solo Showdown?"

Watching David carefully, she was responding to someone who was listening but not paying attention. "The first round eliminations are scheduled for the second week in May. The second round the following week and the final round the first week of June. Like last year, after the student body votes on the winners, the final three contenders shall compete before the general public on June 15. The results of the public's votes will be tabulated while the orchestra performs the rest of the program and shall be announced before the evening is over."

Although David heard every word, his movement about the desk became more agitated. It was becoming more pressing for him to locate whatever it was he was searching for.

"Is there something I can help you find, Professor?"

Scratching his head, he said, "It will turn up someplace."

Myung-hee smiled and ventured a guess as to what it was. "I believe you'll find it on the lectern in the lecture hall, Professor."

David frowned. "Find what?

"Your exercise ball. You left it on the lectern during your discussion this morning."

"And what makes you think I'm looking for that?"

"It's not on your desk now?" she said while trying unsuccessfully to stifle a grin.

David looked a trifle irked as he thought of Carla. "Does everyone know about my exercise ball?" he asked rhetorically, then said, "No, don't answer that." He broke into a smile himself. "Do you mind if I go retrieve it before we get started?

"Not at all."

"I shouldn't be more than ten minutes."

David left Myung-hee alone in his office. Still smiling at the thought of her musical mentor behaving as the definitive absentminded professor, she walked around David's office.

The room was large, but not inviting. The only ornamentation on the walls were photos of his current and former students. He had a bookcase with plenty of reference books, a conference table with several high-backed leather chairs, and his modest wood desk. Nothing about the office said anything about her professor, except the empty stand where his exercise ball should've been. She smiled to herself again as she observed the empty space. She happened to look at the center of David's desk, and that's when she saw it.

Centered in the middle of her professor's desk was a handwritten score laid out in landscape format. She picked up the score for a better look. She was familiar with the standard copyist font but not with this particular hand. It looked pristine and attractive. The title grabbed her attention. It was a string quintet. But skimming through its exposition, the piece was unlike any quintet she'd ever heard of. Scanning the entire front page, she noticed how the flowing motive seemed to grow into a definitive melodic phrase.

The quick-paced *scherzo* in three-quarter time began with the cello. Two measures of doubled eighth notes in ascending arpeggios followed by two measures of single eighth note-eighth rest combinations in descending arpeggios. Noting the overuse of eighth notes, she wondered why the composer didn't consider a six-eight time signature. The composer wanted this piece to move quickly judging from the metronome marking of 158. The first viola answered in this same motive. The phrase seemed to set the pattern for the entire opening subject whose modulations, though occasionally jarring, were quite captivating. This strange work enthralled her. She looked in the upper right-hand corner to see who had composed such a piece. The name was as elegant as the work, but she'd never heard of James Burton West before.

The first movement of the piece took up only a few pages. *It shouldn't take long to copy it,* she thought. She went into Peggy's office and quickly made a copy of the movement and placed it in her book bag before David returned to the office. Unable to get the theme out of her head, she resolved that her group had to play this piece.

But when?

♪

Chapter Twelve

Among the many perks that went along with being the dean of music at UC Davis was having the penthouse office. It was a huge rectangular room on the top floor of the music building distinguished by its unique corner window that made the perfect backdrop for the desk. William Tipton Cobbett III always enjoyed the view.

He never turned to look at the new arrival, because he was expected. Cobbett could hear the footfalls as they traversed the hardwood floor. When he finally chose to acknowledge the man, he did so with a single word. "David."

The assistant dean didn't correct his boss. He merely addressed him in kind. "William."

David earned the right to be addressed as *Doctor*, even by Cobbett, as his boss received his doctorate years later. Cobbett's snobbish address and his appointment as dean over David remained points of contention between the two men. The fact Cobbett held a superior position over his musical contemporary delighted the older man no end. But in all things that mattered, he was David's inferior. Bristling from the use of his first name as a rebuke, Cobbett made an effort to dismiss the insult.

"Please, take a seat," Cobbett blustered.

"Thanks."

"How was your little excursion to Delaware?" he asked feigning interest.

"Uneventful." David didn't feel like a casual conversation, nor was he in a sparring mood. He only wanted to get back to his last agenda item of the day—the spring concert rehearsal.

"Uneventful?" Cobbett parroted in a mocking sort of way. "Something must have piqued your interest for you not to call last week." He considered embellishing his statement with a sarcastic comment but thought better of it.

This was the second time in one day he was chastised for not staying in touch.

Carla's opinion mattered. Cobbett's didn't.

David fought hard to maintain a polite demeanor. "It's a convoluted puzzle for which I don't have all the pieces."

"Sounds intriguing," said Cobbett with an authenticity that made him sound almost human.

"On that point, we can agree."

"Well, that's something anyway."

Grasping the arrogance in Cobbett's tone and having little patience for it, David asked, "To what do I owe the pleasure of your invitation?"

"You didn't want a debriefing of your classes and rehearsal schedules?"

"You couldn't have captured all I needed to know in an email? After all, you took the trouble to send one for this meeting?"

"True, but then I wouldn't have had the added pleasure of your company for the first time in over a week."

David inclined his head in acknowledgment.

With an overblown sense of the dramatic, Cobbett cleared his throat before his booming tenor voice issued forth a proclamation. "I've made a decision with respect to our department's policy on the public performance of unknown works. We're no longer going to do so. Particularly, student compositions."

"And the reason for this extraordinary change in policy?"

Cobbett turned a deeper shade of pink. "Nothing extraordinary about it. Quite simply, I believe we hold a certain reputation for excellence that requires this university to rethink the repertoire it's willing to put forth before the general public. Wouldn't you agree?"

"One would've thought the future of musical excellence was in the hands of our students."

"It is, but not by elevating one student's compositional prowess over another. This university has standing among its peers and the public at large, and I'm going to keep it that way. The public is not interested in student compositions. Unknown works, regardless of their complexity or performance, do not attract audiences."

"Then how do you explain the public acclaim of Elaine Kirkwood's debut piece for clarinet choir last year? Or Clayton Forbes' successful *Concerto for Oboe and Woodwind Ensemble*?"

Unperturbed, Cobbett continued, "This university has a solid reputation showcasing well-established works, and it shall not sully that reputation while I'm dean of music!"

"And how does the performance of successful student pieces do that?"

Frustrated, the dean tried to underscore his point. "I shall *not* allow students to showcase work that may damage the reputation of this university, or am I not making myself clear?"

"Are you sure you're an educator and not a bureaucrat? Because your decision stands to counter everything a passionate educator believes. How can our students learn what's needed to be a complete musician if they're not allowed to explore the entire process?"

"It's for their future success that I take this unpopular action."

"Really? Is it for their future success or yours?"

"How dare you insinuate—" Cobbett gruffly began, but David cut him off.

"I find it fascinating that you would countermand your own words."

"What are you talking about?"

"Not only are you violating the core principles of higher education in general and this institution in particular, but you are violating the introductory remarks you, yourself made when you first came here four years ago."

"What introductory remarks?"

David allowed a smile to appear on his face as he got up from the chair. He looked Cobbett dead in the eye and recited, in the identical cadence and phrasing, his boss's four-year-old words. "The mission of this university's music department is to *fully* develop the talents and abilities of our young musicians in every aspect of musical endeavor. To this end, we shall be second to none in bringing out their peak performance and creativity to the utmost of our ability." To ram his point home, he added, "Now, either your inaugural mission statement was entirely disingenuous or your proclamation today is. Now, which one is it, William?"

Effectively neutered by his subordinate, all he could do was attempt to absorb the feeling of shock that someone would dare to stand up to him. And listen to the footfalls receding into silence as they disappeared beyond his office door.

David started his day in a pleasant mood. It got better when he met with his students and his colleagues. It only took a single meeting with Cobbett to ruin it. Feeling unequal to the task of leading today's rehearsal, he left word with Myung-hee to conduct it one last time before he was able to do it himself.

The disappearing rays of the sun over the roof of his ranch-style home shot past the cloud cover like a decorative Asian fan. David allowed his car to coast into the driveway as he admired nature's colorful tableau. On reflection, it had been a long day that needed resolution. From concerns over the outcome of this year's concert and Cobbett's policy changes, to his anxiety about how well he would perform in this year's Faculty Solo Showdown, David was an emotional wreck. He put on one of Bach's *Brandenburg Concertos* at a low volume before entertaining his pallet with leftovers.

A change of clothing, reheated pasta, and the slow movement of the Bach did little to amend his mood. Perhaps the rich aroma rising from the coffee maker would mark the prelude to an improved demeanor. He poured a cup, mixed it to the perfect shade of brown and took it with him to the recliner. The *Brandenburgs* having ended, he changed the music to the more relaxing *Two and Three Part Inventions*. David dimmed the lights as he retrieved his exercise ball, took a seat, and closed his eyes. The sun had long since slipped below the horizon when Beth called.

"Hello, David?"

"Yes," he said, not realizing who it was at first. "Beth?"

"I was getting ready for bed when I realized I hadn't checked in on you."

"The flight home was relaxing." Then he glanced at the clock. "Aren't we calling a bit late? It must be close to midnight over there."

"I know. But you had a busy week when you were here, and I probably didn't help you slow down any."

He didn't want to bore her with the details. "Thanks for your concern. I just played catch up with class schedules and meetings. What about you? Did you hear anything about your car?"

"The insurance company's going to total it."

"How come?"

"My car was nearly twenty years old. It wasn't worth the cost of overhauling the engine."

"Well, that makes my decision easy."

"What decision?"

"You can do what you want with the insurance money, but the Jeep is yours."

"David, I can't take your car."

"Can't nothing, it's done. The car is yours."

"But I—"

"Look, I can't drive two cars at once, and I already have one. Besides, the Jeep would just sit in the driveway gathering dust if you don't drive it, so it's yours, okay?"

Beth caved with a smile that David heard in her response. "Okay."

"Good! Now that we have that settled, how've *you* been?"

"You're unbelievable! It's only been a couple of days and you miss me already?"

"I have to admit I enjoyed your company. Is that so terrible?"

"No, 'cause I enjoyed yours. When do you think you'll make it back?"

"The academic year ends at the beginning of June, and we have one more concert scheduled after that. Once I finish grading finals, I intend to return for the summer to complete my investigation into our mutual friend."

"I'm glad."

Knowing that Beth's knowledge of the area could be valuable, he asked, "Would you have time to assist? I really could use your help."

"Are you kidding? I'd love to."

"I wouldn't be taking you away from anything, would I?"

"Don't be silly. I think it would be an adventure."

"My colleagues are going over some of Jim's scores as we speak."

"So you got them into the act, too huh?"

"For now, only as far as analyzing the music."

"And then?"

"I might consider inviting one of them to come with me."

"Good idea! Who knows what direction your investigation will take. You may require more help than you realize."

"I do have a particular colleague in mind," he said pensively. "Would that be a problem?"

"Of course not. He would be a welcome addition to the investigation."

"What if *he* was a beautiful woman?"

"Can she stand up to the rigors of detailed research?"

"That's the reason why I'd love to have her with me on this. Would you mind?"

"Hmm. Three is an interesting number, David. You're more open-minded than I thought."

She chuckled first.

He chuckled nervously.

Chapter Thirteen

Usually bustling with activity on any given night, David and Carla's Thursday evening at *Gelmetti's* was unusually quiet. The popular Italian bistro might have averaged thirty-five people the entire night. David was one of them, seated at a table for two. He didn't have long to wait for the occupant of the second chair as Carla came through the restaurant's dungeon-style door.

She was dressed to kill in a tastefully adorned red gown that showed just enough leg and cleavage to warrant the attention of male eyes from all over the restaurant. It was a sleeveless number with a plunging neckline, strategically located crisscrossing tufts of material and a tilted hemline to accentuate her height. The tall woman was an eye magnet, but she wanted to attract the attention of just one pair of eyes.

David was too occupied with the menu to notice Carla as she sauntered in. She was nearly to the table before he bothered to look up at her. Ever the gentleman, he stood up to offer Carla her seat, never removing his gaze.

"Wow! You're a stunner this evening." In all their Thursday evenings together, Carla never put on anything formal. So naturally, David's male ignorance revealed itself in his next question. "Who's the lucky guy?"

Carla kept the smile on her face as she embraced him in greeting then planted the tip of her size seven pump into his shin.

She didn't hit him hard, only enough to make her point. He received it loud and clear, casting that look to her as he sat down, rubbing his sore leg. As he regained his seat and his composure, he said, "Since you never dressed like this for me before, I naturally assumed you had another engagement."

"On *our* Thursday night?"

"Touché. You *do* look quite ravishing this evening."

"Thank you. That was the idea now that I have competition."

"Competition? What are you talking about?"

"Come on, David! Do I have to spell it for you in capital letters?"

"Okay, okay."

"So? Are you gonna spill it?"

Carla leaned over the table with her fists under her jaw and elbows on the table as she waited for his explanation. Luckily, the waitress rescued David from this awkward moment.

Segueing the conversation into their meal, David repeated for Carla what the waitress had offered him when he came in. "The specials tonight are *linguini pescatore* in either a delicate marinara or a bold, spicy seafood gravy or the house *pasta primavera*."

"Which one are you thinking of ordering?" Carla asked.

"I'm leaning toward the *penne arrabbiata*."

Carla turned toward the waitress and said, "The *penne arrabbiata* sounds delicious. Make that two."

"Soup and salad dressing?" asked the young waitress.

"*Pasta fagioli* and thousand island," said Carla. David nodded his approval.

"Would you like a cordial this evening, sir?"

"No, thank you," he responded. "I think an appropriate *Cabernet* served with the meal should suffice."

"Splendid, sir. I'll be out with your bread in a moment."

The second the waitress was out of earshot, Carla assumed her previous posture as if no interruption had occurred. Having delayed the inevitable as long as he could, David continued his reportage.

"Before I bore you with last week's adventure, I wonder if you had an opportunity to review the scores."

Carla looked at David without hinting at what her answer might be.

"You don't have to go into a lengthy analysis, just give me the short answer. For instance, what did you think of *Reverently Isabella*?"

Carla's expression changed from playful sarcasm to a blank stare. Her ability to interpret written music was finely honed; she could hear the music in her head the way most people would listen to a radio. It was apparent to David she was replaying the tune at that moment because she looked lost and in her own world.

"So?" he asked breaking her concentration. "I saw how you left my office the other day. You looked just like you do now."

She snapped out of her glazed expression. "The person who wrote that trio was a troubled soul, David."

"How do you mean?"

"I mean, your friend West was introspective but cursed with a profound sadness."

"I'd have to agree with you."

"It was as though the composer was trying to apologize for something he could never hope to atone for."

"I noticed that, too. Was that the only work that led you to that conclusion?"

"No. Nearly all of his piano works were tinged with this sense of foreboding. It was as if he wanted something he could never have."

"Thank you, Carla."

"For what?"

"You don't know how close to the truth you are."

"What truth?"

"Now that you've seen this man's writings, correspondence, and music, you should understand my odd behavior."

She shot David her best affectation of disbelief. "That hardly seems likely."

"Look, had I tried to explain it over the phone, you wouldn't have believed me."

"Oh, this ought to be good," said Carla as she resumed her distinct trademark posture.

"What I'm going to tell you will shake you to your foundation."

The waitress's timing was perfect. She brought the appetizer over just before he embarked on the summary of his weeklong adventure. When the young woman left, he proceeded according to Carla's previous instruction. No detail was too insignificant to be left out. He laid down all that transpired, starting with his odd meeting in the lawyer's office.

Even before he was finished discussing Talbridge, he noticed a smirk appear on Carla's face.

"What?"

"Your lawyer sounds like someone we know," she said with an air of levity.

David smiled back. "I had that same thought, too."

He went on describing the content of the second correspondence, the Lord De La Warr Bed & Breakfast and its namesake's huge painting above the fireplace. He went into scrupulous detail about that first day of exploration in West's home, the musical discoveries upstairs, the journals, the pencil sketches, and the instruments. He shared with Carla his surprise at the unique architectural use of bookshelves and the massive two-story window with its spectacular view of Cape Henlopen.

Listening to David describe the music, Carla was absorbed. The way he first encountered it. The overwhelming sense of wonder he felt reviewing it. The sheer scope and volume of what he discovered was beyond anything Carla could imagine.

The tone of David's voice was hypnotic in Carla's ears. She became transfixed with a single-minded need to take in every word as if consuming such information was life sustaining.

She perked up a bit as Beth's name was introduced but settled down as he continued to relay how they met and how they interacted throughout his entire visit. She didn't seem to mind when David described his visits to the bank or the archives. That changed when he got to his Thursday evening with Beth. Carla's emotions sprouted to the surface, West's mournful melody of *Reverently Isabella* playing in her head.

Carla visualized David's impromptu concert for a Beth Grey who listened, mesmerized by the pencil-sketched eyes of West's long dead wife. David's descriptive words placed Carla there with the two of them as the scene played out.

Carla's cheeks were damp with tears as he finished his account. She couldn't blame Beth for her being attracted to either West or David. She did blame herself for prejudging him. And Beth. She also blamed herself for not telling David how she felt all these years.

"Thank you, David."

"For what?"

"As I went through West's pieces, I knew it," she said surreptitiously wiping her wet cheek.

"Knew what?"

"That someone who could write such music must have more facets about him than his surface story would suggest."

"Would you like to know more?"

"Naturally!"

"You were the only colleague I even considered asking. I wanted you to know all the facts as I've discovered them because I have something important to ask you."

"Yes?"

"Now that you're up to speed, would you consider coming with me to Delaware for the summer? I could use your help examining scores and conducting further research?"

"I wouldn't miss this for all the chocolate in San Francisco!"

"I was hoping you'd look past my recent behavior long enough to say yes."

Carla was ecstatic about the invitation, but there was something she had to address.

"So, David, do you really like this Beth person?"

"Sure I do. She's a fascinating woman."

"That's not what I mean," she said, locking eyes with David.

Trying to be as honest as he could, he said, "I don't know yet."

"And how do you feel about our relationship?"

Dumbfounded she even have to ask, he said, "Carla, no one could possibly take your place."

"Not exactly the declaration of affection I was looking for."

Clearly irritated with the third degree, he asked, "How long have we known each other?"

"Over ten years now, why?"

"And after all these years, you have *no idea* how I feel about you?"

"Am *I* just as *fascinating?*"

"I've known you longer, which means we know more about each other." In a feeble effort to define their relationship, he said, "You're different."

"Exactly how am I *different*?"

Reaching his boiling point, he blurted out, "Because I'm quite fond of you, Carla. More than I should be, okay? We're more like soulmates than just colleagues, all right? Is that what you wanted to hear?"

"Yes, damn it! A woman still needs to hear the words *occasionally*, ya know."

To purge his exasperation, he took a breath and looked at her. "Carla, I have no friend, man *or woman*, with whom I could more readily confide. You know more about me than anyone, *including* Beth!"

She started to feel a bit better but was still unsure. "So you *do* think of me as someone other than a close colleague?"

"Is that what the eye-popping dress is for? So you could ask me such a question without having to come out and say it?"

Carla just looked at him waiting for a straight answer.

David reached out for her hand and scooped it up in his. He looked into her charcoal eyes as he did Beth's that day. "Can you understand that I've not been myself lately? That I've been thrust into an unusual situation? Can you appreciate the fact I'm still trying to process all of these questions since the day I received that letter? Have you not known me to doggedly work out the solution to a complicated puzzle when presented one?"

"Yes," she said timidly.

"Can you sit there and honestly say I don't trust you with all that I am?"

In an even lower tone, she said, "No."

"Carla, you are the dearest, sweetest, most loyal companion and challenging contemporary any person could ever hope to want in their lives. Married couples would envy what we have!"

At that last pronouncement, Carla took notice and smiled. No longer able to contain herself, she drew closer to David, cradled his cheek in her other hand and kissed him. Not on his cheek but directly on the lips.

"What was that for?"

She smiled at him and basked in the satisfaction. Then he gave her that look.

David spent the short trip home and the rest of the evening in deep thought. Entertaining the idea of a romantic relationship with anyone was the furthest thing from his mind.

His youthful liaisons were always more interesting physically, yet they lacked an emotional and intellectual connection. David's last serious relationship was a sexy young groupie who always hung around his band, Hot Brass Five. He carried on a brief but torrid affair with her, not realizing that she shared her affections with the other members of his group. This revelation ended that relationship as well as the group. The experience left David turned off romantic entanglements for a long time. He maintained a single existence from that point on, preferring to shed human companionship from his life.

Now two opportunities to embrace what he denied himself all these years presented themselves. The thought of companionship with an intellectually stimulating woman was becoming more appealing. His tantalizing quandary, to decide which of these enticing and attractive women he should choose to invest his emotions.

In considering his options, David remembered an ancient Asian proverb: if one wished to learn the true heart of another, they should get them angry. For only by bringing out a person's anger does that individual's true self emerge. David had known Carla long enough to see her exhibit a broad range of emotions, including anger. But what did he know about Beth Grey? Truth be told, she was an unknown quantity.

♪

Chapter Fourteen

The Sacramento Bee proclaimed it "*A Tour de Force!*" The San Francisco Chronicle said of the soloist, "*Myung-hee Chun's interpretation of the Bruch was a masterful performance worthy of Heifetz.*" Here again, in the space of four months, the musicians of UC Davis managed to produce another musical triumph the likes of which would stand alongside the world's greatest orchestras. David and his impressive group of young talent tackled the pieces with dedication, technical accuracy, and public acclaim.

Typical of Myung-hee, she was not concerned with the favorable reviews in the local papers. She focused her attention on organizing the final elimination round of the Faculty Solo Showdown. With the first two rounds out of the way, the last two would now monopolize her time. It wasn't simply the music they had to select for the featured soloists; they also had to coordinate the rehearsal schedule for the orchestra. The accompaniment for these pieces could be as simple as a duet or as complicated as a full orchestra work, but all had to be rehearsed.

The Student Faculty Planning Committee spearheaded the event with Myung-hee at the helm. She was a managerial delight, deftly leading the committee's music-related events to the smallest detail. With her uncompromising involvement, the concertgoing public could expect these next two events to be the most anticipated of the year.

June had arrived with all the blessings of a vibrant and colorful summer. For the students of UC Davis, the academic portion of the year was all but concluded. All that remained now was to wait for their final grades, make their summer plans, and assume their solemn duty to choose those who shall advance to the public performance round of the Faculty Solo Showdown. And of those surviving contestants, one shall determine the theme of next year's concert schedule. With only five contestants left, it was going to be a very heated competition.

Lindsay Morgan's crystal-shattering performance of a Rossini aria garnered the top spot in the last competition. She outshined her nearest competitor according to the votes. The fact she performed so popular an aria helped her standing. Her closest competition was the tight race between Jason Cantu and Carla. The associate professor's abbreviated but brilliant rendition of Liszt's *Totentanz* edged out Carla's Harp performance of a Celtic montage for second place. The last two contestants tied for fourth and fifth place honors. David was one of them. Cobbett was the other. The five performers slated to compete in the final elimination round were now set.

The music building concert hall was filling up fast with an increasingly animated crowd. They were stoked, and it wasn't long before the audience's uniform clapping indicated their growing impatience for the start of the competition.

At the appointed hour, the house lights dimmed signaling the start of the afternoon's program. As a spotlight beamed center stage in anticipation of the host's entrance, a rich amplified voice echoed the following salutation throughout the hall. "Welcome to the final elimination round of UC Davis' Eighth Annual Faculty Solo Showdown."

James Spence's preoccupation with himself, notwithstanding, he had a voice born for the microphone. And he usually managed to capitalize every opportunity to demonstrate it. Exercising his distinctive movie trailer voice, James forged ahead with his proclamation.

"Seventeen competitors have endured the crucible of competition this year, and we've whittled them down to these final five. Only three shall advance from today's contest to the Faculty Solo Showdown before the general public and *you*, the audience, shall choose those lucky three!" The audience cheered loudly.

"It is my distinct pleasure to introduce the host of today's final elimination round, the concertmistress of the UC Davis Symphony Orchestra, Miss *Myung-hee Chun!*"

The center curtain parted allowing the afternoon's host to appear to extended shouts of acclaim. Acknowledging the recognition of the crowd, Myung-hee nodded.

"Thank you so much. You are a gracious audience. Before we begin, I'd like to take this opportunity to recognize this year's Student Faculty Planning Committee members for doing such a fabulous job organizing this event. Like our performers today, their dedicated pursuit of excellence was evident in all phases of the project, and for that we thank them." When the audience settled down, she continued. "This afternoon's winners shall compete in the Faculty Solo Showdown concert two weeks from now. The winner there shall earn the right to control the concert schedule for the upcoming school year. Our first contender is none other than our revered assistant dean of music, Dr. David Whealy!"

The audience cheered and clapped as the curtain opened behind Myung-hee to reveal a contingent of players that made up the chamber orchestra.

David walked out on stage with his cornet, taking Myung-hee's hand as he acknowledged her introduction. She then handed him his envelope. The smile on his face disappeared as he removed the sheet music. It was the third movement of Hummel's *Trumpet Concerto*. He had never played the work before, so this was already going to be a challenge.

His sight-reading skills were excellent, and he was familiar with the music, especially the well-known last movement, which flowed quickly with its emphasis on tonguing technique. The work began with the trumpet's staccato double sixteenth to eighth note pattern. David nailed all the technical aspects of the work from beginning to end. Although his intonation was good, his performance today was not on par with his abilities, and it showed. He realized the subpar standard he set was an easy mark for his contemporaries to best.

Listening from the wings, Cobbett was already sensing victory. His enormous ego already dismissed the others as any real competition. A knowing smile came across his face as his subordinate's performance was somehow lacking this afternoon, and he assumed the students would rate it as such. He stood there mentally crossing out David's name from contention, something he thought the assistant dean was already doing on his own.

David took his bow at the conclusion of the orchestra's final note and acknowledged the crowd's generous applause. He held his instrument in the air as he walked off the stage, waving.

Myung-hee then introduced the dean. "Please welcome to the stage, our dean of music for UC Davis and the next competitor, Dr. William Cobbett."

Unperturbed by the light smattering of applause for the faculty potentate, the dean of music ascended the stage. Myung-hee presented him with his envelope. Cobbett's smile only got wider as he opened it to find a work with which he was thoroughly familiar. He was handed a virtuoso piece of superhuman complexity; Paganini's *La Campanella*.

He placed the sheet music on the stand and with exaggerated movements, drew up his violin, and lightly placed the hairs of the bow on the strings. His technique was flawless. His instrument appeared possessed with a supernatural will of its own. Cobbett's fluid movements and practiced jesting to the audience won them over completely. The dean's performance was nothing short of perfection. The audience reaction confirmed his standing for the moment.

Carla was next up. She received her envelope and noticed it was the *gigue* from Bach's *French Suite No. 3*. The benefit for Carla was that it was a solo work for harp only. In this way, she had complete control over dynamics and tempo. But the drawback would be no accompaniment. Any mistakes she made would be glaringly obvious and all hers.

She launched into the performance with a well-practiced ease. Her execution was inspired and whimsical. She plucked the strings with delicacy at times and with deliberate intent at others. In the end, she electrified the audience with her elegant interpretation.

Jason Cantu's entry was another solo number. Although short, the early E-minor keyboard Sonata of Domenico Scarlatti was far from easy, especially if one had to sight-read it. The associate professor's fingers leapt across the keyboard in a remarkable demonstration of skill and dexterity, and the crowd's enthusiastic applause reflected it.

Myung-hee took up the microphone to introduce the last performer. "And now, our final contestant. Please help me welcome, Dr. Lindsay Morgan."

Lindsay was like David. She was shocked to find Puccini's *O mio babbino caro* as her featured piece. And like David, she had never performed the work before. The only giveaway that she was concerned about her performance was a slight rising of pink in her cheeks as she prepared to sing. But once the opening notes were sounded, she settled down and belted out a convincing performance that recalled the strength of famed soprano, Maria Callas.

Lindsay melted the audience with her rendition. As she sung her final high-pitched note that seemed to disappear into the quiet of the strings, the audience erupted into sustained applause, the loudest of the day.

The audience had their work cut out for them. It would be a very tight decision.

"Ladies and gentlemen, thank you for your attention this afternoon. As the committee tabulates the votes, we shall entertain you with a special presentation."

Myung-hee reached for her violin and tuned it as she signaled the chamber players to do the same. She waited for Clayton Forbes to join her center stage with his oboe. Once in position, Myung-hee raised her bow, sniffed the downbeat, and they proceeded to play Bach's reconstructed *Violin and Oboe Concerto in D minor* with herself and Clayton as the featured soloists. It was a faithful performance that could have stood on its own merit as a separate headlined concert.

The results calculated, the three surviving contestants didn't seem to be a surprise. Carla just edged out Cantu for the third spot at the featured Solo Showdown concert. The next contender was Cobbett, and the obvious crowd pleaser received a standing ovation when her name was read—it was Dr. Lindsay Morgan and judging from the enthusiastic response, she stole the show. All three were called to the stage to receive their second curtain calls and flowers.

♪

Chapter Fifteen

Audra had taken the Smithsonian delegation on a tour of the Old State House across the Green. Two actors in period colonial garb met them as they entered the historic building. The first one introduced himself as Gunning Bedford Jr., one of the Delaware signers of the Constitution and later appointed the first US district judge for the State of Delaware by President Washington. The taller one bowed and called himself Colonel Allen McLane. He was the local American revolutionary, known as the hero of Duck Creek. The CIA officially recognized Colonel McLane as one of the first American patriots documented to use a disguise. In doing so, he successfully managed to conduct a two-week reconnaissance of the British fort at Stony Point, New York.

The two distinguished tour guides escorted the delegation through the first-floor courthouse and then upstairs through the bi-cameral legislature. Peering out of the uneven panes of glass through the second-floor window, each guest, in turn, looked across an open field to the new Legislative Hall, which has served the Delaware General Assembly as their home since 1933.

Upon exiting the Old State House, the colonial actors drew the delegation's attention to a pale blue and yellow sign hanging like a stiff flag out over the corner of a red brick building, not more than a block away from where they all stood. The historic marker identified the original location of the Golden Fleece Tavern. From its steps, the legislature made the announcement that Delaware would be the first state to adopt the new constitution only eighty-one days after it was passed by the 1787 convention. Sadly, the marker was the only remnant of so auspicious an occasion. The original tavern had long since been abandoned to the memory of history. The building had changed hands multiple times before the location finally became a law office.

The tour completed, Audra treated her guests to lunch before returning to the archives for the official start of the conference. Audra saw to the needs of their guests while Marge Tompkins made sure the briefing room was set up and all necessary preparations were tended to.

A lectern complete with a computer remote for the overhead projector was at the front of the room. The conference table was adorned with name tags, pitchers of water, and coffee. In front of each chair was a dossier for each attendee containing an agenda and their respective research assignment. And for their comfort, light refreshments were placed on the back table.

Marge was at the lectern testing the equipment when the lead historians with their research assistants from the Smithsonian and their Delaware Public Archive counterparts entered.

Ever the social director, Marge turned on the charm. "Good afternoon, everyone, and welcome to the Delaware Public Archives. We have a few moments before we get started, so please relax and enjoy the refreshments."

To facilitate team building during the weeklong event, each visiting historian and research assistant was paired up with an archive member. They were absorbed in their individual conversations when Dr. Giles Radnor arrived. He did so with a confidence that matched his well-earned reputation.

A historian and Asian linguistic prodigy, Radnor graduated from Princeton University at seventeen. He was awarded his first doctorate at nineteen. His achievements were indeed remarkable. He was named the youngest laureate to receive the Nobel Prize for Literature for his treatise on early colonial American law. A prolific writer, Radnor was extensively published in all the major newspapers and magazines as well as having several critically acclaimed books to his credit. He also received public recognition from the American Society of Legal History and the Organization of American Historians. His proclivity for the more exotic Asian languages was well-known among the academic community.

Radnor's latest project drew him and his research team to Delaware and the state's archives. The team was working on the formative years of an independent legislature for Delaware and its irreparable break from Philadelphia in 1704. The project was geared toward trying to understand the events that led up to the separation and how two independent colonies' legislatures functioned under a single governor.

As with many individuals of his superior mental discipline, Giles Radnor was a walking fashion faux pas. His predilection for plaid or checked cotton shirts with dress slacks overrode conventional standards. His wiry medium length blond hair and his preference for canvas sneakers only served to further this initial impression of the man. But when you are a tenured curator at the Smithsonian Institute's Division of Political History with more letters after your name than an optometrist's eye chart, most people tend to forgive such eccentricities.

Marge took her cue from Radnor's entrance to introduce her guests. Each visiting researcher had an impressive résumé, and even Marge was visibly struck by their list of accolades as she read them. Each member nodded as they were introduced while Radnor made his way to his seat. He didn't sit long, for Marge finally yielded the floor to her most distinguished guest following a flowery introduction. Radnor's easy manner belied the seriousness of the conference and its necessity to complete its stated aims in all too brief a time.

"Good afternoon, everyone," said Radnor. "On behalf of my colleagues, I'd like to take this opportunity to recognize Marge Tompkins and Audra Bunting for the informative tour this morning and for their herculean efforts in organizing this conference."

The other delegation members echoed Radnor's sentiments.

"The techniques we will share with you this week, along with the documents we brought with us and the considerable resources in your own archives, should reap historic rewards in learning about Delaware's inaugural plunge into self-government."

When Radnor finished his summation of their goals and how to accomplish them, they gathered into their separate groups. They targeted their research into specific time periods and regions. Once

Radnor briefed everyone on what he expected out of them, he let them have at it.

As they split up into their respective groups, Audra went up to Radnor. "Before we get started, could I ask you something?"

"By all means," said Radnor.

"I had someone bring in an artifact they recently inherited. Since you were coming, and knowing of your expertise in this area, I was wondering if you could look into this for me."

"Perhaps, if I knew what it was. Do you have the artifact?"

"Yes, one moment," said Audra as she disappeared into her office.

When she returned, she brought a small box containing David's key. As Audra opened the box, his blinking eyes divulged an intense interest. She passed Radnor the item as he felt the weight of the key in his hand. Turning it over to examine it, he asked Audra, "*Where* did you say you got this again?"

She could see how thoroughly he was looking it over. "A gentleman from Lewes, Delaware said he was handed this key along with his newly inherited property. He lives in California, but I have his contact information should you wish to get more details from him."

Still holding the key in his hand, Radnor was trying to remember where he'd seen something like this before. He thought he recognized its unique shape and size in an obscure reference to a prior investigation involving the mid-seventeenth or eighteenth century, but he wasn't sure.

"May I bring this back with me to the Smithsonian for further study?" asked Radnor.

"I think that's what the owner, Dr. David Whealy, wanted. He left it with me, but I don't know what to do with it. Besides, I believe he would have wanted to see it in the hands of someone with your qualifications to properly investigate the matter first hand."

"Thank you," he said, still staring at the key. "Are you sure he won't mind?"

"I'll contact Dr. Whealy myself to let him know you have it. Like you, he's seeking answers."

"That's kind of you, I appreciate it," he said, trying to recall the specifics of a related investigation he was involved with ten years ago. "I hope I may be of some small assistance in getting those answers."

Radnor reached into his coat pocket to retrieve his cell phone. In a few thumb strokes, the virtual keyboard appeared. It only took him seconds to draft a quick text to his administrative intern back at the Smithsonian.

> *Pls go to the vault. Retrieve box #37M41 from aisle K-3 and leave it on my desk. ty.*
>
> *- Radnor*

♪

Chapter Sixteen

The Student Faculty Planning Committee pulled out all the stops to make this year's ambitious public concert an enjoyable occasion. Everything from quick change set designs to lighting were all choreographed and thoroughly practiced. This was going to be a fun-filled evening and the perfect culmination of a superior musical season.

Carla was first to arrive backstage to check in with Myung-hee. In keeping with the theme of the evening's performance and Carla's chosen work, her dress reflected early eighteenth-century style. The outfit was highly ornamented with a tight-fitting bustier corset and a flowered pale green bodice designed to fit over it. The corset had half-sleeves of exquisitely frilled lace, tied firmly in the center, and laced from the bottom up, accentuating her ample cleavage. The garment was breath-stealing. A complimentary brown wig with spiraled curls draped about her face capped off the look without interfering with her ability to perform.

The out of place refugee from an earlier epoch looked into the gathering to see if she could find David, but he was not in his usual seat.

Concerned, Carla approached Myung-hee. "Have you seen Dr. Whealy?"

"I saw him in his office two hours ago," said the younger woman with her mind clearly on other things. She wasn't as worried about the assistant dean as she was with the final preparations for the evening. "Your harp is already positioned on stage, Dr. Macklin."

"Thank you, my dear," said Carla. She continued to survey the audience as Cobbett and Lindsay crept up behind her.

Lindsay arrived in costume, ready to perform in the opera from which her aria came. She was convincing in her full eighteenth-century military regalia. The officer's coat and shoulder boards with gold fringe lent an air of commissioned authority as did the matching waistcoat, knee breeches, hose, and buckled shoes. The modest white powdered wig she wore was still visible under her black cockade-adorned tricorn hat.

The dean appeared typically dressed in his outdated attire. However, a closer inspection of his period clothing revealed a distinct style was selected, but that wasn't the only glaring anomaly. His entire appearance was unrecognizable in that bushy dark handlebar mustache and homburg that rested with a slight tilt on his head. Rather than trying to appeal to the stereotypical outfit his competition piece tended to elicit, he chose instead, to appear as its creator. Cobbett's featured work was the only famous piece from this Italian composer, yet the familiar work had a distinctive Hungarian flavor.

Turning around, Carla was startled by the newcomers.

"I didn't mean to surprise you," said Lindsay.

"That's all right," said Carla clearly distracted by something.

Curious what her fellow competitors had in mind for a theme should they win, Lindsay asked, "Have either of you decided on a program for next year?"

Cobbett offered an upturned palm toward Carla, yielding the first response to her. Trying not to be rude, she enjoined the conversation. "I thought of exploring Eastern influence on Western music, but I haven't narrowed it down beyond that. How about you two?"

Lindsay responded, "Well, since we don't hear much music from a woman's perspective, I was thinking of showcasing the music of female composers from Elizabeth De La Guerre to Rachel Portman. How about you, Dr. Cobbett? What do you have in mind?"

Cobbett feigned thought by rubbing his chin, his choice for a musical program preordained. "I was leaning toward the composers of the twentieth century."

Carla listened but was preoccupied with searching for David through the sea of faces. "Have either of you seen David?"

"No, I haven't," Lindsay offered.

Carla turned her gaze toward Cobbett for an answer. Naturally, he hadn't seen him either. He confirmed as much with a shake of his head.

She remembered how disappointed David was in his own performance two weeks earlier. A triumph for David this year would have meant his chances of performing West's music would be solidified. With those hopes now dashed, he may have felt too discouraged to show up. Knowing how important this night would be and its impact on next season's programming, she worried David wouldn't come.

The contestants waited in the wings before a packed house. Every seat was filled, the atmosphere electric. Concertgoers who came from as far away as San Francisco waited with breathless anticipation for the contest to begin. The house lights began to dim as the rich voice of James Spence boomed over the speakers.

"Good evening and welcome to this year's Faculty Solo Showdown finale. Three finalists shall vie for the right to select next year's concert schedule and to be named this year's Faculty Solo Showdown Champion. And now, it gives me great pleasure to introduce your host and conductor for the evening, Miss Myung-hee Chun!"

The curtain opened to reveal a chamber orchestra in full costume and ready to perform alongside the first performer. Myung-hee was standing on the podium facing the audience and wearing period-appropriate attire.

"Thank you, James. Ladies and gentlemen, before we begin tonight's festivities, the students and faculty of the UC Davis Music Department would like to offer you our sincere appreciation for your steadfast support over the past year. You have made this our best year ever, and for that, we are exceedingly grateful." Myung-hee allowed the audience to finish their applause before introducing the first competitor.

"Two composers have tackled the French play of *Figaro* at different periods. In *The Barber of Seville*, Rossini took on the courtship of Count Almaviva and Rosina, while Mozart's *Marriage of*

Figaro, composed decades earlier, addressed the period twenty years hence. In her performance this evening, our first artist is doing it in the right order. She had successfully performed as the object of Count Almaviva's desire, Rosina. Tonight, she is Mozart's Cherubino as she delights us with her rendition of *Voi Che Sapete* from Mozart's *The Marriage of Figaro.* Please welcome to the stage, Dr. Lindsay Morgan."

The crowd went crazy when they heard the featured work was to be Cherubino's signature aria. Lindsay walked on the stage to rousing applause. She shook Myung-hee's hand and then turned toward the audience.

Myung-hee lifted her baton as she glanced at Lindsay. They nodded to each other; Myung-hee gave the downbeat, and the musical evening was underway.

Lindsay's sweet but powerful voice penetrated through the soft pizzicato strains of the accompaniment. The flittered timbre of her unique vibrato floated all the way to the upper mezzanine drifting magically into the public's discerning ear. Lindsay's angelic soprano voice and charming interpretation made you forget Cherubino was an infatuated adolescent male.

From opening phrase to closing note, Lindsay nailed it. The audience knew it too, judging from the standing ovation with which they enthusiastically rewarded her. For the first time since the competition began, Cobbett began to sweat, visibly concerned he might not be victorious.

To help change the mood for the next performer, a subtle change in lighting was all it took to give the illusion that the orchestra had instantly changed outfits.

Myung-hee introduced the next work and competitor. "While not considered a virtuoso piece of music, the *Andante allegro* from Handel's *Harp Concerto in B Flat* is a charming and recognizable work to the aficionado of the baroque era. Performing this work for us this evening is Dr. Carla Macklin."

Carla strode briskly onstage to the adulation of the crowd. Someone shouted from one of the upper levels, "Go, Carla!"

Executing an acknowledging nod to the source of the disturbance, Carla smiled as she waved back to them. She received Myung-hee's welcoming hand and took her seat to tune her harp with the orchestra. When Carla signaled her readiness, the conductor raised her baton.

Although not a complicated piece, it was quite refined. There was something regal about the work and Carla made the most of it. Orchestra and soloist played off each other sublimely. She still had the power to draw in the listener and to carry the delicate theme even within the unaccompanied solo phrases, the mark of a strong soloist. The execution of the *ritardando* in the final chords was done with such majestic intensity it seemed to herald the arrival of royalty.

Cobbett watched and listened with an unnatural patience. If he had interpreted the audience reaction correctly just now, his only competition was Lindsay. The applause for Carla's performance, while sincere and appreciative, was far from all encompassing.

Now it was Cobbett's turn. He sensed victory. He believed the competition was his to lose. And he wasn't going to lose. He had too much riding on the outcome to blow it now.

Again, Myung-hee turned her attention toward the audience. "The unfortunate phenomenon of the one-hit wonder is not confined to pop culture. It is indeed regrettable that the composer of the iconic piece you are about to hear was never known for the numerous operettas and ballets he wrote. What's more illuminating is that the unbridled Gypsy passion of this renowned work would not be considered stereotypical of his native Italy. But lucky for us, Vittorio Monti was faithful to the muse of his heart rather than the strict convention of nationalism. It gives me great pleasure to introduce our own dean of music, Dr. William Tipton Cobbett III, and his interpretation of Monti's spirited virtuoso violin piece... *Czardas.*"

From the audience's wild reaction, they knew the music well and were expecting something quite unique. The Monti look-alike was about to oblige.

Cobbett proceeded to shock the audience with a perfectly executed performance. The free flowing ad-lib opening gave him the space he needed to set the tempo and tone of the orchestra's accompaniment and set it he did.

At the completion of an exaggerated cadenza introduction, he glanced at the audience, rapidly flicked an eyebrow, and slowly issued the theme's four-note opening.

Cobbett's rigid stance gave way to a man consumed by what he played. The music carried him from one side of the stage to the other, eventually settling at center stage. He winked as he reached the end of the introduction, to begin the exposition of the main *presto* theme.

Exaggerating his sniff to the orchestra, he set a lightning tempo. This had the effect of not only bringing in the accompaniment but also drawing in the audience. Familiar with the piece, they began clapping with the first and third beats as Cobbett answered with the solo accent on the second and fourth before ripping into the *ostinato*.

The speed of Cobbett's bowing was phenomenal. His only mistake may have been having too much rosin on his bow. The friction buildup was such that before he was finished with the piece, strands of bow hair had broken off, floating back and forth like fine feathers as he scraped the bow across the strings.

As Cobbett's down-bow stroked out its last note, a profoundly surprised audience let their raucous adulation known. His ovation was genuine and long. Who knew his acting ability could match his musical prowess.

A brief intermission followed Cobbett's performance. The audience was asked to select their winner and pass their votes to the student representative near the aisle. Each student added their sections votes and then passed the results along to an organizer who consolidated the vote totals.

The chamber orchestra performed four more pieces to complete the evening. When the last work was performed, Myung-hee traded her baton for the microphone.

"Ladies and gentlemen. Based on your reactions this evening, I don't believe either of our top two performers are going to be a surprise to you, only the order. Our first runner-up performed for you Mozart's *Voi Che Sapete*, Dr. Lindsay Morgan."

Again, Lindsay was rewarded with a heart-felt ovation.

"And now, ladies and gentlemen. The winner...of this year's Faculty Solo Showdown...is...our dean of music, Dr. William Tipton Cobbett III!"

Thunderous applause ensued.

Cobbett's thin smile grew wider as he raised his head to acknowledge their cheers, then he bowed deeply to the audience.

A lone observer in the last corner seat of the upper mezzanine watched the entire proceeding with disappointment at first. His disappointment turned to disgust as his boss and growing arch nemesis was crowned champion.

The Eighth Annual Faculty Solo Showdown was now in the books. Having taken top honors and proven the superior performer in this contest, William Tipton Cobbett III would now have total control over the musical agenda, and he was determined to press that advantage. The lone observer's responsibility for next year's concert schedule was relieved. He could now pursue the mystery of James Burton West with renewed vigor.

♪

Chapter Seventeen

David stood in the quiet of his ranch-style home in the Sacramento suburbs with the smell of fresh brewed coffee waking his senses. The academic year was all but over. He only had to complete one final week of academic housekeeping before he would be on his way to Delaware. He needed to relax and put his disappointing performance at the showdown behind him.

Peering into the living room, he caught sight of West's journals perched on the armrest of the sofa. After pouring his cup of coffee, he moved into the living room. He scooped up the journals and looked through the first one to confirm it contained only lengthy program notes of West's musical output. Setting it aside he took up the next one.

The initial entry was undated. That is to say, it only had a day and month, but no year. This approach seemed to characterize the early entries as though time simply didn't matter to the author. David skimmed through this first true journal and found that the entries were addressed to no one in particular.

It wasn't until he read the last few entries in the last journal he noticed West had properly identified a recipient for his discussions. And that person was David.

For some reason, after an undetermined amount of time, West needed to *talk* to someone. He wasn't comfortable with real people like Beth, so he put his thoughts in writing. His inaugural entry was an interesting read.

To the unaffected reader,   *April 23rd*

I've been contemplating the idea of keeping some kind of personal journal for the past few months.

The idea occurred to me during one of my jaunts. I was in New Mexico, I think. I don't remember now (thus, the need to commit my thoughts to paper).

I'd really let myself go over the last few years. My hair became a scraggly mess. As the unkempt look at my age seemed undignified, I resolved to do something about it.

I pulled off the highway and drove my Jeep through the little town, reducing my speed to the obligatory 25 mph. In the distance, I saw the familiar spinning of a barber pole at the far corner of the street. As I approached a traffic signal, a flock of birds, sparrows maybe, took flight directly in front of me. They shot upward like dark confetti executing all manner of movement in complete unison. They darted to and fro with the precision of synchronized swimmers. After a brief pause to admire their performance, I proceeded to my unscheduled appointment at the barbershop.

I sat there in the barber chair watching the specs of my clipped hair rain down across my face to land gently upon the black expanse of the barber cape. The image struck me as a snow shower. I hadn't noticed how gray my hair had become. The sparrows' dark-flecked exhibition moments earlier reminded me of my former, more youthful-colored locks. These contrasting visuals clearly illustrated to me that time was not on my side. I needed to commit my thoughts to paper—before it was too late.

David was totally mesmerized. Unable to put the down the journal, he found himself drawn in by the depth of West's narratives. The early entries were quite brief. West was remarkably selective in what he chose to document for posterity. David readily passed up the shorter entries for the lengthier ones.

West's muses were wide and varied. Though he rarely addressed his mood, he discussed his creative motivations, his travels, and the odd reminiscence. On numerous occasions, these entries offered David a window into West's compositional thought processes. A few of them were only tantalizing hints to his creative genius.

October 24th

Finally! These past few months have been very productive. Today I managed to pen the final note of a string of works that capped a month-long creative impasse.

West's facility for teasing David with such tidbits of information was sufficient to engage his interest. Reading of the author's excitement at the completion of more works brought David closer to his benefactor and forced him to forget his emotional and physical exhaustion. West's narratives painted a distinctive picture with crystal clarity. David was the silent observer, present with West as he penned his thoughts to an unknown stranger.

Though some of West's narratives were vague, others went into precise detail and were more akin to the composer's thoroughly described program notes in his first journal. On one rare occasion where West used a complete date, David discovered the entry not only exposed West's penchant for discussing musical ideas but his ability to express his patriotic fervor through artistic and musical symbolism.

September 18th, 1997

Earlier this month, I began to reflect on the significance of this date. I've done much to eradicate the memory of my military experience, yet the restructuring of the defense of this nation under the National Security Act of 1947 should be acknowledged—somehow. I had already made a sketch of the old Army Air Corps star and wing shortly before my retirement from active duty. Last week, I started work on a sketch that not only recognized the Air Force's 50th Anniversary but also captured a montage reflective of my 23 years of service.

Today, as I was putting the finishing touches on the final idea, a rhythmic musical motive came to me. I found it difficult to concentrate on the sketch without hearing the pulsating rhythm in my head. It only took me a few minutes to sketch the first page of the fanfare and a second of thematic material.

In one of the few times West's entries were connected to each other, the next entry dated one week later, completed the discussion.

September 24th, 1997

The new fanfare is now complete owing its instrumentation to three trumpets, three horns, three trombones, and tuba with snare drum accompaniment.

In the spirit of Air Force heraldry, the lone trumpet signifies the Air Force's initial "solo flight" as a separate military service. After the second statement of the motive by the solo trumpet, the horns enter. Their chordal structure signifies the majesty of the Air Force's indomitable spirit. By the end of the first phrase, a confident Air Force team comes into full voice. The secondary motive suggests the flexibility of the Air Force. The brief development section lends itself to describing the Air Force's ever-evolving mission. With the reprise of the main theme, the solo trumpet theme is now a polyphony of sound representative of a mature Air Force. The work concludes with a statement of the Air Force Song.

Each voice contains three parts that represent the active, reserve and guard components of the Air Force both past and present. The voices themselves are representative of the various team members that make up our nation's Air Force. The trumpets are the officers, the leadership of Air Force. The horns stand for the Air Force spouses and dependents whose support is never forgotten. The trombones represent our Air Force civilians whose direct contributions are pivotal to the success of our young service. The tuba, indicative of the Enlisted Corps, the "backbone" of our Nation's Air Force. And finally, the snare drum, representing the pulse of the US Air Force, carrying its bold mission into the 21st century.

He looked through the first journal of cataloged works to see if he could find the write-up. He skimmed the journal and found it listed under opus 73. It was entitled the *USAF 50th Anniversary Fanfare*, and the program notes were a word for word transcription from this journal. Apparently, the first journal was the last he considered writing. This entry was the first, and only time West put a program note in these journals.

West made the distinction between a program note and a journal entry. When he discussed the circumstances surrounding the creation of a new work, the work itself would be described in great detail within the program notes.

However, the content of these volumes took on varied and sundry subjects. As David continued to peruse through the carefully documented volume, he found an entry that Beth Grey might be interested in. He had to remind himself to tell her when he saw her.

April 18th

I was returning home from a stroll on the beach this morning when I met my new neighbor. She was trying to unload some furniture into the corner house across from mine. Watching her struggle with such a burdensome task alone, I wondered why the men in her life abandoned so charming and attractive a woman to her own devices.

She was sincerely appreciative of my offer of assistance in moving her heavy articles. To reciprocate, she offered me dinner, but alas, I had to decline. It wasn't my intention to be rude, but my morning walk was quite musically productive, for the ending of the piece I was working on had been plaguing me for the past few days. I was finally able to work out a satisfactory resolution for the work that morning but didn't have time to render the ideas to paper when I met her. While I still had the ending clear in my head, I had to ensure I did so before her alluring distraction vanquished the ideas completely.

I must admit that in that short space of time, I was taken by her strength of personal character to say nothing of her infectious charm and beauty. But for the abrupt way I ended our initial encounter, we might've explored a deeper friendship. If only.

He wondered why West didn't elaborate on that final thought. Most of his entries discussed a litany of matters, which, on the surface, didn't seem to make sense to David. Odd though they were, David enjoyed reading these atypical accounts.

March 15th

When I was twelve years old, my grandfather showed me a timeworn letter fragment (the unsigned first page). It was purported to be from an early descendant whose father was a famous Thomas of some historical significance. Contained in the letter was an odd phrase, which neither my grandfather nor I ever understood. The phrase, recreated here exactly as I remembered it was, "In my Solitude, the secret shall remain forever." The purpose of the letter was unclear. It may have been in response to a query of some kind. There was mention of the author's property and his "current status," although he never said what that status was. I also found the use of phrasing and capitalization a bit odd until my grandfather told me that their manner of writing in the eighteenth century was not standardized. What we would consider grammatical mistakes today was commonplace during that period.

A few pages past that entry, he ran across another tantalizing account that deepened the mystery further. Here again, was a reference to the iron key David already had, and the gold signet ring that he had yet to find. Since there was so much importance attached to this object, it was something he was keen to locate, but like the correspondence West provided him, no clue as to the ring's whereabouts would be forthcoming in this entry either.

May 3rd

Rummaging through my father's effects sometime after he passed, I came across a couple of curiosities. The first was a gold signet ring allegedly handed down from the very first property owner. I couldn't make anything of the design since it was so badly worn. I could only decipher its oval boundary and a

119

strange impression on the top and bottom of the oval with three discernible circles in the middle band and an odd phrase in Latin below it. I never saw anything like it before.

The second was this oversized iron key. The only distinguishing feature beyond its age was its size. A relic of some bygone era, it seemed to have meant something to my father since he felt the need to keep it. Why it was so important, he never told me. He never said anything about the ring either. They must have had some significance to our family since he kept them locked away in his trunk, but what was it?

Seeing how neat and tidy West kept his home, David wondered where his benefactor could've been rummaging as he found himself reading the final written pages of the third journal. He also noticed that the author began to use complete dates. And that wasn't all. Something else had changed. The entries now addressed *him* specifically.

To Dr. David C. Whealy,   *January 21st, 2008*

Although you do not know me, I've been a fan of yours since your Hot Brass Five days. I happened to run across a documentary that featured you, and as a consequence, I believe you to be the most qualified person in whom I may confide.

I must admit to a marked preference to keep much to myself, yet I also find it increasingly necessary to open up to someone, since merely "speaking" to an empty book holds little rewards.

*Your temperament, your brutal honesty, and your
eclectic musical taste make you the ideal recipient
for my life's work and my solitary ruminations.*

For the first time, David felt a personal connection with a man who, until now, was simply a name on some letters and a storyteller to an unnamed person in some journals. From this point on, Jim West was his one-way pen pal. A storyteller whose sole intended audience was David.

He quickly read the few remaining pages until he reached the end of the last journal. The first entry addressed him formally. The last two by his given name which caught his attention.

Dr. Whealy,

Today I passed a milestone. Two hundred individual opuses. An event of this magnitude I'd normally share with Isabella. I can see her sweet smile grow wider as she acknowledged the accomplishment. It's at times like this that her absence is so keenly felt. She, above anyone else in my life, could understand the importance of such a milestone.

The only thing that would make this achievement greater would be academic recognition from an authoritative source, like you, to declare the works of any redeemable value.

If they are not, then they should be consigned to the flames of oblivion.

Here was the first tangible clue that referred to the destruction of his works should they have no intrinsic value. Why, the entry didn't say. He kept reading to see if any explanation would be forthcoming.

David,

I must apologize to you. I've been remiss in my appreciation to you for your patience and your unrealized friendship. It's with deep regret that I never took the opportunity to meet you face to face. Please forgive me?

Both my health and creativity have taken a downturn of late, and I fear these mutually exclusive topics are somehow related. I refuse to go to a doctor. I haven't been to one in years. I simply don't see the need, especially since I can't seem to write the quality of work to which I've grown accustomed.

My end shall come, no doubt, when the creative sustenance within my soul is depleted.

David,

I find myself written out. New musical ideas are fading with age. Old ones seem to be replaying in my head, originality strangely absent from these uninspired themes. Perhaps my life and my music have run their course. Perhaps this life is done with me. Perhaps

This was the last journal entry of James Burton West. And it was this entry that woke David up because Jim's thought was left unfinished. To his dismay, there was no further mention of why David should destroy West's music in the event of an unfavorable evaluation.

Turning to look at the clock, he noticed it was nearly two in the morning. The hours he'd spent reading West's journals had him so enthralled he lost all track of time.

He wasn't feeling tired, but it was too late to call Beth. Pouring himself a sherry, he contemplated what he needed to put the final punctuation mark on this academic year before summer break. His loss in the faculty competition meant he was relieved of the responsibility for next year's concert schedule. He was now free to concentrate on his trip to Delaware.

Sipping from his glass, his eyes drifted toward his laptop. A brief search and a few mouse clicks later, David had confirmation for two round-trip tickets to Baltimore.

♪

Chapter Eighteen

David and Carla picked up a rental car and headed south on I-97 toward Route 50. They took lunch at a seafood place on the Chesapeake Bay island of Kent before heading toward Delaware, but Carla wasn't too enamored with the meal.

Taking in the beauty of their drive along the Delmarva Peninsula, she periodically glanced at David, who seemed to have retreated into himself. "You look rather quiet today. Anything wrong?"

"Just thinking."

"About?"

"I reread West's correspondence trying to make sense of the clues he sprinkled in among his journals."

"Yeah? And?"

"You remember. In one of his letters, he said he would provide an explanation as to why I should destroy his works if their destruction was warranted?"

"I remember that one, sure. Why?"

"Well, I've read through his three journals but couldn't find that explanation anywhere."

"Did he say where you could find it?"

"No, he didn't."

"Then I'd say you have another mystery on your hands."

He threw her a sarcastic expression. "Thanks."

"You said you found his journals stacked neatly on the corner of his desk right?"

"Right."

"His music meticulously organized in both the music folders and in the file cabinets, right?"

"Right."

"His home well-maintained with everything in its place?"

"What are you getting at?" he asked, frustrated with the rapid-fire questioning.

"Humor me a bit longer, will ya?"

"All right," he said with a hint of resignation.

"Where did you find his scores?"

"They were located in two lateral files, recessed among the bookshelves. Why?"

"Did you notice them at first?"

"No, I didn't. So what you mean is, not everything is at it seems in this redesigned home?"

"Exactly! Your pal West devised an ingenious way to reveal his innermost secrets when he wanted to, and only to the right person."

"And how are we to find these innermost secrets?"

"I don't know yet, but one thing is sure."

"What's that?"

"There's another journal."

He looked at Carla incredulously. "How do you know that?"

"Come on, David. Think! Too many unanswered questions remain, and presumably, he's been quite open about himself in these other journals, right?"

"Yeah?"

"Then it stands to reason he'd be very specific about what he wanted to share with you. You did say he didn't begin to refer to you by name until the last few pages of the third journal."

"That's right," he said, still not getting what Carla was saying.

"So he either left you another correspondence, which is highly unlikely given his short letters never went into great detail—"

"Or?"

"Or he left you a journal that would have given him the space needed to expound on the explanation you've been looking for. Thus, there's another journal you haven't found yet."

David pondered this notion as the newly paved blacktop marked their crossing into Delaware. The two colleagues remained silent as David considered her words, trying to figure out where West may have placed such a crucial journal.

Surveying the flat open spaces of her new surroundings, she broke the silence first. "Were there any other clues West wrote in his journals or correspondence that we should investigate while we're here?"

"The key I was given is now in the hands of some Smithsonian expert. The signet ring I haven't found yet."

"What would you like to do first?"

"I'd like to go through West's music first. That task will take us a while."

"And then?"

"We have to find out about this letter fragment."

"What letter fragment?"

"Sorry, just read about it myself in his latest journal. He said his grandfather referred to this letter that mentioned an enigmatic ancestor named Thomas. I have no idea how to proceed from that."

"Well, let's think about it. If his estate was in the family since 1724, shouldn't we begin our inquiry there?"

"What if his progenitor was from a time before that?"

"Hmm, you've got a point there," she responded. "We could narrow our inquiry considerably if we found the complete letter."

Offering her a tantalizing clue, he said, "West's journal did say it contained an odd phrase."

"Really? Do you remember what it was?"

"The quote was, '*In my solitude, the secret shall remain forever.*'"

"That's odd all right. Was there anything else?"

"That's all I can remember for now," said David as the two fell into a thoughtful silence until they made it into Lewes. Before they headed to the house, they pulled into Five Points market to get some groceries. While on the checkout line, David tried to contact Beth, but no luck.

"Were you able to get ahold of her yet?"

"No, and I'm starting to get worried."

"Is it a landline or a cell?"

"That's what I don't understand. It's her cell number."

"That's weird. She could be charging it?" Carla suggested.

"You could be right. But she hasn't responded in days."

Now both were worried.

The straight road to the house was a familiar sight to David as the West estate came into view. As they reached the far curve of Frontage Road, David looked into Beth's driveway but didn't see a vehicle. He glanced up his driveway hoping it was there, but again nothing. *She must have kept the Jeep*, he thought.

"I wonder where she went."

"She could be on vacation, you know. After all, it is summer."

"Beth didn't say she was going on vacation."

"She might not know you well enough to tell you that."

"You could be right," he said. They gathered up their belongings and groceries and brought them into the house. David gave Carla a brief tour of the first floor. "You can have the master bedroom with the en suite, and I'll take the guest room."

"Thank you."

Although she was given the complete description of the room, she was still taken aback by the sheer magnitude of the second floor's character when he took her upstairs. She scanned the walls from left to right, then her eyes drifted to the Bösendorfer sitting dead center in the middle of the room. Wasting no time, she quickly took a seat at the piano and began to play arpeggio exercises in ever-increasing half steps.

Her hand crossings looked effortless to David who took in the sight with unvarnished awe. The fluid movements of Carla's arms had a dance-like quality that captured his attention. When she finished, she looked up at David, winked, and transitioned into her competition piece, the *gigue*. Her instantaneous segue from boring exercise routine to expression-filled performance was profound. David let her enjoy herself while he went downstairs to make dinner.

Soon, the house was filled with the aroma of something delicious. It made its way to the second floor enticing her hunger, interrupting her performance.

"What smells good?" she asked leaning over the balcony.

David smiled to himself, "Thai red curry."

"How did you whip up something like that so fast?"

"I already had the rice, coconut milk, curry paste, and seasoning. All I needed was the fresh chicken which we picked up and the time to cook it."

"That beats my time in the kitchen!"

"It'll be ready in ten minutes. Are you hungry?"

"I could eat again, sure. Besides, the cook at that seafood place must have had an off day."

As David set the table and selected an appropriate table wine, Carla came downstairs. She didn't see it until she got near the bottom of the staircase. That's when she noticed the pencil sketch portrait of Isabella West. She remembered David's detailed description of the home and how he explored its rooms and the vivid, lifelike detail in West's visual art. But she was no less impressed to witness his ability first-hand.

"Your benefactor's talents were extraordinary on many fronts."

"Yes, they were. And tomorrow, we have the opportunity to prove the pieces I brought back were only the beginning."

"What's the plan of attack?"

"How about you start at the beginning opus numbers, I'll start at the end, and we'll meet somewhere in the middle?"

"That's a good plan for the music, but what about the missing ring and the letter fragment?"

"That's where Beth could come in," he said handing Carla her plate. "She doesn't know much about written music, but she knows the area. Maybe we could enlist her help researching the other clues before we all go to the archives."

"The archives?"

"That's right," he said, taking a seat to enjoy his dinner. "The Delaware Public Archives would be a great place to pick up the trail."

"Of course," she agreed. "Well, I'm famished."

They ate quickly. Yielding to full stomachs and exhaustion, they both retired early.

♪

Chapter Nineteen

David was awakened by the smell of maple-smoked bacon. Carla had gotten out of bed earlier and decided he needed to sleep in.

"Good morning. Finally decided to get up I see."

"When did you get up?"

She looked at the clock then replied, "Oh, two hours ago."

"Why didn't you make breakfast earlier?"

Smirking, she said, "I didn't want to wake you. I got you up now, didn't I?"

His facial features held a hint of that look as he turned his attention to the full coffee maker. "Thanks for the consideration," he said, pouring himself a cup. "You want one?"

"Sure."

Pouring Carla a mug of liquid motivation, he asked, "How did you sleep?"

"Like a baby. So what's on the agenda this morning?"

"We could begin straight away by examining his scores? Have you seen the CD library yet?"

"I have. West was quite the audiophile, wasn't he?"

"That he was. Let me show you how to use the sound system, so you can use it whenever you want."

"If our first task is to evaluate his musical output, wouldn't it make more sense to do it quietly? Without disruption?"

"Of course, you're right."

Too excited to wait much longer, they finished their bacon and egg breakfast and migrated to the second floor to begin their task.

The midmorning sunlight was splayed across the mahogany floor. Carla sat at the desk with a stack of scores retrieved from the upper lateral file while David was ensconced in a high back office chair next to the lower lateral file and began going through the scores backward. Having already examined West's other works in the folders, she noticed his earlier works weren't as sophisticated as the later ones. Some of the pieces skipped opus numbers between scores as they were either in the three music folders or the pieces David brought with him to California. She picked up each one in turn and read them.

As David pulled out another score to review, he turned and looked at the focused intensity in Carla's eyes. They were moving left to right as if she were speed-reading a newspaper. David smiled to himself watching Carla, taking her task so seriously. She caught sight of him staring at her.

"What?"

"Nothing."

The two of them, engrossed in the music, didn't notice how the sun had arched across the sky, its light sinking below the horizon.

"Hey, you! Guess what?"

"What?" she asked absentmindedly, not looking David's way.

"It's eleven o'clock!"

"I'm not ready for lunch yet."

"No, sweet cheeks, it's eleven *p.m.*," he enunciated.

"Wow, I didn't realize we've been working that long!"

Carla suggested a light snack before going to bed.

This was their routine over the next two days. Wake with the sun, breakfast, and a long day of score reviews with perhaps a snack, more music review, then a light meal before bed.

Meal times not only let them engage in expanded discussions over West's varied musical taste and style but also gave them a much-needed break. They also tried to make contact with Beth throughout the day but without success.

By the end of the third day of nonstop score evaluations, both were losing their focus. David saw Carla hunched over the desk examining a score. He could tell being in the same position for hours on end was working against her. She confirmed it by rubbing her tired neck with her free hand.

"Anything interesting over there?" he queried.

"I have to say," she was interrupted by a yawn, "your pal West's compositional skill seems to drastically improve with each new work. I find myself having to go over his earlier works to confirm it."

Carla was visibly exhausted. "Do you want to call it a day?" he asked.

"My mind says no, but my eyes, legs, and back say differently."

He put down the score he was reading and went over to Carla. "I tell you what. I'll pop the cork on some red table wine and get dinner ready. Why don't you amuse yourself by exploring Jim's music library?"

"Excellent idea. *Anything* different would be a good idea about now." Carla selected some of West's soft jazz for a change of pace. She had his scores in her brain for the past three days and as good as they were she needed a stylistic break. The smell of dinner was once again drifting through the house. Coming into the kitchen, she said, "What's that? It smells great!"

"Homemade cheese ravioli and marinara."

"You're going to make someone an excellent housewife someday," said Carla jokingly.

"Are you applying for the job of *someone?*"

"You know I would," she answered. But this time, she was serious.

They ate dinner and discussed the music they reviewed. West was a serious phenomenon worthy of discovery. David already thought his colleagues would come to the same conclusion when they reported on their homework.

They enjoyed dinner, washed down with a tasty red wine. Three days of exertion was plainly evident in their manner; the conversation dwindled to nothing. David used his napkin to remove the remnants of sauce from his lips when he noticed Carla looking at him quite strangely.

"What is it?"

"Could I ask you a deeply personal question?"

"When have you ever felt you couldn't?"

"I'll take that as a yes," she said, fixing her intense gaze into his eyes. "In all the years we've known each other, why have you never made a pass at me?"

Eyeing her back, he replied, "It's not because I hadn't thought of it."

His answer put a smile on her face. She knew that was as close to a sensual compliment as she'd ever heard from him regarding any woman. "So you find me attractive?" she asked coyly.

"Absolutely, Carla," he said, aroused by the seductive tone of her questions. "But why would someone of your considerable wit, youthful beauty, and intelligence waste their affections on a man like me?"

She asked playfully, "What's wrong with you? Are you an ax murderer or something? We're only ten years apart! It's not as if there's six years difference where the Chinese zodiac would say we're incompatible."

He offered her a hint of that look. "Come on, Carla. You know why."

She sat staring at David waiting for him to respond to her logical conclusions.

"You know I could give you several reasons you would dismiss out of hand, but convention would have to top the list. How would you feel if I were to carry on an open relationship with, oh, let's say Antara? Would you feel comfortable with a colleague openly dating someone who is essentially your supervisor?"

"I suppose not. But you're not the boss are you?"

"Close enough for a perceived relationship to become a problem. Right?"

"Point taken," she conceded, thinking she knew who wouldn't be a problem for him to date. "Then there *is* someone else."

Knowing who she was fishing for, David diffused her assumption right then and there. "No, there isn't. I've not had a relationship for several years, now, and you know it. For the time being, my energies must be focused on exploring this mystery called James Burton West. Not even a relationship with Beth is possible as long as I'm in the middle of this, okay?"

Seeking to make a tactical retreat now that her competition was mentioned, Carla changed her demeanor and the subject. "The marinara was excellent, David."

"Would you like anything else? Coffee? Tea?"

"No, thanks. Goodness, we've been going at it now for three straight days, and I think the combination of daily reading and jet lag finally got to me."

In a sympathetic tone, he said, "Listen, you go on and get ready for bed. I'll clean up here."

"Are you sure?"

"Yeah, I got this. Go on, get outta here," he said with a smirk.

She threw her hands up to signal her surrender. "If you insist, but first a shower."

David watched her as she disappeared into the master bedroom. He shook his head and smiled, thinking he was a fortunate man to have such a magnificent woman attracted to him. If only he could separate himself from his arcane sense of propriety.

When he thought about it, Beth was pleasant company, but she was all wrong for him. She wasn't musically inclined. She didn't live in California. And she didn't have in-depth, personal knowledge of him at his most intimate level. Carla did.

He said it to Carla already. *Married couples would envy what we have.* David just denied the most important aspect of their relationship—to physically express genuine love and affection for someone he's come to care for deeply.

David wasn't paying attention when he heard Carla's voice announce she was heading off to bed. As he turned to address her, he was floored at what he saw.

Carla emerged from the bedroom, her almond-shaped charcoal eyes staring intently at him. She was a pure Amazon beauty; her straight jet-black hair parted in the middle cascading down about her shoulders. Her firmly muscled, copper-toned body was accentuated by the delicate clothing she was hardly wearing; a thigh-length translucent black lace robe with plunging neckline that barely covered her ample breasts. Her purple satin bra and matching boy short panties hugged her so completely, they looked painted on. The dark outline of Carla's body was visible through her robe due to the light emanating from the master bedroom behind her.

He couldn't help staring at her like a bridegroom who beheld his wanton bride moments before they'd consummate their union. The involuntary stirring of his body betrayed the chivalrous manner he desired to maintain.

"I don't want to regret not doing this," she said. With that, Carla reached up and caressed his cheek with the open palm of one hand and said, "Good night, sweet man."

She was so close David could feel the heat emanating from her nearly naked body. She then brushed her lips against his in a light, experimental kiss. Interpreting no resistance to her advance, she used the index finger and thumb of her other hand to guide David's chin as she planted a deep open and loving kiss squarely on his mouth. It was the kind of kiss that was usually proceeded by or followed up with the words *I love you*.

She embraced him, his arms slowly wrapping around her. His feelings gave him little choice as he surrendered to the moment. He gently caressed the shapeliness of her tight warm body as his own reacted in ways it hadn't in years. She knew then, at least, he wanted her physically. Now, if she could get his mind and his heart to follow.

Both headed off to their separate rooms after their embrace. Neither of them slept for the next several hours with the memory of so passionate and seductive a kiss still fresh on their minds.

She replayed the kiss over in her head. For her, any lingering doubt as to her feelings and desires were shed. She knew from that moment on that she loved David—mind, body, and soul.

For David however, his sleepless night was only beginning.

He unsuccessfully concentrated on his exercise ball to get his thoughts off that kiss. Try as he might, he couldn't turn his thoughts away from the time he spent with a charming woman named Beth Grey. Thinking of his week with Beth in relation to his near ten years with Carla, Beth's hug to Carla's kiss, it was no contest.

Beth's touch, although pleasurable, came without chemistry. David's limited experiences with emotional relationships didn't offer much by way of comparisons. But there was something in the way

Carla touched him. The seductive technique she used to manipulate that kiss manifested a physical reaction from him.

And he liked it.

The groupie with whom he had the most stimulating physical relationship in his life never elicited that kind of deep emotional feeling. She was shallow and uninteresting. That relationship was a catastrophic failure of the heart. Rather than dwell on it, he decided to concentrate on his career. The thought of ever using his heart again wasn't even on his mind when Beth Grey entered his life. After he'd met her, the idea of Carla's growing interest in him forced David to confront and evaluate his feelings for both women.

He had to admit that despite the prospect of exploring a stimulating relationship with a woman like Beth, he was forced to examine his entire relationship with Carla. With her, every aspect of a successful relationship was there—history, compatibility, and now with the evidence of this kiss, chemistry.

The clock ticked past two in the morning before his eyes could no longer remain open. David's mind wandered aimlessly as his vision blurred. Exhaustion overtook him, and soon his eyes closed for a final time, his head turning on the pillow and his exercise ball slipping noiselessly from his hand to the carpet.

The first early morning thunderstorm knocked out power along the Lewes grid, but the two investigators hadn't noticed it. Both of them slept in.

By the time David woke up, it was nearly ten in the morning. His alarm clock was a loud rumbling of thunder from the second wave of thunderstorms that was forecasted to last the remainder of the day.

He noticed the flavor of scented candles along with the aroma of fresh brewed coffee. He looked around but didn't see Carla. That's when he heard the voice from upstairs.

"It's about time you decided to grace me with your presence," she called down to him. "Did you sleep well?"

"I did *finally* doze off last night," he said with a hint of sarcasm that was not lost on her. "What time did you get up?"

"Not long before you did. I just put up the coffee if you want some."

David made his cup and went upstairs. "Did you eat breakfast?"

"No," she murmured. "I wasn't hungry this morning."

"I could get some bagels and cream cheese if you want."

"That's all right," she said, once again replying in a subdued tone. "You don't have to make a special trip for me."

Thinking that his hesitant reaction to their goodnight kiss had brought on this new emotional reserve of hers, he figured he should address the situation. "Carla?"

"Yeah?"

"I believe it's my turn to ask that personal question."

Her thoughtful expression gave way to a knowing smile. "Let me make this easy for you."

She was reading him again, prepared to lay out his argument for him. Before she launched into her explanation, he struck a familiar pose. He leaned against the wall, folded his arms and waited.

She grabbed the next West piece in the stack. "To be quite honest, I can't turn off my feelings for you, but I understand where you're coming from and I can respect that."

"I appreciate it." He relaxed and went back to work on the next score in his stack.

"So long as you're not offended by my occasional expressions of endearment, then I can wait. But don't make me wait too long, okay?"

His nod came with a smile.

She returned it with an expression of guarded patience before resuming her examination of the next work.

"I was just—" She was in midsentence when the matter she was reading caught her eye. The piece was written for only three oboes with a tempo marking of *Andante espressivo*. It was scored in the key of A-flat despite the atonal quality of the work. With no introductory material to distract her, the distinct motive grabbed her attention, as did the title, *The Sunder*. Carla reread the initial phrase.

David continued reading the score he had in his hand, intent on what she was saying before she was suddenly silenced. "You were just what?" he asked, still not looking at her. Carla didn't hear him. She was engrossed in the strange interplay of harmony between these soft toned oboes. Sweet, distant, and strangely beautiful, the double reed chorus of the second subject was quite soothing until the voices began to peel off in various directions. This piece was correctly titled. And right away, she understood the symbolism of the three instruments. The three voices moving harmoniously for a time, then torn apart. Much like West's family was sundered.

Off into the distance, she heard an echo of a familiar voice. "Carla? Carla?"

Snapping out of her trance, she shook her head and responded, "Yes?"

"Are you all right?"

"Yeah. It's this piece." She brought the music to the piano. "Here, listen to this."

Carla's fingers delicately caressed the keys as she performed the theme, occasionally looking at David to test his reaction.

His concentration ruined, he turned and listened to Carla's performance. Again, Jim's music seemed to be a direct reflection of the inner turmoil he felt for the loss of his family. Judging from the early opus number, it must have been written around the time he lost them.

"Well? What do you think?"

She could tell he was considering the work before he ventured an opinion. Showing a thoughtful demeanor, he asked, "What opus number was that?"

Stealing a quick glance at the score, she replied, "Thirty-one, why?"

"I'd be very interested to see what his program notes said about this work."

"So would I."

David retrieved West's first journal of program notes so he could see what the composer himself had said about this piece. Quickly leafing through the early pages, he found the entry for the work. It was short but compelling.

The Sunder
(Opus 31)

It was the 31st of July, a black day indeed, and the impetus for the piece. Even the catalog number contains such symbolic significance that I couldn't ignore the implication. The date, the genesis of my sour mood, provided the theme's motivation. The rays of the rising sun being ripped into its constituent colors through the prism of a window pane provided the inspiration for the title, along with the unpleasant memories of that day.

The melody and its intricate harmonies came naturally as their memories arose in my mind's eye. The apparitions before me guided my hand as each note was penned. This was the first and only work that came so easily, and so fast, it was completed in one day!

Carla studied David's face as the color drained from it. The memory of what she played on the piano and the words he read were still whirling in his head when something suddenly clicked. He'd seen the date July 31 in connection with his benefactor before. That was the same date entered in block 16 for all three certificates of death.

As David was making that particular connection, Beethoven's familiar anthem rang out. Someone was at the door.

"I'll answer it," Carla volunteered. "I have to answer the call of nature anyway."

Less than three minutes later, Dr. Carla Macklin found herself face to face with Beth Grey.

♪

Chapter Twenty

Giles Radnor's office may have been located in the Smithsonian institution's main building, but it was no larger than a walk-in closet with historical *objet d'art* strewn about the shelves where he kept his reference books. His desk was no bigger than a card table holding his research at the moment, his tablet, and perhaps a cup of tea.

He was assigned a college student intern to function as his administrative assistant. Although he saw her occasionally during the course of his day, Shannon McClintock proved herself to be a most valuable assistant over the past year. She secured the cataloged box Radnor had requested from the archives and placed it on his desk. A light service tray with a hot pot of ginseng tea and an upturned cup was next to it. He smiled as he saw the steam rising from the spout. He took out his cell phone and sent her a thank you text. She responded in kind and replied if he needed anything further, she was at the Museum of Natural History Library.

Radnor poured himself a cup of tea and went straight to work. He retrieved a small box from his overcoat that contained the cloth-covered key Audra had entrusted to him and laid it opened on the desk for further inspection. He took the lid off the box Shannon had retrieved and removed a three-ring binder of document-protected papers and artifact photos. Their spines indicated the building and room of the referenced exhibit. These particular binders were from a recently added exhibit to the National Museum of American History: The Absolute Monarchies period of Europe during the seventeenth century.

He scrutinized the key before placing the binder on his lap. Flipping through its pages, he hoped the clue he sought awaited him there. It could be a minor reference contained in an obscure write-up or the memory of some abstract photo from one of the various displays of the period, which might spark his normally acute memory. He wasn't sure, but he was certain the solution was in this box of binders.

About fifteen pages into the third binder, the muffled sound of calypso music emanating from the cell phone in his coat pocket indicated a call from his fellow researcher, Dr. Calvin Selby.

Cal was Radnor's junior by only three years, but he looked much younger. Despite his jovial demeanor that sometimes tried the elder man's patience, it was a mutually beneficial relationship both men found rewarding. Even when they got on each other's nerves, they never lost sight of what was truly important. Spirited banter in the course of a debate was expected. However, they always managed to maintain a professional respect for each other's position and opinions.

"Ah, the wandering minstrel returns!" exclaimed Cal. "I hope you're ready to get back to work now that your three-state junket is over."

Chuckling sarcastically, Radnor responded, "I wouldn't necessarily call it a junket, but it was an informative trip. In fact, we learned more in the past three months about early colonial government on the Delmarva Peninsula than we've learned in our last three years of study here."

"Is that so?"

"Before we get into that, would you mind explaining to me what possible conundrum could so egregiously monopolize your attention as to require my *immediate* assistance?"

"Caught you at a bad time, did I?"

"As usual, your facility for understatement continues to exceed all bounds," Radnor said teasingly. "Now are you going to tell me what you need or am I going to have to guess?"

"You're not the least bit interested if Connolly's replacement gets hired?"

"Then human resources found a replacement for Anne?"

"No, not yet. When I spoke with Henderson at HR last week, he told me he interviewed ten applicants. He also scheduled three more interviews this week with two callbacks for the more promising candidates."

Demonstrating his legendary knack for multitasking, Radnor kept his concentration on the flipped pages. "It appears he's working on it."

"I hope so," Cal lamented. "Finding another qualified researcher with Connolly's skills, passion, and meticulous eye for detail won't be easy."

Looking back at his long association with Anne Connolly, Radnor thought of how he enjoyed working with so dedicated a researcher. He was fortunate to share this last quest at the Delaware Public Archives with his cherished colleague and friend. She was a consummate professional with an insatiable curiosity. She was also the only woman in his life he'd allow to get close. Her expressive sapphire blue eyes left an indelible impression on Radnor. Unfortunately for him, in the same year he felt their relationship might blossom into something more, he learned of her betrothal to a college sweetheart.

Now married, she chose to follow her new husband abroad, thus leaving a terrible vacancy in the office and his heart. A heaviness overcame him as he thought about the prospect of a personal and professional life without his colleague and friend. "She will be sorely missed."

"You could always look at the bright side."

"There's a bright side?"

"You still have me, don't you?" Cal stated in a lighthearted voice.

Radnor's retort carried the distinct air of exasperation. "That's not the same thing."

Detecting that a wordless boundary may have been reached, Cal switched the topic of conversation to Radnor's trip. "You still haven't explained what you were able to get from the Delaware Public Archives."

"We found some documents from the Maryland Historical Society and the Pennsylvania Archives that might assist Delaware's director, Marge Tompkins, with the missing years of their early legislative period. However, they haven't said if the documents or references were anything earth-shattering. Their lead researcher,

Audra Bunting, said she would provide me with a report if there were any findings of note."

"Were you able to uncover anything that shed light on how two colonial legislatures functioned under one governor?"

Before he could respond, he turned to the next page and found something that struck him as familiar. "Hey, Cal, can I get back to you?" Radnor asked as he leaned over the book to get a closer look.

"Sure. How about we get together for lunch? You could fill me in later."

"That works for me. The *Castle Café* at noon?"

"It's a date," Cal said jokingly.

"Right," he said blandly and hung up.

There in the write-up for the King Louis XIV display, he found what he remembered seeing. Contained in a small, inset photo over the portrait of the legendary French king was a black rectangular box eighteen inches long and ten inches high with something protruding from the center of its lid. Radnor held a magnifying glass over the area to get a better look, but the poor quality of the picture made a detailed examination impossible. The object appeared to be much like the key Radnor had in his possession, but without a more detailed photo of the area, any definitive finding would be inconclusive.

Since Shannon was still in the Natural History Library, he called her.

"Hello?"

"It's Radnor. Do you have time to locate a photo for me?"

"Sure, Dr. Radnor. I finished collating those documents you asked for."

"Perfect, thanks. You might want to drop those off at the office before you begin this task, so you won't be lugging around a ream of paper."

"Can do. Oh, what photo do you need me to find?"

"I'll send you a picture message. See if you can locate a larger copy of it for me, would you?"

"What's the subject?"

"It's from the monarch exhibit. I need a good copy of that inset photo from the portrait of Louis XIV on the east end of the exhibit at the American History Museum."

"No problem. But I do have to meet someone over at the Library of Congress later this afternoon, so if I can't find it here in the library, I should be able to find it there."

The Library of Congress would be a more productive resource than the Smithsonian's own library for this errand, he thought. "Excellent idea, Shannon. If you find it there instead, just shoot me a copy via email. And thanks again." He used the camera on his cell phone to send her the picture with the subject line *"Here it is."*

The menu wasn't the reason Radnor wanted to meet his colleague at the *Castle Café* but for its proximity to his office. He wasn't interested in lunch so much as wishing to share his findings with Cal. Also discussing Anne Connolly over lunch provided them an opportunity to commiserate over her departure.

Cal was already at the table when Radnor came around the corner. The older man's slow gait made him appear tired. "You seem no less the worse for wear," said Cal.

"And you look like yesterday's dinner," responded Radnor noting the unusual pallor in his younger colleague's face. "Did you even go home last night?"

"I've been here since four this morning. The amount of material your team finally chose to unload on me was considerable. Now I have to pour through it to see what's relevant. And you?"

"Getting my feet wet again. Going through some of these documents, I have a few ideas that might point you in the right direction."

"For instance?"

"Proceeding from what we already know, William Penn's plans for claiming a definitive proprietorship over Delaware were thwarted when James II was deposed in the Glorious Revolution in 1688. Problems with piracy along the Delaware Bay coupled with Penn's exclusionary Frame of Government limiting Delaware's legislative power forced him to come up with his Charter of Privileges in 1701. This opened the door for Delaware's separation in 1704. At the council meeting of April 11, 1704, Delaware assemblymen were declared nonmembers. Enraged, they left the council never to return. The first separate assembly met with John Evans as Proprietary Governor on May 22, 1704. We knew all this before the state conferences."

"All that jives," said Cal. "Any surprises?"

"We managed to locate ledger receipts from the Blue Hen Tavern in New Castle and an unidentified public house in present day Elsmere. They clearly showed that the assembly met in these locations along with their preferred location at the New Castle Courthouse. References to these and other taverns in the personal correspondence of assembly members into the mid-1720s confirm these meetings took place, but there's still much about their conduct we don't know. The surviving minutes of these meetings are few, but they do tell us much about their parliamentary procedures."

"That's not much to go on," said Cal to a distracted Radnor. "Giles, what's wrong? You seem preoccupied, and I don't think it has anything to do with Connolly."

"Can't put anything over on you."

"What's up?"

"I've stumbled on something that's getting me sidetracked."

"Anything I can do to help?"

"Thanks, but I have Shannon working on it."

"It's research related, then?"

"You could say that," Radnor said with a halfhearted smile. "I was presented with an artifact I thought I'd seen before when we were working on the absolute monarchies period."

"Sounds intriguing! What artifact?"

"It's a large iron key about six inches long with a heavy bow and a thick, tapered shank. Its collar and throating are unusual, to say the least, and it has a trapezoid-shaped bit. When I cut you off so abruptly this morning, I thought I'd found a picture of it. The photo was poorly blown up. I asked Shannon to track down a sharper copy for me."

"What picture?"

"It's the blurred inset photo over the portrait of King Louis XIV, why?"

"Just curious. My grasp of European monarchies isn't what it should be." Radnor's blank stare informed Cal that his friend's thoughts weren't in the here and now. "Giles? You all right?"

Allowing the crease of a smile to appear on his face, he said, "I will be. I didn't realize how much I'm going to miss Anne. She was more than a colleague to me, Cal. Now, I won't be able to…" He trailed off.

Rescuing Radnor from an awkward moment, Cal said, "Look, if anyone can find a replacement for Connolly, Henderson can do it."

"I don't think anyone can replace Anne."

Conceding the point, Cal nodded. "You're right, of course. Well, I've got to get back to that stack of documents your team left me. Why don't you come over to the house tonight for dinner? Amanda and I would love to have you."

"Thanks, Cal, but I have too much on my plate today. How about a rain check?"

"You got it."

Radnor made his way to the stairs for the two flights up to his office when he received an incoming call. He dug out his phone and checked the caller's name. It was Shannon. In his typical deadpan delivery, he asked, "Did you find it?"

"I couldn't locate the exact picture you wanted, Dr. Radnor. But I've sent you an email with a clear photo of the box in question. There was no key in that picture, but the box is an exact duplicate to the one in the picture you sent me."

Disappointed he wasn't able to make a comparison to the key he had in his possession, he acknowledged the young woman's efforts on his behalf. "Thanks. Where did you find it?"

"In the Library of Congress. It was from a photo exposé on the reign of King Louis XIV."

"Excellent job, my dear!"

"Will there be anything else, Dr. Radnor?"

"No, that'll do it, Shannon. Take the rest of the day off and thank you."

Radnor made his way back to the office and pulled up the email on his tablet. The photo she'd sent was a spot-on match to the box pictured in the inset photo. This clearer picture was the strongest evidence that Radnor was getting closer to solving the mystery of this key. Under the emailed picture was the following caption:

> *This iron strongbox, made by Klaus von Richthofen,*
> *was presented to Louis XIV by Leopold I in 1685.*
> *It is currently on permanent display at the Louvre*
> *in Paris.*

If that didn't make his day, the note in the body of Shannon's email certainly did.

> *Dr. Radnor,*
>
> *I understand from my friend that the Metropolitan Museum of Art plans on exhibiting the Art of the Holy Roman Empire this fall. Wasn't Leopold I a Holy Roman Emperor?*
>
> *— Shannon*

He smiled to himself thinking that Shannon was a most treasured assistant indeed.

Chapter Twenty – One

"Beth! What a surprise!" said the tall, attractive young woman.

"Excuse me?" asked a startled Beth Grey. This stranger's overt familiarity seemed out of place for someone who never laid eyes on her before. Beth's protective instincts went right into high gear. "How do you know who I am?"

"I'm sorry, we haven't been formally introduced. I'm David's friend from UC Davis, Carla Macklin. I'm pleased to meet you."

"You didn't answer my question."

"You are as David described you."

"Oh?" She said feeling a bit embarrassed. "And how was that?"

"If I recall his description, he said you were a shade over five feet seven, blond, blue-eyed, fit, intelligent, and strikingly beautiful with a quick wit. He was obviously right."

Beth's voice and blood pressure both rose as she responded, "He said all that, did he? And you can tell I'm this person by the mere expedient of opening a door?" Beth didn't know who to be more upset with at this point—Carla for her matter-of-fact description or David for going into such detail about her to a complete stranger.

Breaking into a smile, Carla expounded on her deductive reasoning. "Not exactly. We were both worried when we couldn't get ahold of you. We expected to see you upon our arrival, but we were surprised to find you were still out. He told me you drove a copper-colored Jeep. As I find that particular color Jeep parked in the driveway, and it's unlikely we'd expect another visitor with the exact same vehicle, the logical conclusion is that its driver was Beth Grey and that you must be her."

"It's Bethany, actually. However, most people quickly learn that to address me in that fashion would be considered unwise."

David turned the corner to find the two women in the midst of their verbal joust. Judging from her posture, Beth seemed to be a trifle irked. Nevertheless, he greeted Beth with a hug. "What happened to you? We were worried sick."

"I got back so late last night, I didn't want to wake you."

"Care to join us? We were just getting ready to break for lunch," Carla offered.

"I had a late breakfast," she said in a less sarcastic tone. Beth still regarded Carla with a hint of suspicion trying to determine if she were friend or foe. "I wanted to stop by to tell you why I was unable to contact you earlier."

Carla took her nature break while David headed into the kitchen for some cold drinks. They all sat down in the living room as Beth began to explain.

"One of my closest friends and former coworkers, who now lives in College Park, Maryland, had a family emergency. She asked me to take care of her Airedales, Jumbo and Gypsy for the week. I finished packing my suitcase when I received a call for a job interview. Before I came to Delaware, I had applied for a position as a historian with some government agency website, but nothing ever came of it.

"Well, they contacted me last week and conducted a phone interview. While I was talking to them, my phone signaled the battery was dying. I plugged the cell into the charger and completed the interview over the next thirty minutes. I scheduled a face-to-face meeting and finished packing for the trip. Unfortunately, I didn't pack the phone. I left it turned on and in the charger. Not a recommended action according to the instructions.

"I totally forgot about the cell phone until I was already in Maryland. When I got back, the phone's circuitry was fried. I felt terrible that I couldn't call you because the only place I had your number was in my cell. Sorry, David."

"We're glad our worries were unfounded. You're here now, and you're safe. That's all that matters." He seemed to catch on that Beth wasn't enamored with Carla. He knew his colleague could be abrasive at first if you didn't know how to take her. He gave Beth enough credit that she would eventually figure that out on her own. "Why don't you regale us with how your interview went?"

"I'm probably not going to get it."

"What makes you say that?" he asked.

"Well, for one thing, the job wasn't located at College Park where I thought it was, it's in Washington. Even if they selected me for the position, I don't feel like moving again."

"Is it what you want?" asked Carla.

"I once thought so," Beth replied.

"You certainly got me excited when you were discussing Delaware history. I learned much from you the last time I was here," said David.

"I like my consulting work, but it's work. Doing historical research has always captivated me. That's another reason why I'm so keen to learn about Jim. Everything you've uncovered about him so far is quite intriguing."

"Then you'll be happy to know that Carla and I have spent the past week going over Jim's music. That's all we had time for."

Detecting her opening, Beth took it. "Then does your invitation still stand?"

With a broad smile, David said, "That it does. I thought you could help us search the house for any clues we may have missed. We still haven't found the ring. And in one of Jim's journals, he made mention of a letter fragment his grandfather had found that was from the son of a renowned Thomas from Delaware history. Carla also believes that there's another journal we haven't found yet."

"Wow, a real treasure hunt! That sounds fun. Where do we start?"

"Why don't we all go upstairs so we can give the room a good going over?" David suggested. "The room itself hasn't been explored, so perhaps Carla and I could take a break from the music, and we could all explore the room together. How does that sound?"

"Sounds great to me!" Beth said.

Following another satisfying meal from *Chez* David, they went to work.

The three detectives stood at the top of the staircase surveying the task that lay ahead of them. The initial target of their search would be the books in the outermost bookshelves. The wall behind Jim's desk was populated by encyclopedias and other reference books, while the opposite wall held a massive array of hardcover books. In the middle were the bookshelves that contained CDs and vinyl records. Housed in a lower central location of the far wall were the lateral files that contained the cache of Jim's musical scores. Recessed in the wall nearest to them was the stereo system. The desk of solid walnut was modest and tastefully designed but with few drawers.

"Who wants to do what?" David asked them.

Carla, determined to put her theory to the test, went straight for the far wall's library of books.

"I'll get started on the opposite side," Beth offered. She went to the far right side bookcase to get started, all the while keeping a close eye on Carla.

"I guess that means I get what's left," he said almost sarcastically. He headed toward the piano before he moved to the desk. Most piano benches had a storage space under their seats, so he thought he might find something under its soft, leather-upholstered seat. He checked but found the two small swatches of soft cloth used to clean the piano. Finding little else, he moved his investigation over to Jim's walnut desk.

Carla located a small stepladder so she could reach the uppermost shelf to begin her search. Starting at the top left, she slowly ran two fingers across the book spines, taking in the titles for reference.

Beth applied a different technique to her research. She removed each book and flipped through its pages for any hidden clues. She inspected several books before turning to Carla. "What's your story?"

Carla threw Beth a quizzical look. "What are you talking about?"

"Well, you seem to know all about me, and I know little to nothing about you. Who you are or where you come from? It seems only fitting."

"Fair enough. I'm originally from a small town near Seattle. My dad's family hailed from New Orleans and descended from Haitian-Creole and Brazilian traditions."

"Wow, that's some combination," Beth conceded.

"Unfortunately for me, my dad didn't pass on any of his culinary Haitian-Creole genes, but I did manage to get my passionate zest for life and his hot-blooded Brazilian temper."

"I can vouch for the latter," said David, chiming in.

Momentarily throwing charcoal darts at him, she continued to address Beth's question. "He was the first in our family to receive a scholarship and graduate college. He earned his engineering degree at San Jose State and worked in the aviation industry here in Seattle."

"What about your mother?"

"My mom's parents were from Kuala Lumpur."

"So that's where you got such lovely eyes," offered Beth.

She glanced at David again. "Thanks. At least someone thinks so. I tend to take after my mom in that department. I got her Asian face and his dark complexion."

"If I may say so, you're a beautiful blend of your parents."

"That's nice of you to say," Carla said.

"Let's not forget about his infamous temper," David added as he rifled through the desk.

Carla thumbed her hand toward David like a hitchhiker. "When he gets that way I usually smack him over the noggin with a rolled up newspaper."

Beth was amused by Carla's *bon mot* at David's expense. "How did your mom happen to meet your dad?"

"After my mom's parents emigrated from Malaysia in the mid-'40s, they settled in Seattle and opened a small dental practice. She was born and raised there. Following in their footsteps, she went to school and became a dentist, taking over the family practice. My dad was a patient of hers before they started dating. My mom had high hopes I would continue the tradition, but something happened that changed my life."

"What was that?" Beth queried.

"It was my ninth birthday. My parents wanted to do something special for me that day, so they took me to see a performance of the Seattle Symphony. The highlight of the evening was the debut of a young teenage pianist. I watched in awe as this young girl, only a few years older than me, performed Grieg's *Piano Concerto in A minor*, and in front of a live audience.

"My irrevocable journey down the musical path came that night. When the conductor pointed to the timpani player, he embarked upon a crescendo that was symbolic of my growing excitement for music. The timpani roll grew from *pianissimo* to *fortissimo* so rapidly, I was mesmerized by the sound. When the young girl's hands came thundering down upon the keyboard in an authoritative pronouncement of the A minor chord, it jolted me in my chair. Her opening cadenza was boldly executed and summoned the attention of all present. She produced the sweetest melody from her tiny fingers that I'd ever heard in my life. I couldn't get the sound of Grieg's only piano concerto out of my head for weeks afterward.

"I was determined to get the music and learn to play it, to express my feelings in musical terms. Ever since, I dreamed of performing such music in front of a live audience. I wanted to give people what this young girl gave to me."

Beth watched Carla's face as she described this childhood experience. Her voice was in the here and now, but her eyes seemed fixed on this past event that forged her destiny. As Carla went into detail about herself, Beth was surprised to find how affable Carla was. The younger woman was confident and well-spoken. Something Beth always had trouble with despite her ability to project such traits. She could now see how David would be attracted to Carla. Observing how the two interacted with each other, Beth believed they played off one another beautifully. This is what happens with time and exposure to each other. Chemistry.

Beth came to realize her initial reaction to Carla was unfairly based on her mistrust of new people. Her disastrous experiences with the men in her life have made her overly protective and given to self-preservation. Beth usually took lots of time to get to know someone before she was comfortable enough to open up to them. Jim was the same way, she found out, thanks in large part to her new friend, David. If he had enough confidence in Carla to bring her along on this quest, she couldn't be all bad.

"I'm sorry, Carla. I didn't mean for us to get off on the wrong foot."

"No worries. I sometimes have an unfortunate effect on people when they first meet me. Friends?"

"Friends," said Beth.

They nodded to each other from across the room, knowing that this new friendship would need time to grow into the words they just exchanged with each other.

"And what have you been doing over there besides eavesdropping on our conversation?" Carla asked David.

"Going over the CD library to see what we could be listening to while we work before I hit the desk in earnest. Why?"

"We're doing the work while you sit there kibitzing," Carla observed as her fingers continued their gentle slide across the bindings of yet another row of books. She began a new row at around eye level. As she got midway into the row, her fingers stopped on an unusual leather-bound book with no words written on its spine.

She slowly turned a pair of satisfied eyes to David as if she discovered the lost city of Atlantis.

David didn't understand. "What?"

"Oh no," she said. "I think you should see this for yourself."

Yielding the honors to David, she got out of his way so he could retrieve this mysterious book. He reached up and drew the book out with two fingers and grasped it from the shelf. David inspected the brown leather cover. It had an oval relief containing an embossed coat of arms. Its intricate design sported a knight's helmet facing left with an ornate plume emanating from its top and spreading out to encircle the shield below it. The shield was bisected by a curved line. The shield's design had three prancing leopards, one centered at the bottom and one on each corner of the top. The florid design of the scroll that underscored the shield and plume contained only one word. And that word was *West*.

♪

Chapter Twenty – Two

David was unprepared for what awaited him as he opened the cover of the dusty journal cracked with age. Brimming with curiosity, the two women flanked him to read the content. In Jim's meticulously metered hand was the following doleful declaration:

> *To the unaffected reader,*
>
> *This old volume, handed me by my grandfather, shall be the repository of all the dark chapters of my life. Of all the bitter ruminations smoldering in my memory that should only be shared with a select few or one. That person, I am hopeful to discover before it's too late. A confidant with whom I might entrust the delicate content of this journal.*

David was familiar enough with Jim's writing style to detect the subtle differences between the other journals and this one. Although the initial entry's address to the unaffected reader was similar to the journals, no further salutations were offered on any subsequent entry. Neither did he date the entries in any way whatsoever. The only way the reader could tell Jim began a new idea or thought was by the extra space between the narratives.

There was one more glaring difference. These entries were suddenly imbued with a darker, more ominous tinge. And Jim began with the most gut-wrenching entry a sober man could ever hope to calmly relate.

> *I remember distinctly the exact moment my first life ended—and my new one began. As with most*

transformative moments in one's life that border on cliché, this one started with that dreaded knock at the door.

That last wonderful morning I spent with my family on the day of my retirement from active duty, July 31st of 1993, was perfection. The boys were excited, and Isabella never looked more beautiful, with the possible exception of our wedding day. I hadn't slept well the night before. A turbulent flood of images from twenty-three years of experiences, both good and bad, came rushing into my head as I contemplated my last official day in uniform and a life of retirement.

I awoke late. The kitchen was already abuzz with activity. Isabella made my favorite Belgian waffles with bacon on the side, Ethan brewed the Columbian coffee, and Alexander cleaned and set the table. I don't recall the specifics of our breakfast conversation, but I do remember with crystal clarity the love and laughs we shared. All they wanted from me was to enjoy this very special day.

It was to that end, Isabella said they had to leave early to finalize some surprise plans and to take care of some last-minute errands before the ceremony. I was still in my robe as they headed out the door. I don't know what possessed me to do it, but I got up, walked over to the window and watched as Alexander got behind the wheel and started the car. Ethan took his position in the back seat as Isabella opened the front passenger-side door.

Before getting into the vehicle, she turned to look at me. Then she did something she'd never done before. She blew me a kiss.

I smiled in spite of myself as I returned it with an outstretched palm. As the car headed down the road, I thought to myself how blessed a man I was.

Over the next few hours, I spent the time getting prepared for my final day as an active duty member. Tomorrow, I'd be known by the simple term of veteran. Or by the more enviable title of Isabella's husband. I reviewed the speech she helped me with, before checking my uniform to make sure everything was ready.

In this solitary moment, as I took inventory of my twenty-three-year career, the weight of the day began to grow heavy upon me. Flashes of memories from Vietnam to the First Gulf War. From all the transfers to all the TDYs...

"TDYs?" Carla asked out loud. "What are TDYs?"

Coming from a military family, David knew what Jim meant. "It's a military acronym meaning temporary duty. That means he was placed on temporary assignment someplace."

"Sorry, I didn't know."

Both women peering over his shoulder, they all continued to read the candid account.

...all the TDYs. From the impact my supervisors made upon me to the impact I was privileged enough to make on the junior members of our young service, the faces of so many people came rushing into my head. I felt overwhelmed by the ceremony that would soon commence.

I had put on my service dress jacket when the doorbell rang. What happened next occurred with such astonishing speed, my brain was unable to process it in any logical order at the time.

As I opened the front door, I beheld two men in uniform and a third behind them who wore black. At first, I believed them to be military training instructors because of their campaign Stetsons, but the battleship gray uniforms offered up a more disquieting possibility. The gold badge on the taller man's chest confirmed he was a state trooper.

Still believing that this was all a set up by Isabella, I asked them if she'd put them up to providing a police escort to the ceremony. But the grim expressions on their faces held a very different message. It was then I noticed the neck of the third man standing behind the two officers. The stiff black collar he wore had a square patch of white in the middle.

I had observed scenes like this before, but I was never a party to one and certainly not the object of their attention until now. The only portion of their conversation that I can remember with any clarity was when they asked me my name.

"Master Sergeant James West?" asked the tall trooper in a stern, diminished tone.

I answered, "Yes?"

He then uttered words that would forever be seared into my memory. The words that carved out my heart and destroyed my soul. The last words I could recall clearly for the rest of the day.

"Sir, we regret to inform you…"

The rest was a confusing jumble of words. Rival cartels, drug war, mistaken identity, and unwitting victims.

When I came to my senses again, I found myself lying on the sofa with these three men standing nearby asking me if I was all right. I'd passed out, and they had brought me inside. At that moment, I didn't know who I was, where I was, or what was going on.

I looked out the window to see the bright sunshine. The same rays that had warmed the faces of Alexander, Ethan, and Isabella not more than a few hours ago were now shining on three new faces. Nameless strangers whose ominous appearance stripped away the three most important layers of meaning in my life. From that moment until the sun had set that day, I was in a fog, unable to distinguish the lapse of time.

That last sunset—was cruel. This characterization is the only charitable way to describe it. As I stood there, gazing at the myriad incarnations of the colors orange and blue, I couldn't get the last vision of Isabella, Ethan, and Alexander out of my head.

I stood there, motionless and numb, observing the way the waning sunlight suffused through the smattering of billowy white and gray clouds. Soon the burnt orange cloud cover, overlaid upon a background of an azure blue sky, began to merge into a subtle darkness. One that now matched the pitch black of my empty soul.

It would be weeks before I would learn of the arrest of those who murdered my family. It was months later before I learned of their conviction and sentencing. But those facts would be of little consolation to me as I embarked upon my post-military life—alone.

Visibly shaken, David had finished the story. He felt a hand suddenly grab his shoulder. He looked up to see Beth with her other hand over her mouth covering a gasp; her cheeks wet with tears. On the other side of David, Carla was finishing the last paragraph with moist eyes and damp cheeks.

"Are you guys okay?"

Looking over at the pencil sketches of Jim's family, Beth's memory of the last time she was in the house learning about her neighbor, seemed to catch up to her all at once. "I'm sorry, David. To finally learn what happened to his family—" Beth couldn't continue.

"We can stop reading if it upsets you," he suggested.

Still feeling uneasy, Beth said, "I don't think I'd be able to approach this book again if we stopped now."

They all got comfortable on the sofa downstairs and took up where they left off, with the next graphic story about how James Burton West garnered his military decorations.

The last time I lost someone close to me was in the jungles of Southeast Asia.

We had touched down quickly with the aft door of the aircraft open to allow our team to hop out to retrieve the twelve dignitaries. We exited quickly from the slow-moving aircraft and ran for the Quonset hut that served as their forward base of operations. Most of them were civilians attached to State Department, but that's all we knew. Their status wasn't the issue, however. It was their presence in Cambodia that garnered a raised eyebrow from our copilot, Lieutenant Allen, when the mission was briefed that morning.

The aircraft commander repositioned the open cargo door in front of the building to give us the optimum angle to get our charges safely aboard. Ernie escorted his group of three to the aircraft first, before dashing back to the hut to get three more. The two of us alternated in this way, getting the first nine civilians safely aboard amid the outbreak of small arms fire.

On his last pass with his final three charges, he was hit in the thigh and abdomen and fell to the ground in a hail of bullets. I managed to get the last three on board when all hell broke loose. We were picking up fire from every direction. With the aircraft beginning its departure, I wasted no time running back for Ernie. He was moaning in pain but still conscious as I lifted him up on my shoulders. I bolted for the open door of our AC-130 gunship as fast as my legs could carry us. As I made my second step onto the ramp, I felt a sharp sting through my left shoulder, but that wasn't what made me lose my balance. Something hit Ernie, knocking both of us down onto the ramp. The aircraft commander had ordered the ramp and door closed as he was bringing the engines to takeoff power. I don't remember anything after that until I awoke in the hospital a few days later. Lieutenant Allen, I found out, was mortally wounded as the aircraft first came under attack. But that wasn't the worst of it. I also found out that Ernie's head was taken off by an RPG that continued past us and into the Quonset hut before it exploded. It's also what knocked Ernie and I down. He never knew what hit him.

Jesse Ernesto Ortega was born two hours ahead of me in the same hospital. Our families lived within a mile of each other. They became friends and consequently, so did we. Ernie and his family were regular visitors to our home.

Ernie and I were inseparable in school. We got our driver's licenses together. We grew up together and played football, soccer, and baseball together.

I introduced him to his first girlfriend to whom he was later engaged.

Ernie and I graduated from Cape High School together, enlisted in the Air Force together, and were assigned to the same unit together. Sadly, we went on the same fateful mission together. He was, for all intents and purposes, the most valued friend I ever had.

And they had the audacity to decorate me for this mission. I never led the so-called counter attack they credited me with. Nor did I ever wear the medals they presented me for our actions on that day… because I didn't earn or deserve them!

As he flipped through the journal, they were all unnerved to witness how many of these narratives filled the remaining pages. The stories they'd read chilled them to the bone. The quiet nature of this man belied the dark passages lurking beneath the surface, hidden between the lines of his pristine paragraphs, visually stunning sketches, and musical notes.

It was toward the end of the book that David came across the account he was so anxious to find. The *in-due-course* explanation as to why his works were never made public.

It was September 1991, six months after our decisive victory in the First Gulf War. I had arrived at a makeshift base outside the city of Riyadh in Saudi Arabia. My assignment was to set up a training office for the provisional installation.

On this particular occasion, the unit first sergeant asked me to assist her in setting up the commander's call. This monthly forum for the unit commander to brief the status of the unit also provided a much-needed opportunity to recognize personnel achievements.

It was quite apparent to me that our presence on Saudi soil was barely tolerated. Restrictions to what we could say, do, or display was rigorously enforced. For example, we weren't allowed to display our national ensign above the tents where we were housed. In fact, even our accommodations were a direct reflection of their derision toward our presence. The Saudi side of the air base had hardened facilities with real gold inlay on the marble floors and handrails. The only hardened structure on our side was the sunroof over the air terminal, and we were relegated to living and working in temper tents.

That notwithstanding, however, I wasn't aware of any prohibition to our music, so…

Working with the Land Mobile Radio maintenance officer – a major – they helped me set up the public address and sound system for our upcoming commander's call. They had an old Korg keyboard plugged into the public address set up. To test the equipment, I played the national anthem. As I was absorbed in the performance, the building's personnel stopped what they were doing to listen, including the major.

I wasn't paying attention at the time, but once I finished, I was stunned to see tears in their eyes. All of their eyes. The major had been in country since the outset of Desert Storm. It was the first time he'd heard our national anthem since his deployment for Operation Desert Shield, three months before the war started.

My country, the one I swore an oath to "defend against all enemies, foreign and domestic," has died a cruel and agonizing death. Somehow, the trait dearest to us as Americans had lost its luster. She has abandoned her principles and eliminated common sense from her collective consciousness. In our nation and our government, now held in high esteem, resides obfuscation and deceit, while honor has no place. Loyalty, so long as it's demonstrated with flawless precision toward hate of country, is prized while those whose sacrifice for love of country are ignored, mischaracterized, and vilified.

In my detailed studies of musical history, I've discovered that music has always had the ability to bring forth pride in the American patriot. But those with ill-designing intent for propaganda purposes can also use music.

The persistent voices of ghosts from the condemnation of '48 are gently whispering their portentous warning into my ear with increasing regularity. It is for this reason, and my growing antipathy for the new world order, I have taken the extraordinary step of retaining all of my work from public view and performance.

I do this since I believe those in power shall never see me as a viable artist in my own right. My political views, outmoded by "conventional wisdom," have become arcane and out of step with prevailing social norms.

The three emotionally drained investigators just looked at each other with puzzled stares. They'd spent nearly eight hours bearing witness to the horrific accounts as documented by a tormented James Burton West. The darker stories of his benefactor were harrowing to be sure, and David was not immune to their effects. He wondered how someone who'd gone through so many personal trials could maintain his sanity long enough to write such touching music. Looking at his two companions, he noticed the dampness under their eyes. It was evident that any further investigation would have to wait for another day. The three of them were all in.

Beth was the first to notice the total absence of sunlight in the room. She quickly glanced at her watch. "Oh my! I didn't know it was that late," she said as she got up with a stretch. "I have to be to work in the morning, so I better head home."

"Are you sure you won't stay for dinner?" David asked.

"No, that's all right," she said appreciatively. "I'll grab a light snack before I go to bed."

Carla asked, "Will you be joining us tomorrow? We'd love to have you."

Slowly developing an appreciation for the younger woman's personality, she responded, "I'd love to, Carla, thanks. That's very sweet of you."

David got up to walk Beth to the door. But when he set the journal down, something that was stuck between the last page and the back cover had fallen out. He picked up the object to examine it. It was a page of yellowed parchment; he estimated to be much older than any he'd received from Jim. It was the refined quality of linen, folded in thirds, with an illegible wax seal. The shallow depth of the impression made a close inspection with the naked eye difficult at best.

"Beth, do you have a magnifying glass and a laptop?" asked David.

"Yes, I do. I'll bring them with me tomorrow. It has a WiFi adapter, so we can do some follow-up research right from here," Beth suggested.

"That would be great," he said.

They all looked at each other with tired eyes and agreed that any secrets this letter could reveal would have to wait until tomorrow.

The investigators chose to put an end to their day. Beth had gone home. David and Carla sat at the kitchen island eating a light salad in the quiet darkness. They were glad this sad day was over. Even though David hardly said two words to Beth all day, Carla managed to proffer the inevitable question.

"You like her, don't you?"

"Who, Beth?"

Tilting her head down as if looking over an imaginary set of reading glasses, she tossed David a skeptical look. "Who do you think I meant?"

"Yes, of course I do. Don't you?"

"The jury's still out on that one."

♪

Chapter Twenty – Three

David read the fragment once to himself, then once more aloud to Carla trying to make sense out of it. He found the garish handwriting unconventional and difficult to read.

Dear William,

I write with urgent news. Pennsylvania has now joined Delaware in adopting the new constitution. This action places me in considerable danger of losing nearly all my holdings despite my father Thomas's historic import and influence in the lower counties. My current status can only serve to work against me in achieving any relief from my losses, but I still have a strong hand to play with the Delaware General Assembly. In my Solitude, the secret shall remain forever. Knowing that the property of Lewes-on-the-water is safely in your hands, due in large part to that secret is entirely satisfactory to me. They shall have no claim against you or your property. Still, my requests to salvage my claim on the strip of property off the Schuylkill have not met with a favorable response from the Pennsylvania Legislature. I have little recourse but to seek appropriate relief from the Crown. To do so requires me to make such an appeal in person. Having tended to my affairs, I shall be bound for England sometime next month.

Still in her fleece pajamas due to the early morning chill, Carla went to the kitchen to toast a bagel and pour her coffee while she listened to David's narration. She took up residence on the sofa and looked across the table at David with a thoughtful expression.

"What do you make of it?" he asked, handing Carla the letter to read for herself.

She looked over the fragment carefully before actually reading it. Then she set the document on the table and stretched out on the sofa to get comfortable. "Hmm. The obvious question is, who wrote this letter? A detailed analysis of the clues the author left us might help answer that question."

"What clues? The letter is unsigned. There's no date. No surname for the addressee or the so-called historic Thomas. And the impression stamped in the wax is probably illegible, so what clues are you talking about?"

Carla grinned. "Let's set aside the faded wax impression for the time being. To whom was the letter written? When was it written? Who was this influential Thomas of historic import? You mean to tell me these questions never entered your mind?"

"Questions? Yes, but are they clues? I doubt it."

"The questions *are* the clues, David! And addressing them first might point us in the right direction to solve the other ones that present themselves. Questions such as, why was the property off the Schuylkill so important that he had to address the Pennsylvania Legislature? What did he mean by that odd phrase '*In my solitude, the secret shall remain forever?*' Why did he feel the need to go to England for his remedy?"

"Wait a second. How do you know the author was a man?"

"The handwriting is uniquely masculine, not feminine. The topic, tense, and meter of the conversation is distinctly political. With few exceptions such as Abigail Adams, most women didn't involve themselves in the politics of the 1700s. The fact the author discusses property and using strong methods with the legislature or the king to retain said property suggests a man."

"Sounds plausible," he conceded. "But who was this William?"

"I'm not sure, but one thing we do know is, this William had possession of the property located at Lewes-on-the-water. In this

167

case, I believe the resources at the Delaware Public Archives should prove illuminating."

"Okay, what about when it was written?"

Carla scanned the letter again. "The author's *news* is that Pennsylvania had just adopted or ratified the new constitution. Since Delaware ratified the Constitution on December 7, 1787, and that date is plainly written on the state's flag, I think we can assume the date of this letter was either December 1787 or January 1788."

"All right, would you mind telling me how you knew that date was on Delaware's flag?"

"Do you remember when we passed by the Lewes Volunteer Fire Department?"

"Yeah, so?"

"You didn't see Old Glory flying on one flag pole and the Delaware state flag on the other?"

Once again, yielding to her powers of observation he said, "I'm impressed! Now, what can we do with that information?"

"Now that we know the estimated date of the letter, we can narrow down our search for the appropriate William and Thomas," she suggested.

"Well, here's where my knowledge of early American history gets dicey."

Looking at David as if she were addressing Cobbett, she asked, "Dicey?"

"Too much exposure to your friend the dean." He quickly segued into his response to her original question. "I couldn't even fathom a guess as to which William played a role at the time. The only two Thomases that ring any bells for me are Jefferson and Paine."

Carla stared at David, processing his offhand remark about her alleged attachment to Cobbett, she grinned at him. "Were either of them particularly important to Pennsylvania or Delaware?"

"I don't know, maybe not."

The Carla stare was bearing down hard on him.

"Okay, you got me. Are there any questions that escape you?"

"Yes, actually. I wonder what leverage the author thought he had over the Delaware Legislature that he believed he could press to his advantage? And I think if we find the answer to why the Schuylkill property was so important, we'll find the answer to that question."

David watched Carla as her eyes told a story of burning concentration. Her lips pursed, and her eyes squinted as she let them drifted down toward the letter. Curious, she picked it up again. "What is it?"

"I didn't pay too much attention to that wax impression when I first looked at it. I want to see if I could make anything out in the daylight." Straining her eyes to examine the seal as best she could, it was still too faint for a detailed evaluation.

Relaxing back into the recliner, he said, "Hopefully Beth's magnifying glass will give us a better look." With his elbow resting on the arm of the chair and his fist under his chin, the corners of David's mouth constricted as he pondered what Carla said. His thoughts returned to Carla's question; was either Jefferson or Paine *particularly important to Pennsylvania or Delaware?* "I've got it!"

"Got what?"

"Remember I told you that I stayed at the bed-and-breakfast of Delaware's namesake when I came here?"

"Yeah?"

"Remember I told you that his portrait hung over the bed-and-breakfast's fireplace?"

"Uh-huh?"

"It was the portrait of Lord De La Warr himself. The plaque below his portrait said he was the Third Baron De La Warr and his name was Sir Thomas West!"

Taking some time away from a solid week of investigating, David took Carla out for a brief tour of Lewes and the surrounding area of the lower Delaware coast. He even took her to see the suspect portrait of Sir Thomas West at the bed-and-breakfast. They soon found themselves at the Second Street Tavern for a late lunch. It wasn't quite their Thursday evening meal, but after spending days at the house with no break, it was a nice change of pace and environment. They had just ordered their meals when Carla began to stare at David. Knowing this particular mannerism of Carla's, he expected her to say something either profound or ludicrous.

"I never imagined how picturesque the East Coast could be," she volunteered.

"I was quite taken by the beautiful sunrises and fresh salt air, myself."

"Oh yeah, I could get used to this. Moderate weather, beaches, fishing..."

Almost on cue, he pointed past the lighted intersection. "Then you're in luck. Across that bridge over there is a line of charter fishing boats."

"Really? I remember the first time my dad took me out deep sea fishing when I was little. We'll have to go out before we leave."

"I'll make the reservations. I always wanted to try out that striper recipe. Now I'll have my chance."

Carla suddenly chuckled to herself.

"What?"

"I was thinking about the faculty fishing trip we took three years ago, remember?"

"Remember?" he asked his face flushing with embarrassment. "How can I forget? It took everyone well over a month to stop teasing me about it!"

She sat fully erect with her eyes cast down. "I don't know what you're getting all upset about. You should be proud! You landed the biggest catch of the day!"

"That *catch* was a hook in my pants."

Placing her elbows on the table, knitting her fingers together and resting her chin on the back of her hands, she looked at him and said in a sultry voice, "And what a nice looking catch it was, too." Carla flicked her eyebrows.

"Not funny," he said sternly.

"It was a little funny. Besides, you didn't suffer any lasting injury except to the only pair of jeans you own!"

"Yeah, well this time, I won't be catching anything but stripers."

"You'll be fortunate not to catch a summer cold."

"We'll see. It all depends on what we get done, first."

"Is the fishing better on the East Coast?"

"I have no idea. Aside from my conductor's conference in DC a few years ago, I hadn't spent any time here."

"Ever been interested in the East Coast before?"

"Never gave it much thought until this whole business began. My family's roots are in California. We've been Californians since the mid-1800s. What about you?"

"I've always wanted to but usually managed a convenient excuse to put it off."

"You never told me you wanted to come here?"

"There's a lot I've never shared with you about me." Her smile inferred she was willing to do so.

"Do you have family here?"

"No, I don't."

"Then what is it that draws you here?"

"My family mostly," she said in a matter-of-fact tone.

"But you just said—"

"My parents have always been a huge influence in my life, David. They are proud of their cultural heritage. A pride they've passed on to me. Even so, they felt it necessary for me to understand the history of our adopted country. So I thought what better place to start than from whence that spark of liberty was first ignited?"

"You've got a point there." Carla's words touched the memory of the military side of his family. David wanted to serve, but issues with his feet medically disqualified him. "Is it the colonial period of America that you're most interested in?"

"No, not especially. But it's always a good idea to start at the beginning."

"Well, if what we've uncovered so far is any indication, you will know more about the colonial era than you expected."

"David, I'm sorry."

"Sorry? For what?"

"I don't think I ever thanked you for the invitation."

"I wouldn't be this far along without your help."

At that comment, she chuckled. "Yeah, I could picture you calling me every five minutes trying to discern the clues you continually overlooked."

"I'd also be way behind in my examination of Jim's musical output were it not for you."

"To be honest, without the lure of West's music, I might not have come with you."

"I know, and I'm sorry, too. You weren't exactly thrilled with my odd behavior these past few months."

"Odd doesn't begin to cover it." The waitress arrived with their meals as she started to say, "You *were* being quite the ass—"

"Yes, I was," he admitted, interrupting her publically inappropriate metaphor.

From the moment she walked into the house, Beth could tell there was something more between David and Carla than either would let on. Something that clicked. Something that worked. She saw it in how they interacted. She saw it in how they looked at each other. It was something she'd wanted to achieve with Jim. That something was chemistry.

Not wanting to dwell on this observation, she concentrated instead on deciphering this letter and the deepening mystery that surrounded her former neighbor, James Burton West.

Beth arrived with laptop and magnifying glass in hand ready to get to work. She set the laptop down on the kitchen island and said, "I'll bet you guys got a lot accomplished today. Were you able to glean anything from that letter?"

David volunteered, "We were able to get pretty far even though the letter was undated and the wax impression unreadable."

"I've been curious about that letter all day! May I see it?"

David handed Beth the letter and watched with intense fascination as she brought the glass close to the seal to scrutinize it. In the middle of the oval impression was a tiny well-defined circle. On the bottom of the oval appeared to be a banner with faded ends. In the center of the banner was distinct lettering. What looked like a partial capital letter *D* was followed by the letters *um*, but the next set of letters was clear and read *Clavum*. The last legible letter looked more like an upside down capital *L*.

"It appears to be a Latin phrase. But Latin for what?" Beth queried.

"Don't look at me," Carla said in a hands-up gesture. "Dead languages are not my *forte*."

He gave Carla a teasing look. "You sounded like you had all the answers earlier." David turned toward Beth and ran down the list of Carla's deductions. "With minimal information, Carla was able to determine that the letter was likely written by a man either in December 1787 or January 1788, and the addressee William was the owner of the property in Lewes."

When Beth finished reading the letter, she looked at the two of them and nodded to Carla's deductions. She turned to David and asked, "Did you come up with any ideas on who this Thomas might be?"

David said, "I suspect it could be Sir Thomas West."

"Although the surname is compelling, I think we can eliminate that Thomas from the list based on your analysis of the date of authorship."

"Why?" he asked.

"History bug that I am, I researched the state's origins when I first came here. Sir Thomas West died crossing the Atlantic on a return trip to Jamestown in 1618. And I don't think any of his children would have lived long enough to write the letter if the date you came up with is accurate. That evidence alone would eliminate him from the list."

"Okay then, let's kick the idea around and see who else we come up with," David suggested. "How many renowned Thomases of that period had anything to do with Delaware?"

"Let's find out," Beth said as she took to her laptop so they could begin to whittle down the list of probable Thomases. "Who are we looking up first?"

"David brought up Thomas Jefferson and Thomas Paine. How about them?"

"I don't believe it was either Jefferson or Paine," Beth offered.

Carla bristled at Beth's dismissive attitude at first until she remembered how she suggested to David neither Jefferson nor Paine was the best choice. "And what would lead you to that conclusion?"

"Not only did Jefferson have little to do with Delaware, neither he nor Paine was at the Constitutional Convention in 1787. Jefferson was minister to France at the time, not to mention his only known male child died in childbirth long before the letter was written."

The idea dawned on him they were concentrating too much on the suspected father Thomas and not the letter's author. "What about Thomas Paine? Did he have any sons?"

"Let me see," Beth said as her rapid keystrokes made loud clacking sounds. It took her only seconds to pull up the information on her laptop. "Yes, as I suspected. Not only was Thomas Paine in London at the time of the convention, his wife and newborn son died in childbirth. He had no other children."

"Were there any other influential Thomases during that period?" asked David.

"Let me look that up," Beth offered, taking a bit longer than before. "Thomas Mifflin and Thomas Fitzsimons were from the Pennsylvania delegation to the Constitutional Convention, but according to this, there were no Thomases from Delaware. The only Thomas as a delegate from Delaware was during the Second Continental Congress in 1776 for the Declaration of Independence. That would have been Thomas McKean. We could look him up to see if he fits the profile?"

"Sure, why not?" David said. "Let's be thorough about this."

Nodding to David, she let her fingers clack away on the keyboard as she pulled up Thomas McKean's bio on her laptop. "Wow, it says here Thomas McKean had eleven children."

"Do any of them fit the timeline?" asked Carla.

"Based on what it says here, of the three males that survived to adulthood, Thomas Junior would have been nine years old when the letter was written. And there's nothing to indicate either Joseph or Robert ever left the country. Since the author said he settled his affairs and left for England on or about 1788, I'd say Thomas McKean isn't the Thomas we're looking for either."

Frustrated by the dwindling list of possible candidates, he asked, "Then how about the two Pennsylvania delegates Mifflin and Fitzsimons? It has to be one of them."

Beth spent almost twenty minutes researching several sites before coming up with annotated biographies on both men. She read the entries, seeking facts that would either confirm their ties to the author or strike them from the list. "Ugh! It looks as though neither man qualifies as our Thomas. Thomas Mifflin had four children, all girls and Thomas Fitzsimons had none."

"We're getting nowhere with this line of inquiry," he said reluctantly.

Snapping her fingers, Carla said, "Maybe we're going about this all wrong. Perhaps we'll be able to close in on our target Thomas when we figure out who William was."

"I agree," Beth intimated. "We should be able to track down the addressee, William through tax and deed records at the archives, since we have a target date to go by."

"All right," David said smoothly. "We have a plan of action for the William question. How are we going to address why the property off the...how do you pronounce that word?"

"It's pronounced *skoo-kle*," Beth corrected. "The Schuylkill River is next to Philadelphia."

"Right," he said looking at Carla strangely for her previous mispronunciation. "Why was the Schuylkill River property so important to the author?"

Carla reminded David, "Didn't you want to ask her about that odd phrase, *'in my solitude, the secret shall remain forever*'? Not only did the author make such a confusing statement, he also capitalized the word, solitude."

"May I see the letter again?"

"Sure," said Carla, handing Beth the letter.

Rereading the entire fragment, Beth suggested something neither of them considered.

"Although we could go round and round on the intent of this phrase, I don't believe there's anything mysterious about the capital S. Standardized spelling was not standard practice in letters of the period. It's widely known even our founding fathers' correspondence were rife with misspellings and improper capitalizations. Even the font of printed pages of the time made an *S* look more like an uncrossed lower case *f*. Take, for instance, the Bill of Rights. In the word *Congress*, the first *s* is written larger than the second. Today, a capital S would have made the word Solitude a proper noun. It may have been a simple mistake."

David turned his attention from Beth to Carla. "Well, at least we have an idea where Jim's sense of writing style was influenced. Nearly all of his correspondence was in florid eighteenth-century style complete with a wax stamp."

Carla was visibly dissatisfied with their lack of progress. "Yeah, outside of the fact the author was a man, and the letter was written in December 1787, we're no closer to solving this thing than we were this morning."

Chapter Twenty – Four

David peered across the open expanse of the archives looking for Audra Bunting but didn't see her. He went over to the staff member behind the curved information desk to inquire about her.

"How may I help you, sir?" asked the maroon-smocked attendant.

"Excuse me, but do you know if Audra Bunting is in today?"

"She's not normally here on Saturday, but I can check to see if she's in her office. In the meantime, may I be of some assistance?"

"It's possible she left something for me. Could you check to see if she left a message or a package for a David Whealy?"

"Sure, give me a moment."

"Thank you. I'll be right over there," he said pointing to the table where his two fellow investigators had already established their base of operations.

David jotted down a few ideas to narrow their focus of inquiry and to make productive use of their limited time. Initially centering their research around Sussex County and on the William in question, he suggested using the estimated year of the letter's origin, 1787 as a starting point. All that remained was to determine who would do what. David began with the tax and census records in the card catalogs, while Beth took on the index binders for the birth and death records along with the probate indexes. Carla wanted to familiarize herself with the layout of the archives before settling to work on the record of wills and deeds. Once the division of labor was decided, they each set off to their respective tasks.

Standing in front of the card catalogs for Sussex County, David observed his musical colleague with an air of amusement. She went about her exploring with the insatiable curiosity of an obsessed child.

He shook his head as he continued sifting through row after row of 3 x 5 cards that were printed using an old typewriter. Making it past the second row of cards, he felt a tap on his shoulder. It was the attendant.

"Sir, Ms. Bunting isn't available, but she left you this." The attendant handed David a manila envelope with his name on it.

"Thank you." David opened it and found a short note from Audra informing him the key along with his contact information was in the capable hands of a Dr. Giles Radnor from the Smithsonian. He put the note back into the envelope and placed it on the table they were working from so he wouldn't lose it. It was then he glanced up at Beth and noticed the look of worry on her face. "Hey, what's the matter?"

"I just wish I could join you here during the week."

"That's all right. At least they're open one Saturday a month. With your help, I think we'll stand a better chance of identifying this William from the letter."

"What if we don't?"

"I'm sure we'll find something."

"Records from that long ago are spotty or incomplete at best and our time for research is limited. The riddles this letter presents may never be solved, today or ever."

"You don't think something useful will present itself with a little effort?"

"All I'm saying is don't get your hopes up. Genuine research takes time. More time than you could realistically budget for your short stay here."

"Point taken." Investing the time needed to solve this new conundrum unexpectedly derailed his examination of West's music. David considered the file cabinet full of scores, the abundant amount of work still left to do and the limited timeframe with which to do it. He realized they only had a month left before he and Carla must return to the university.

"Tell you what. Since I'm not going anywhere, I promise to use my free time to track down every clue we find."

"You don't have to do that."

"I'm in this, David," she said with steadfast determination. "Jim was a friend, albeit a distant one. The best way to honor his memory is to help you figure this out."

"I appreciate that."

Carla returned to the table and lamented, "It's a shame they won't let us bring a laptop into the archives. Documenting our findings would be easier."

Defending archive policy, he said, "I understand their concern for bringing pens, electronic devices, and bags into the archives. It's a way of protecting the source documents, many of which are original books, maps, and other historical items. Well, shall we get busy?"

Anxious to get started, Carla said, "Let's do this!"

They scattered about their tasks trying to identify the mysterious addressee, William. Looking through the Sussex County card catalogs, David located the tax records for addresses in the Lewes Hundred, but no names were connected to any of them. He decided to cross-reference the tax data with the record of deeds and census records, and that's when he got a promising hit. The owner and taxpayer of the property called Lewes-on-the-water and listed on the census record of 1790 was William West. Taken off guard by the familiar surname, David rushed over to share his findings.

"Hey, you two," he said as he held out a small piece of paper with the familiar name on it. "Check this out."

Carla's expression reflected the words that issued from her lips. "You've got to be kidding."

"That was almost too easy," said Beth. "If only the rest of our results could come that fast."

"I hope so," David agreed. With the name of the letter's addressee believed solved, he returned to the record of deeds to continue his research.

He noted that the census records reflected William West's name connected to the property from 1780 to 1810. But sifting through the tax records before 1780, he noticed something odd. Not only had William West's name dropped off the tax rolls, but he also found no evidence of revenue received from the Lewes Hundred between the years 1723 and 1780. Unable to make any further headway through the tax records, the record of deeds or the census records, David turned his inquiry to the birth records.

He backtracked the birth records of 1780 and earlier to see if he could find out when William West was born and found nothing. It was as though William West didn't exist before 1780. David was puzzled, but then again the records from that period were fragmented and incomplete, just as Beth indicated. Failing to find a birth record on William West, he took on the daunting task of going over marriage records, but this also became a fruitless exercise.

Meanwhile, armed with a full name to conduct her inquiry, Carla was now able to continue her search in the record of wills and deeds with renewed optimism. Not seeing the name West in her limited search of the probate record, she began looking for evidence of a will in this name.

Beth used the new clue to comb through death records she'd already searched, using the year 1790 as a starting point. After two hours of diligent effort, she managed to find a significant clue. Two Wests from Lewes died only four days apart from each other in April 1813; William, fifty-six years old and Cynthia, fifty-one. Suspicious this wasn't a natural occurrence, she asked Carla to check the month of April 1813 in the coroner and probate indexes. Beth used the index library near the archives entrance to locate the reference number for the roll of microfilm she needed. Finding the correct reference number, she disappeared into the microfilm room to find the roll she needed.

Filled with nervous excitement, she found a seat in front of an unoccupied microfilm projector, quickly loaded the roll of film into the reader's slot and scrolled the knob to advance the microfilm. In short order, Beth found a page from the *Wilmington Gazette*, dated April 12, 1813, that held her answer. She printed the copy of the article to keep with the rest of their collected notes. The horrific headline read *"Lewes Residents Killed in Attack."* Contained within the story was the following report.

Cynthia West has expired from injuries received during the British assault on the town of Lewes five days ago. The April 7th attack destroyed West's home and killed her husband, William. Their son Robert, aged 32 years, was not harmed.

When she emerged, Beth went over to Carla and asked her to check the coroner's inquest references for Sussex County to confirm her findings, while she went back to the viewing room to retrieve the microfilm from the reader.

It took Carla a bit longer to wade through the sea of reference material before she managed to find the most basic of information concerning Cynthia West. The coroner's inquest index contained the cause and dates of death in brief entries, detailing the extent of William and Cynthia West's injuries. The entries were short, but they corroborated Beth's newspaper story. She took the reference book over to the information desk to ask the clerk for a copy of the pages. Once she had copies for David's growing file, she rejoined them at the table.

"Were you able to find something?" Beth asked.

"I think so, but I'm not sure it does anything but verify your information," Carla said.

David piped in. "I know you said we shouldn't get our hopes up, Beth, but based on the ages you gave me, I looked up the birth records for a William West born in 1757 or '58 and a Cynthia born in 1762 or '63. I may not have found William West, but I did find a Cynthia named Belmore, born in the county of New Castle in 1762 that otherwise matches the timeline." David pulled out his pocket watch to check the time. They had less than an hour left before the archives closed, so they had to work fast. "Let's do one last check of the records before they close."

"Sure," Beth volunteered. "But what are we looking for?"

Realizing they had to limit their search, David sat down to summarize their efforts in a chronological outline. He gathered all the evidence along with the clues he remembered from Jim's correspondence and drafted a timeline relevant to the information they discovered.

"Let's start with the earliest year, 1723. That was the last year revenue was collected from the Lewes Hundred until it resumed in 1780, fifty-seven years later. Based on his age and the year he died, William West was born in either 1757 or '58. However, since I was unable to find a birth certificate, it could mean the documents were either lost, or he wasn't born in Delaware."

"That's likely given the fluid movement of the population at that time," Beth said.

Smiling up at Beth for her favorable evaluation of his deductions, he continued his narrative. "Since the only Cynthia born in Delaware old enough to have been West's wife was a Cynthia Belmore, born February 6, 1762, in New Castle, she would be the most logical candidate. But without a marriage certificate to prove it, we won't know for sure."

"Yeah, you're right," Carla said. "We'll have to come back to the archives."

This was the kind of stumbling block Beth warned David about, but she held her tongue for the time being.

"In 1780, William West was first identified as owning Lewes-on-the-water. Their son, Robert West was born around the same year. Next on our timeline was the letter written in 1787 to William from an unidentified man, presumably from Philadelphia, since he had such quick knowledge of their ratification of the Constitution. Both William and Cynthia West meet their end as a result of the British attack on Lewes, Delaware on April 7, 1813. He was fifty-six and she was fifty-one when they died, leaving their thirty-two-year-old son, Robert. Now, did I miss anything?"

"I don't think so," said Carla.

"The question is, with only forty-five minutes before they close, do we have time to find a marriage certificate for William and Cynthia West or any information on their son, Robert?" asked Beth.

"We can try," David suggested.

Carla volunteered, "I'll search for the marriage certificate."

Beth nodded. "I'll look in the death and probate records."

That left David to scrutinize the birth records.

They concentrated their effort by canvassing the Sussex county records, but it was almost a useless gesture. David had enough time to review the birth records but found nothing on a Robert West. Carla's search netted the same negative results. Aside from confirming her discovery on William and Cynthia West as she went through the card catalog of recorded deaths for the county, Beth found no certificates of death for either Robert West or Cynthia Belmore. The sheer size of the reference for wills and probate records prohibited Beth from completing her task of locating any documentation with the name Cynthia Belmore or Robert West, and they still had two more counties of records to search. That would have to wait for another day. A staff member had announced the archives' imminent closure.

The ride back to Lewes was a quiet one at first. The sound of soft jazz on the radio relaxed the mentally fatigued trio. David took his time driving back to the house with Carla riding shotgun and Beth observing the duo from the backseat.

David stared at the road. Carla stared into space. Beth broke the silence first.

"What are you thinking, Carla?"

"I'm thinking that I'm disappointed."

"Why so?"

"I thought we'd have an easier time extracting useful information from this archives. I didn't expect so large a data gap in our research."

Beth smiled. "As I suggested to David before we started, gaps in the historical record are more common than most people realize. We have to remember, the further back in time we go, the easier it is for us to find gaps in documentation."

"But as a repository for all salient historical data, shouldn't a place like the Delaware Public Archives be as complete as possible?"

"Yes, but finding relevant data that far back is problematic at best. For instance, the revised Great Seal of the State of Delaware contains three specific years: 1704, 1776, and 1787. We know all too well the significance of the latter two. But the first date's significance hinges on the events of May 22, 1704."

"What's the significance of the first date?" Carla asked with genuine curiosity.

"We only know what happened on that date because there is evidence that on May 22, 1704, the proprietor of Pennsylvania met with the new legislative body of the lower counties in New Castle, Delaware. We have no definitive proof as to who made up the assembly, where they met or what they did between that date and 1739."

Carla did the math in her head. "That's a thirty-five-year gap in the historical record. Is there any chance of finding records that chronicled their doings during that period?"

Beth said with a hint of optimism, "There's always a chance. However, the more time passes, the more difficult it shall be to locate any of those records."

It wasn't the answer Carla was fishing for, but it was an answer. "David, didn't you say that West—" She stopped abruptly. Thinking her dispassionate reference to Beth's late friend was somehow an insult, she rephrased her question. "Didn't you say that Jim's family owned that property since 1724?"

"Yes. Jim revealed as much in his first correspondence. Why?"

"Wouldn't that mean William and Cynthia weren't the first West's to have owned the property?"

Beth caught on. "If *they* weren't the first owners, then who are we looking for?"

Glancing into the rearview mirror at Beth, he quipped, "Excellent question."

David came to a logical conclusion. "I believe the answer we're looking for is contained in that letter. From its tone, the author had *something* to do with the property. The owner must have been either the author, which is improbable given he and William appear to have been contemporaries, or more likely the Thomas to whom the author referred."

They'd passed Five Points when Beth reached for her newfangled cell phone the wireless agent convinced her to get and noticed that she had failed to turn it back on. Unlocking her phone, its pleasant chime informed her it was functioning. But a second chime accompanied the words *Missed Call* on the face of the phone. When she checked the unfamiliar seven-digit number, it was followed by the words *College Park, MD.*

Beth was visibly distressed. "I'm sorry, but I'll have to forego dinner this evening."

"Why? What is it?" Carla asked her.

"Nothing," she said at first. In a forlorn voice, she added, "Hopefully."

♪

Chapter Twenty – Five

The week following the trio's daylong research at the archives had passed quickly. David and Carla heard nothing from Beth after they dropped her off at her house. She'd called David to let him know she had to go back to the DC area for a few days, but she didn't say why.

Taking up the task of score reviews once again, Carla was better than three-quarters of the way through her file drawer of music and David was halfway into his. Even with their admirable efforts, it was dawning on them their window of opportunity was closing, and they wouldn't finish their task before they had to return to California. David already planned on bringing back the more impressive scores.

Confining herself to the examination of the work in front of her, she did her best to ignore David's rattling around downstairs. She became so involved in a large-scale piece of music, she was able to tune out every other sound except for the majestic brass section playing in her head. The notes she was reading began to play effortlessly as the beautifully constructed motive West composed passed among the various instruments. With each transition of melodic responsibility came a modulation. She was so fascinated by the subtle changes in musical color, she felt transported from that small room into the concert hall at the Mondavi. That is until a loud crash abruptly replaced the music.

"Are you all right down there?"

"Yeah," he said, looking down at the mess he created. "I never did like the color of this kitchen tile. That's why I chose this particular moment in time to decorate the floor with the new jar of sea salt we bought yesterday."

An amused Carla only shook her head and went back to work on the score. Not seeing any cleaning supplies in the kitchen the last time he was in the house, David decided to inspect the closet near the front door.

That's when he saw it.

Right next to a broom and dustpan was an umbrella stand with three objects in it. The first was a common black umbrella with a wooden crook handle. Next to the umbrella was a black-shafted, hand made shillelagh with an oversized light brown knob handle. Its owner must have favored the shillelagh since the handle's finish was nearly worn off. David removed the stick to look at the iron ferrule and noted it was worn down to a nub. But it was the last item in the stand that drew his attention. He replaced the shillelagh and grabbed the item from its resting place. It was this item he just had to show Carla.

Armed with a broom, a dustpan, and his latest discovery, he went back into the kitchen to clean up the salt and broken shards of jar off the floor. The sound of broken glass scraping across the tile and the other disjointed noises coming from downstairs was getting on Carla's nerves.

"What are you doing down there?"

"Cleaning up," he called back to her. Unable to prepare his original suggestion for lunch without sea salt, he deferred to his other idea. After he completed his sanitation duties, he made some light finger sandwiches, pleasing to the eye and delightful to the palate. "Are you hungry?"

"I could eat, sure," came the response from the second floor.

Carla heard him coming up the stairs. He had a tray of drinks with finger sandwiches in one hand and in the other was a long dark object capped with shiny metal.

"What's that?"

"Since we worked through lunch today, I thought a light snack would be in order."

"No, that!" she exclaimed, pointing to the item he held in his other hand.

Holding it up proudly, he said, "I found this in the broom closet near the front door."

"Let me see it."

David handed her the newly discovered artifact for her examination. She scrutinized the stylish gentleman's walking stick with keen interest. It was topped by an ornate ten-inch-long silver-and-gold handle that matched the girth of the stick where it connected to the wooden shaft. The metal handle's diameter grew gradually from the shaft to its rounded end. It was composed of alternating rings of gold and silver. The unusual design had three intricately decorated thick silver rings, the thickest of which was in the center of the handle. Separating each silver ring was a satin finished gold ring. Each end of the metal handle was made of gold. A thicker ring of unadorned gold connected the handle to the shaft while the other end was a rounded, bulbous top made of the same color.

"Now *this* is a work of art. Where do you think West got it?"

"I have no idea. But I know that it's coming with me."

"What do *you* plan on doing with it?" Carla asked with a sarcastic bent.

"If your father, the dean, can go about in his old-fashioned suits and ridiculous hats, then perhaps it's time for me to accessorize my attire as well. Of course, you *know* William would kill to have a stick like this. By my beating him to the punch, he'd have no wind left in his sails for one-upmanship."

"Whose father?" she asked playfully.

They both had a good laugh at Cobbett's expense.

"That looks delicious," Carla said, as she set aside her work to partake in the lunch David brought up with him. As she ate the first sandwich, Carla's expression became a prelude to yet another intuitive observation.

"You were a genuine detective Saturday."

"How's that?"

"I didn't know you were that into family histories. You were methodical, detailed, and quite scientific in your approach to the research we conducted at the archives," explained Carla as she reached for another sandwich. A skeptical look came across his face again, so she felt she had to qualify her remark. "One would have thought you were a genealogist." Tipping her glass of wine toward him, she added, "You were quite impressive."

"Actually, my father was the genealogist of the family."

"Really?"

"He was the one who did the most extensive research into our family line. He traced it back to 1818 before the trail was lost."

"You never told me that before," she said, curling up into the small chair they had wrested from the guest bedroom on the first floor. "And?"

David let the desk chair recline as he leaned back. "Let me see now. If I recall my father's research, he found out the earliest known Whealy lived on the East Coast. His name was Payton, and he was born in Philadelphia in 1818. He married a singer named Diane Marlow, the daughter of Richard and Elizabeth Marlow. Payton and Diane had three children, two sons, and a daughter. But the eldest son, Edward, chose to move to California in 1860 to pursue his entrepreneurial aspirations and it was from him that I am descended."

"I remember you discussing your family from California, but what about your family on the East Coast? Did your father ever learn what happened to them?"

"Regrettably, there's little documentation concerning Diane Marlow's forebears. He was only able to find Diane's father, Richard. He'd made a respectable living as a skilled carpenter. And her mother, Elizabeth, was the only Methodist in a family of Protestants. The only information he was able to find on Elizabeth was that she might have died in either January or June of 1858, and she was buried in an undisclosed location somewhere on the East Coast, but that was it."

"What about Payton and Diane's other children? Do you know if any of their descendants survive today?"

"I don't know why he stopped looking into that side of the family history, but he did. I suppose I could resurrect his effort if I had the time or the interest to do so."

"Well, based on what I've seen you do so far, I wouldn't doubt that you could find them if they exist."

David was about to respond to her appraisal of his abilities when he received a text from an unwelcomed source—William Tipton Cobbett III with a list of program pieces slated for the season's debut concert.

Looking down at the message, he turned to Carla shaking his head. "You're not going to believe this."

"Oh, let me guess." Carla planted her feet firmly on the floor, knitted her fingers together, forearms on her thighs, and stared at David. "Your father?"

"That's not funny."

He read the text message twice before he handed the phone to Carla. She looked at the list with ambivalence wondering what David's problem was.

"What's wrong with the *English Folk Song Suite* or the *English Dances?*" She kept reading the list. "I even enjoy Holst's *First Suite in E flat.* I think it deserves greater consideration for performance than his *Planets.*" She finished reading then turned to look at David's sullen face. "What?"

"I hope I'm wrong and he isn't as petty as I believe him to be."

"Okay, I'm lost. What are you driving at?"

"Tell me you haven't noticed a distinct change in his attitude at the end of the last semester?"

"Nothing out of the ordinary, why?"

"You haven't noticed a difference in how he interacts with people after his receipt of the Gold Baton Award?" Not knowing the award's significance, David explained it to her. "A Gold Baton recipient typically gets priority placement to any job offer they wish to put in for, and the principal director of the London Symphony Orchestra is retiring next year."

She tried to put two and two together. "What does his award have to do with these pieces?"

"Read the remaining program."

Elgar's *Nimrod* and Benjamin Britten's *Young Person's Guide to the Orchestra* were the last remaining works on the list, but she still didn't get it.

"What are the names of the composers William came up with?" he asked, giving her a hint.

"Vaughn Williams, Gustav Holst, Edward Elgar, Sir Malcolm Arnold and Sir Benjamin Britten. That looks to be everyone."

"Yeah?"

"What's the matter with that list? They're all composers from the 20th century?"

"And all *English* composers."

That gave Carla something new to chew on besides her last sandwich.

Getting ready for their last Thursday evening dinner in Delaware before they had to head back to the West Coast, David planned on treating Carla to the stuffed blue crab dinner at the restaurant near the Lord De La Warr. They were about to leave the house when his cell rang. It was Beth.

"David?"

"Yes," he said simply, realizing who it was.

"I have some great and not-so-great news."

"Oh? What news?"

Detecting a slight tenseness in his tone, she asked, "Have I done something wrong?"

"You left for DC without saying a word. We were concerned when we didn't hear from you."

"I apologize, David. I honestly do. Watching you and Carla's devotion to the task and each other made me feel a bit out of place. I felt slighted where no slight was intended by either of you. I realize that now. You were the consummate gentleman, and I was wrong not to confide in you."

...devotion...to each other...

Those words stuck in his head from the moment she uttered them. He also noted she didn't include Carla in that last statement. Not wanting to get into it right then and there, he said, "Don't worry about it. And I take it from your uneasiness your news is not that great?"

"I'm not sure yet. I may have landed the job I wanted, doing what we did in the archives, as a historian!"

"Is that right? Where?"

"That's the crummy part. Remember I told you about the position I applied for on that government website?"

"I remember."

"You won't believe this, but they had me interview for it three times now! The way they're going about this whole thing sounds as if they want to hire me."

"That's great!" The delay in her response told him otherwise. "Isn't it?"

"It would be if I didn't have to move. The DC area is far too congested for my taste. I hate being uprooted again."

David felt empathy for Beth's plight. He recognized a bit of himself in her behavior and didn't like what he saw. He started to grasp the hurt he inflicted on Carla after his return from his first trip to Delaware. "That's quite the conundrum. What do you plan to do?"

"They haven't officially selected me for the job, but they seem to be leaning that way. I'm not sure if I should accept, but I figure I'd better have an answer for them once they've made their decision."

Carla emerged from the master bedroom refreshed and ready to head out the door. That's when she noticed David was still on the phone. Not wanting to be rude but curious as to the identity of the caller, she mouthed the question, *Who is it?*

David covered the microphone and whispered, "It's Beth." He continued his discussion trying to address her problem. "What does your heart say?"

His question was met with silence from Beth and an exasperated look from Carla. She heard David's unexpected question, but not understanding the context, she stared at him hoping to glean more information from his responses.

"Beth? Did you hear me?"

"I heard you. I don't have an answer for you because I don't know the answer myself."

"Look, it's getting late, and we were headed out for dinner. Care to join us?"

"Where are you going?"

"That seafood place near the Lord De La Warr?"

"Oh, the *Poseidon's Bounty*? Their tilapia is the best. I can meet you there in half an hour?"

"We'll see you there," he said before ending the call.

Satisfied as to the direction of their conversation, Carla chose to change the subject. She eyed David as if wishing to devour him where he stood. "You look quite dashing this evening, sir!"

"What was *that* look for?"

She just smiled.

The crowd at *Poseidon's Bounty* was respectable for a Thursday evening, but there were still a few tables open. Beth arrived late enough to find David and Carla already seated and nursing their drinks.

"I'm sorry," Beth said. "Our last client had a complicated issue that took me a while to resolve."

Remembering Beth's last marathon meeting, he asked, "I hope you were able to eat today?"

"Today? Yes. Earlier this week? No."

Wanting to feel included in the conversation, Carla asked a question she already knew the answer to. "What was it you did again?"

"I'm a consultant for a Chicago-based advertising firm."

"Really? Chicago? What would draw their interest here in Delaware?"

"They were only interested in Delaware's business-friendly incorporation laws at first," Beth began. "After the chief financial officer got back from his first business trip to Wilmington, he suggested setting up an office near Rehoboth Beach. It's become a very lucrative opportunity while providing the company an East Coast presence."

"You seem to have a great head for business," said Carla frankly. "With such an intimate familiarity of your firm's decision-making acumen and your instinct for troubleshooting client issues, you must be highly placed in your organization."

"No," Beth admitted. "I'm only a midlevel account planner."

"And a good one, too," complemented Carla. "Judging from the emphasis they place on you and your ability to solve delicate problems."

"I *hope* the firm recognizes my value when it comes to successfully dealing with difficult clients."

"Tell me, how does a savvy Chicago businesswoman end up with such a keen interest in Delaware history?" asked Carla, who became an unwelcomed inquisitor.

Before she could respond to Carla's purposeful nettling, David tried to diffuse the situation. "You said you had some great and not-so-great news?"

Keeping her gaze in Carla's direction but answering David, she said, "Yes, I did." Beth's expression of annoyance disappeared as she wrapped her mind around the question at hand. "It's not definite yet, but I may have been selected for that job in College Park. The only catch is they want me to move there."

The question wasn't necessarily for David's benefit but to force a change of subject and to fill Carla in on the content of Beth's earlier call. Realizing what the consequences of her acceptance would mean, Carla's look of curiosity changed to a relaxed satisfaction. "You would be leaving then?"

Determined to hold superiority in her verbal riposte, Beth replied, "Not if I have anything to say about it. My skills don't come cheap. If they want me, it'll cost them."

Carla sought another honorable retreat, this time from her worthy adversary. She tried to strike a more conciliatory tone. "You *should* hold the value of your skills in high esteem. You've earned it."

"I wonder if you could explain how you knew I had *earned* it? Aside from any anecdotes you may have been privy to, you know nothing about me."

Stunned at the tone and direction their conversation was taking, David could only sit in utter silence as the effusive drama unfolded.

Lobbing the verbal grenade back in Carla's direction, Beth watched to see if she would fall onto it or somehow manage to evade its destructive intent.

Carla sat back in her chair. "You're right, of course. Aside from your success as the business woman your former agency was so desperate to retain they paid to move you here, I know nothing about you," she admitted. "How can anyone get to know you, if you don't know yourself?"

Beth could do nothing but sit there turning five shades of red. Looking at Carla, she thought to herself, *I never told David the real reason I moved to Delaware, so how does she know? Or is this just a clever device on her part to get me to reveal my secret?* After her internal deliberation, she said resolutely, "Trust is not something I'm willing to simply hand over because you ask for it. Trust must be earned."

Carla allowed her impatience to color her response. "I can understand being cautiously skeptical of new people, but how is it possible for anyone to trust *you* if you're not willing to be truthful with your friends? This self-protection thing plays well for a few rounds, but it doesn't win you the fight, nor does it win you any friendships." Then as if to skewer Beth with the killing thrust, she asked the mortal question, "What are you so afraid of?"

Carla's question reopened a wound Beth was loath to explain. Successfully able to deflect Carla's question, Beth demonstrated her only real strength in this contest, her silence. A silence that, outside of some brief commentary on how well the food was prepared, defined the remainder of the evening.

Chapter Twenty — Six

David sat quietly in his car after pulling into his reserved parking spot near the music building. Ten minutes flew by as he thought about last Thursday evening's squabble between Beth and Carla. In their altercation, he recognized what first attracted him to these women; they were both able to maintain a healthy sense of self-worth without sacrificing their femininity. Although Carla seemed to have the upper hand in their tense exchange, Beth still managed to elude Carla's best efforts to extract a meaningful answer from her. But trying to assign logic to what happened between these two had all the fascination of calculating an algorithm. So he chose not to.

The new semester was here, and he needed to get busy. Spending the summer in Delaware, he ignored his lesson plans. Cobbett would be furious if he knew David wasn't prepared for the academic year. Completing the semester schedule in a few hours was the easy part. Evaluating the musical strengths of the new student population was going to take longer. Doing so gave him the upper hand to decide if the repertoire chosen by last year's Faculty Solo Showdown champion would be a success or a failure.

Cobbett's reserved space was still empty, which meant the dean was occupied with his plethora of morning meetings. He grabbed the valise containing some of the reviewed scores and his new walking stick before he made his way into the building.

All the evidence he needed to prove Peggy had an enjoyable summer was etched on her peeling pink nose and tanned face. Antara sat in the chair next to Peggy's desk.

"Good morning, ladies," said David. They both responded in kind. Referring to Peggy, he said, "I guess I don't have to ask if *you* had a great time this summer. The only question would be where."

Peggy's stoic expression relaxed a bit. "Stan and I just got back from an enjoyable ten-day cruise to Puerto Vallarta. On the last day of the trip, I fell asleep on the promenade deck." Then she pointed at her nose.

David shook his head. "At least the trip was fun." Addressing Antara, he asked, "And did you go anyplace exciting this summer?"

The diminutive woman's soft, translucent brown eyes were trained on David from the moment he walked into the cramped reception area. Antara's reserved personality showed in the accented elocution of her speech and her distinct yet subdued sense of fashion. The light color lipstick she favored offset her near flawless skin. But it wasn't her modest looks that captured and kept an observer's attention. It was her eyes.

Framed in eyeliner, delicate shading, and finely tweezed eyebrows, Antara's twin soul seekers were enough to project a soothing effect on anyone who looked at her.

"I didn't have anything planned this summer, so I went to Lake Tahoe to relax with those interesting scores you handed me." Taking a particular interest in the stick David had, Antara said offhandedly, "That's new."

Although the stick was new to him, he didn't know how old it was. With no knowledge of the subject, he couldn't tell if it were made yesterday or was a carefully preserved relic from some European aristocrat.

He held out the metal-topped staff to Antara. "I happened upon it in the home I inherited. Can you make anything of it?"

David was always keen to temper his superior position over the other professors with a mutual respect for their talents and abilities. For this reason, he respected their opinions regarding West's work. It was reasonable for David to assume he would receive an honest appraisal about the music and the stick.

She spent most of her time examining the rings of the topper. Running her fingers over the silver portion, she said, "The extensive detail would suggest this stick was handmade. The artwork on the smaller rings is extraordinary. This tire tread design in the center resembles the hilt of a sword without the hand guard."

David was surprised at her assessment. "I wouldn't have thought of that."

"Skilled artisans used to hide small daggers within their walking sticks for the defense of the owner. This could be one of them, but I don't see any mechanisms to open it."

"I don't think it separates."

"There's usually a switch or key feature on the handle somewhere, but I can't find one. It's a handsome piece, though." Looking at David, she handed the stick back to him.

"Thank you, Antara, for that detailed assessment." Antara nodded before moving into David's office. Addressing his assistant, he asked, "What's the schedule look like?"

Peggy looked at her notes. "Antara is in your office now since she has a prior engagement for lunch. You have a nine o'clock with the Student Faculty Planning Committee, new student orientation at ten, a working lunch at noon with all the department heads followed by the campus paper interview, syllabus reviews, and a three o'clock with Dr. Cobbett."

"Is it possible for you to block out some time for me to breathe?" he asked jokingly. All he got in return was a cynical stare. "Yeah, I know. Welcome to another fun-filled academic year."

He accepted his list of appointments from Peggy and retired to his office for the marathon of meetings about to begin. His first appointment with Antara was going to be a pleasure. The last one with the dean, he wasn't so sure.

David approached the conference table where Antara and her portion of West's scores were waiting for him. "I see you have your hands full today, so we'll make this quick. It's too bad we shall miss you for lunch."

"It took me two months to schedule my annual physical, so I don't want to miss it."

"You do what you must," he said understandingly.

"I hope you don't mind, but after reading the first few pieces, I couldn't help sharing these with the rest of the department."

"I'm glad you took the initiative. What was their overall consensus?"

"Most of them were as impressed as I was."

"Anything about the work that stood out for them?"

Antara referred to the stack in front of her. "Despite the eclectic nature of the pieces, this composer's work is distinct and identifiable."

David didn't remember either he or Carla considering that aspect of his benefactor's music. When he tried to remember the patterns of chord progression and the composer's need for melodic flow in each piece, he understood what she was talking about.

"In fact, Professor Cantu summarized the music's warm effect as introspective and inviting, but occasionally forlorn."

Typical of Antara's high regard for her colleagues, she placed their opinion first. Again, that tactic wasn't lost on David, for he knew Antara well enough. He'd have to coax her for an appraisal. "What did you think of it yourself?"

Now David was asking something Dr. Antara Singh was reticent to admit. When she expressed her opinion, she usually did so with a poetic cadence. He sat across from her expecting another philosophical gem to come from her lips. She didn't disappoint.

Antara divided her stack of scores into two even piles. Placing her left hand on one pile, she offered the first insightful clue to her own evaluation. "Like the notes of the first piece I reviewed, the core of this composer's music touched every happiness I have yet to live." Gently caressing the other pile with her right hand, she added, "He also managed to touch every tear I have yet to shed."

That last statement took David right back to the night when he played West's music for Beth. The night Beth blankly stared into a very different set of expressive eyes. The eyes of Isabella West.

It was nearly nine o'clock when he wound up his meeting with Antara. There was only enough time for him to check his email before the next meeting. The feedback on West's music had been coming in from all quarters since the end of July. Like Antara, all the department heads shared West's music with their colleagues. He was getting evaluations from almost every professor in the music department. This proliferation of effort was what David expected. If he ever hoped to get this man's music out in front of the public, he was going to need their support. Without it, he wouldn't be able to convince an irascible dean to break his own rules and perform this unknown composer's works.

He scanned the responses from the department heads first since the agenda wouldn't allow them to discuss their evaluations during the working lunch. Julia's email essentially said the same thing as Jason Cantu's summary, but she went further. She described West's quartets as having all the refinement of Haydn, the precision of Mozart, and the complexity of Beethoven all rolled into one. His later quartets exhibited a preference for modern complexity that transcended the barriers of musical form and function while maintaining a melodic line.

Lindsay echoed Julia's interpretation. She said West's music was powerful but musically despondent as if the composer were trying to ask forgiveness from someone who could never grant it. Lindsay's analysis had a familiar ring to it.

Henry Tanaka's assessment was less complimentary. Henry was well-known as the George Bernard Shaw of the UC Davis Music Department and a staunch advocate for the strict interpretation of music as penned by the composer. The only thing that irked Henry more than a misinterpreted performance was a critic who used the term *important* to describe a piece of music. To him, that vague description was beyond lazy. He savaged the users of the term because they were never able to express why a particular piece was so *important*. The head of the woodwind department wasn't enamored with West's earlier efforts, considering them too shallow in the development section. Still, he had to admit being thoroughly impressed by West's more mature works despite their eccentric originality.

When David got to Henry's last sentence, he grinned. That was when the music department's harshest critic dared to say that the music was bold, inventive, and thus worthy of performance.

David couldn't ignore how every analysis seemed to add up to the same conclusions drawn by both he and Carla. They all found merit in the music of this previously unknown composer called James Burton West.

As he finished reading Henry's email, Peggy poked her head in the office. "The attendees for your next meeting are here."

"Send them in."

Myung-hee took her seat across the conference table from the assistant dean for the last time as president of the Student Faculty Planning Committee. Clayton Forbes, Holly Runyon, and last year's newcomer, Preston Stoddard, represented the students on the committee. Carla and Jason Cantu sat in for the faculty.

David reached across his desk to retrieve a notepad before he acknowledged the veteran concertmistress. "The meeting's all yours, Myung-hee."

"Thank you, Professor." Taking on a businesslike demeanor, she grasped the reins and assumed control as David knew she would. "Before we get into the details of the first concert, I want to make sure that all nominations for this year's planning committee executive board are turned into Clayton no later than the close of business Friday. That will give the nominees over a month to campaign. Elections are scheduled for the Monday following the fall concert. Has anyone shown interest in any of the committee positions?"

Preston said, "I'll throw my hat in the ring, so to speak."

"Which board position would you like to be nominated for?"

"I'd be good with vice president," he answered.

"Thanks, Preston. Anyone else?" Hearing no other nominations, she checked off that agenda item and moved on. "Our first round of rehearsals for the fall concert is scheduled next week. Dr. Cobbett supplied me with the program for the first concert, which promises to be a fun, lighthearted event." Unsure of her next move, she looked at David for encouragement "The dean withheld the committee's power to decide the remaining concert schedule for the rest of the academic year."

"Did Dr. Cobbett tell you why he'd do such a thing?"

"No, he didn't," she said meekly. "He gave me the impression he wanted to speak to you about it first."

The three puzzled faculty members looked at each other.

"I'm not sure why he wouldn't allow the committee to do their job," said David, "but I have a meeting with the dean this afternoon. I'll address it with him then."

Relieved, Myung-hee said, "I appreciate that."

"Since we're unable to discuss the remaining schedule, are you planning anything different for this opening concert?"

"No, not really," said Myung-hee regaining her confidence. "The doors open at 6:00 p.m., an hour before the start of the concert. Gelmetti's has agreed to cater the affair." She then recognized her fellow student seated to her right. "Clayton has arranged several pieces for string quintet in keeping with this year's theme. We'll use them for the gathering music."

David inclined his head, encouraging Myung-hee to press on.

"The featured opening works are Vaughn Williams' *English Folk Song Suite*, Holst's *First Suite in E flat* and we'll round off the first half of the evening with both sets of *English Dances* by Sir Malcolm Arnold."

"That's about forty minutes worth of music. Who've you asked to conduct the concert?"

"Since he was last year's Solo Showdown champion, we were hoping to enlist Dr. Cobbett if he's willing."

"I'm sure he would be delighted to take the baton." David thought since this year's theme was Cobbett's idea, the dean might insist upon having as much conductor time as possible. "So far, so good."

"After the intermission, Edward Elgar's *Nimrod* will function as the *entr'acte*. The second half of the concert shall feature Tippett's *Fantasia Concertante* before we close the concert with Britten's *Young Person's Guide to the Orchestra*. All in all, we believe this concert shall set the musical standard for the year."

David noticed the change in the program from Cobbett's text. They needed to add the piece by Sir Michael Tippett, or the length of the program would be too brief. "Again, that's just over forty minutes worth of music. What's your plan for an encore?"

The student representatives looked at each other. Preston piped up first. "That's why we need your help, Professor."

"Why is that?"

"The piece we want to perform was written by Kenneth J. Alford," Preston volunteered.

David recognized the pseudonym of the early twentieth-century composer. "Hmm. Better known as Lt. F. J. Ricketts, England's answer to John Philip Sousa. Then the work you've selected is the *Colonel Bogey March*?"

"We figured it would put an upbeat ending on the entire evening," Myung-hee suggested.

"Well, the dean already saw fit to incorporate Sir Malcolm Arnold into the mix of composers, so I don't see why he'd object."

None of the student committee members caught the connection, but so long as the assistant dean was in agreement, they'd proceed with printing tickets and programs for the concert. Generally, the encore wasn't listed on the program. Regardless, they still had to obtain the assistant dean's permission to order the music and to work it into the rehearsal schedule.

After the near two-hour working lunch, the exhausted department heads got up out of their chairs and filed out of David's office. Hearing his colleagues depart, David moved his meeting notes to his desk. When he turned to leave himself for his appointment with the campus paper, Julia was standing in the doorway.

"Do you have a moment?"

"I'm late for another appointment," he cautioned her. "What can I do for you?"

"Have you had the opportunity to review the pieces Dr. Cobbett wanted me to order this year?"

"Dr. Cobbett? I wasn't aware he was selecting the musical program for the year. He was only supposed to choose the theme, not the programs."

"I thought so, too. That's why I was confused when Carla told me none of the upcoming concert pieces were mentioned during the Student Faculty Planning Committee meeting today."

"Do you have the list of music the dean wants?"

"Let me check," Julia said as she sifted through her briefcase. "I'm working with the finance department to order the score rentals right now, and I have to do so with enough lead time for rehearsals."

"As you so diligently accomplish every year. Aside from how cagy the dean can be with the planning committee regarding his choices, you appear to be concerned for another reason," David guessed.

"I am, actually. Nearly all of them were large ensemble works like symphonies. He has no solo, virtuoso, or chamber pieces scheduled. Do you know why?"

The routine of the day's agenda and a full stomach had exhausted the assistant dean. He hated days filled with meetings, and he still had three more to attend. But something in Julia's question disturbed him enough to brush away the growing cobwebs.

With such enormous talents as Myung-hee Chun, Elaine Kirkwood, Holly Runyon, and Aaron Godwin all graduating this year, the university had a responsibility to showcase their talents. If ever there was a college draft opportunity for talented young musicians, their last academic year was it. This was the university's last chance to feature their exceptional talent, which could make or break a budding professional career. The students knew this, so why couldn't Cobbett figure it out? Or did he want to?

"No, I have no idea," David said.

"Here it is," she said, handing him the list.

David scrutinized it. Among the works he was familiar with were Arthur Bliss' *A Colour Symphony*, Frederick Delius' *Florida Suite*, and William Walton's *Symphony No. 1* as well as his *Crown Imperial* coronation march. There were a few more he was unfamiliar with, but something was wrong with the preponderance of these choices.

Works from composers like Bliss, Delius, and Walton all fit the criteria for this year's theme of twentieth-century composers. However, they were all English composers. Cobbett had even planned a night with Edward Elgar for the spring concert series, which would have featured all three symphonies and the complete *Enigma Variations*.

David didn't have to expend too many brain cells to determine who the dean was trying to impress and why. The dean's carefully guided musical selections only served to confirm what disturbed David after Cobbett sent him that text message.

Neither his colleagues nor his talented students would stand for that. "Thank you for bringing this to my attention, Julia. I'm meeting with him at three today. I'll take care of it then."

"Thank you," she said and left.

Not far behind her, David grabbed his new accessory that was leaning on the corner of his desk. He walked out saluting Peggy with the tip of the stick in his hand and said, "I'm off to the media department for the interview, then to my appointment with the dean."

"When shall I expect you back?"

"Don't wait up."

Peggy knew her boss well enough. He was going straight home from that last meeting.

Stella, the younger of Cobbett's two administrative assistants, was out for the day. David would have to deal with the less affable one named Trudy. He had little patience for self-absorbed people, but he vowed to be pleasant. To test the waters, he ventured a benign personal greeting.

"Good afternoon, Trudy."

The woman at the receiving end was all business, no time for pleasantries or idle banter. She was rigid, soulless, and devoid of personality. In other words, a perfect receptionist for the dean. Not bothering to look up, she said, "Dr. Cobbett just walked in a minute ago. He should be ready to receive you in about ten minutes."

"Thank you," he said as he took a seat placing his stick across his lap.

Cobbett could always be counted on to follow his peculiar habits to the letter. For someone so fanatical about punctuality, the concept of being late for his own appointment was a frustrating experience. Not having control over a situation afflicted him to where artificial help was indicated. Trudy understood what that entailed.

The man dressed in the out-of-fashion suit secured a tiny pill from a prescription bottle in his desk drawer and quickly washed it down with water. He would only entertain this visitor once he felt confident the medicine had taken effect.

"Send him in now," came the order over the intercom.

"The dean will see you now," Trudy said, looking up at David for the first time.

The assistant dean drew himself up to his full height in front of Trudy. In a move that was becoming natural to him, he tossed her a salute with his stick before he walked toward the entrance to Cobbett's inner sanctum. Normally unfazed by distraction, she couldn't take her eyes off David's cane. He wondered what her boss was going to make of his new accessory.

With his back to the man moving toward him, Cobbett could hear the distinct addition of a grace note to the percussion of his visitor's footfalls. At first, the dean thought he recognized David's identifiable step, but this new sound cast that assumption into doubt.

Still surveying the campus through the window, the dean assumed both the identity of his visitor and a gracious manner. "I trust you had a good summer."

David came to the office expecting Cobbett's usual antagonistic approach. Noting the sincerity in the dean's voice, he chose to respond in kind. "I actually had an enjoyable one, William. What about you?"

The dean slowly turned around as he greeted David. "Well, if you really must know—" Cobbett's sentence was paused for half a heartbeat the moment his eyes came to rest on the object in David's hand. The skip in cadence was hardly noticeable, but David caught it. "I spent my summer taking care of a few renovations around the house." Cobbett gestured for David to sit as he took his own seat.

David placed the walking stick between the palms of his hands as he sat down. "Oh really? I didn't know you were a handyman."

"Well, not me personally, you understand. The deck to the back yard was becoming unusable, so I had a new one built with composite material."

"Sounds expensive."

"It's much stronger than natural wood and colorful to boot. You should stop by sometime to help me break in my new barbecue grill."

Was William Tipton Cobbett III really asking someone from work to his home and in a social capacity? David wasn't about to waste this opportunity. "I may have to take you up on that, William. How did your meetings go at Mrak Hall?"

"Hours of dry-witted speakers discussing budget limitations isn't how I'd have chosen to spend my morning." The pleasantries over with, the dean launched into the cryptic reason for his meeting. "However, where goes the university, so goes the music department."

"May I assume from the tone of your statement that we're headed for an unexpected detour?"

"Funny you put it that way. I want to float this one by you. Apparently, our department must come up with an alternate plan for our annual field trip to Vienna. During the financial part of the meeting, the chancellor regretfully informed us the university's budget could no longer sustain the increased cost of off-site airfare."

"What do you suggest?"

"My recommendation would be to cancel the trip altogether and come up with a different option. What is your view?"

"Do you want to make that decision summarily?"

"What choice do we have?"

"You seem quite set on unilaterally cutting the trip, unless your use of the term, *float* was meant to suggest an alternative?"

The dean didn't catch David's allusion at first, but when he got it, his scowl was unmistakable. "No, I was not suggesting a cruise. Even if I were, where would they go? The Vienna Philharmonic is not in the South Pacific."

"If the executive board doesn't need an answer right away, shouldn't that decision be brought before the next regular session of the planning committee?"

"I'm sure the next regular session would suffice. But the decision must be first on their agenda."

"I'll attend to it."

The dean nodded in agreement, then stood up to resume his stance by the window. Like so many of Cobbett's visitors, David understood this body language well. It meant the conversation was over. William Tipton Cobbett III said so. If he were going to bring up Julia's concerns, now would be the best time since the iron was as hot as it was going to get.

"I do have one more concern, William."

The dean was already surveying the campus from his window perch. Inexplicably, he turned around to face his seated visitor. Something he never did, except to emphasize a point he was making. "That being?"

David recognized the Cobbett of old written large in the older man's attempt to impart a regal bearing. "I assume there's a reason why you went above your mandate as Solo Showdown champion."

"To what mandate are you referring?"

"The Solo Showdown champion's responsibility for the new season's musical content was always limited to the theme, not the selections."

"Should the champion not be able to come up with suggestions to go along with the theme?"

"Suggestions?" David pondered the word. "The works on that list you handed Julia to order for the rest of the concert season were mere suggestions? What about the committee's responsibility to come up with specific pieces for the concert season based on your *suggestions*?"

"I would hope they would seriously consider my *suggestions*. Besides, since they frequently address smaller ensemble works, I thought it prudent to address the larger venues," said Cobbett.

Outside of those who attend the concerts in person, only the larger featured music for a performance was publically advertised in advance. The warm-up ensembles and encore pieces never made it in the programs. This gave Cobbett some form of control over what he wanted people to see. Most especially, the managing director of the London Symphony.

Knowing this, David played his hunch. "Then I take it you won't mind if the committee is allowed to perform their primary function to select the music for the remaining year?"

"So long as the pieces are from well-established composers that fit the criteria of this year's theme, I don't care."

♪

Chapter Twenty – Seven

Members of the Student Faculty Planning Committee and their volunteers arrived early to prepare the grand lobby and the stage of Jackson Hall for the commencement of the concert season. Two volunteers took to setting up the stage according to the seating chart, while three others ensured all the parts needed for the evening's performance were placed in the proper order on the music stands. Leading the effort in her swansong as committee president was Myung-hee Chun.

This was her opportunity to mentor her successor whoever it was going to be. All three candidates for the position were present to assist her in this undertaking; the impressive cellist sophomore Renatta Johnson, the irrepressible James Spence, and the newest bassoon player to the orchestra, Preston Stoddard.

Renatta was involved in directing the setup of the lobby and familiarizing the caterers with the layout to make their jobs easier. Naturally, James Spence was inspecting the sound system. Assisting Myung-hee on stage was Preston.

He finished double-checking the conductor's scores on the rostrum when he noticed a short, slightly corpulent figure emerge from stage left. The silhouette materialized into a recognizable person as the house lights bathed the figure in illumination. Holding a fancy garment bag in one hand and some envelopes in the other, the newcomer made a beeline for Preston.

"Are you learning anything from our illustrious concertmistress?" the faculty member asked.

"I never realized how much work she put into this job, professor," said Preston as he was going over the conductor scores for the last half of the evening's performance.

"Someone is going to have some large shoes to fill, Mr. Stoddard," said the newcomer. "Not only must we find a worthy successor to Miss Chun's indispensable leadership as president, but we'll also need an equally capable concertmaster."

Preston agreed.

Panning the stage with searching eyes, the newcomer segued into his question. "By the by, you wouldn't happen to have seen her, would you?"

"She was here a moment ago," said Preston scanning the hall. "She might be in the lobby helping Renatta. Do you want me to find her for you?"

"Please."

"Sure thing, Professor."

"Thank you," said the faculty member as he stood on the podium. He briefly watched Preston disappear on his errand before tending to the business of reviewing the music on the conductor's stand. The right side held the first hour's music, while the left the entr'acte and the second half of the evening's program. His fingers walked through the scores until he got to the unannounced piece selected for the encore. His jaw dropped when he read the title, the *Colonel Bogey March* by Kenneth J. Alford.

A tightness grabbed William Tipton Cobbett III by the chest as he reread the title. He thought he'd made his feelings quite clear on the subject of musical soundtracks. He hated them. He did not believe they embraced the compositional standard, which was why he would never allow their performance during his tenure. Next to violating his new edict prohibiting the performance of unknown, untested music, ignoring this cardinal rule would bring the wrath of Cobbett. The dean's ironclad rule against such music was well-known among the faculty and therefore assumed to have been de facto guidance for the committee.

Appearing from the lobby, the concertmistress hurried down the aisle toward the stage. She purposefully kept a respectable distance from the dean who remained on the podium. In this way, she wouldn't have to look down at her professor. Something Cobbett should've appreciated.

The dean allowed a thin smile to cross his lips. "Miss Chun, I found these two pieces of mail in with my stack yesterday. I believe you may find them of interest." With that, he held them out for her inspection.

The young woman's eyes were then drawn to the envelopes in Cobbett's hand. Both were addressed to her. One was from the administrative director of the Houston Symphony and the other from Benaroya Hall in Seattle.

"If it isn't too early for congratulations, may I say I happen to know the retiring concertmaster of the Seattle Symphony. You would be a perfect fit to replace him should you choose to accept their offer."

Myung-hee Chun was floored, to say the least. With her mind totally absorbed in her current activities, she wasn't prepared to receive such welcome news. Stunned into near silence, all she could manage was, "I don't know what to say."

Trying his hand at humor, but missing horribly, he said, "You could say thank you?"

"Thank you."

Changing the subject, he asked, "How are the preparations proceeding?"

She'd completed her final inspection of the lobby and was satisfied with Renatta's work. Noticing the percussion section finished, she said, "We're all set, Dr. Cobbett."

"Excellent," said the dean. He turned as if to leave but stopped. Not bothering to look back at Myung-hee, he asked, "And the encore piece?"

"Oh, don't worry, Dr. Cobbett. We thoroughly rehearsed all the pieces in the program. We placed emphasis on that one since you wouldn't have conducted the piece prior to the concert. The last dress rehearsal was flawless."

"Of that, I have no doubt, Miss Chun," he said. Facing the young woman, he nodded his assent. Still not satisfied, he removed the questionable score from the folder and scanned it casually. "May I ask whose idea was it to include the *Colonel Bogey March* in with the program?"

"Preston made the suggestion. It's the perfect selection to end the evening."

"Did the assistant dean voice any objections?" probed Cobbett, looking to see if his subordinate made any effort at all to enforce the dean's mandates.

"Professor Whealy said it was all right."

"I see." Cobbett's haggles rose. "Well, we're certainly going to miss you around here, Miss Chun. Luckily, we'll have one more opportunity to benefit from your exceptional talents before you leave us."

Blushing at the unexpected compliment, all she could muster was a humble "Thank you."

To anyone who'd ever seen it, the glass façade of the Mondavi Center paid architectural homage to New York's Metropolitan Opera. Its transparent outer wall showing the cutaway of all three floors, the multiple staircases, the doors into Jackson Hall, and the grand lobby all complimented its East Coast cousin.

An evening at the Mondavi was a happening worthy of the finest gala affair. All manner of glitterati made up the typical concertgoer at the season's debut concert. From government officials to visiting Hollywood royalty, if you weren't seen at the Mondavi for the new season's inaugural concert, you weren't part of the *in* crowd. Even the governor and his wife managed to be on hand for the festivities.

Flowing evening gowns and tie and tails were the order of the day. The buffet tables were decked out with an abundant assortment of light snacks and hors d'oeuvres. The wait staff cruised the lobby, balancing trays as they went about with every imaginable drink from cognac to citrus smoothies. The mandatory umbrella tilted along the rim was a standard garnish.

The soft drone of conversation began to pick up volume as more people arrived in the lobby. The only competition for one's attention was a small group of string players situated near the inner doorway into Jackson Hall. They set themselves up and began playing a series of Clayton Forbes' arrangements of twentieth-century music.

The group was led by the concertmistress in her waning days at Davis, Miss Myung-hee Chun. The violinist next to Myung-hee was her young protégé in his second year at the university, and her personal choice to succeed her, Eric Vasquez. With Robert Caulfield's graduation last year, Renatta Johnson's deft bowing provided a seamless transition at the cellist's position.

They had been favoring the oblivious public with charming but forgettable pieces for the moment. Most people went about their business eating, drinking, and conversing. When the group finished performing each piece, the crowd would reward them with light applause before returning to their dull conversations.

Myung-hee regarded the clock to see if they had time enough for the remaining pieces. With room for one last work, Myung-hee looked at her fellow players and gave them the signal. Renatta nodded with a knowing smile as she and her fellow musicians shuffled the music on their stands. She knew this piece would showcase her technical prowess on the cello. Myung-hee looked around at the gathering and scanned the faces of her fellow performers one last time before she lifted her bow.

Since the opening measures were cello only, she simply counted out the tempo, sniffed the downbeat for Renatta, and they were off to the races. The quick tempo of the *scherzo* began softly in *mezzo piano* but quickly grew in dynamics and intensity. Each instrument entered in turn, building the primary motive until the first *mezzo forte* chord shift. By the beginning of the second statement of the phrase, the crowd nearest the group began to take notice as the exquisite sounds of this strangely designed quintet permeated the lobby.

In a visual reminiscent of falling dominoes, the diminished tinkling of glasses, the squelched conversation, and turning heads radiated outward from the center of the disturbance—the music coming from the quintet. By the time the last domino fell, only the refrain of the *scherzo* echoed through the lobby unchallenged by any other sound.

The curiously attractive theme swept from player to player, ripping through each measure, at times with jarring intensity. The sheer power coming from such a modest force was something the savvy audience had never heard before, and they were transfixed by every note of it.

By the time the recapitulation arrived, the group commanded the complete attention of the entire gathering including David as he appeared from the left staircase and Cobbett as he entered on the right side of the lobby. Neither of them was happy but for different reasons. David was shocked that Myung-hee would steal the music from his office. Cobbett was furious because his edict was ignored. For now, both men's anger would have to wait to be quelled.

The final chord hadn't ceased before the lobby erupted in spontaneous and enthusiastic applause. Shouts of adulation were heard everywhere, and David took note for future reference. The group stood up and acknowledged the appreciation of the assemblage.

The performers busied themselves packing up their instruments and equipment from the main entrance to the hall when an unknown woman approached Myung-hee. "If this is a prelude of the music you plan on treating us with, this will be your best year yet."

The San Francisco critic who lauded the quintet's performance in the lobby remembered her words for the article that appeared in the paper the next day. Headlined critics throughout the country would echo her complimentary overture.

The UC Davis Symphony Orchestra always wooed the crowd with their robust interpretation of challenging large-scale musical repertoire. Critics naturally raved about the technical brilliance of this season's spirited debut performance and appreciated the rousing pieces selected for the program. But an honest chronicler of the goings on at the UC Davis Music Department had to realize something remarkable was happening with its smaller organized groups and with their constituent members.

The universal acclaim for this unknown chamber piece played by the quintet was a total surprise, one that served to draw the unwanted attention and ire of the dean.

Cobbett never saw the potential in smaller groups. Not even the London Symphony gained any notoriety from its smaller ensembles. This to Cobbett was a waste of musical effort.

The dean's opinion didn't matter to the San Francisco critic. She recognized something special in this last work the quintet performed. Its style was unlike anything she'd ever heard before. A fresh, bold approach that screamed for an audience. For those unable to attend future performances in person, she would make it her business to inform the public of what it was they missed.

Because this quintet had shared something remarkable.

Something fresh, new, and exciting was introduced.

Some*one* of previously unknown origin was introduced.

And her devoted readers were going to be introduced to this unknown person...soon.

Chapter Twenty – Eight

Peggy peered into David's office. "There's a change to the change. I had to move your two to two thirty, and the dean now wants to see you at five, instead of four."

"Thanks, Peggy."

In a hushed whisper, she added, "And Myung-hee is here, whenever you're ready."

She couldn't miss the look of pain on the assistant dean's face as he looked up from his paperwork. "Show her in."

While waiting in Peggy's outer office, Myung-hee had time to reflect on what she'd done. As she stood up, she began to feel ashamed of her impulsive act. She'd gravely disappointed the one person she most valued in her academic life. The one she could always count on to be proud of her. This, too, began to weigh heavily upon her as she took the last few steps toward the door. Retribution was now at hand. Consequences were about to be meted out. Though it wasn't going to be pleasant, she'd accept them.

The imposing assistant dean stood at the head of the conference table as the contrite young woman approached bearing her embarrassment firmly on her hunched shoulders.

To make the meeting easier to endure for the both of them, he gestured for her to take a seat at the conference table as he took the one across from her. David calmly laced his fingers together and brought them to his lips as he stared at an unspecified spot on the table.

Breaking the unbearable silence, she stammered, "I'm sorry for not asking you before I copied the quintet from your desk. I was only—"

David interrupted her with a raised hand, measuring his next words carefully. "Having borne witness to your musical and personal development over the past four years, Myung-hee, I *know* you appreciate the gravity of your offense."

She could only nod, her lowered eyes staring blindly at the table.

Presenting a fatherly image, he said, "I was not only surprised by your uncharacteristic action, I was disappointed that you didn't trust me enough to simply ask me if you could copy it."

"You're right, Professor," she said sheepishly. "I should have asked. I never dreamed of disappointing you." She raised her eyes to meet his for the first time since she came in. A tear traced its path along her cheek. "I've breached the trust you once had in me, and no matter what happens now, and I could never hope to regain it."

"Truth be told, you executed what I was trying to figure out how to do myself."

Astonished, she wiped the wetness from her face and eked out the word "Really?"

"You don't know this, but I had the faculty evaluate some of the music I brought back."

"How many compositions were there?"

"You'd be surprised," said David teasingly. "Luckily for you, I had the opportunity to appraise this quintet *before* you copied it." Watching to gauge her reaction, he quipped with a comical inflection, "I fully intended to get this music out in front of the public on my own, but *you* kicked in the door and beat me to the punch!"

His attempt to soften the mood had the desired effect. She smiled.

Successfully altering the flow of the discussion, David reached across his desk for a small green folder as he said, "Your only misstep was to debut this work so anonymously. I wanted everyone to know who wrote this piece." Waiting for her to meet his gaze, he added thoughtfully, "Perhaps yours was the best way after all."

"How do you mean?"

"There's nothing wrong with a bit of mystery. Besides, after what they wrote in the paper the other day, I'm hardly in a position to criticize your approach."

Detecting forgiveness in his tone, Myung-hee said, "Then you're not mad at me, Professor?"

"Everyone deserves a mulligan now and then," said David, employing the familiar golf metaphor to absolve the young woman. "Myung-hee, I want you to remember your final academic performance in triumph, not shame. To ensure you do, I have a favor to ask."

In an effort to do anything to erase the memory of her transgression, she said, "Of course! What is it?"

David slid the folder across the table to her.

She opened it cautiously not knowing what she would find. The eyes of the newest concertmistress for the Seattle Symphony Orchestra almost popped out of her head as she beheld the same distinct handwriting that penned the string quintet her group played. For staring back at her was the title page of an even larger work.

A violin concerto by the same unpublished composer.

The contrast in the dean's administrative assistants couldn't have been sharper; Stella was bright, cheery, and welcoming. Trudy was her opposite number—dark, unbending, and cold.

Mere yards away from each other, the two women were definitive examples of yin and yang. Trudy's dotted trigram leaned heavily toward the darker yin side, while the three unbroken lines of Stella's trigram represented a strong yang identity. Despite their opposing natures, the two women complimented each other just as the traditional Daoist symbol suggested.

Where Stella felt uncomfortable with detailed administrative duties, Trudy was an exacting taskmaster. But where Trudy's interpersonal skills were, for lack of a better term, wanting, Stella more than made up for the deficiency.

It was Trudy who was forced to reschedule David's appointment since Stella was away from her desk at the time of Cobbett's request. Trudy would rather have cut out her tongue than use it to speak with anyone, even though she was required to do so in her administrative capacity. Stella would've made the change without batting an eye.

The identity of the messenger notwithstanding, David knew the real source of the message.

It was Cobbett.

This last-minute change had only one calculated meaning. *I'm in control. You're not.* Despite this, David was not about to give his boss a perceived psychological edge.

He had a good idea why this meeting was taking place, and he was prepared for it. He intended to show up fifteen minutes late because Cobbett would have made him wait at least that long in the outer office for his tongue-lashing.

Stella had already called down to Peggy to inform her that David was late for his appointment, when the assistant dean burst into the office with driving intent. Under normal circumstances, he would have acknowledged the two women with a pleasantry or two, but not today. He walked past them and into Cobbett's office. His timing was impeccable.

In that same instant, Cobbett's voice thundered through the intercom, "Send him in, now!"

"Don't bother, William, I'm already here," said David as he continued to make his way toward the chair nearest Cobbett's desk. He hesitated before he took his seat, planting his new toy in front of him and crossing both palms over its topper. David sat there savoring the older man's attempt at trying to wipe the look of horror off his face. Firing the first salvo, he asked, "I assume you wish to take issue with the quintet's musical choices at Friday night's performance?"

"Brilliant diagnosis, David," the dean said, trying to regain his composure. His eyes once again locked onto his assistant dean's walking stick, but only for a New York minute. "But perhaps, first, you might enlighten me as to how the music from a movie managed to make it into Friday night's performance?"

"I don't recall any movie music?"

"Then I'll put it bluntly: How did the music to the *Bridge on the River Kwai* make it into the performance Friday evening?"

"Since you already set the precedent by having the composer of *Bridge*, Sir Malcolm Arnold on the program, I'm sure the music he included with his score shouldn't have been a problem. After all, the

Colonel Bogey March wasn't composed for the film but by a British officer. And in 1914!"

Cobbett ignored the point. "You know my feelings about film music."

"Every professor in this department is well aware of your low regard for film music. But since you selected this particular film's composer for the printed program, you can't blame the committee for including *Colonel Bogey* for the encore, especially since it fit the theme *you* chose in the first place."

"That's not the problem. The issue is *your* inability to enforce my biggest pet peeve with the committee—extolling the virtues of film music."

"And how did I do that?"

"Your lecture on the dawn of film music, for instance."

"Oh, so now you're amending your prohibition from just performing to include instruction?"

Cobbett couldn't contain himself, his face flushed with anger. Needing a moment, he turned around to look out the window. "No, I'm not. I just think you spend far too much time on such a shallow subject."

"Aren't we supposed to offer a more comprehensive musical education?"

"I don't consider music for TV, movies, or ad jingles the acme of what passes for curriculum at this university!"

"Right, that's why you once chose to feature the *William Tell Overture*, a work from the world's most borrowed-upon composer, Rossini," David countered.

"I assume you'll be arriving somewhere close to a point soon," Cobbett said indignantly.

"TV and film composers have blurred the lines of their music since the dawn of the genre."

Folding his arms in a wordless expression of skepticism, Cobbett raised an eyebrow.

"Ever see a Bugs Bunny cartoon?" David shot back.

Cobbett could only guffaw.

David wasted no time jumping on that opening. "Like the Looney Tunes composer, Carl Stalling, even Shostakovich quoted Rossini's famous theme in one of his symphonies. Composers have used themes of other composers to create works like Brahms' *Variations on a Theme by Haydn* and Rachmaninoff's *Rhapsody on a Theme of Paganini*. Even today's composers use quotes from other famous works."

David paused to give Cobbett a chance to respond.

He didn't.

"These works have become part and parcel of the musical lexicon. Should we excise them from the repertoire because some past director chose to use a concert piece for their TV show or movie project? By that logic, Shostakovich would never be performed here, since the science fiction B-movies of the '50s extensively quoted his *Symphony 5*, to say nothing of his own expedition into the genre with his soundtracks for *The Gadfly* and the *Maxim Trilogy*. Didn't this university perform the Shostakovich *Symphony 5* three years ago?"

David's well-thought-out argument notwithstanding, the dean remained obstinate. "How is your justification relevant to the *Colonel Bogey* and why it was featured as the encore piece?"

"It was *you* who invited the inclusion for two reasons. One, you insisted on adding *Bridge's* composer, Sir Malcolm Arnold, to the program, thereby breaking your own rules, and two, the original composer of *Colonel Bogey*, F. J. Ricketts, had nothing to do with the movie. He simply fell perfectly into the requirements for this year's theme. A theme *you* chose."

Reduced to abject frustration for losing his argument, Cobbett said, "I don't care! You still know my stand on this university performing soundtracks."

"And you know mine," David insisted. "The composer of today's motion picture score *is* the opera composer of yesteryear. Remember, we did both Rossini's *William Tell* and the *Barber of Seville* overtures a few years back. They're not only vibrant and accessible pieces of music for today's audience but their performance made for an enjoyable afternoon. And again, the choice to feature these pieces used for the *Lone Ranger* and several Bugs Bunny cartoons was *yours*, not mine."

"For the record, David, I consider the TV or motion picture score no more than an accent. A musical representation designed to mimic the action on the screen. It's punctuation. Nothing more."

"I'll remind you of that, the next time this university receives a rave review for its exceptional interpretation of a *punctuation*."

Neither man yielded the advantage, though a veiled smile did appear on the face of the dean.

Believing he achieved a victory, Cobbett said, "Now, about that surprise the quintet dropped on the crowd in the lobby."

"You've never bothered yourself with the university's smaller ensembles before. Why are you worried about them now?"

"Quite simply because anything put forth before our audience carries with it the reputation of this university," said Cobbett with a newfound assertiveness. "And the gatekeeper to such a sterling reputation is *you*."

"And how do you expect *me* to do that?" David fired back.

"As facilitator to the Student Faculty Planning Committee, I *expect* you to carry out my wishes regarding musical decorum."

David settled back in his chair, tilted his head back, and raised his eyebrows in a nonverbal query.

Cobbett detested the gesture and David knew it. It only served to make Cobbett look inferior. And William Tipton Cobbett III would never accept being anyone's inferior.

Mimicking David's nonverbal behavior, Cobbett comfortably settled into his high-backed leather chair. "Perhaps I didn't make myself clear the last time we broached this subject."

"I believe you were quite clear—no student compositions," said David plainly.

"That's not what I meant, and you damn well know it!" the dean roared back.

"Well then, perhaps you should be more precise in how you put your demands."

"It's a simple *request*, David. No unknown or unpublished works shall be performed by either students or faculty of this university so long as they're doing so in a representative character. Am I clear?"

"Funny, but that's not what you said before. You *said* you didn't want unknown or unpublished works printed on the program and the quintet's lineup was never published in any program."

Cobbett's pink cheeks were turning a bright crimson. "What did I say that made you believe that?"

To drive a dagger into the heart of Cobbett's argument, David used his boss's own words. "To quote you *exactly*, you said, '*So long as the pieces are from* well-established *composers that fit the criteria of this year's theme, I don't care.*'"

Cobbett never appreciated having his own words rammed down his throat. Especially if the source was his own subordinate. "Then if you would be so kind as to tell me how this composer was well-established and fit the criteria?"

Using another move that upset Cobbett plenty, David rubbed his chin thoughtfully. "Let's see now. As I recall, the man who wrote the quintet was born in 1952, so that qualifies him as a twentieth-century composer befitting the only criteria you announced. The only real question remaining is, what do you consider a dyed-in-the-wool composer?"

The dean stammered, "Then who is this composer and why haven't I heard of him?"

Twirling his walking stick in the fingers of his left hand, David said, "You haven't heard of him because no one had. Yet. However, it's still not a disqualifying feature to your restrictions."

"This composer of yours wouldn't happen to be a student, would it? One of your more nobler gestures, no doubt?"

"No, I actually followed that guidance."

"Then, who the hell is it?" demanded the dean.

"Who the hell *was* it," David corrected.

"Very well. If no one knows who this person *was*, then how could he be considered a *well-established* composer?"

"Define well-established."

"Someone with a known track record for composing traditional forms of music."

"Someone such as?"

"Beethoven."

"Fine, what about the sketch fragments of Beethoven's *Tenth Symphony*? If someone were to find his completed autograph score for that symphony, a work that isn't known and was never published, wouldn't you wish to be the first to perform it?"

Cobbett just sat there.

"We all know Beethoven because he was a prolific composer, right?"

"Of course."

"Would it not follow that if someone were a prolific painter, they would be an artist?"

"Yes."

"Composed hundreds of sonnets, a poet?"

"Perhaps."

"Then, regardless if they were unpopular or unpublished, so long as they had an unmistakable and distinct bent toward their art, they would be that artist, wouldn't you agree?"

"Beethoven was a prolific, well-established composer. That was his vocation."

"You didn't complain last year when the quartet played Borodin."

"Now, what are you talking about?"

"Alexander Borodin's primary vocation wasn't composition. He was a surgeon and chemist. He was even purported to have lost a symphony among his many experiments."

"I assume there's a point to all this?" asked an exasperated Cobbett.

"How could a successful chemist become a force noted as one of the *Mighty Handful*, who carved his indelible stamp on Russian musical identity with the likes of Balakirev, Cui, Mussorgsky, and Rimsky-Korsakov?"

"I suppose, it's possible to be both."

"Then I ask you one more time, is it possible for this unknown composer to have written a wealth of quality music, not have had it published, yet deserve the approbation of an audience?"

"Perhaps. But I would need to evaluate the work, myself."

"Fair enough," David said. "I'll bring you his journal of collected works, and you can choose which scores you'd like to evaluate. I'm quite sure you will find something of worth out of his two hundred plus pieces. You'll also conclude that the prolific composer in question never wrote a single jingle, movie or TV theme."

Cobbett could only sneer.

Chapter Twenty – Nine

Beth Grey had one of those red-letter days at the office. One of the company's most valued and lucrative clients nearly closed their account with her firm. Had they done so, it would've been her fault. Once again, trust was at the crux of the problem.

It all stemmed from the fact she left her new cell phone turned on and at full volume; a peculiar and significant enmity of the client in question. From there, the delicate meeting spiraled out of control. She had reset the phone to vibrate, but it was too late. It took Beth almost an hour to placate her disgruntled client enough to speak with them rationally. She managed to salvage their relationship with the company, but not with her.

The ride home was a nonstop replay of the trainwreck series of events that led to her leaving the office early. By the time she got home, the throbbing in her head was all-consuming.

With no appetite to speak of, she went straight to her bedroom, leaving her pumps, her purse, and a trail of clothing on the floor as she went. After grabbing some painkillers to quell her growing headache, she turned on the hot water and poured some bath oil in the tub so she could soak this horrendous day out of her body.

As the oil drained from its bottle, she caught sight of her full nude profile in the mirror. *Not bad for a fifty-six-year-old*, she thought to herself. She only wished Jim had thought so. Or David. The first relationship could never happen, and the other wasn't likely.

At the thought of the California music professor, she contemplated the mediocre progress she was making on his behalf. Her weekly trips to the archives over the past few months were more like progress through elimination.

Beth was unable to find any birth records on file for a Robert West much less locate any proof that Cynthia Belmore was the Cynthia who married William West. The only substantial lead she was able to procure was an 1847 certificate of death for Robert West. But once again, there wasn't any evidence this was the son of William and Cynthia West.

Running these results in her head, she came to the inevitable conclusion that restricting her search to only the Delaware Public Archives was limiting her success. She needed to expand her pool of historical resources, which meant she would have to move her investigation to the state archives of Maryland and Pennsylvania.

The futility of expending useless energy on issues she couldn't resolve, like the catastrophe at work, only served to make her headache worse.

Instead, she let her mind return to the reverie of that last embrace with David as she prepared to submerge herself into the tub. Thoughts of his gentle embrace. The warmth of his bare chest against her tear-streaked face. His seductive manly scent.

The silky smoothness of the oiled water penetrated her parched skin as she lowered her athletic body into the fragranced mixture. She authorized herself a full twenty minutes of uninterrupted aquatic bliss before treating her neck to another twenty minutes of shiatsu massage, courtesy of her new massage pillow.

Her body reacted favorably to this rare form of pampering, her mind drifting further into the allure of fantasy. Lost in a labyrinth of the exquisite sensations generated by the gyrating circular neck pillow humming in her ears, she never heard the other vibrating device that competed for her attention.

From inside a dark corner of her purse, five muffled thrums emanated from her cell phone before they ceased. A moment later, another one.

Following the gratuitous five rings, a familiar voicemail feature announced itself. Unable to talk to her in person, Henderson from the Smithsonian's human resources department left a message for Beth Grey to call him at her earliest convenience.

To schedule her new employee's orientation.

♪

Chapter Thirty

Radnor had been to many places in his life, but the great hall of New York's Metropolitan Museum of Art wasn't one of them. Ascending the stairs near the East 82nd Street entrance, he marveled at the four massive sets of dual pillars in front of him. Beyond the main entrance was the great hall, whose four entries were distinguished by four Ionian topped columns. With eight grand arches, a mosaic marble floor, and an octagon-shaped information desk, the great hall was a grand work of art in and of itself. The three dome-shaped ceilings were capped with circular convex skylights that bathed the entire hall in sunlight. Against the logical physics of its design, Radnor thought it ironic the room's architect couldn't have devised something more appealing for the domed windows other than partitioning them like an apple corer-slicer.

Directly opposite from where he came in, and on the other side of the information desk was a sign that proclaimed the beginning of the exposition for the Holy Roman Empire.

The sheer size of this exhibit was breathtaking, encompassing the empire's entire run from its origin in 962 to its collapse in 1806. All manner of sacred and secular objects were on display in the first-floor European Sculpture and Decorative Arts rooms. Rare and beautiful objects such as the Orb to the Holy Roman Emperor and its impressive jeweled crown and scepter were among the central articles of imperial regalia on display.

From the crowning of Otto I to the abdication of Francis II, the museum set up an impressive array of portraits, apparel, and other artifacts from the numerous houses and dynasties that led the empire throughout its reign. The immense size of the exhibit required some of the displays to be moved into the Medieval Sculpture Hall.

To mark the boundary of the exhibit, the evolution of the empire's various banners throughout its existence were festooned on straight polls overhead at regular intervals. Heavily gravitating toward a yellow background with the caricatured figure of a twin-headed wiry black bird with red claws, the image was the *idée fixe* that distinguished the Holy Roman Empire.

Radnor negotiated his way to a small group of tourists about to embark on their tour along the serpentine route through the exhibit. As they went, he listened with a discerning ear, waiting for the guide to get to the object of his trip to New York.

Then they came upon it.

The rectangular box encased in glass in the center of the room was made up of crisscrossing strips of metal secured by large button head rivets. The lid was similarly adorned, with a large key protruding from its center. He didn't see the key at first, but it was there.

The college student tour guide did a respectable job spouting off a comprehensive array of trivia about the objects she was describing. Even so, it was evident to Radnor that despite her ability to relay such information in an entertaining way, she was only speaking from a prepared script. If the rehearsed speeches were the sum of her knowledge, she wouldn't be able to field any of his questions.

The tour group formed a semicircle around the box and their guide as they waited for her scholarly dissertation. "This item has a curious history. Referred to by the name of its creator, this iron strongbox is one of several that were specifically designed by a little-known blacksmith and artisan named Klaus von Richthofen. He received his commission to create these boxes from Leopold I, who intended them for the eight electors of greater Germany and all the crowned monarchs of Europe at the time, in a failed attempt to bring a final peace to the European continent. The only difference between them was a cloth tapestry placed over the locking mechanism containing the coat of arms unique to each recipient. This particular one, as the photograph in the corner shows, belongs to the emperor as the tapestry is of the double-headed eagle over a yellow field."

Seeing there were no questions from the tour group, she moved them on to the next display, one member electing to remain behind to admire this particular artifact.

Radnor was only inches away from it now. Through the glass barrier, he got an excellent look at the black iron box, its pitted rust spots dotting the entire surface. The front latch, designed to secure the lid from the outside, was open with no padlock. However, the shape of a familiar key was jutting out from its lid.

From what he could see, this key was identical to the one he had in his possession. The question was, did it have a trapezoid shaped bit similar to the key Audra Bunting presented him?

While Radnor stood there considering this question, he felt a light tapping on his shoulder. Turning around, he met the curator of the European Sculpture and Decorative Arts Department, Paul Batiste.

The curator recognized the esteemed Dr. Giles Radnor with his outlandish hair, plaid shirt, and canvas sneakers. The iconic profile of the celebrated historian had been featured in so many magazines he could claim instant celebrity status. Strangely, neither the tour group nor his twenty-something tour guide knew who he was.

"Dr. Giles Radnor?" the man queried as he offered his hand. "Paul Batiste. It's an honor."

Radnor smiled broadly taking Batiste's hand. "The pleasure is all mine. Thank you for seeing me on such short notice, but didn't we have a later appointment?"

"We did, but with your indulgence, I have a family crisis I must deal with, so I thought I'd stop by now to answer whatever questions you may have."

"If it's an emergency, we can postpone. I'll be here over the next couple of days before I must head back to Washington."

"It's not an emergency, but it will require the balance of my day," said the apologetic curator. "I understand you have questions regarding this piece?" Batiste pointed to the box in the glass.

"Yes, I do. We're putting together an absolute monarchs collection for the American Museum building when I came across a photo of this box inset over a portrait of King Louis XIV. The picture's corresponding article about the iron box contained no useful information. I was wondering if you could tell me the back story of this box."

"How much do you know already?"

"Not much, I'm afraid."

"What did the guide tell you about it?"

A reluctant Radnor said, "She covered some general facts about its creator, and that this particular one belonged to Leopold I. Beyond that, nothing of value."

Seeming a bit disappointed but not surprised by her performance, Batiste went into professor mode. Taking a step back, he folded his arms and looked at the black iron treasure behind the glass before he launched into his informative lecture.

"Leopold I held a grand vision from the moment he was elected emperor of the Holy Roman Empire in 1658. He entertained the idea of recreating the Pax Romana in a failed bid to quell the infighting between the various electors. Leopold was making inroads with his plan when the unthinkable happened.

"In 1683, Ottoman Turks led by Sultan Mehmet IV invaded Austria. Outraged by this deplorable act, the emperor vowed to do something about it. After successfully repelling the invaders, he decided to expand his peace plan to include the absolute monarchs of Europe as well as his quarrelsome electors and his former enemy, the Turkish sultan.

"Leopold had already commissioned the reclusive but talented blacksmith Klaus von Richthofen to create identical keepsakes intended for each of the eight electors of greater Germany. The emperor approved the design of an iron strongbox that would be identical in every way, except for the cloth coat of arms under the lid representative of each elector. By creating these nearly identical keepsakes, it was assumed all would feel a sense of shared kinship and thus result in a lasting peace on the European continent.

"The emperor expanded Richthofen's original commission to twenty-five, but he was only able to complete fourteen of them before he died in 1685."

"That's an abundance of information for one display," Radnor lauded. "And you have this sort of in-depth knowledge on every piece?"

"Knowing you had a particular interest in this one, I did my homework."

"What happened to the other thirteen boxes?"

"I can only vouch for the ones belonging to the Deutsche Museum," said Batiste. "They currently hold seven of them, which includes six of the eight electors and the one owned by Sultan Mehmet IV of the Ottoman Empire."

"And the other two elector boxes?"

"Given to the archbishops of Mainz and Trier and on extended loan to the Vatican Museum."

"Do you know who received the remaining boxes?"

Batiste looked thoughtfully at the display again as he pondered the question. "If memory serves, only four other absolute monarchs ever received the boxes produced."

"Do you know if any other museums have them?"

"The Annexe of Amsterdam have two more, the Museo del Prado has one, and the one you already know about in the Louvre."

Quickly doing the math, Radnor said, "That's only thirteen. What happened to the fourteenth box?"

"All indications point to the emperor's intention to give a box to Charles II, the king of England. But like Richthofen, Charles II died in 1685. James II succeeded him. There's no evidence Charles II ever received a box, and I couldn't answer to whether James II ever received one either. You could check with the Kensington Museum or the Tower of London."

"This may sound strange, but I've never actually seen the inside of one of these boxes."

Smiling, Batiste took out a small keychain and used the silver key to unlock the sliding glass door to get to the box inside. He reached up and grabbed the massive key on top of the box and turned it. It made a loud clicking sound as the locking mechanism released. Radnor observed as Batiste removed the key from the lid paying close attention to the key's bit. It was trapezoid-shaped.

Lifting the heavy lid, the hinges creaked as the curator brought it to its full extension, revealing the cloth tapestry inside. It was the miniature yellow banner of the Holy Roman Empire pictured in the photo in the display case next to the box.

"Do you know if the other boxes came complete with their keys?" Radnor asked.

"I can only tell you all nine of the boxes belonging to the Deutsche and Vatican Museums have their keys. As for the remaining boxes, I couldn't say."

The sun had begun to set over the back side of the Metropolitan Museum of Art, casting a dark orange hue on the Marymount School buildings along 5th Avenue opposite the museum's main entrance. Radnor took notice of the strange colorations as he left the museum to catch a cab to his hotel.

He raised his arm and hailed a yellow taxi with practiced ease. "The Plaza Hotel, please," he informed the cabby. Radnor peered out the window at the flow of traffic but didn't see it. He was too busy processing the fascinating account of the Richthofen boxes as told by Dr. Paul Batiste. He thought about the nine boxes with keys and hypothesized about the fate of the other five.

That's when he took out his cell to call Shannon. He had some new homework for her to do. Then he removed David's key from his pocket and stared at it.

In the palm of his hand may well be the key to one of the last five Richthofen boxes.

Chapter Thirty – One

Dr. Giles Radnor made his way past the Enid A. Haupt Garden as he approached the south entrance of the centerpiece of the Smithsonian, the Castle. The Smithsonian's first building fit its name, with its asymmetrical spires, lattice adorned windows, and maroon battlements. Appearances aside, it functioned as the museum's central administrative complex.

The majesty of the Castle stood in stark contrast to its financial reality. Cuts in the museum's fiscal budget prevented Radnor from taking anyone with him to the Holy Roman Empire exhibit. He was still lamenting that lost opportunity as he entered the building.

A creature of habit, Radnor stopped by the *Castle Café* to grab something to eat. Heading back to his cubbyhole of an office, he bumped into Cal, the younger man absorbed in thought.

"Cal? Are you all right?"

"Fine."

"You don't seem *fine*. But, if you don't want to talk about it." Radnor let his last statement hang there, waiting for the reply he knew would come.

Cal's eyes wandered as he tried to find the words. "I just got off the phone with Henderson. His news is a mixed bag."

"Naturally. So what's the upshot?"

"He's found a successor for Connolly."

"I take it from the length of the frown on your face that the other shoe is about to drop?"

"Cute," said Cal blandly. "The limitations in this year's budget means we won't be able to fund her relocation from Delaware or her locality pay. She must either accept the job with the condition she operate from her current location or decline it outright."

"Why doesn't HR just hire someone else?"

"That's the rub. If we're unable to retain the new hire, Miss Grey, the answer from the bean counters is we will *lose* her position entirely!"

"So she either accepts the conditions of her employment or we will summarily lose her position?"

"That's essentially it, yes," said Cal, not wanting to prolong his disappointment any longer.

"What about the grant proposal? Wouldn't that cover the cost of her relocation and locality pay?"

"Yeah, but we still have an issue with the application. The proposal never made it through the Congressional process."

"Resubmit!"

"We can't. The deadline for this year has passed."

"If this institution can find money for grants to support the National Science Foundation and the National Endowment for the Arts and Humanities, why can't we locate funding to retain the services of *one person*? That's outrageous!"

"Agreed. If she doesn't accept, we'll be without Connolly's position for the rest of the year."

"You're a veritable font of good tidings today."

Trying to screw on a smile, Cal said, "Well, I'd love to stay and chat, but I have a full dance card today. Catch up with you for lunch?"

"The *Café* at noon?"

Dr. Calvin Selby, looking as though someone gave him a roundhouse to the stomach, just nodded.

The harmonious beginning to Radnor's day had turned decidedly discordant at this news, but he hoped his chance at salvaging any optimism might already be waiting for him upstairs.

Arriving at his office, he noticed the aroma of freshly brewed tea as he spied Shannon's report on the desk.

The one universal constant was his faithful intern's infallible timing. Radnor had grown to depend on the young woman, especially as Anne's blossoming personal life increased her detachment from Radnor.

A political science major at Georgetown University, Shannon McClintock applied for internship with the Smithsonian as a Research Associate during her sophomore year. Since then, she's served Radnor with pride and distinction. Perhaps the disturbing news about Anne's replacement would be the only hiccup in an otherwise productive day.

Radnor hung up his cloak and placed a leather dossier on his desk. Opening the dossier, he sifted through the notes he'd made detailing the manufacture and distribution of the so-called Richthofen boxes as described by Batiste.

As thorough as the curator was in his account, there were still a few questions Radnor wanted Batiste to have answered; chief among them was the fate of the fourteenth box.

With more time to think, Radnor wondered who the other eleven intended recipients might have been if the emperor's original order was for twenty-five boxes. And what induced the emperor to settle on these boxes as a way of establishing his new Pax Romana?

He read his notes first before corroborating them against the report Shannon had compiled. His initial homework for her was to report on the locations of all the Richthofen boxes and the whereabouts of their keys. Typical of Shannon's reports, it was easy to read and concise.

A Report for Dr. Giles Radnor
by Shannon McClintock

Inquiry into the manufacture and location of the
fourteen strongboxes created by Klaus von Richthofen
as commissioned by Leopold I, king of Bohemia
and emperor of the Holy Roman Empire.

Klaus von Richthofen - Born, February 6, 1648, in Dresden, Saxony. Died, March 29, 1685, in Prague, Bohemia. Credited with constructing one of the first iron lockboxes specifically designed for use by the financial institutions of the period, Richthofen fashioned fourteen strongboxes at the behest of the Holy Roman Emperor, with a highly sophisticated locking mechanism unlike any before it.

Of the fourteen boxes created, only thirteen recipients were ever documented to have received them. The eight elector recipients were the archbishops of Cologne, Mainz, and Trier; the electors of Saxony and Palatine; the prince elector of Bavaria; the great elector of Brandenburg; and the king of Bohemia, Leopold I. The four absolute monarch recipients were the kings of France, Spain, Sweden, and Denmark. And one went to the sultan of the Ottoman Empire.

The recipients, their titles, and location of their Richthofen boxes are as follows:

Recipient	Title	Location
Leopold I	The King of Bohemia	Deutsche Museum
Mehmet IV	The Sultan of the Ottoman Empire	Deutsche Museum
Frederick William	The Great Elector of Brandenburg	Deutsche Museum
Maximilian II	The Prince Elector of Bavaria	Deutsche Museum
Philip William	The Elector of Palatine	Deutsche Museum
John George III	The Elector of Saxony	Deutsche Museum
Maximilian Henry	The Archbishop of Cologne	Deutsche Museum
Franz von Ingelheim	The Archbishop of Mainz	Vatican Museum

Hugo von Orsbeck	The Archbishop of Trier	Vatican Museum
Louis XIV	The King of France	The Louvre
Charles II	The King of Spain	The Museo del Prado
Karl XI	The King of Sweden	The Annexe of Amsterdam
Christian V	The King of Denmark	The Annexe of Amsterdam

The curator of the Metropolitan Museum of Art, Dr. Paul Batiste, had confirmed that all seven boxes belonging to the Deutsche Museum are complete with their keys.

The Louvre, the Vatican Museum, and the Annexe of Amsterdam have all verified that their Richthofen boxes—five in all—are on display, complete with their keys.

I made inquiries with the Kensington Museum and the Tower of London to see if a Richthofen box ever made it into the hands of Charles II or James II and, if so, where it might be (the logical assumption being the intended recipient of the fourteenth box was from England).

At the time of this report, we still await word from the Museo del Prado regarding the Richthofen box given to Charles II of Spain.

Radnor was in the process of digesting her report when the perky young intern with all that youthful energy entered the room.

"This is most excellent, my dear."

The red-faced woman responded, "But the report was incomplete, sir."

"Shannon, your reputation around here remains unblemished. I read your report with satisfaction. I trust your update can put a final resolution to your last two bullets."

"That's the reason I'm here. I received an email from the Museo del Prado ten minutes ago. They have both the box and its key. But as to the question of which English monarch received a box, well, it's a bit more complicated. In preparation for their answer, one way or another, I did some digging."

"What did you come up with?"

The young woman took out her notepad and began reading. "A year after the death of the English Charles II in 1685, two independent sources reported finding documents related to the king's arguments supporting Catholicism in an iron strongbox. What made the discovery noteworthy was they were written in the king's own hand."

"Sounds straightforward enough," Radnor admitted. "What would complicate the discovery?"

"The box described by both sources is different from the Richthofen box. It wasn't locked from its lid but accessed and latched from the side. Its exterior was smooth, not laden with strips of metal or dotted with large rivets. And the English Charles II died in early 1685, and the first of these boxes weren't handed out until later in the year, so it would have been impossible for Charles II to have received one."

"If it was an English monarch who received the last box, that would point toward James II as the most logical recipient wouldn't it?"

"It would, but again, we have no description of James II's strongbox that had mysteriously vanished under curious circumstances in 1723."

"What?" Radnor said, in amazement.

Shannon sifted through her book bag to retrieve her research journal. She skimmed through several pages before she came to it.

"Ah, here it is. When James II died in 1701 at the royal château of the Saint-Germain-en-Laye in France, a detailed inventory of his belongings was conducted. An iron box of unknown origin and description was listed among the items. In 1723, an unidentified agent in possession of a British royal warrant was granted permission from King Louis XV to access the Saint-Germain-en-Laye to conduct an investigation for the British Crown. After this questionable investigation had concluded, the iron box turned up missing. No one knew what became of it, nor of the mysterious agent."

"That's a fascinating story."

"All of my research is cross-referenced, Dr. Radnor."

"Of that, I'm sure. Was there anything else?"

"There is one more account which only serves to confirm that the box is actually missing."

"And that is?"

Reading again from her penciled note in the margin of her journal, she said, "In 1789 during the French Revolution, James II's tomb at the Chapel of Saint Edmund in Jacques, Paris, was raided. When the perpetrators were captured and interrogated by French authorities, they told investigators they were searching for an iron strongbox, expecting to find some form of treasure."

Radnor tapped a finger over his lips. "What makes this story relevant to our missing box?"

"It was the description of the box they were looking for that drew my attention to this account—a heavy rectangular box of high-end value. The box was characterized by crisscrossing strips of metal with large rivet heads equally spaced around the lid face and its edges. And they described the inside of the lid as having a cloth covering with the crest of James II on it."

Although not the definitive evidence he was looking for, the circumstantial evidence was overwhelming that James II was the recipient of the last Richthofen box.

And Dr. David C. Whealy owned the last remaining key.

♪

Chapter Thirty – Two

Freelance reporter for the lifestyle section of many Bay Area newspapers, Ashley Sobon, was a busy lady.

Sobon's stagnant career in journalism received a well-deserved boost with her coverage of the Mondavi Center opening in 2002. Her inspiring words, picked up by the Associated Press for publication across the country, first brought the quality of the university's music program and the magnificence of its newest performance hall to public attention, thus catapulting her name to national prominence.

With a solid reputation for covering the music scene around the Bay Area, she made it a point to be on hand whenever and wherever there was a scheduled performance by the UC Davis Symphony Orchestra. Musically, she thought she'd seen it all.

That was until she witnessed the raw power five performers were able to produce at the university's concert season opener.

Not wishing to leave it at that, Sobon chose to make amends for her understandable oversight with an initial article addressing how the average concertgoer typically ignores smaller recitals and chamber groups.

In the weeks following that concert, Sobon became a fixture at the university's various music program offerings. She conducted interviews with staff, faculty, and students in a concentrated effort to make certain the university's music department remained center stage and in the public ear.

She put forth articles that played right into David's plans for finding an audience for West's music. Had he bothered to read them, William Tipton Cobbett III would have been incensed.

Sobon's literary contributions were about to shine a spotlight on the chamber groups that had received such poor attention in the past from her colleagues in the Fourth Estate.

The Language of Music
By Ashley Sobon

The art of language is a journalist's stock-in-trade. And the human condition is blessed with nearly 200 forms of verbal and written communication expressly defined as language.

But there is one powerful language that transcends the spoken word. It's a language that speaks with uncompromising power and universal understanding among every sentient being.

The language of music.

It's also instructive to realize that within the root form of any language, there are offshoots of that form. A dialect, an accent, or a vocabulary derived from the primary source of that root language.

And just as language has such intricate derivative relationships, so too is the way of music.

Recalling Davis' inaugural concert this year, my thoughts continue to dwell on the quintet's warm-up performance and the as yet unnamed piece that captivated the assemblage in the lobby that night.

Having such an unassuming force grasp and hold our attention, drawing us toward their unfamiliar musical vocabulary, I realize I've spent my available commentary on only one musical dialect. The dialect of the root orchestral form. Like most critics, I completely ignored the other rich forms of musical expression that exist in the smaller venues, such as the chamber orchestra, a duet, or even a trio.

Call it a musical bias if you must, but based on attendance alone, most of us tend to dismiss these disarmingly entertaining smaller groups. We do so at the risk of diminishing our musical enjoyment.

Few performances of recent memory could compare to the superior command of musical elocution as was demonstrated by the UC Davis Music Department at this year's concert season opener. But hearing them speak with such an authoritative voice that night was a seminal experience.

So naturally, I was curious to see what other dialect, accent, or musical vocabulary they had to offer.

Dr. Henry Tanaka of UC Davis said, "The university provides several venues for our students to explore chamber performance."

Touring the locations with Dr. Tanaka, one got the idea that more was going on than the red-letter concerts typically publicized. Locations such as Freeborn Hall or Wright Hall at the main music building make it easy for various chamber ensembles to organize, rehearse, and perform a myriad of intimate venues and musical styles from classical to jazz.

If that weren't enough, Tanaka admitted you don't have to stay on-campus to enjoy what the music department at Davis has to offer.

"We have four on-campus locations conducive to chamber performance. The oldest of these is the Wyatt Pavilion

Theater. In addition, the community has graciously offered us the use of two churches in Davis and one in Sacramento," Tanaka said.

"We've scheduled three more chamber events between now and the December concert," said Tanaka.

And this reporter plans to be at all of them.

The Power of Five
By Ashley Sobon

A happening at the Vanderhoef is all about ambiance.

Located inside the Mondavi Center, the Vanderhoef Studio Theater offers a cozy alternative to the tie and tails venue of the concert hall. It can easily be set up to accommodate either a theater in the round or dining configuration. And the best part is, the room provides the intimacy required to make the audience feel included.

Visually, the inside of this impressive theater may be dark and brooding with lighting reminiscent of a boxing ring, but the variety of seating choices are all designed with the listener in mind.

Acoustically, the proximity of the performers to the audience, along with the unique design of the studio's interior, creates the perfect reverberation for small ensembles. All that's required to produce a quality sound recording, even in the presence of a packed 200-seat audience, would be strategically located microphones within its 3,000-square-foot space. Here again, the beneficiary of such considerations, is, of course, the audience. No distracting echoes or hollow sounds to disrupt the performance of the players or the enjoyment of those assembled.

However, the facility itself is nothing without the diligent efforts of the well-tuned and practiced performer. Friday evening, the listening public was treated to just such a performance.

Five talented individuals under the direction of Elaine Kirkwood – playing clarinet – skillfully approached a challenging 90-minute program and made it thoroughly enjoyable, proving that last night's happening could be a charming alternative from the usual dinner and a movie.

Kirkwood and her wind quintet treated the audience to a technically brilliant, yet playful interpretation of pieces by Samuel Barber, Paul Hindemith, Carl Nielsen, and Gustav Holst. Though managing to hold the listener's attention throughout the evening, the standout performances were of the Nielsen and Holst.

Best known for the timpani-infused fourth *temperament* of his 2nd symphony, Nielsen's only wind quintet has no melodic lines that lend themselves to instant memorization. Generally not a staple of musical literature, Kirkwood and her fellow players brought a whimsy and depth of feeling to the performance worthy of laying down on vinyl (or at least the CD equivalent).

Written 13 years before his highly successful *Planets*, Holst's charming wind quintet is an understated and underperformed work today. In contrast to Nielsen's work, elements of Holst's opening *allegro moderato* harkens to later movements of his more famous work. While all four pieces complimented each other on various levels, they were more atmospheric than melodic. That being said, nothing could take away from the flawless performance of Kirkwood's group.

Upon reaching a satisfactory conclusion to the evening, Kirkwood and her fellow performers humbly acceded to a request for an encore. It was this encore work that received the greatest reception and the only standing ovation the entire evening.

Not that the typical concertgoer would have recognized any of the works on the program, but this one piece seemed to stand out from the others as having an unmistakable identity to its melodic style, despite the fact the piece's composer was never mentioned. Hmm…curious.

UC Davis Holds Ensembles Workshop
By Ashley Sobon

UC Davis held their annual Chamber Players Workshop this past weekend, displaying once again why they so richly deserve public adulation.

Hosted by the assistant dean of music, Dr. David Whealy and facilitated this year by Dr. Henry Tanaka, yesterday's annual event afforded the casual observer the opportunity to witness various examples of surviving and extinct forms of chamber ensembles and their instrumentation.

In an experimental new move, Tanaka said that university seniors would lead some of the master classes traditionally taught by the faculty.

Tanaka described this pioneering effort, first proffered by the Student Faculty Planning Committee, as offering a greater leadership challenge to the students. "In their new role as instructor, they will hopefully gain a new appreciation for the experience of actually teaching underclassmen," said Tanaka.

"We are very fortunate to have such gifted students capable of leading individual classes," said Whealy.

Cellist Renatta Johnson not only showed off the versatility of her instrument within a chamber group but also introduced and demonstrated the antiquated *viola da gamba* to the modern listener. An unusual precursor to the cello, its deeper bodied construction sported snakelike *f*-holes, with a wider tailpiece and a wider, fretted fingerboard to support the three extra strings.

"The first time I ever saw someone play this instrument was at a candlelight performance at Colonial Williamsburg," said Johnson.

Oboist Clayton Forbes conducted a fascinating demonstration of the double reed instruments. His contributions included everything from wind trios for oboe, flute, and clarinet, to octets and a combination of wind and strings. He concluded his session with a short duo he composed himself and a strangely constructed oboe trio he called *The Sunder*.

Admittedly more comfortable composing, Forbes seemed most at home in front of a lectern. A prolific arranger, Forbes is heavily relied upon to provide a stunning array of assorted orchestrations for events similar to this and on short notice.

"It's not as bad as all that, really," said Forbes. "Most of the arrangements I'm asked to come up with are changes in instrumentation from the scores they already have."

Each individual workshop brought something to the entire event, but it was the staged finale at Wright Hall that stole the show. This portion of the event featured two new unfamiliar works. The first was a forlorn piece scored for two oboes, two English horns, bassoon, and harp. The second, much more optimistic, was an overture for a larger than average group of wind instruments. Its lighthearted classical-era styling evoked Rossini and was a welcome change of emotion from the mournful double reed and harp sounds of the *Farewell Lullaby* played earlier.

"All in all, I believe today was another remarkable example of finely honed performances by our young men and women here at Davis," said Tanaka. "I couldn't be happier."

Reverently Isabella?
By Ashley Sobon

Three faculty members from UC Davis delighted shoppers at the Arden Fair Mall in Sacramento yesterday with an exhibition of their musical prowess in advance of their much-anticipated winter concert.

Violinist Dr. Julia Winslow, cellist and adjunct professor Paige Styles, and pianist Dr. Carla Macklin electrified the crowd with sterling performances of piano trios by Mendelssohn, Franck, and Schubert.

The usually bustling throng of shoppers was so enchanted by the sweet sounds emanating from the three musicians, they created a thick, unmovable circle surrounding the performers. From the second and third floors, heads peered over the railings, joining in the hush that followed as the performers began to play the well-known second movement of Schubert's *Piano Trio*.

They completed their announced performance to enthusiastic applause. But that wasn't the surprise.

After the trio acknowledged the appreciation of the impromptu gathering, Dr. Macklin stood to address them. Thanking them for taking the time to listen to their concert and bending to their requests for an encore, she then said something to the crowd before assuming her seat. Something quite enlightening.

"It took some considerable prodding, but with the reluctant permission of our assistant dean, Dr. Whealy, we're proud to offer you a work which had never been performed in front of an audience. We are pleased to debut for you, a piece called, *Reverently Isabella*," said Macklin.

The work's title was all she would say. Once again, the name of the composer was kept from the public.

The crowd fell silent from the instant the piano issued forth the first eight chords. As the inconsolably sweet theme was picked up by the cello, then the violin, it developed into a theme and variation the listener couldn't help but be drawn into.

Observing the crowd as the trio played this new work, one couldn't mistake the expression of deep sadness in the eyes of some of the listeners closest to the performers as the soothing effect of the theme seemed to touch distant and heartfelt memories.

When asked the name of the composer, Dr. Whealy would only promise to reveal his name at the winter concert. We'll see if he's prepared to follow through.

Someone of such deeply moving musical caliber must be shared with the world.

Chapter Thirty – Three

"Could you get Carla on the phone for me please?"

Peggy was answering another call when David's request came in over the intercom. "That call will have to wait. I have a Miss Beth Grey on the line."

"Thanks. I'll take it." Seconds later, a soft female voice was on the other end. "Hello, Beth."

"David, how've you been?"

"Keepin' busy, you know. We're in rehearsals for the winter concert. What are you up to?"

"David, you're not going to believe this."

"I will if you tell me."

"Nice. Hey, do you remember the historian job I told you about in DC?"

"Yeah, what about it?"

"Well, I got it!"

"I suppose I'm going to lose the only neighbor I know. When do you move?"

"That's the beauty of it!"

Her ambiguous statement was met with silence. David's lack of response could only mean he didn't understand.

"They don't want me to move! They expect me to work from home, using the tristate area as a satellite location."

"What does that mean?"

"It means I'm to conduct research at the archives of Delaware, Maryland, and Pennsylvania for the Smithsonian and to report my findings from the comfort of my own home! I only have to drive out to Washington on a quarterly basis for meetings and other administrative duties. Isn't that wonderful?"

"I'm proud of you, Beth. I knew you could do it. It's what you wanted, isn't it?"

"Yes, and that's not even the best part," she said with mischief in her voice.

"And what would that be?"

"My first assignment is to assist the Smithsonian in researching Delaware's early foray into self-government. I've been able to spend more time tracking down the clues we came up with on that letter."

"Don't tell me you found something?"

"As a matter of fact. If you recall, we only had time to look for Robert West's death certificate in the Sussex County records. Well, I found it in the records for Kent County. Robert West died of consumption in 1847. I was unable to find his birth certificate, but I found that he married a woman named Amanda Porter in 1800. Amanda was born in New Castle County in 1781. Robert and Amanda had two children, a son Charles born in 1802 and a daughter Elizabeth born in 1803."

"My goodness, you have been busy, haven't you?"

"All in a day's work."

"I hope you don't get into trouble doing private research on their dime."

"Oh, don't worry. I'm heavily engaged in the research into this shared governor business between Pennsylvania and Delaware. And that's another reason why I called."

"Which is?"

"I leave for Philadelphia tomorrow. Perhaps something will turn up there that could shed some light on those unanswered questions about that letter."

"You'll do that for me?"

"Sure, why not?"

"Thank you, Beth."

"What for?"

"For keeping me informed. And for being a good friend."

"You're quite welcome, sir," said Beth playfully, trying to repress her grin as she hung up.

David was no sooner finished with his conversation with Beth when Peggy called over the intercom again. "The dean called. He wants to see you straight away."

"Call him back and tell him I'm on my way. And since I'll be late for rehearsals this afternoon, could you offer Carla my apologies for not getting back to her and ask her if she wouldn't mind taking over my rehearsal until I get back?"

Peggy acknowledged his request.

Cobbett walked briskly into his office with a stack of newspapers under his arm. The dean's eyes darted toward the clock on the wall as he approached the door to his private office. It was only after he was satisfied his administrative assistants had returned from lunch on time, that he favored them with a terse nod. "Good afternoon, ladies."

"Good afternoon," was their unison reply.

Before he disappeared into his inner sanctum, he looked to Stella and asked, "Would you bring in a fresh pot please?"

"Yes, sir."

Turning his attention toward Trudy, Cobbett said, "Unless the building is on fire, I want you to hold all my calls for the rest of the afternoon."

"What would you have me to say you're doing?"

"Nursing a migraine," said Cobbett, squinting his eyes and squeezing the bridge of his nose, "which, as it turns out, is a short stroll from the truth."

"I could get you something for that," offered Trudy.

"No, thank you, dear. The caffeine in the coffee should suffice. When Dr. Whealy arrives, send him straight in, won't you?"

"All right," said Trudy. *Dear,* she thought to herself. *Who is he kidding? He really must be out of sorts if he's referring to me as, dear.*

Cobbett slowly removed his brown fedora and put it on its peg next to the felt bowler. He made his way to the desk, placing the newspapers on the corner next to a stack of opened mail, and a journal containing the collected works of some East Coast native called James Burton West.

Reaching into the middle drawer, he found his prescription bottle empty. *Damn*, he thought. To have to enter this particular meeting without artificial help. He could only wait until Stella arrived with his fresh pot of coffee.

The strong scent of brewed Arabica beans meant she was coming into the room with his remedy.

"Thank you, Stella."

"Is there anything else I can get you, Dr. Cobbett?"

"You can make sure the door is closed on your way out?" he said with just enough edge to his sarcasm that made Stella question whether he was serious or not. She was going to say something, but she correctly read the meaning in his dark, sunken eyes.

He watched as she scurried through the threshold into the outer office. But before she could close the door, a well-dressed man carrying a silver and gold-topped walking stick replaced her silhouette in the doorway.

"Well, William," he said amusingly. "I hope you realize this unscheduled meeting of yours interrupted my rehearsal, which should have begun ten minutes ago. What is it this time?"

His underling's insufferable attitude was taking its toll on Cobbett's already frayed patience. His pharmaceutically induced reinforcement unavailable, he had to draw on his own weakened constitution to endure his subordinate's verbal parries.

Doing his best to keep his emotions in check, Cobbett addressed David. "Would you mind telling me why my directives and mandates are continually ignored by virtually everyone in this department?"

"What are you talking about?"

The dean nodded toward the newspapers on his desk. "I don't believe I need to review any of Miss Sobon's articles for you to understand where I'm coming from."

"I'm afraid, William, that since that quintet was first offered up to the public, interest in its composer was bound to happen. Wouldn't you agree?"

His face darkened considerably. "Tell me something. Does compliance with *any* regulation issued by proper authority present a problem for you?"

"Not regulations that make sense. Now, if you would please be so kind as to indicate which so-called regulation I violated, so we can get this over with and I can get back to work?"

"You know damn well you intentionally skirted my mandate. It stops now!"

"And the encore that's already rehearsed and ready?"

"Scrap it!" he thundered. "The advertised program itself is nearly two hours long anyway. We don't need an encore."

"Ah, but you have the reputation of the university to consider, William. Remember?"

"Our reputation doesn't depend on an encore."

"We've set the expectation of providing an encore at the completion of every concert. That's our reputation, William. You wish to scuttle it now?"

"All right then, replace it with something else," Cobbett demanded.

"With what? We have no other music on hand that would be performance ready by Friday."

Feeling his blood pressure begin to skyrocket, Cobbett did something he wasn't in the habit of doing in the presence of visitors; he sat down. A nonverbal capitulation. David had won.

"Very well," Cobbett relented. The older man appeared to be staring at a spot on his desk near the journal. "Look at these."

"At what? The letters?"

"There are twenty of them, at *least*. Nearly every one of them favors your position on this matter."

"Are you all right, William?"

"No, I'm not all right!" he said raising voice. "Mainly because I've been inundated with letters supportive of this West character's quintet. Everyone from high-dollar contributors to the governor's wife has written in requesting to know the name of this piece and who wrote it."

"I'd say the overwhelming tide for granting their request should be honored. What do you think?" He waited in silence as the dean contemplated his options. "Well? Are you going to grant their requests or not?"

The resignation in his voice was unmistakable. "I see no other alternative," said Cobbett as he stood up. "You may perform his quintet per their request and one of his works as an encore for this last concert, but know this. I'm drawing a line in the sand. This is it! No more performances of this man's work after Friday night. Do I make myself abundantly clear?"

David thought, *We shall see.*

This year's winter concert set a precedent for the university. For the second year in a row, the winter concert sold out every last seat for the evening. Requests for standing room in the back of Jackson Hall were made and politely refused.

During the preconcert festivities, four string performers occupied the attention of devoted concertgoers with excerpts from quartets by Prokofiev and Barber. Halfway through their allotted time, they introduced an excerpt from a new unfamiliar quartet.

Its quick paced melodic statement grabbed the attention of the crowd, like the quintet before it at the season opener. Judging from their intense appreciation of this last piece, the audience preferred it to the earlier offerings. Suddenly, from behind the hall doors emerged another viola player. That's when the packed lobby erupted in spontaneous cheers because they knew what was coming.

The staccato of Renatta's rising double eighth note arpeggio opening was met with rousing applause. William Tipton Cobbett III granted the public's exuberant requests for a reprise of West's string quintet. And they were ecstatic.

Only minutes after the soft gong's timely cue, the patrons were seated, the house lights dimmed, the stage lights came up, and the performers entered with instruments in hand. Once situated, the concertmistress rose from her chair and nodded to Clayton Forbes to sound his A note to tune the woodwind and brass sections. As they completed their adjustments, Clayton played his A note again; then the string players followed suit. The orchestra waited for one more scene to play out.

The performers rose for the entrance of the conductor from stage left. Conductor and concertmistress exchanged a handshake before the man with the baton acknowledged the audience.

Dashing in his white-tie, wing-collared shirt and waistcoat with black tails, David's recent haircut gave him a sharper appearance than normal. He turned his attention back to the orchestra and raised his hands. With the vigorous downbeat of his walnut handled baton, the musical evening was under way.

The scheduled program spanned the outer fringe of standard musical repertoire. The concert opened with the *Coronation March* of Edward Elgar. Its majestic exposition soon yielded to a sublime second theme with a rich development section before returning to its original motive and a stately conclusion.

Frederick Delius' *Walk to the Paradise Garden* was the perfect counterpoint to the dignified pomp and ceremony of the Elgar. Musically, the evening's second selection was a gentle caress of long flowing notes tastefully building up romantic tension. Beautifully scored, the ending was all but a lullaby as the sweet kiss of high strings and long, soft tones of the wind section drifted into the ear, bidding the listener a very restful good night.

For those that did fall asleep, Sir Michael Tippett's *Divertimento on Sellinger's Round* quickly followed by the *Things to Come Suite* by William Bliss contained enough rhythmic and thematic variety to capture and hold the patron's attention for the remainder of the first half of the program.

The *Crown Imperial Coronation March* of William Walton served as the entr'acte. As was the function of the Elgar, Walton's march was intended to focus the attention of the audience onto the stage in a specific and majestic way. The march was the perfect overture to his *Symphony 1*, the last work on the program that brought the musical evening to an exciting and emphatic close.

From formal and majestic to lush and evocative, the performance was well received by the crowd, albeit more subdued than normal.

David signaled the orchestra to rise as he turned around to bow to the audience.

Following the custom, David departed stage left with Myung-hee right at his heels, while the orchestra remained standing. The audience continued their record-breaking, high-decibel clapping as David returned to the stage.

He bowed to the audience, looked stage left, and beckoned to the person behind the curtain. Myung-hee came out in a stunning white evening gown with violin in hand. She acknowledged the crowd with a gentle nod before David shook her hand and ascended the podium.

Watching from his private box above, Cobbett was quite content with how the evening was unfolding.

David gave the downbeat to kick off the new work. The soft accent of low strings in *tremolo*, a horn chorus met by soft timpani, rolling to a crescendo, punctuated with a string section *sforzando*. As the string section reached its peak, their *tremolo* quickly diminished into a sustained *pianissimo*. Floating above the strains of the string section, a solitary oboe played a brisk but mournful melody. The oboe's romantic motive became the principle theme that was developed into textbook *sonata-allegro* form. At the recapitulation of the introduction, the soloist pronounced the melody rather than the oboe. And pronounce it she did.

Myung-hee's gypsy-like interpretation quickly whisked the audience from complacency to excitement as the Hungarian-style theme she emoted continued to capture their imaginations.

The echo from the work's emphatic ending precipitated a standing ovation from an exhilarated audience. Both soloist and conductor left the stage once again.

Believing it was over, Cobbett smiled to himself.

David returned to the conductor's rostrum again, but this time, he had a microphone with him. As he spoke for the first time since the concert began, Cobbett's frown grew roots.

"Thank you. And good evening ladies and gentlemen. Before we continue, I wish to recognize our concertmistress and soloist for the evening, Miss Myung-hee Chun."

When Myung-hee came back out onto the stage, the audience went crazy. David gladly waited for the enthusiastic throng to express their appreciation for the young violinist's exceptional performance.

"For the past four years, Miss Chun was a fixture as first chair violinist and concertmistress. We've been blessed to have her with us. Her leadership, performing skill and passion for her art, will be missed by us all as she assumes the mantle of concertmistress for the Seattle Symphony Orchestra."

Again, the audience responded with fervent applause.

"The man whose work you heard and whose quintet held you spellbound in the lobby isn't well known to the public at large. So allow me to acquaint you with him."

Cobbett became livid that David would choose to single out one student over the others. But watching his underling defy his orders about the encore made his face turn an unmistakable shade of crimson.

Knowing his actions countered Cobbett's wishes pleased David to no end as he entered into a brief biographical narrative of the man who gave them this music. While he did so, the orchestra was augmented by a huge chorus assembling behind them.

"His name was James Burton West, and he was a twenty-three-year Air Force veteran who became a reluctant composer. West began his military career as a loadmaster on an AC-130 gunship during the Vietnam War. It was during that time he embarked on the fateful mission where he garnered some of our nation's highest honors, but at a cost that wounded his soul; his friend's life.

"Married to a classically trained pianist, the former Isabella Rodriquez, they were the proud parents of two handsome young men. The elder son, Ethan, was a cellist. The younger, Alexander, was a violinist. They harped on their father to write the music they knew he could write, but his military obligations prevented him from doing so.

"On the very day of West's retirement from active duty, he had to endure their loss in a random act of violence. From that point on, he sequestered himself from society, racked with grief.

"He lived a private, unassuming existence for the next nineteen years making periodic and anonymous donations to charities around the country. An artist of extraordinary talent, he also made numerous true-to-life pencil sketches of landscapes, montages, and of his family.

"He loved his country, but he loved his family even more. For he kept his promise, dedicating the remainder of his life to write the music he'd promised them he'd write. Contained in his Delaware home is the testament to his love of family—the surviving handwritten scores to well over two-hundred pieces of quality music. Works that include the piece you are about to hear. It's a symphonic poem called *Hymn*."

Following some light applause, David turned around, raised his baton, and engaged the low strings to open the work.

Cobbett was fuming at this point, but he could do nothing until the concert was over.

The lonely C-minor entrance of the low strings matched West's feelings of remorse and sorrow. The strained motive enjoined by the high strings ended the initial cadence on a grand pause, punctuated by low brass. The audience was breathless waiting for the piece to start again.

The angelic sopranos initiated a statement of the primary theme. Deep male voices blended themselves with the high voices in a delightful syncopation of rhythm, the original melodic idea of which enchanted the audience. As the initial cadence to this new idea concluded, the crowd then did something out of step with formal concert etiquette; they applauded in midperformance.

A lengthy ovation ensued at the sound of the last chords. Among those to stand first was the governor's wife in her regular box near stage right. Visitors from Hollywood royalty in their orchestra seats engaged in the rousing adulation, as did Ashley Sobon in her reserved box near stage left, and one other person.

A concertgoer who managed to arrive undetected, took his seat in the upper mezzanine. A man who took notes. A man who had flown in from London the night before, in attendance on orders from the executive director of the London Symphony Orchestra.

Chapter Thirty – Four

The cheers from the third curtain call could still be heard as David made his way to the conductor's office, stage left. But Cobbett was already there, waiting for him.

The dean's anger would no longer be contained. Still seething, he could hardly wait to express his extreme displeasure. He had to make sure his assistant dean understood who the alpha male was in this scenario. To underscore the point, he was already seated behind the desk when David came through the door.

"I hope you are quite pleased with yourself," Cobbett said bluntly.

"Naturally. And the one thing you can't do is undo it."

"Nevertheless, I can still take steps to ensure it never happens again."

"Steps? Such as?"

"As you seem reluctant to follow my lead, I can always replace you with a more compliant second who can do as they are instructed."

"Too bad my tenured position will prevent that possibility."

"Eventuality."

"Fantasy!"

Outraged at being verbally slapped in the face, Cobbett said, "We shall see what the chancellor and the executive board have to say about this. I'm confident they won't look kindly on your insubordinate conduct. I'm quite sure they'll back my recommendation that you be summarily removed from your position."

"Based on what?"

"Based on your open defiance and how it reflects poorly on the reputation of this university. We can't have that."

"You mean *your* reputation, don't you? I have to wonder why you're even here. Certainly not for the benefit of those you're supposed to educate?"

"The beauty of my decision is that, one, I don't have to justify myself. Two, the responsibility for interpreting the *mission statement* of this department is mine alone, so it says what I want it to say. And finally, I've already made my decision. Do I make myself clear?"

"Then you make mine a simple one." David turned his back on him and went to leave. Just like that day in the office of Simon Talbridge, when he reached for the door, he stopped. Turning around, he burned his steely-eyed gaze at Cobbett. "You'll have my *full* resignation on your desk in the morning."

The unexpected news hit Peggy hard. It was difficult for her to maintain her composure while discharging her duties that morning. The two of them had been a team since her arrival. She had David's patterns and habits down to a science. To have little or no time to adjust to this new situation was unsettling.

David wasn't only leaving his post. He was leaving the university. It wasn't the way he wanted to leave. His guiding principles of education were uncompromising. He would rather resign than sacrifice those principles to satisfy what he believed in his heart to be cheating his students out of a quality education.

Peggy may not have known what led to his decision, but her astute intuition told her that something had been wrong between him and the dean for at least a year. Suddenly it all came to a head. It was what it was. She couldn't change it.

David had been in his office with the door closed for about an hour when Peggy fielded the first of several calls for the former assistant dean.

"Dr. Whealy, you have a call from a Dr. Beverly Christian, the dean of music at the University of Delaware."

"Please take down whatever message they have, Peggy. I'm no longer the assistant dean, nor do I speak for this university."

"I understand." Knowing David as long as she had, Peggy could easily tune into his mood. He was less than his jovial self, and when he got this way, it was best he didn't speak to anyone. "Do you want me to hold your other calls?"

"That would be a good idea. Thanks, Peggy. You're a treasure."

"What about visitors?"

"Them, too."

She supposed that meant to put the stall on them as well.

Of course, that tactic worked on everyone. Except Carla.

He was in the process of cleaning out his desk into the boxes he had on the conference table when he looked up to see Carla standing in the doorway with her hand on her hip.

"I heard it, but I had to see it to believe it."

"He left me little choice," said David as he returned to his packing.

"You're not even gonna put up a fight?"

"In case you haven't noticed, I've been doing that for most of the year. Ever since William picked up that award, he's completely abandoned his scholarly principles. I'm not going to have my hands tied trying to educate our students. His unreasonable rules I could deal with, but his decision to remove me from my position for no reason other than spite was the last straw."

"He must have made a hell of a pitch for you to just surrender," said Carla sarcastically. "What are you going to do now?"

"Long term? I don't know."

"Short term, then? You're going back to Delaware, aren't you?"

"Now would be a good time. I still have a mystery to solve, you know."

Carla looked around the room and noticed David hadn't yet removed the framed pictures of all his past students. Tossing her head toward one, she intimated, "And what about them?"

"It's for them that I'm doing this."

"Really?" she said sarcastically. "For them? Or for yourself?"

Carla's deft use of David's own words to Cobbett was cutting.

"Carla, if I'm prohibited from teaching in the only way I know how, I would be lying to myself and cheating them. Do you understand?"

She exhaled her exasperation and shook her head.

"Besides, now I can dedicate my energies to solving this mystery and getting West's music out in front of the general public, especially now that they're aware of him."

"And you'll do this without me now, I suppose?"

Tossing her a hurt glance, he went back to packing.

"What are you going to do about your homes? Are you going to stay here in California or are you moving to Delaware?"

"I haven't decided. I like the idea of having a place on both coasts. I never thought about it, but I think Delaware is beginning to grow on me."

"Don't you mean Beth is beginning to grow on you?"

David reserved a hot look for Carla since she seemed to be guiding the conversation in that direction. "I already told you, I'm not interested in seeking a relationship *with anyone* until this thing is over."

"After Friday night, I don't think the press are going to stop hounding you about him or his music."

"Possibly not. In any event, I still have to find that missing ring, solve the mystery of that old key, and champion his music. That should keep me somewhat occupied."

"I guess that means I'll have to fight the good fight here."

"And so you will, as the new assistant dean of music."

"What?"

"That was part of my resignation statement. I wanted to make sure the university was in good hands. I can't think of any reason why he would deny that request."

"Why didn't Lindsay Morgan get the nod? Or Henry Tanaka?"

"Because deep down, even your father knows who the most qualified person is."

She managed a quick smile. "Thanks, but you know what I'd rather have."

His sympathetic look turned into a smile.

She returned it.

The Associated Press picked up Sobon's article covering the winter concert. And because this cub reporter chose to go on a crusade over the works of some strange, unknown composer, William Tipton Cobbett III believed his chances of securing the post with the London Symphony were now dashed.

Thanks to her favorable write-up advancing West's music in the Lifestyle section of nearly every major newspaper in the country, Westmania went viral. Critics began to ask the inevitable question: *Who was James Burton West?*

The best man to the answer that question was no longer on the job and nowhere to be found. But that didn't stop reporters like Ashley Sobon from trying to find out.

Chapter Thirty – Five

The driveway of James Burton West loomed large as David approached the hairpin turn of Frontage Road. He pulled his car up next to the garage, shut the engine off, and just sat there taking in everything that happened during the past few days. Feeling all the tension that built up in his neck finally release, he went inside the house, a place he was now able to call home.

He glanced at his pocket watch and noticed the business day hadn't yet ended. Hoping to take care of a few household errands, he made some calls. Bad timing plagued his attempt at productivity this late in the day.

He left a message for Walter Kelly to get back with him so he might continue the home's utilities funding. He tried to get hold of Dr. Beverly Christian at the University of Delaware, but all he got was her voicemail. Failing that, he made an attempt to contact Beth to let her know he was back in town, but again, no answer. Three calls, three strikes.

Unsuccessful on all fronts, he freshened up with a shower and a change of clothes before heading out to Five Points to pick up some groceries.

David was in the produce section when he received several calls in rapid succession. The first was Walter Kelly in response to his request. The second was a wrong number. The third came in as he rounded the corner of the condiment aisle.

"Hello, David?"

The combination of background noise and jet lag kept him from recognizing the voice. "Yes?"

"It's Beth. I'm sorry I missed your call."

"That's all right. I called to find out what you're up to?"

"I'm actually on my way back from Philly."

"What time do you think you'll get in?"

"Traffic is light today. I figure I'll be home in about another hour, why?"

"I'm in the Five Points market if you need anything."

"You're here in Delaware?" she said excitedly.

"It's a long story. I'll have to fill you in some time."

"How about over dinner?"

With a quick glance at his watch, he said, "It's already six thirty. Are you sure it wouldn't be too late?"

"Don't be silly. On this job, I set my own hours."

"I've been meaning to ask, how's it been?"

"Productive," was all she would say.

"Sounds intriguing. And cryptic." Not wanting to keep her on the phone while she was driving, he asked, "What time should I expect you?"

"How about eight?"

"Eight it is."

David was in the process of breading the thinly sliced pork cutlets he'd prepared when *Ode to Joy* rang in his ears.

Not standing on ceremony, Beth came in quickly, gave David a peck on the cheek, and handed him a copy of the local paper. "You sure made a splash with Jim's music, didn't you?" Making her way to the kitchen island, she put her laptop on the table.

"What—" He was dumbfounded by her whirlwind entrance until he read the front-page story. The headline of the Lifestyles segment read "*Local Composer Subject of National Query.*"

"I'm surprised you haven't been flooded with requests for information about Jim or his music."

David chuckled. Beth didn't know about the striking turn of events following his triumph on the stage.

"What's so funny?"

"I'm not here because of Christmas break, Beth," he began, "I resigned."

"You what? Why? What happened?"

"William Tipton Cobbett III happened. It's a long story, but the boiled down version is this; I'm not going to supplant my teaching style or sacrifice the value of my students' education for any grand designs of a man who had only himself to promote."

Thinking back over her own life's tribulations, Beth began to relate to David's plight. She didn't want anyone else to pry into her secrets, so she felt compelled to acquiesce to David's short explanation. "Sorry to hear it. What will you do now?"

"I am going to solve this mystery surrounding our mutual friend."

Beth smiled broadly. "Funny you mention that. It's why I brought the laptop over."

David flipped the pork cutlet over in the skillet with the deft touch of a seasoned chef.

"What would you like with your cutlet?"

"What do you have?"

"Corn, mashed potatoes, or a light salad?"

"Caesar?"

"Coming right up." David went to work on a head of lettuce.

"As I told you earlier, my new job so far has been quite productive, but I didn't necessarily say for whom."

David looked at her with a questioning eyebrow.

"Remember I told you my new assignment is to research early political activity in Delaware? Well, along with finding several documents that were of interest to the Smithsonian, I also located a few that were of interest to our investigation of that letter."

"You're kidding? What documents?"

"You remember where our investigation left off?"

"We were looking into the origins of William and Cynthia West and their son, Robert, when we ran out of time."

"If you recall, I discovered Robert West's death certificate, marriage certificate, and the fact he and his bride Amanda had two children, Charles and Elizabeth."

"That's right."

"Well, I've subsequently discovered an obituary that reported Amanda's death abroad in 1852, which is why I couldn't find her death certificate on file."

"Were you able to locate their children?"

"There was quite an extensive record on their son, Charles. He married an Anna Pennington in 1827, and they had a son named Avery born in 1835. Charles's records were much more complete than Elizabeth's, however.

"The only documentation I could find was a notice in the newspaper announcing the birth of an Elizabeth West at their home in Lewes on April 2, 1803. The trail to locate anything more on Elizabeth grew cold after that. It's as though she never existed, if not for that article."

"Were you able to find Robert's birth certificate?"

"No. I even looked into the county orphans' court index to see if Robert's name appeared, but he wasn't there."

"What were you able to find up in Philadelphia?"

"That's the exciting part! Now I know why our friend William West couldn't be found anywhere in Delaware. It's because he was from Philadelphia."

"You found him there?"

"Our William was born in Philadelphia in 1757. He married the Cynthia Belmore we found from New Castle. Church records indicate they were married in the Old Cathedral Church of West Philadelphia on December 5, 1778."

"That's a bit of detailed work, Beth. I can see why you wanted to become a historian."

The corners of her mouth came up. "Why, thank you! Oh, and I found another tidbit of history that should interest you. How much do you know about America's involvement in the War of 1812?"

"Not much I'm afraid. Why?"

"Without getting too far into the weeds for an explanation, I'll try to simplify the account." She glanced at the laptop's screen to read her notes. "On the first of June 1812, President James Madison sent a letter to Congress detailing the belligerent actions of the British. The increased predation of the British Navy against American merchant ships on the high seas constituted one front, while their supplying of weapons to the Ohio tribes under Chief Tecumseh was the other. Continual kidnapping and impressments of American merchant ship crews was the last straw for Madison.

"A month and a half later on July 18, after much deliberation, Congress voted to declare war for the first time since the Constitution was ratified." Beth looked back at David, placing emphasis on her next statement. "The delegation from Delaware voted no."

"That's fascinating, but how does this history lesson apply to our investigation?"

"In April of 1813, the flagship HMS *Portiers* led a blockade of the Chesapeake and Delaware Bays and the subsequent assault on the town of Lewes. But it was her sister ship, the HMS *Stalwart*, that laid claim to inflicting the only appreciable damage to the town."

"You're still not telling me the why?"

"David, remember the articles from the archives? This was how William and Cynthia West met their end. Their house was destroyed in the attack and Robert held the British responsible and thus sought revenge for their loss."

"Based on what?"

Beth turned the laptop around so David could read the front-page article she was talking about. "I ran across a broadside account that tells of Robert West's attempt to embarrass Delaware's federalist congressman and the two federalist senators who voted against the declaration. Apparently, he'd hired a privateer captain named Tunney to locate and destroy the British frigate responsible for the destruction of his home. A subsequent broadside reported that the British ship went down with all hands six weeks later."

David read the account with fascination.

"I also managed to find one other article that contains a passing reference to Jim's property. During the great storm of 1889, what we now know to be a hurricane, the house was damaged once again. Avery West completed a significant restoration of the home a year later."

"I can now see why the Smithsonian was so keen to retain your services."

"I appreciate that, David. I really do!" Satisfied by the meal, Beth said, "Well, it's getting late, and I have an early morning."

"Where are you off to now?"

"It's my first trip to DC to report my findings, and they want me there at eight in the morning, so I'd better go."

David escorted Beth to the door. Giving her a little hug, he said, "Thanks again for all your hard work. I wouldn't be this far along without you."

Beth returned the hug and turned to leave. All of a sudden, she snapped her fingers, pointed at David, and said, "Oh, I almost forgot. Audra Bunting would like to meet with you. Something about some documents that you might be interested in."

Shockwaves reverberated throughout musical academia as news of David's abrupt resignation was made public. The former assistant dean's office was inundated with job offers and requests for copies of West's work, but he wasn't there to receive any of it.

The hardest hit by the news, however, were the students who read the paper during the holiday break. The rest would soon find out upon their return.

Unable to grasp why this happened in the wake of such a successful concert, the shock of the student population soon turned to anger with no place to vent their bestial fury. Their only hope at redemption rested on Carla's shoulders. She now had to lead the department and the planning committee. And she would need to employ scandalous methods to get David back into the fold with an obstinate William Cobbett in the front office.

With the right game plan, she might have a chance at doing just that.

Chapter Thirty – Six

Milling around the faculty lounge, most of the music professors were grouped around the tables talking among themselves in hushed tones, visibly shaken over the news. Several more were huddled around the water cooler commiserating.

The faculty had to put up with one more administrative day while the student population departed for their Christmas break right after the concert. They weren't aware of the altercation that occurred between David and Cobbett until Sobon's latest article hit the newsstands.

Into this pathetic gathering, Jason Cantu entered with another copy of the newspaper. He spotted Carla nursing a cup of coffee at the far end of the room and approached her.

"Have you seen this yet, Carla?" asked Jason, handing her the paper. "The students aren't going to like this one bit." She only read the beginning before she handed the paper back to him.

> Abrupt Resignation Follows Musical Triumph
> By Ashley Sobon
>
> On the eve of his greatest musical success, Dr. David Whealy inexplicably resigned from UC Davis yesterday. The campus is trying to come to terms with Whealy's departure amid the revelation of a tussle between himself and the dean of music, Dr. William Cobbett.

"Yes, I did," said Carla. Her deliberate response required no interpretation from anyone in the room. She was pissed.

How did this reporter find out so damned fast? The article, published only days after the concert, was a blow to the unbounded success of the musical evening.

The department garnered a modest success introducing West's music over the past few months by the use of smaller venues. They expected the two large-scale pieces performed at the concert to be the *fait accompli* to Cobbett's censorship of his works, yet this outcome became the unexpected result.

Carla scanned the long faces that were prevalent around the faculty lounge. The university didn't need this kind of controversy in the wake of such a musical *coup*. They needed a shot in the arm, and they needed it right now.

Taking decisive action, she stood up and addressed her colleagues in the open lounge. "I want to see all the department heads in the assistant dean's office in one hour. Bring your game faces and your notepads. And leave your negativity at the door. You won't be needing it."

With that, the new assistant dean of music marched out of the room.

The intuitive administrator that she was, Peggy set up the conference table ahead of the meeting. On her way back from the supply room, she ran into Carla.

"Will there be anything else, Dr. Macklin?"

"No thanks, Peggy."

"Do you want me to send them in as they arrive?" asked the pensive older woman.

Carla sensed her discomfort. "It will be all right, Peggy. Just go about your job as you did for David and everything will be all right, I promise."

"It's only—" Peggy began, but her emotions wouldn't allow her to finish her statement.

"I know. I feel the same way, too."

Peggy did what she was told. She proceeded with her workday as she always had. Reading her emails, Peggy noticed one the dean highlighted as urgent. Opening it, she read its contents to Carla while she was still standing there.

"Dr. Cobbett wants a meeting of all the department heads at noon today."

"Which is why I'm meeting with everyone now," countered Carla.

Smiling at the veracity of the young woman, Peggy said, "Great idea."

Julia Winslow was the only department head not in the faculty lounge when Carla made her startling announcement. But hearing of Carla's tenacity from one of her associate professors, she arrived with youthful optimism that something positive was going to come of this meeting.

"You're expected, Dr. Winslow. Want me to get you something?"

"No thanks, Peggy," said Julia. "Do you know why we're having two meetings? One with Dr. Macklin and the other with the dean?"

"It's not my place to say. I believe Dr. Macklin is going to address that subject during the meeting."

Julia acknowledged Peggy's statement as Carla walked in with Henry. Jason, Lindsay, and Antara showed up shortly after that.

"Okay, let's get this over with," said Carla as she escorted everyone into the office. "Please take your seats, and I'll let you in on the reason for this unscheduled meeting."

The command in Carla's voice came through loud and clear. They all looked at Carla as if she was going to perform a stupefying magic trick. Perhaps, she was.

"As you may or may not be aware, I was asked to assume Dr. Whealy's duties until a new assistant dean is appointed. In the interim, Jason will be filling in for me while I'm here, so I've asked him to join us this morning."

Lindsay spoke first. "Does anyone know why Dr. Whealy left? What's going on?"

"Yeah, and what's this afternoon's meeting with the dean all about?" asked Henry.

"I'll tell you what's not going on," said Carla. "We're not going to allow this decision to stand. But before we go any further, if there's anyone else with a better idea how we fix this, I'm willing to entertain it. But you'd better speak up right now."

No one said a word. They just stared at Carla with marked fascination.

"All right, here's what we're going to do."

Trudy and Stella waited at the head of the conference table for the attendees to show. They were used to accomplishing Cobbett's every whim from the moment he arrived. Naturally, he was going to be fashionably late. But that privilege was his alone. No one else dared be tardy for a meeting scheduled by William Tipton Cobbett III.

Antara, Julia, Jason, and Henry were the first to show up, followed by Lindsay and Carla. Trudy escorted the attendees to their seats as Stella kept a watchful eye out for their boss.

Following the agreed-upon game plan, not a word would be uttered by any of them until Carla spoke to the dean first. And only after she addressed them individually.

Stella was used to premeeting discussions that went on before her boss showed up, but today, they were as silent as an oil painting. No one so much as looked around the room.

They waited five more minutes before Stella's eyes informed the group of the dean's arrival.

"Good afternoon, everyone," the dean's voice boomed across the conference table. "I wanted to review the events of last week so we can dispense with any rumors to the contrary."

The game plan was now in effect. With some luck, it would have the desired results.

Cobbett pressed on with his monologue. "Dr. Whealy has resigned his position for personal reasons. Effective today, I've asked Dr. Macklin to assume his duties until we're able to nominate and select his replacement."

"His successor," Carla said smoothly.

Cobbett and his former assistant dean had an unspoken understanding. If David felt the need to challenge the dean's authority, he would only do so in private. Carla set a different standard. Public or private, it didn't matter. If you were wrong in her estimation, she called you on it. Her decision to do so, and in this venue, warned Cobbett she wasn't going to pull any punches as to where she stood on anything.

Darting a scornful glance at the new assistant dean, Cobbett simply yielded to her edification. "Of course. His *successor*." The dean continued as he moved his gaze from Carla to the group. "As I was saying, there was a breakdown of communication between me and you because my stated position wasn't made clear by my former assistant. So I will repeat it for you now."

No one moved. No one shook their head, no one nodded, no one fidgeted in their seats or uttered a sound as was previously agreed. Carla took in what Cobbett was laying out while waiting for the right time to strike. Meanwhile, she allowed him to wax arrogant.

"This university will maintain its stellar reputation by ensuring that only works by well-established composers are performed. We won't experiment with that reputation by popularizing unknown composers or unpublished music. Is that clear to everyone?"

Once again, no one moved or said a word.

The dean's complexion was taking on a rosy hue with every statement that went unanswered. His frustration was mounting, but he tried not to show it.

He attempted to force a reaction, but it wasn't the one he expected. "Carla, would you at least agree to this policy on principle?"

Carla folded her arms and looked at him, raising an eyebrow. She too understood Cobbett well enough to know this nonverbal behavior always caused the dean to bristle.

"Look, the person in the position of authority is responsible for the decisions and actions of their department. I take this responsibility quite seriously," said Cobbett, directing his next comment toward Carla. "Can you understand that? Or did I make an error in judgment in selecting Dr. Whealy's replacement?"

"*Successor*," she said again with emphasis.

By now, Cobbett was all set to lose his temper. He made a motion as if he were going to launch into another verbal aria when Carla silenced him.

"Are you done?" she said with her arms still folded.

Stunned by her insolence, Cobbett could only sit there, turning beat red.

"Because here's what *you* are going to do. One: you're going to live up to the tenets of the mission statement as written and not your continually modified interpretation of it. As a reminder, I'll restate it for you, and I quote: the mission of this university's music department is to fully develop the talents and abilities of our young musicians in every aspect of musical endeavor. To this end, we will be second to none in bringing out their peak performance and creativity to the utmost of our ability, unquote.

"Two: you are going to formally apologize to Dr. Whealy, both in person and in writing, and request his immediate reinstatement to this university in whatever capacity he wishes to serve, including *your* position if he wants it.

"And three: based on the overwhelming response from the faculty and students of UC Davis and the critical acclaim of the general public, the music of James Burton West will be featured in any and all future performance venues this university sees fit to include."

To accentuate what came next, Carla rose from her chair and walked confidently toward Cobbett, who was backing up in his. As she got closer to him she held up a piece of paper as evidence, bore her penetrating stare into his eyes, and coolly and calmly said, "Because if you don't comply with every demand, this letter of no confidence in your ability to represent this university as dean of music and subsequent request for your immediate removal signed by all of us, shall go to the chancellor for presentation to the board."

"You can't—"

"*Doctor* Cobbett. I've already made them aware of your insidious behavior, and I know how they're going to vote!"

For the first time in Cobbett's miserable lifetime, he felt his position threatened.

"Do I make *my*self clear or do you feel the need to *test* me?"

With his mouth partially opened, he scanned the conference table and to his horror saw the looks of satisfaction on the faces of all present. After which there was no fight left in him. He could only offer a reluctant nod.

"I thought as much." Handing Cobbett her cell phone, she said, "His number is here on my phone. You can call him right now. We'll wait."

♪

Chapter Thirty – Seven

Audra Bunting once again found herself waiting for Dr. David Whealy near the cylindrical entrance of the archives. Marge Tompkins had sent the rest of the skeleton crew home. She wished Audra a Merry Christmas before she departed. The interior of the archives was peaceful and quiet on this last business day before the Christmas break.

A gray overcast sky added to the chill of the afternoon. A moderate snow the night before was topped with streaking wisps of fresh powder floating over the parking lot. It swirled and settled around a small berm left by a recent attempt at plowing the road. The crispness of the cold, dry air made Audra's sinuses ache. It had been a cold day with the mercury forecast to drop into the teens later that evening.

Her patience was soon rewarded as she saw David's car pull into the parking space near the building. The last time she met David, she felt apprehensive, not knowing what to expect from such a well-known celebrity.

This time she felt comfortable. This time she had something of possible value to add to his investigation. And this time, David suggested he had something of value for her.

"Dr. Whe—" she began. But remembering David's request for a less formal term of address, she smiled. "David, so good of you to come." Then she caught sight of his new accessory. "That's an interesting addition to your stylized wardrobe."

Holding out his walking stick to give Audra a better look, he said, "This was yet another gift from my Lewes benefactor, hidden in a broom closet."

"I've never seen anything like it before. And on you, it looks smashing!"

David chuckled. "Let's say it completes the look."

She laughed with him before she turned the conversation over to the business at hand. "I realize it's late, so I won't keep you any longer than necessary."

"Not at all. I'm here in Delaware longer than you might expect."

"Why do you say that?"

"I'm no longer with the university."

"I'm sorry to hear that. What happened?"

"Let's just say I can attend to the estate for longer than I anticipated."

"If that means you'll be joining us here in Delaware, then nothing could please me more."

"I won't be going anywhere until I get to the bottom of this mystery."

Audra lightened her expression. "Then I hope to that end, the following summary is an early Christmas present for you."

David inclined his head in satisfied agreement.

Grasping his arm, Audra escorted David to the lockers. Even though it was the two of them, following archive procedure was still a must. Securing his coat, walking stick, and cell phone, he and Audra entered through the metal detector and into the main research room to find a thick binder on one of the tables. The only thing he brought inside with him was the unsigned letter fragment with the strange wax stamp.

Audra motioned for David to take a seat at the head of the table while she sat in the chair next to him. Drawing up the binder, she said, "Piecing together the early days of the Delaware General Assembly, we may have discovered something that has a direct bearing on your property, so I wanted to share that with you."

"I appreciate that, but I hope I'm not putting you out, especially around the holidays."

"Think nothing of it, David. You share such beautifully weaved stories through your music, allow me to do as much for you with a story that may hold some of your answers."

Relaxed for the first time since the summer when he and Carla were going over West's scores, he sat back in the chair with laced fingers. His body language informed Audra he was ready to take in whatever she was about to relate.

Audra flipped open the binder, assumed the character of a lecturer, and began her story.

"Before Delaware became a proprietorship of William Penn in 1681, the Dutch controlled much of what we know as Pennsylvania along with the Delmarva Peninsula and established themselves near Lewes in 1631.

"After the Duke of York extended William Penn the proprietorship of the lower counties, as Delaware was known then, an ongoing feud between him and Lord Baltimore of the House of Calvert ensued. Unable to reach an agreement, Penn sailed for London in 1684 to resolve this dispute directly with the king, but he was too late. Charles II died only months after Penn's arrival, and the former Duke of York became James II in 1685.

"The new king's three-year reign was a turbulent one that ended in the Great Revolution of 1688. William and Mary were elevated to king and queen. James II lived out his days in France until his death in 1701.

"Before he left England, there was some speculation that James II drafted and signed a land grant favoring Penn over Lord Baltimore effectively ending the dispute. However, the document, if it ever existed, was never given to Penn. He ran out of time to plead his case with James II. Unaware of the possible land grant, Penn worked tirelessly but unsuccessfully to argue his case. First with William and Mary. Then the courts of London.

"Meanwhile, pirate attacks on Lewes and other towns along the Delaware coast were causing increased tension between Philadelphia and the lower counties. From the time William Penn returned to America in 1699, he worked to maintain his fragile hold on his proprietorship. But at this late date, he realized it was hopeless.

"In 1701, Penn created a new charter for his Frame of Government. The charter contained a codicil that if the lower counties couldn't reconcile with Philadelphia in three years, they would be allowed their own independent assembly. On May 22, 1704, that's what happened."

David was mesmerized by the story. It gave him a historical tapestry in which he could see how all the individual threads of research were woven into a fabric that made sense. Now, if he could do the same thing with the clues he had been able to deduce to this point.

"I get the feeling it wasn't as simple as that."

"You're more right than you know," she said. "After the lower counties attained their legislative independence, the new assembly's poor record keeping and lack of a standard meeting place led to problems tracking their activities."

Curious as to why there was so much confusion, David asked, "If one governor oversaw both general assemblies, why was there such a disparity in their record keeping?"

"Bravo, David. You've been doing your research. Although they shared a common proprietary governor, the lower counties were not obligated to send copies of their minutes, legislation, or legal codes to either Philadelphia or London. Consequently, we are left with a void in their legislative record that lasted until 1739."

Replaying her last statement in his head, David rubbed his chin. "All of this is quite interesting, but what is the link to my property in Lewes?"

"I believe I may have found it," Audra responded. "With the death of William Penn in 1718, it was up to his sons, John, Thomas, and Richard, to carry on the fight for their proprietary rights over Delaware. Perhaps one of them accomplished what William was unable to."

With a puzzled look, David said, "Our research to date never came up with any links to the Penn family. However, we did find a gap in the Lewes tax records between 1723 and 1780."

"We know that when new tax districts were proffered in 1719, Lewes was on the rolls consecutively until 1723. Between then and 1780, the Lewes Hundred seemed to have evaporated from any and all documentation, including the tax rolls. One thing's for certain. Once Lewes was removed from the tax rolls in 1724, no evidence surfaced to uncover why this occurred. That's until a descendant of Delaware Assemblyman Silas Coates came forward with the following letters."

She handed David copies of the two letters that were written in 1724.

"These letters by the Lewes assemblyman are the earliest known records we have from the fledgling assembly since their separation from Philadelphia in 1704. Although the first one's intent is not entirely clear, the second mentions a *Penn resolution* in the same year that the Lewes Hundred ceased paying taxes."

"What was the Penn Resolution?"

"I'm not sure, but whatever it was impacted Coates' elected position to the point he had to resign. I'm willing to lay odds that the resolution had something to do with either limiting the Penn family's tax liability or expanding their proprietorship in Lewes."

"What makes you say that?"

"Didn't you say you found a gap in the Lewes tax record between 1723 and 1780?"

"Yes, we did," said David. "Why, is that significant?"

"It's an educated guess, but if the Penns did own that property in Lewes, and this resolution had anything to do with that fifty-seven-year gap in tax revenue, then the resumption of the tax may have coincided with the institution of the Divestment Act of 1779, which forced the Penn family to surrender their unsold properties."

David tried to make sense of this new evidence. "Do these letters prove that my property belonged to the Penn family originally?"

"I'm not sure what these letters have to do with your property particularly, but it's quite clear they discussed a resolution that affected the Lewes Hundred since it disappeared from the tax record about the same time these letters were written."

David thought back on the day they spent in the archives researching information gleaned from the letter fragment. David's attention lighted upon the name of the middle son. "There's a *famous Thomas of historic import* mentioned in one of West's journal entries. It's also the exact phrase used in this letter fragment that I have for you," said David. He retrieved the letter from his suit pocket and handed it to her. She received it with intense interest.

"Where did you get this?"

"I found it in the back of one of West's journals, but there was only this one page."

David relayed the list of clues he, Beth, and Carla were able to come up with. That the author was a man. That through contextual clues and the suggested time frame of 1787, it's plausible the author was the son of the Thomas mentioned in the letter.

After giving the matter some thought, Audra said, "There isn't enough data in this letter for me to come to a definitive answer. However, I know of someone who could give you that answer."

Audra went over to the information desk and called Dr. Giles Radnor on the off chance he might still be in his office. It rang twice before someone answered.

"Radnor."

"Dr. Radnor, it's Audra Bunting."

"Merry Christmas, Miss Bunting, and thank you for your latest summary. I received it in the post the other day."

"Celebrating the holidays by working again, I see."

"You caught me on the way out, but that's okay. What may I do for you?"

"I'm here now with Dr. David Whealy, the owner of the key you're investigating. I wonder if you could make some time to see him. I could give him the copies of the Silas Coates letters I neglected to include with the summary?"

"I'd like that. We can schedule something right after the New Year," said Radnor as he reviewed his schedule. "How about 9:00 a.m. on the third?"

"Sounds good. I'll tell him," Audra said. "Thanks again, and have a safe New Year."

"You do the same."

David wished Audra a happy holiday season and departed the archives as light snow flurries filtered down from the sky.

He started the car before he realized he had forgotten to check his cell phone.

Pulling it out of his coat pocket, he looked to find a message on its face and saw he had two missed calls.

Both were from Carla.

Chapter Thirty – Eight

The phone was ringing on the other end, but there was no answer. David never left his phone more than a few feet away from him at any given time, which could mean only two things—either he's recharging it or he's in an area where his phone has no signal.

Carla's intense stare never left Cobbett's eyes as he tried yet again to reach David on her cell. "It's no use, Carla. He's not answering."

"I don't want you to leave a message. I want to hear you *tell* him!" she roared.

Carla's imposing physical presence was magnified by her looming position over the seated Cobbett. Despite their planned actions, the others were still surprised by Carla standing up for David, the students, and the entire faculty in this matter, all by herself.

Cobbett attempted the call again. As he waited for a response, his eyes roamed the conference table at the other department heads. They appeared to condone what Carla was doing to him.

"I'm sorry, Carla, but there's no answer."

"Fine, you can call later. But we're not done yet." She went back to her seat, retrieved another piece of paper with a short statement written on it, and placed it in front of the dean. "Here. Now open your email and send this to all faculty members with a copy going to the chancellor and all of the board members. I assume you have their email addresses?"

"Of course," said a disgusted Cobbett.

"That's good. Because if you didn't, I happen to have them right here."

Carla watched the dean as he picked up the paper and allowed his eyes to quickly run through the memo. As they did, they got larger, and his state of exasperation was a treat to behold.

"If you think I'm going to send this—"

She cut him off in midsentence, "You had *better* send this or all of us are going to march directly from here to the chancellor's office with *another* letter. And you can be sure you will *not* savor the results. Now, I suggest you get typing."

With that, she folded her arms and waited. The others turned their focused attention from Carla to the dean. None of them looked ready to compromise.

Cornered into a position from which there was no escape, Cobbett labored an exhale indicating his abject surrender.

He swiveled in his chair to access the keyboard. The dean gave them a look of suspicion, but seeing their resolve, he began to type.

> To all music department faculty members:
>
> Due to the tremendous volume of positive responses we received from the general public, we are suspending the remaining concert schedule for the coming year in favor of highlighting the unpublished cataloged works of James Burton West.
>
> This is an opportunity that we simply cannot pass up.
>
> The details will be handled through the Student Faculty Planning Committee, facilitated by Dr. Carla Macklin. Questions regarding implementation will be channeled through her.
>
> William Tipton Cobbett III
> Dean of Music, UC Davis

Once he pressed Send, he turned back toward Carla. "Young lady, you're sadly mistaken if you think this is the end of it."

Matching his level of confidence, she replied, "Like you were mistaken when you thought that no one would call you on your self-absorbed plans?" To seal the deal on their game plan, Carla addressed each of her colleagues in turn.

"Julia?"

Thoroughly enjoying the situation, Julia said, "I contacted resource management and canceled the order for all upcoming concert scores."

"Very good," said Carla. "Henry?"

"I was able to convince Mr. Stoddard, the new president of the planning committee, to contact the rest of the student members to gauge their interest. Before this meeting, he told me that their voice vote in the affirmative was unanimous."

"That's wonderful. Jason?"

The associate professor, still reeling that he was even part of this conference, settled down long enough to relay his portion of the plan. "I've asked several music scoring companies about the possibility of enlisting their help in transcribing parts from the West scores. Because of the recent publicity, three of them have offered to do it below standard university rates."

"Excellent. Antara?"

The little woman with the large alluring eyes said, "New flyers with appropriate advertising are already in the works, and the student paper was given a heads up. By the end of the break, both the student body and the faculty will be made aware of the change."

"Perfect. And Lindsay?"

"Based on the message Dr. Cobbett sent out, I've drafted a press release in the dean's name citing the message approving the change. It's scheduled to hit all the major papers in the morning."

"Outstanding!"

Injecting his impatience, Cobbett said, "Now, if you're quite finished with your witless badinage, I do have other pressing matters to attend to."

Carla regarded her colleagues. They appeared satisfied they had each contributed to the demise of Cobbett's self-centered plans. She was about to tell the dean their business was concluded when a familiar ringtone announced itself. It was the one she reserved for David, the third movement of the Hummel *Trumpet Concerto*.

Smiling at her co-conspirators, she answered it, "David? Yes, I called. Or more precisely, Dr. Cobbett called. Yeah, that's right. He has something to say to you." Carla covered the microphone and said to the dean, "Remember, you're not only apologizing to him, you're also reinstating him." Then she handed him the phone.

The dean openly grimaced. "David?"

"Yes, William. What is it?"

Cobbett's eyes glanced up at Carla. "I may have been hasty in seeking your dismissal."

"What are you trying to say?"

Carla slowly mouthed the word *apologize* to the dean.

"What I'm trying to say...is..." The words wouldn't come because it wasn't natural for him to say them. They were being coerced from him. "I'm...I regret what I said to you."

Carla mouthed the word *apologize* again.

"David, I...apologize."

"I didn't realize that those words spoken in that particular order were ever in your vocabulary, William. I'm shocked," said David in an off-hand manner.

"Will you accept them? Would you consider returning to the university?"

"Have a great Christmas break, William. I'll get back to ya."

The phone went dead. The silence that followed David's noncommittal reply was unsettling. Cobbett did what he was asked, yet there was no definitive response. For the first time, he felt stranded in uncharted territory.

Once thought to be his impregnable fortress of power, the penthouse office of the music building managed to turn into a prison in the space of one thirty-minute meeting. A meeting he called for. An uncertain Cobbett handed a confident Carla Macklin her phone.

Carla looked around the room one last time, as they all nodded in agreement. Drawing her pointed gaze at the dean, she asked, "Questions?" Receiving satisfied looks from the small gathering and only a blank stare from a dejected Cobbett, she added, "I thought not. Well, if there's nothing else, enjoy your two-week break." Projecting her best David Whealy, Carla acknowledged the seated dean with one word on her way out. "William."

Once again seated around the conference table in David's old office, after successfully bluffing their way around the room, it was time for Carla and company to put into practice that which they had dreamed up only hours ago.

As assistant dean, Carla had the dubious honor of facilitating the Student Faculty Planning Committee, but Henry took the lead to contact Preston Stoddard to schedule a meeting as soon as classes began next month.

Julia sent an email to resource management canceling the remaining concert scores.

Jason coordinated with a scoring company from San Francisco to get West's scores transcribed into parts.

Antara worked with the student paper to make the campus aware of the new performance schedule.

And Lindsay reworked Cobbett's message into the promised press release.

All that was mere game plan was now realized and put into place. The only thing left was to see how Cobbett was going to react as Carla's plan was implemented.

Carla had no doubts. The dean wasn't going to react favorably.

Chapter Thirty – Nine

The Smithsonian Institution's library system is a leviathan of individual libraries, each with its specific research discipline or mission. Out of that multitude, Shannon confined herself to the one library that just might hold the answers her mentor was looking for.

The National Museum of American History Library may not be as large a resource as the Library of Congress, but it boasted a curious assortment of source material covering a wide array of cultural and political topics.

Shannon spent the entire morning and most of the afternoon in this library seeking any further evidence to support the notion that James II was the recipient of the last Richthofen box, but her efforts were futile.

Most of the detailed account concerning the ransacking of the Saint-Germain-en-Laye was uncovered using the resources at the Library of Congress. Believing the answer was still there, Shannon methodically investigated her hypothesis by systematically exploring every possible resource the library had to offer, beginning with their online resources, and ending at the Kluge Center. She spent nearly a month combing through the law library alone, but in all instances, she came up short.

Out of ideas, she sent a message to Radnor. *"I've had no luck tracking down details about the missing box from the Saint-Germain-en-Laye. Short of heading off to Paris, do you have any suggestions where I might look next?"* It was only then she realized she hadn't eaten lunch. She left the library's Adams building and headed for a restaurant on Southeast Pennsylvania Avenue to quell her noisy stomach and to wait for a reply from Radnor.

By the time his response came, it was too late to do anything. For the resource in question was the Smithsonian's Research Annex located in Landover, Maryland. Situated on the periphery of Washington's east beltway, the annex was only open until 4:00 p.m. and then only by appointment. It was already a quarter to four.

Radnor's text contained the information she needed to secure an appointment and to locate the facility. He also said the annex was closed during the holidays. Now all she could do was wait. And waiting was not counted among Shannon's favorite activities.

With the dean's staff now on their holiday leave, Cobbett was able to suffer the indignity of his thwarted plans alone. Forced to relive how his mutinous department heads countermanded his wishes, the next two weeks were the longest of his life.

The blueblood lifestyle that came natural to Cobbett was alien to his current circumstances. To endure the shame of what they did to him was torture, and it left him with a feeling even his artificial help couldn't remedy.

During that two-week timeframe, his car was the only one in the music building's parking lot. Living a solitary existence had its benefits, but over the next couple of weeks, it was more a prison. Prevented from implementing his planned strategy, Cobbett was relegated to reading his emails, which had diminished during the holidays.

Not having his staff available was another distracting irritant. There's no one to whom he could readily delegate his pantheon of menial tasks.

On the days when mail was placed in Stella's inbox, he scanned it for any external envelopes that may contain a London return address. But so far, he found nothing.

Sitting on his throne atop Valhalla, William Tipton Cobbett III tried to devise a way out of his current dilemma, but the trap his department heads set for him was airtight.

This is ridiculous, he thought to himself. *There's nothing to do, so why am I here?*

Observing the clock on the wall, he noticed it was time for high tea. Perhaps that's what he required to regain his sense of self. Deciding to call it a day, Cobbett grabbed his felt bowler on the way out of his inner sanctuary.

He already turned the key to the glass door of the outer office when he happened to look in Stella's inbox. The mailroom made one last delivery before the year ended. Seeing the banded correspondence, he went back inside to retrieve it. The dean was so disgusted over recent events he never noticed the odd letter nestled among the others as he grabbed the bundle and left.

Shannon exited US 50 onto the industrial park service road near Washington's east beltway looking for the annex. From its appearance, no one would've guessed such an important building was hidden behind two commercial distribution centers.

The only way to access the annex was to negotiate the narrow fenced-in driveway between the private company buildings to the security checkpoint at the far end. She parked her car near the entrance to the enormous, one-story annex. The facility looked more like a warehouse than a research library, but that perception was challenged once the intern stepped inside.

The annex curator, a miserly-looking old gentleman, met Shannon by the doorway and set her up with a research station and gave her a quick overview of the library and its available resources. She thanked him for his help and set about the task at hand.

A methodical researcher, Shannon focused her efforts gathering as much detailed information as she was able to find before transferring what she discovered onto one of three distinct geographic timelines—French, British, and the lower counties. Operating from the assumption that James II was the recipient of the missing Richthofen box, she narrowed her quest to prove it.

Shannon began her search with the British reference books. When she found a relevant citation, she would log it in her notes, cite the reference, then plot the incident on one of the timelines.

It took her nearly two hours of unrelenting work before she found something that put her on the right track.

After jotting down all the details she needed, Shannon annotated her British timeline accordingly.

Above the year 1723, she placed the names of George I, king of England, and Sir Robert Walpole, first and longest serving British prime minister. She transferred the years 1721 and 1742 onto her timeline to indicate Walpole's tenure as prime minister.

Connecting numerous years between 1688 and 1745, she affixed the label Jacobite uprisings and above the dates 1840 to the present she wrote "Royal Warrants." She annotated the dates 1749 to the present as "Agents of the Crown" before turning her attention to the French line of inquiry.

Again, several hours of diligent work yielded useful information taking up several pages of notes, which she summarized and annotated on her French timeline.

As she did with the British timeline, she began with the year 1723 in the middle and worked her way outward. Above that year, she placed the name Louis XV, age thirteen, king of France. Joining the years 1715 to 1774, she wrote reign of Louis XV. She labeled the years between 1715 and 1723 with the name "Philippe d'Orléans, Regent of France."

Other dates Shannon affixed on her French timeline were 1701, 1789, and 1848. Above them, she wrote the death of James II, the first French Revolution, and the February Revolution respectively. She also delineated the year 1723 three more times: February, August, and October.

Before taking a break, Shannon perused through a rare set of preserved documents discovered in among a collection of Delaware colonial papers. One of them was a bill from a tavern in New Castle dated 1722, that had a listing of names on the reverse with the words *yea* or *nay* written next to them.

The faded ink from which the majority of the names were written made their legibility nearly impossible. However, the name of Silas Coates was a standout.

She wasn't able to determine what the vote was about, but it was enough to expose the early assembly's crudity and cavalier attitude for official documentation.

Shannon happened to glance at her watch. The annex was about to close. Approaching the curator, she asked if it was possible to schedule another day.

The frown on his face said no, but his gentle nod said otherwise.

♪

Chapter Forty

Pulling into one of the few remaining parking spots on the one-way street of Jefferson Drive on the southeast side of the National Mall, David couldn't take his eyes off the Smithsonian's main building. He marveled at the grandeur of the famed red-castled architecture as he walked through its impressive archway entrance. Radnor wanted David to meet him at the *Castle Café* for a spot of tea before they retired to his office.

The smartly dressed former college professor carried with him West's old valise with the unsigned letter fragment, copies of the Silas Coates letters, and all of West's journals and correspondence he had received, in case any of it could prove useful to Radnor. David may not have enough information for the eminent historian to unravel these new conundrums, but at least he was going to find out what Radnor learned about the key.

Finding the Smithsonian scholar already at a small table near one of the tall lattice-filled windows enjoying his cup of green tea, David approached him. "Dr. Radnor?"

"You must be Dr. Whealy. This is indeed a pleasure."

Receiving a heartier handshake than he expected, David responded with like firmness.

"Won't you join me?" said the older man, stretching his arm out toward a chair. "I had the good fortune to attend one of your concerts a few years back, and I enjoyed it tremendously."

"I'm flattered," said David with genuine humility.

"I was treated to a faithful interpretation of the reconstructed *Oboe Concertos* of J.S. Bach, courtesy of your talented orchestra."

David dipped his head in modest acceptance of so florid a compliment. It took a while for David to get accustomed to hearing such well-phrased oratory from a man whose tailor evidently followed the beat of a very different drummer. "If you enjoyed their performance, then I can only accept the credit on their behalf."

"As you wish. I hope my directions didn't send you too far off the beaten track."

"Your instructions were flawless, thank you."

"You know, when I initially provided you with the directions, I found it quite the coincidence that I had to give the same directions to our newest researcher from Delaware. Perhaps you know her."

"Who is it?"

"Miss Beth Grey?"

"Really? She lives across the street from me. She told me she had a new job with the Smithsonian, but she didn't say she would be working with you. I'm sure going to miss her."

"Unfortunately for us, she'll be working from her Delaware home."

Beth had told David of her employment arrangements, but he didn't want to let on that he was already aware. "She's not coming here, then?"

"Alas, she's not. Miss Grey will function as a satellite liaison between us and the historical resources of the three states that make up the Delmarva Peninsula. With the new technologies we've adopted to further our research efforts, she'd be more productive on-location."

"That's understandable."

"Her familiarity with the Delmarva Peninsula shall be a great asset to the Smithsonian. If you don't mind, I'd like to involve her in this business."

"She's been a tremendous help to me so far. Naturally, I'd love to have her along on this."

"Indeed," said Radnor, appearing quite pleased that the Smithsonian's newest researcher was already on the case. "Your key and my research notes are in the office, if you don't mind the claustrophobic nature of its space?"

"No, I don't mind." David wasn't interested in brunch so much as he was eager to learn about the key he entrusted to Audra and Radnor.

The two men quickly moved their meeting to Radnor's office, where Shannon had already left a tea service with two cups and a hot pot of freshly brewed tea.

"Why, that sweet young lady."

"Who?"

"My college intern, Shannon. She's proven herself indispensable for every project I've assigned to her. Of course, I'm going to miss her, too, when she leaves." Radnor's expression went blank as he thought of Anne Connolly. "However, with the welcome news of Miss Grey's preliminary involvement in this business, I'm sure she will do an admirable a job."

"I'm quite sure she'll surprise you."

He squeezed into the small seat next to Radnor's desk. Trying to get as comfortable as he could, David laid the valise on his lap and set his walking stick against the bookcase. The historian did a double take as the sunlight glistening off the metal topper caught his eye. Radnor had never seen such an attractive walking stick before.

Settling into his seat, he offered David a cup of tea. "Before we get into the subject of your key, I understand you found another artifact?"

"I did, yes. It's not the ring Mr. West said he left with the key, but we found this letter fragment in one of his journals." David opened the valise and took out the unsigned letter and handed it to Radnor.

"Hmm, this looks interesting." Radnor examined the partial wax impression before taking up the narrative. He took his time reading the fragment, yet his conclusions ran quick and thorough. Conclusions that Carla, Beth, and David hadn't thought of before.

"Can you make anything of it?"

"To begin with, this was written in December 1787, based on the fact that Pennsylvania ratified the Constitution on the twelfth of December, 1787. The author wasted no time in spreading the *urgent news*. The addressee isn't related to the author since he refers to his father as, *my* father Thomas rather than *our* father. And it's obvious the author had once owned the property at *Lewes-on-the-water*."

"We suspected it was written to one of the early occupants of the property. With Beth's help, we were able to whittle down the list of historic Thomases from a list of probables."

"Is that so? Who did you come up with?"

"We quickly eliminated both Jefferson and Paine. Through a process of elimination, we excluded Pennsylvania delegates, Mifflin and Fitzsimons, the Delaware delegate, McKean, and even the baron Lord De La Warr, Sir Thomas West. None fit the timeline or the clues left behind by this fragment."

"What was the hypothesis you were working under?"

"We concentrated on the renowned Thomases of the period we were familiar with," David replied. "We brainstormed a list of names and researched them. We were forced to eliminate every name we came up with.

"Did you consider any British Thomases?"

"We assumed the Thomas in question was from the side of the revolutionaries."

Radnor smiled before he detailed the flaw in this conjecture. "Reading the unsigned letter, one can see how the American victory in the war and its subsequent adoption of the new constitution, adversely affected the person who penned this letter. As a result, I doubt very much the author was on the side of the revolutionaries."

David was clearly stunned. "Is that so? And how did you determine that?"

"By mentioning that he was in danger of losing his holdings and that the king of England was his only shot at keeping it. This would lead me to believe he sided with the British cause."

"Interesting. So, how do we determine which Thomas he was talking about?"

"Why don't we use your approach?" suggested Radnor. "If we restrict our consideration to known British Thomases of the period, we may just solve this puzzle."

"Great. I don't recall many *American* Thomases of the period, much less British ones."

"I think we can narrow the field down significantly," Radnor said with confidence. "There weren't many famous Thomases on the side of the British whose actions would agree with the tenor and timeline of your letter, so I think we can identify those few."

"Sounds promising. Who?"

"The one that most obviously presents himself would be Thomas Gage."

"I don't remember him," said David, demonstrating his lack of colonial knowledge.

"General Gage came from an aristocratic English family, so he would fit the spirit of the letter. He was known to have fought alongside George Washington during the French and Indian War but remained loyal to the Crown. As Governor of Massachusetts in 1775, Gage ordered British troops to confiscate the weapons cache the rebels obtained from Concord. The result was the first skirmish of the Revolutionary War at Lexington. On the heels of his failures during the Siege of Boston, Gage was ordered to return to England."

"Hmm, now that you mention his name, I don't know why I didn't remember him."

"Then there was Thomas Graves."

"Now I *know* I've never heard of *him*."

Radnor embarked on another informative recitation. "Thomas Graves was the First Baron Graves. He is remembered as the admiral who suffered defeat at the hands of the Comte de Grasse in the Battle of the Chesapeake, which forced the British to surrender at Yorktown. Although he had a son named Thomas, the boy would have been twelve at the time of this letter, which would make him an unlikely candidate.

"Were there any other politically active British Thomases at that time?"

"I think the closest ones to qualify, would have to be either Thomas Pitt or the middle son of William Penn."

"Would that be the man Pittsburgh was named after?"

"No, not him. Pittsburgh was named after Pitt's grandson, William Pitt." Radnor warmed his tea, offered David more, then continued his story. "Thomas Pitt's biography aligns better with your timeline, but his machinations and exploits were more geared toward the Middle East than to the American colonies. His claim to fame, from which his nickname *Diamond* was derived, was the purchase of an uncut gem that eventually became the Regent Diamond and is now part of the French Crown Jewels. He ultimately used the fortune he made off the diamond to purchase land in England. He had no interest in the Delmarva peninsula."

"We can eliminate all of these candidates from what you've said about them," said David, disappointed.

Sitting back in his chair, Radnor reviewed the list of possible candidates in his head. His eyes were staring blankly at David before their spark returned. "Which one of these Thomases had anything to do with your property on the Lewes Hundred?"

"None that I can see."

Once again, a smile played on Radnor's face. "We didn't discuss Thomas Penn, did we?"

"Now that you mention it, no we didn't."

"It's this last Thomas, whose historical position seems best suited to all the facets of your letter thus far."

"If we only had some evidence or confirmation."

"It's possible we may already have that evidence. Thomas Penn succeeded his father, William, as proprietor of Pennsylvania. It's entirely possible he is the prime candidate since his son, John, settled in Philadelphia for a short time and may have had some propertied interests on the Delmarva Peninsula until he left for England."

"Then Thomas Penn is the most credible candidate."

"Perhaps. Alone, this letter fragment doesn't provide us with enough data. Do you have the letters Audra Bunting entrusted to you?"

"Yes, I have them right here," said David as he retrieved both the Silas Coates' letters.

With great interest, Radnor accepted and read them. He examined the content, style of prose, and the flourished colonial handwriting. The initial letter seemed promising.

It was dated the same year James Burton West indicated his family had owned the property at Lewes-on-the-water. However, the only real clues were the date and the district from which the signatory assemblyman hailed—in this case, the Lewes Hundred. The rest of the letter's content was ambiguous at best.

> *Mr. President,*   *February 4th, 1724*
>
> *In the matter presented to this Assembly, Tuesday last, I must dutifully tender my most strenuous objection. The Resolution brought before this Assembly was not in order, as we have no confirmation from the Crown that the document in question was genuine.*
>
> *Silas Coates, Esq.*
> *Assemblyman, the Lewes Hundred*
> *God Save the King*

Rubbing his chin with a nervous index finger, Radnor raised an eyebrow and said, "I must confess that this first document tells us very little. It does, however, pose several intriguing questions, like who was Silas Coates and what document would the king be required to verify?"

"Maybe the other letter might shed some light on the subject resolution discussed in the previous letter."

"Let's see." Radnor took up the second letter.

> *Mr. President,*   *February 18th, 1724*
>
> *By what right does this Assembly appropriate land it does not own so it may cede it over to the proprietor? The recent vote of this Assembly to hand over virtually the entire Hundred by the simple expedient of legislation is the highest form of malfeasance, if not an outright criminal act.*
>
> *Just learning of Governor Sir William Keith's affixed signature on the Penn Resolution, which has now carved the epitaph upon my elected position, I find*

*it necessary to dutifully tender my resignation from
this Assembly.*

Silas Coates, Esq.
Former Assemblyman, the Lewes Hundred
God Save the King

As he finished the letter, Radnor's head nodded as he reread the word *proprietor*. Then he reread the phrase *the Penn Resolution*. He was quite aware of Governor Sir William Keith's proprietorship over Pennsylvania and the lower three counties on the Delaware in 1724, but until today, he never actually witnessed definitive proof of this dual leadership.

"These letters, aside from providing a window into the inner workings of how two colonies shared one governor, also offers direct evidence that the Hundred, which Coates was talking about, was his district. If it wasn't, I'm sure he wouldn't have been so melodramatic about the loss of his *elected position.*"

"Could the Penn, Silas Coates was talking about in the second letter, actually be William Penn's son, Thomas?"

"Second son, actually. It seems plausible, though. The unsigned letter, together with the evidence of the Silas Coates letters, does seem to point to only one Thomas that fits all the parameters."

"Then we've narrowed it down to the right man?"

"Out of all the Thomases we've examined, Thomas Penn would appear to be the only logical choice. We may also hypothesize that the author of this letter was either John or Granville Penn since both brothers would stand to lose much if England lost the war."

Seeing how his guest appeared exhausted by this verbal exercise, Radnor changed the subject. "We dissected that question. Now, how about that key?"

"I was wondering when we were going to get to that. Have you been able to discover anything about it?"

Opening the drawer in front of him, Radnor produced a small box containing David's small treasure and handed it to him. "I believe this is yours."

David offered his gratitude. "You know, with the exception of his estate, his music, and his correspondence, this key is all I have left of him. He made mention of a signet ring, but we never found it."

Radnor sensed David's disappointment. "That key had an interesting history,"

For David's benefit, Radnor went through the entire history of Leopold I commissioning of the fourteen Richthofen boxes. He went into great detail about how they were created and why, who eventually ended up with them, and the fact the last Richthofen box and its key turned up missing.

The Smithsonian scholar discussed how he believed the missing box might have ended up in the possession of King James II, at the Saint-Germain-en-Laye, and that an agent of the Crown may have taken it from its last known location.

Radnor summarized, "Circumstantial evidence would indicate that in 1723, the box came up missing. Then a year later, Thomas Penn managed to gain possession of the Lewes Hundred."

David finally understood how the key and the letters all seemed to tie into the mystery. He also understood the timing of Radnor's smile when Penn's name was suspected of being the target Thomas of the letter fragment. It had to be more than mere coincidence.

When Radnor finished his lengthy explanation, his focus returned to David's walking stick. "That's a stylish gentleman's stick you have there. May I?"

Handing it over to Radnor, he said, "It was in the same house where I inherited the key. I've asked around, but no one can make anything of it. I don't even know if it's genuine or a knock-off."

Radnor took hold of the stick. "What a handsome specimen." Rotating it as he observed its entire length from handle to ferrule, an audible *hmm* could be heard escaping his throat.

As the older man was examining the walking stick, David added, "One of my colleagues suggested the tire tracks might be the hilt of a hidden dagger."

"It's possible, but I don't see where the maker placed the mechanism." All of a sudden, Radnor placed the stick ferrule down on the floor and began twisting it between the palms of his hands, taking great pains to analyze the odd designs etched into the silver rings.

Its silver middle resembled an unusual tire tread. He noted six distinct bars of angled herringbone lines. The top three bars were composed of lines that curved right and made a series of *S*-shaped lines, while the three bottom bars of lines curved left and formed a series of backward *S*-shaped lines. The six bars together made a large V-style tire track pointing left or a complex, oversized *less than* symbol. Not able to make much of this design, Radnor moved his eyes to the smaller bands.

The two smaller silver bands were split by five square blocks, which went around their circumference. Unique to each were intricate designs in relief. At first blush, he didn't recognize them, until he took out his jeweler's monocle to inspect the finely partitioned blocks closer. That's when he noticed something familiar about them.

Because of the cursive nature of the silverwork, he almost missed it. With some surprise, he said, "Unless I miss my guess, these are *hanzi* or Chinese characters."

Comparing the two rings, he noticed that the *hanzi* in four of the five blocks were identical.

半 球 飓 风

Only the fifth *hanzi* was different on each of the smaller rings, but Radnor believed he knew why. He also believed he knew the meaning of the first similar character of each ring.

Radnor pointed at the odd symbols to show David, "You see these two characters?"

"Yeah?" said David as he looked at the distorted, cursive representations of the Chinese script, 北 on the top ring and 南 on the bottom.

"They're the defining characters for each line," he began. Pointing to each *hanzi* as he referred to them, Radnor said, "This one, *bei*, means north, while this one, *nan*, means south."

"When placed before the other *hanzi* I'm familiar with, it reads, *northern half* and *southern half* respectively."

Stymied by three of the characters, the Smithsonian scholar turned to grab a reference book from the shelf behind him. He skimmed the index looking for something, then quickly turned to a page somewhere midway into the book. David watched his roaming eyes as he scanned the page searching for the English definition to the *hanzi* he was looking for.

Trying not to be rude, Radnor explained what he was doing as he was doing it. "The problem here, Dr. Whealy, is that the English language uses only twenty-six letters in its alphabet. The Chinese writing system utilizes over sixty thousand individual *hanzi*, which makes their writing system one of the most sophisticated in the world. Both the Koreans and the Japanese borrowed about two thousand of these *hanzi* and adapted them for their use. But thanks to the ingenious work of King Sejong in the fifteenth century, Koreans now have their own scientifically designed writing system called *hangul*, made up of only twenty-four characters."

He was about to say something else, when he flipped another page. "Bingo! I thought so!"

"You found something?"

"Yes, a huge something." Radnor turned the book around for David's inspection. "Do you see this series of *hanzi*?"

"Yes."

"These characters, 北半球, or *běi bàn qiú*, means 'northern hemisphere.' These characters here, 南半球, or *nán bàn qiú*, are interpreted as 'southern hemisphere.'"

"Okay, so what do we do with that information?"

"That's only the first part of the phrase. Do you see these other two characters here?" asked Radnor, pointing to the characters, 飓 and 风.

"Yeah?"

"The first one I can't identify in this dictionary, but the other one is, *fēng*, and it means wind. Although I have not identified this last character, I'll wager this full string of *hanzi*, 北半球飓风, is *běi bàn qiú jù fēng* or northern hemisphere typhoon, and this bottom string, 南半球飓风, is *nán bàn qiú jù fēng* or southern hemisphere typhoon. But I wonder what the middle ring's design has to do with these markings?"

Again, Radnor scrutinized the tire tracks of the central ring, and that's when he noticed something from one of his intellectual discussions with his weather-minded colleague, Dr. Calvin Selby. Still not sure, a confused look reflected in his face.

"What is it?" David asked

Wordless, Radnor grabbed a piece of scratch paper and recreated the central handle's tire track design. Superimposing a circle over a portion of it, the total image popped out at him, like the globe his colleague once showed him.

"Look at this area, here," Radnor pointed to the circled area of tire tracks on the paper. "This represents the earth, and these six striations represent the wind cells known as the trade winds, the westerlies, and the polar easterlies. Do you follow?"

"I think so."

"That being the case, then this isn't an unusual set of tire tracks, but an ingenious way of describing the workings of the Coriolis effect."

"The what?"

"It's the name of the force that governs the direction of a hurricane's rotation in the different hemispheres."

"Why would someone go through all that trouble to manufacture a stick like this?"

"The last of the great silversmiths working anywhere near Delaware at the time would have been around 1850. However, based on the markings on this stick, I'd place its manufacture well after that date. But whoever created this piece was a gifted silversmith. They also had an affinity for Chinese calligraphy and an abiding love of meteorology."

"Does that mean it's genuine?"

"Oh, it's genuine all right. I dare say it's a one of a kind. Perhaps a special order or a gift from the maker to someone close to them."

"But why would someone create such a stick, and what was the connection to my benefactor?"

"I don't know the correlation. But, if according to the Coriolis effect, hurricanes in the northern hemisphere rotate counterclockwise, then my guess is this upper ring should be able to rotate the same way."

With that, he moved the upper ring counterclockwise. To the surprise of both men, it moved one click and sprung back to its original position. Nothing happened.

"Try the bottom one," suggested David.

Radnor worked the bottom ring. It wouldn't move counterclockwise, but it did move one click clockwise, the usual direction of a southern hemisphere hurricane, before it, too, sprung back to its original position.

Radnor and David shared a mutual gaze of satisfaction, as though both men simultaneously managed to solve the so-called remarkable proof of Pierre de Fermat. Turning the upper silver ring one click counterclockwise at the same time he rotated the lower one a click clockwise, something definitely happened.

The top of the stick popped open about half an inch. Radnor moved the top further to reveal an object that was hidden inside the topper.

It was a gold signet ring with the words *Dum Clavum Teneam* inscribed inside its oval shape.

Chapter Forty – One

The campus of UC Davis was awash with activity following the winter break. Professors were busying themselves putting the finishing touches on their lectures and lesson plans as the students were converging on the campus from every corner of the country.

Carefully making her way past the throng of students haphazardly crossing the streets, Carla rolled her Audi hardtop convertible into the nearest available parking spot adjacent to Mrak Hall. This wasn't the intended destination she planned on this morning, but a last minute detour, per the chancellor's urging. Carla had little choice in the matter.

Anyone so summoned to the chancellor's office understood this was never a good thing. The intention of this meeting was plain to Carla; she was expected to pay the piper for her excoriation of William Tipton Cobbett III.

Her parents had always told her if one wasn't inclined to accept the consequences of their actions, then one shouldn't engage in behavior that may incur them.

The way the entire department had treated the dean was far from professional. Their actions notwithstanding, they all agreed something drastic needed to be done. The faculty of the music department was tired of having to endure the tyranny of the dean, to say nothing of how his management style adversely affected the quality of the university's musical education. But then again, she didn't know the substance of the meeting, so it may not be as bad as she was thinking.

A blast of crisp cool air met Carla's face as she exited the warm compartment of her vehicle. She was about to learn whether her gamble to fix the problems of her department was worth it.

Carla allowed her eyes to scroll up to the heavens and to take a deep breath before she went into Mrak Hall and her appointment with destiny.

David was enjoying his stay in the nation's capital touring its prized museums and iconic landmarks. Being forced to endure yet another day without a word from Radnor about the signet ring left David no choice but to play tourist.

The Smithsonian scholar and his colleagues were working on the latest West discovery, and David was hoping they'd come up with some encouraging news soon.

Meanwhile, he found no end to his amusements in this paradoxical city. Cradle to the American Republic, the city was steeped in rich history but bathed in political intrigue. Imbued with such partisan divisions in recent memory, he thought no sane person would wish to venture forth into that treacherous morass.

Choosing to dress down today, David skipped his trademark suit-de-jour for a more relaxed, off-duty professor look. A light, camelhair over a collarless shirt and slacks completed his look. Thinking about his choices for breakfast, he stuffed his smartphone into his jacket as it came to life.

Answering it without looking at who was calling, he simply said, "Hello?"

"David? Radnor."

"Good morning. You caught me on my way out."

"Oh? Did I catch you at a bad time?"

"I was heading off to breakfast, then the American History Museum, why?"

"How amenable are you to an alternate location? Say, the library near the rotunda of the National Museum of Natural History around eleven?"

"Okay, I'll bite. Is there a particular reason why I should go there instead?"

"Only a hunch, but if you bring that letter fragment with you, I believe I may have unlocked the secret of both it and your ring."

"Absolutely!"

"Of course, I'll need Shannon's report on that mysterious agent and the library's resources to verify it, but if what she told me over the phone is accurate, her report will bear out my hypothesis."

"Now that's worth a change in plans," said David with refreshed excitement.

Preston Stoddard now held Myung-hee's old seat at the head of the conference table in David's former office, some old and new members of the Student Faculty Planning Committee in attendance. Notably absent from this unique gathering was its facilitator, the assistant dean.

Preston Stoddard wasn't a natural leader, but he could always draw on his parents' superb example of Marine Corps leadership. And even though he wasn't military minded, his parents instilled in him that success in any endeavor was a matter of initiative.

Half-conceding the decision to the most senior faculty member there, Preston said, "With your indulgence, Dr. Tanaka, I think we should proceed."

With the meeting already running thirty minutes late, Henry said, "It's your meeting, Mr. Stoddard. Go right ahead. We'll fill Dr. Macklin in on any particulars she missed."

"Thank you. As everyone by now already knows, our remaining concert schedule was scrapped. We have no programs or schedules, other than to perform the music of this James West." His take-charge opening statement was impressive. Myung-hee would've been proud of her successor. Looking around the room, Preston asked, "Does anyone here know who this composer is?"

Softening his expression, Henry looked around at his faculty colleagues. They tendered him a knowing nod before he offered an explanation.

"Most of you students weren't made aware of why Dr. Whealy left for the East Coast so unexpectedly last year. The rumors were he was attending a funeral for a family member. When Dr. Whealy returned, he'd brought back many autograph scores from a composer previously unheard of. He then told us the pieces we were looking at were only the tip of the iceberg. The man's catalog contained over two hundred unpublished works."

At that astounding revelation, the shock of surprise registering on the student members' faces was nearly universal. Even Renatta Johnson who was in on the quintet was silently agape.

Henry continued, "Dr. Whealy asked us to review the music, which was an eclectic assortment of pieces from chamber to full orchestra. Like you, we were stunned. Suffice to say, we have more than enough music to keep us busy for the next year."

Preston finally broke the silent exchange of blank stares following Henry's tale. "Dr. Tanaka, how many of these pieces do you have now, and do they come with any parts?"

"Of the works we have, there are two symphonic poems, two overtures; one for full orchestra and the other for winds only, and several smaller chamber pieces for double reeds, wind quintets, and string quartets. Though no parts accompanied many of the larger works, Professor Cantu is working on that problem right now. How's that project going, Jason?"

Jason grinned. "Galaxy Music Company is working on several pieces for full orchestra along with a few chamber works. And hopefully, with Mr. Forbes' assistance, we'll have a few string quartets to add to the mix."

Clayton injected an affirmative nod to the discussion.

Preston nodded his acceptance.

Remembering something about the piano works, Lindsay added, "If I recall, Dr. Whealy said that all the piano works already came complete with their parts. We shouldn't need to do anything with those pieces, do we?"

Henry answered, "I think Dr. Macklin would be in a better position to answer that. We can ask her when she returns."

"Our only problem would be to decide which ones we want to perform," Lindsay added.

Carefully taking in the discussion, Preston asked, "In that case, is anyone prepared to suggest the content of the upcoming spring concert series?"

The faculty members all seemed to be wearing strange smiles on their faces.

David met up with Radnor and his intern near the tusked bull elephant in the center of the museum's rotunda. Wasting no time, Shannon escorted them to the library, brought out her research, and spread it out over their reserved corner tabletop.

"That's a lot of work," said David.

Glowing with pride, Radnor said, "When my intern here began to relate what she found over the phone, I thought it best she share her results with both of us at the same time."

"I appreciate the consideration."

Radnor extended his hand toward Shannon inviting her to proceed.

Being in the presence of her illustrious mentor was nerve-racking enough, but having someone of David's celebrity with him made Shannon more nervous than usual.

"Okay, using 1723 as a focal point, I found the previous report of an unidentified agent being in possession of a British royal warrant to be unfounded."

"Why is that?" asked David.

"British Crown grants are more textiles oriented than legal. And they didn't reach prominence until the Victorian era, so the timeline doesn't support that claim."

"Very good, Shannon," said Radnor, encouraging the young woman to go on.

"If this mysterious agent represented British authority, then there must be documentation. According to the Kensington Museum, no such authority had been granted for an investigation outside of England at that time. French records were more descriptive of his identity, so I went with them." Shannon referred to the three timelines on the table as she explained her deductions. "I focused my premise on identifying the mysterious agent and finding out what happened to the box he claimed went missing."

Radnor and David leaned over opposite ends of the table to follow along with her explanation.

"King Louis XV ascended the throne at age five, which meant the actual power in France was vested in a regent named Philippe d'Orléans. In February 1723, Louis XV reached the age of thirteen, the age of majority, and the young monarch assumed power from the regent.

"Since it was the young monarch's first genuine year in power, the French Parliament elected to scrutinize his actions that year. His audiences were observed and recorded to see who were granted them and why. It's from these records that I found something quite interesting.

"In August 1723, a man claiming to be an agent of the British prime minister requested permission to access the royal château of Saint-Germain-en-Laye. The reason given, and documented in the French log, was an investigation into a plot concerning the heirs of James II be allowed to commence on the grounds of the château.

"In October 1723, that same agent published his findings with the French monarch in a report that was suppressed or lost until 1848."

"Were you able to find it?" asked David.

"I have it here," she replied, tapping her research file. "It states that the agent found no evidence of Jacobite activity, but that an iron box fitting the description of the last Richthofen box, and known to be among James II's effects when he died in 1701, wasn't found."

"Jacobite activity? What does that mean?" asked David.

Radnor replied, "The Jacobite rebellions stemmed from a desire among their followers to reinstate the Stuart line of British kings descended from James II. Their periodic uprisings were a constant threat to the Hanover line of English kings."

"But what does the term Jacobite have to do with James II?" David asked.

"The name *Iacobus*, or Jacob, is the Latin form of James," explained Radnor.

"Oh," said David absent-mindedly as if the two had shared an inside joke he was not privy to.

Shannon referred to the timeline again. "In fact, backtracking through English history to 1721, the first and longest-serving British prime minister, Sir Robert Walpole, uncovered a plot by the bishop of Rochester, Francis Atterbury, that put the sect on the defensive from that point on. During the first year of Sir Walpole's tenure, he even managed to expose a few sympathizers within the English Parliament.

"The most infamous of which was Lord Bolingbroke, whose Jacobite sympathies forced him to flee to France. His public return to England in 1723 may have given our mysterious agent the ruse he needed to gain access to the Saint-Germain-en-Laye to conduct his clandestine activities."

"Then you identified the prime minister's agent?" asked David.

"No, I hadn't. The written record kept by the regent was illegible and contrary to the French record, England denies ever sending an agent to France in 1723."

"Perhaps, but doesn't this report also leave no doubt as to the identity of the recipient of the last Richthofen box? It was James II, wasn't it?" asked David.

"It looks that way, Dr. Whealy," suggested Shannon. "The only question remaining would be where the last Richthofen box is now?"

Looking at the documentation on the table, David noticed that she never addressed the bottom timeline. Referring to it, David asked, "Then what's this?"

"This represents the General Assembly of the lower counties," said Shannon. "As you can see, I have the date 1722 listed. It happened to coincide with a tavern receipt that contained a list of names on the back."

"What makes this receipt significant?" Davis queried.

Radnor responded, "This is further evidence that Silas Coates was part of that assembly. Although most names are illegible, his name stands out. And Silas Coates was the assemblyman from the Lewes Hundred who resigned in protest in 1724 with the passage of the Penn Resolution. Remember those letters we discussed the other day?"

David silently acknowledged.

Radnor continued, "It was this circumstantial evidence that would seem to implicate our friend Thomas Penn as the only logical person who fits the age, timeframe, and circumstances of your unsigned letter and those of the former assemblyman, Silas Coates. It's also logical to assume that Thomas Penn was the agent who went to France."

"How do you figure that?" asked David.

"Consider this," Radnor suggested, "Isn't it suspicious that between the 1701 inventory of James II's effects and this agent's declaration of the box's disappearance, no one had bothered to question the inventory's validity until he showed up? And since this agent's curious appearance, no one had been able to find the box?"

David could only return a blank stare.

Radnor tried to clarify his deductions from the beginning. "For the entire three years of James II's reign between 1685 and 1688, William Penn tried, however unsuccessfully, to obtain uncontested possession of the lower counties through a Crown grant, but according to all accounts that grant never existed."

"I still don't understand. What's the connection between William Penn's land troubles and the missing box?" asked David.

"Think about it," said Radnor. "It could only be a fantastic coincidence that in October 1723, a box belonging to James II was declared missing and less than four months later, a resolution in Penn's name was passed and signed by the proprietary governor and in that same year the Lewes Hundred was relieved of all tax liability until the Divestment Act of 1779."

At the mention of the divestment act, the lightbulb finally came on as David remembered this phrase from the letter fragment—*my current status can only serve to work against me in achieving any relief from my losses...*

"Ms. Bunting alluded to that when we were discussing the gap in the Lewes tax records. She said the Penn family was required to surrender all their unsold property to the states," said David.

"That's essentially correct," said Radnor.

"So something important must have been in that box. Something that holds the answer to why Penn was able to obtain the Lewes Hundred so quickly wouldn't it?"

"Possibly," said Radnor rubbing his chin. "Be that as it may, I think we're well on our way to corroborating my hypothesis."

"That being?"

"The one you dropped into my lap. That a descendant of William Penn did, in fact, own the Lewes Hundred," suggested Radnor. "Whether or not my hypothesis is correct may well depend on the letter fragment you have in your possession. Did you bring it with you?"

David retrieved the fragment from his coat pocket and handed it to Radnor.

Drawing his attention to the wax impression first, the older man picked up the reference book Shannon had previously reserved for them. The book was an encyclopedia with enlarged photos of family crests. Radnor flipped through to the index, found the page number, and turned to a photo of an identical representation of David's ring.

"If you look here, you will notice the single bar with three circles inside with the banner under a shield with the phrase, *Dum Clavum Teneam*, Latin for *While I hold the helm*. This was the well-used phrase of the Penn family since William's time. Notice how an oval shape encircles the entire crest."

While David was examining the photo, Radnor pulled out a small plastic bag with a clump of sculptor's clay. Radnor's eyes registered concentration as he laid the clay out on the table. Reaching for David's ring, he asked, "May I?"

David handed over the ring with a skeptical look on his face. At least he was skeptical until Radnor stamped the ring into the clay then removed it to reveal a familiar design.

"Now, compare this clay impression with that of the wax one on the letter," suggested Radnor.

David's eyes grew wide as he aligned the two impressions. The two were an exact match. Moving the ring over the wax impression on the letter, he noticed it fit like a glove.

Radnor passed his jeweler's monocle over to David so he could examine the clay impression.

"Take a look at the words in the banner," instructed Radnor. "See how the font and spacing compare to your letter's wax impression?"

"They're the same," said David. His thoughts drifted to the journals West left behind. He remembered that the ring was *handed down from the very first property owner, some famous Thomas of historic import.*

"David? What is it?" asked Radnor.

He tapped his finger over the fragment and said, "Read it."

Radnor reread the page with the relish of Champollion deciphering the hieroglyphs.

As Radnor took in the old fragment's secrets, David was lost in a whirlwind of recollections. From Jim's journal entries to the conversations he'd had with both Beth and Carla, David glimpsed snippets from these mental sources.

Among those momentary shards of information that flickered through his mind was the fact West's estate was *in the family since 1724.* That Jim's journal pointedly stated that the "*letter fragment… was from the son of a renowned Thomas from Delaware history.*"

The content of the fragment that hinted at a solution for David was, "*This action places me in considerable danger of losing nearly all my holdings despite my father Thomas's historic import and influence in the lower counties.*"

What could its author be talking about other than the property of Lewes-on-the-water? He even said as much in the passage…"*knowing that the property of Lewes-on-the-water is safely in your hands…is entirely satisfactory to me…They shall have no claim against…your property.*"

The puzzle was coming together nicely, but David was still unable to rectify all the circumstantial evidence they had uncovered with the odd statement even James Burton West had trouble with "*In my Solitude, the secret shall remain forever.*"

What the hell did that mean?

The look of satisfaction in Radnor's upturned head woke David from his short reverie. And the older man's summary solidified their mutual train of thought.

"If this ring did belong to the Penn family and it sealed this letter, then according to this fragment, they must have owned the Lewes property at one time."

"Okay, if that's true, then who wrote this letter?"

"If I may draw your attention to this phrase, you'll find your answer," a sanguine Radnor said.

David craned his neck to read the sentence the older man had his finger on "*In my Solitude, the secret shall remain forever.*"

"Neither my friend Carla nor I could make heads or tails of that particular phrase. Even Miss Grey said it could've been the result of the lack of standardized spelling in colonial correspondence."

"Not when you consider the remaining content, it's not," said Radnor confidently.

Shannon's expression revealed no clue as to what Radnor was talking about.

Taking hold of the letter, David reread the portion of the fragment Radnor alluded to. In doing so, his review of that phrase only served to confuse him "*In my Solitude, the secret shall remain forever...the strip of property off the Schuylkill.*"

David glanced at Shannon to see if she knew the solution. She just shrugged her shoulders.

"Don't you see? The phrase *In my Solitude* isn't misspelled," an excited Radnor clarified. "It's capitalized for a reason."

"You mean it stands for something?" queried David.

"It most certainly does. Of the two sons of Thomas Penn, this new evidence eliminates Granville as our suspect author and makes his older brother, John, our prime candidate!"

Passing the letter and ring over to its rightful owner, an unmistakable air of satisfaction radiated from Radnor. He folded his arms as if placing a final punctuation on his feeling of contentment. "Dr. Whealy, I also believe we may well have located the box that goes along with your key."

Shannon and David looked at each. "Do you think so?" David asked Radnor.

"To confirm it, we'll need to go on another field trip."

"Figures," said David with a look of skepticism.

"Are you two up for a short trip in the morning?" asked Radnor.

"I can't, Dr. Radnor," said a disappointed Shannon McClintock, "I have class tomorrow."

Radnor could only return a scowl toward his resourceful intern. "What about you, David? Are you game?"

"Where to this time?"

"How does the Philadelphia Zoo grab you?"

"Where?"

The committee meeting was breaking up when Carla blustered into the office like a woman on a mission. "Sorry for the interruption, folks, but I had an unscheduled meeting with the chancellor."

"That's fine," said Lindsay. "We were wrapping up anyway." Seeing that Carla was in some form of distress, she asked, "Is everything all right?"

"After a fashion," Carla said cryptically. "How did the meeting go?"

Appearing more optimistic now that the committee officially blessed what they did with Cobbett, Lindsay said, "It went better than expected. The game plan is officially in the works."

"I appreciate that, Lindsay. That's a load off my mind," said a relieved Carla. Then she addressed Henry. "If you have a moment, I want to have a word with you."

"Sure," said Henry. He stayed back as everyone else filed out of the office. "What's up?"

"Henry, if you would do me a huge favor and take on this committee for me as its lead facilitator I'd appreciate it."

"Isn't that traditionally the job of the assistant dean?"

"That's right, it is. Because you are now the assistant dean. Congratulations."

Henry was flabbergasted. "Don't think me ungrateful, but why? What happened?"

"The first answer is because I need someone to fill in temporarily until I can resolve a personal matter. Besides, you've earned it. As for the second, I will be exploring new career options. As the resident of the office upstairs."

Henry and Carla came out of David's old office to break the news to Peggy who was finally told what was going on.

The bewildered administrative assistant was struck speechless for a second or two. "That job didn't last long. Does this mean you move out today?"

"Before I go anywhere Peggy, I'll be taking a sabbatical courtesy of the chancellor," Carla said with determination.

"Why? What's going on?"

"I'm going to Delaware. I'm going to see what I can do about getting that exercise ball either back on the desk in the next room… or better yet, into Cobbett's old cave of an office."

♪

Chapter Forty – Two

Carla's red-eye flight landed in Baltimore shortly after eleven in the morning. Using David's directions, she found herself pulling onto Frontage road in under two hours.

She considered calling, but under the circumstances, she preferred to surprise him. With the key to West's house still hanging from her keychain, she would make herself at home in the event he wasn't there.

Cobbett's lackluster apology and insincere request to resume his duties at the university left a bad taste in David's mouth, and Carla knew it. David was in a much better position now, and she knew that, too. Kindly authorized by the chancellor, this trip not only gave her a chance to convince him to return to the university but also offered her a renewed opportunity to launch into a deeper, more rewarding relationship with her long-time colleague and weekly dinner companion.

Then there was Beth Grey, the amorous adversary for David's affections. If Carla was to take her challenge directly to the source, she needed to do it in person.

At their last encounter, Carla found the chink in Beth's armor—a secret so horrendous, she couldn't even bring herself to tell David. Beth gave the game away the last time they met and this time, Carla was determined to pry that secret from her.

If David wanted this woman, she loved him enough not to stand in the way of that. But Beth Grey wasn't going to win without a fight. Before Carla would allow this stranger to steal David, she was going to make sure her dear friend knew who it was he planned on getting involved with.

Seeing no vehicle in the driveway, she allowed herself to relax. The plan was unfolding as Carla intended. She had to work out how she was going to deal with his refusal to come back now that Cobbett was no longer an issue. Even if he'd only accept a position as professor emeritus, at least he would be there in California and not a continent away from her.

Beethoven's familiar anthem echoed through the house as Carla finished her shower. She threw on a sleeveless terry wrap and answered the door. It was her erstwhile antagonist. No time like the present to determine if that designation was destined to be permanent or not.

"I was about to get dinner ready," said Carla in a disinterested tone, "come on in."

Beth complied, not sure how to take Carla's appearance or cold demeanor.

"Give me a minute. I just got out of the shower." She headed for the master bedroom to change, leaving Beth alone in the great room, a waning blaze in the fireplace on its last log. Calling through the closed door, Carla asked, "Have you eaten yet?"

Beth's terse answer was swift. "Yes!" she called back.

Beth looked around the room, taking a closer look at the pencil sketches of her friend, Jim. She stared at one of them, a grayscale representation of the new Cape Henlopen lighthouse. She couldn't help but be impressed with the accuracy of his unerring hand. There it was, off into the distance, in the upper central portion of the framed sketching that caught Beth's eye. In the foreground was a weathered picket fence surrounding a carpet of sand that stretched out toward the tide pooled beach.

Beyond the barrier between sand and sea, on a man-made stone-reinforced shoal, it stood. An uneven tuft of spare, leafless brush underscored the central object of the sketching—the short, stubby sentinel that replaced its taller, leaner, eight-sided predecessor.

Originally located on Cape Henlopen's Great Dune outcropping, the old lighthouse, which stood for over 160 years, became a casualty of time, erosion, and finally a storm in 1926. No longer capable of sustaining the ravages of wind and wave, she ultimately succumbed to the will of the sea and pitched into its welcoming arms.

West's homage to the older lighthouse was displayed in the little sketching he had made and placed next to the larger new one.

Beth moved on to another sketching a few feet away. This one was a montage that captured West's years in the Air Force. There were twenty-three scenes that made up the overall design, one for each year of his active duty service. Almost imperceptibly, he'd overlaid the original Hap Arnold Star and Wing over the entire work as a way of knitting together all the scenes.

Centered inside the circle of the star was the portrait of a pleasant-looking young man. It wasn't a self-portrait or anyone from West's family. This person must have been important to Jim since his image held a prominent location in the sketching.

He was wearing a dark blue service jacket with circled US insignia on the lapels and a black-billed, dark blue service cap with a circled eagle on it. He also wore one of those easy smiles that made you want to walk right up to him and strike up a conversation. And that's when Beth noticed something strange. Out of every pencil sketch that decorated the walls, this image was the only one that Jim had depicted in color. Not even Jim's family was so honored.

The proverbial bucket of cold water then hit her in the face. This must have been Ernie Ortega, Jim's best friend. The man he couldn't save in the jungles of Cambodia. That was all it took for her emotions to well up to the surface again.

From her lower left, a voice said, "Odd, isn't it?"

With cat-like stealth, Carla had made her way into the room, knelt down in front of the fireplace and began to stoke the fire with another log.

Startled at first by the unexpected pronouncement, Beth asked, "What's odd?"

"That you're the third person to be so drawn to this particular picture. David and I did the same thing. Strange, since it doesn't hold a central place in the room, yet out of all his works, this young man is the only subject West rendered in color."

The story of how Jim's childhood friend met his horrible end quickly flooded back into her memory. "It's Ernie, isn't it?"

"Bravo," said Carla in an off-hand manner. After tending the fire to bring up the temperature in the chilly room, Carla moved into the kitchen to work on dinner.

Beth looked askance at her host as if the younger woman was being condescending or facetious. Perhaps she was.

"To what do I owe the pleasure of your company this evening?" Carla asked, taking chef's knife in hand to trim the crust off a loaf of freshly baked sourdough bread.

"Seeing a car in the driveway, I naturally thought David made his way back from Washington." Not bothering to look in Carla's direction, she moved on to the next pencil sketch on the wall as she responded with cutting ease. "I didn't expect to find you."

There was an uncomfortable silence as Carla worked feverishly in the kitchen. She retrieved a package of smoked bacon, a jar of mayo, and a plum tomato from the fridge. Carla began to cook the bacon and toast the bread. Her skillful chopping made short work of the tomato and head of lettuce.

Beth looked Carla's way as the smell of smoked bacon made its way to Beth's nose. "I realize California is three hours behind us but isn't it a little late for breakfast?"

"I'm not making breakfast. They're BLT club sandwiches on toast. Would you like one?"

"Maybe," was her short answer, but she was unable to resist the bacon's smoky aroma and yielded to her salivating taste buds.

Observing that the fireplace's warm blaze wasn't enough to take the chill out of her guest's bones, Carla offered some liquid heat. "How 'bout some hot chocolate to warm you up?"

"Hot chocolate sounds great, thanks."

"You got it."

"Do all Californians usually prefer breakfast for dinner?"

"We tend to consume what our appetites pine for," Carla shot back.

Not sure how to take that one, she just ignored the intimation.

Another of her mom's sayings began to play in her head: *Carla, don't begin a testy conversation with a disagreeable person without feeding them first. It's the great equalizer.*

Carla took up the chief's knife one last time to quarter the two sandwiches she made, plated them, and set them on their respective trays before she poured the cups of hot chocolate.

"Soup's up." Giving her guest the honored place at the table, Carla took up the corner seat from her.

"You've got to be kidding," said Beth as she noticed an added bonus on the tray. "You whipped up miso soup with double-decker BLT club sandwiches and hot cocoa that fast?"

"I've always been taught that tense conversation is made less stressful with palatable food."

The advice must have been sound. Beth smiled for the first time since coming into the house.

"I have to say, I do like my sandwiches that way. Who taught you how to cut off the crust like that?"

"The same person. My mom's culinary admonitions are the main reason why David and I first got to know each other."

Now that was a story Beth simply had to hear. She grabbed a sandwich, taking a nibble from it first, then giving the younger storyteller her full attention.

"I had just joined the staff at Davis as an associate professor. I was teaching a class on music theory at the time, discussing modal structure. Nearly all of my students grasped the concept. That is, all but one rather troubled student.

"I worked with him for well over a month, but no matter what I tried or how I approached him, he just couldn't seem to grasp the material. I was sure he would fail the semester. One of the other associate professors suggested I seek out David's advice.

"I must admit, at the time, I didn't think much of the idea. I found David to be standoffish and rigid. Anytime I would see him in the faculty lounge, he kept to himself. He rarely engaged in conversation with junior professors, much less seasoned ones. I figured him for a loner. But once I approached him, he was engaging and a patient listener."

"I thought that, too," Beth injected.

Carla let out a discernible *hmm*. "Believe it or not, it was his suggestion that we have dinner to discuss it. It was a Thursday night."

"Oh," said Beth as recognition of that auspicious day came into focus.

"As you probably figured out by now, we managed to resolve my student's issue, but we kept up our Thursday evening ritual. And we've shared many Thursday evenings since."

Carla allowed the corner of her mouth to twist into a smirk. "The problem with my student may have been over, but through the fullness of time, our conversations grew more generalized. Mainly discussing the music department, the pieces we were rehearsing, how each of our careers got started, etcetera.

"Then we began to move our discussions into more personal topics. Before long, we were discussing our likes, dislikes, and eventually our former personal relationships."

Beth had been waiting for this one.

"One evening we got into a terrible fight. It started off like any other Thursday, but it soon devolved into a contest to see who could raise the bar of despicable behavior the highest.

"My logic that day was so short-circuited with anger, I must admit the topic escapes me even now. But it was one of the few times David won the argument." As she thought about what she just said, Carla looked at Beth. "And if you repeat that to him, I'll deny it! As far as I'm concerned, he lost, okay?"

Beth's walls of self-protection were crumbling right before Carla's eyes. Beth didn't know how this young woman managed to do it, but she did. No one had invested the time to expose themselves to her in such a profound way. Beth would soon find out that Carla's admission came with a price.

"So, knowing David as I do, I think it's safe to say I can judge his moods better than anyone."

"You don't have to convince me of your deep friendship, Carla. I can see it in his eyes when he looks at you. And I believe you're right."

"About what?"

"Your mom's fondness for food as a device to engage a conversation, but I would add one more thing."

"That being?"

"The individuals in the contest must be predisposed to address their views honestly." She managed to say it before she thought about the content of her words, but it was too late. Carla picked up on it immediately.

"Then that would mean you're prepared to do so as well, right?"

"I suppose," responded Beth in a quieter voice.

"So why did you come here?"

"I received a call from Dr. Radnor a bit ago, requesting that I meet him and David at the Philadelphia Zoo tomorrow morning. Naturally, I assumed the car in the driveway was David's, like I said earlier. I was curious as to what he found out during his visit to Washington."

"Then I take it Radnor was less than forthcoming with any details?"

"I don't know. I only met him once. Briefly."

"That's interesting," said Carla taking her golden opportunity, "but that's not what I meant."

Beth stared at her cup of hot chocolate. "I'm not sure what you mean."

Seeing her opening, Carla played her last card in a calm but determined manner and hit pay dirt. "You told us that before you came *here* to Delaware, you applied for a position as a historian with some government agency website, and nothing ever came of it."

"Yes."

"What you failed to point out was that you hadn't applied for a federal position but directly to the State of Delaware. This to me defies explanation, unless there was a specific reason for you to come here. A reason you've kept secret all this time. Why *did* you come to Delaware? It's not the reason you gave David. Is it?"

She couldn't put it off any longer.

Reasoning that Carla had no ulterior motive other than to look out for her dear friend, she finally surrendered the secret that kept her at arm's length from every relationship she ever made in her life.

"No, it's not," she said, her thoughts drifting. Beth couldn't take her eyes off the steam rising from her cup. Her mounting defenses caused her to surround the cup with her hands.

Noting the other woman's utter vulnerability, Carla reached out and placed her hand on Beth's wrist and gave it a gentle squeeze in a show of compassion.

Beth rubbed the wetness from her cheek before she began. "About sixteen years ago, during a routine physical examination, I was told my blood type was B negative. Not exactly a shocking revelation in and of itself, but I'd always thought my blood type to be A since my parents were both blood type A. Medically speaking if I was blood type B, then they couldn't possibly be my biological parents."

Carla's intuitive nature picked up on the ramifications of Beth's revelation, but she allowed her emotional visitor to continue.

"When I confronted them with this information, my mother broke down and finally told me the truth. That she and my father had adopted me soon after I was born. At the time, the agency didn't tell my parents where I came from.

"On my first birthday, they received an unsigned letter from my biological father. It was this letter that my mother let me read when I confronted them with what I knew. That essentially made me who I am today—a cautious and less than trusting person."

"What did the letter say?" Carla asked with genuine concern.

"It stated that my biological parents were young, married professionals. My biological mother's pregnancy was perfect. The attending physician told her that there was never any danger of carrying me to term.

"My biological father was ecstatic, but my biological mother was not. She was only six weeks into the pregnancy when she found out, far too soon to even determine the sex of her child, but that didn't matter to her. She wanted nothing to do with having me.

"My real father managed to convince his wife that there were many couples out there who badly wanted to have what she was willing to throw away—a child of their own. A child to love and to carry on their family line."

Beth had to steel herself against the pain of telling Carla the hurt-filled truth. "My real father said that his wife 'begrudgingly agreed' to see the pregnancy to fruition. She refused to even look at me after I was born."

All Carla could do was listen. When Beth did look up at her, she saw written in Carla's eyes a delicate empathy that touched her soul.

Beth smiled. "It's one thing when the most precious people in your universe, the people you've always known as mother and father, lie to you your whole life. But it's quite another to learn that your biological mother wanted nothing to do with you. The only clue to the letter's origin was its postmark: Millsboro, Delaware."

Understanding enveloped Carla as she took in that last piece of the puzzle. "Beth, I'm sorry. This was the burden you kept locked away in your heart all this time?"

Words failed her at that moment. She could only nod.

"Why didn't you tell David the truth?"

"Once I knew the truth, I was afraid anyone who found out would think less of me."

"If you want a relationship with someone to have a chance at succeeding, don't you think you should build that relationship on trust?"

"I realize that now," Beth began. "It's probably why my first marriage would've failed had my first husband not have died and why my second marriage failed. It's also why I can't see myself ending up with David."

The logic of that last reason escaped Carla. "Why would David not want a relationship with someone of your charming personality?"

"You're sweet, Carla, thank you for that," said the teary-eyed woman. "No, I couldn't succeed with David, because of one important element that is completely lacking."

Carla shook her head in the common expression that said, *Well?*

"Chemistry. You and David have it. Unfortunately, David and I don't."

"Oh," said Carla flatly. Then Carla regaled her visitor with the events of the evening at *Gelmetti's* and what took place between her and David.

"What is it with guys today, Carla? Are they that blockheaded they can't see when someone is interested in them? I understand now why Jim wasn't interested. He was too wrapped up in his own grief to see another woman in the place of his beloved Isabella."

Carla added to Beth's thought. "And David was too wrapped up in his profession to see any woman as anything other than a colleague."

Beth and Carla looked at each other and said at the same time, "Men!"

Sharing a giggle at David and Jim's expense, the two women reached for each other's hands.

With the life-long barrier Beth erected against healthy relationships now destroyed, she wanted to build on this new foundation. "Hey, I have a great idea."

"What?"

"Radnor wants me to meet him and David at the Philadelphia zoo in the morning. Why don't you come with me? Then the four of us could track down the clues they were working on at the Smithsonian. What do you say?"

Carla smiled broadly and nodded.

Chapter Forty – Three

Morning rush hour along Philadelphia's I-95 corridor was expected, but still aggravating. Beth's Jeep was crawling at a snail's pace until they made it past the airport and onto industrial drive. Once there, the flow of traffic moved smoothly through South 26th Street, onto I-76, and finally to the zoo. Making their way up the west side of the Schuylkill River, they traversed the congested arteries of the City of Brotherly Love, its recognizable skyline arching away from their vantage point until it disappeared altogether.

Admiring the river's spillway to their right and the quaint line of brightly colored colonial homes on the opposite shoreline, Beth nearly missed the exit for Girard Avenue. Riding shotgun, an alert Carla quickly noticed the sign, giving Beth enough time to negotiate the move to the off-ramp.

"What did you say the name of that parking area was?" asked Carla.

"It's the Tiger parking lot on 34th Street near the north entrance."

The lot was on the other side of the exit's acute, right-angled merge onto 34th Street, which prevented them from making a legal left turn. The zoo's Channel 6 balloon loomed large across the street informing the women they were at their destination. To get to the right parking lot, she could either drive north a block or two then turn around or...

Carla wasn't able to caution her in time. Beth made her decision, then her turn.

Judging the traffic to be light enough, Beth glanced in both directions before initiating the illegal maneuver. After receiving a less than complimentary scowl from Carla, she drove the extra tenth of a mile to the Tiger parking lot.

"Ever considered a career as a stunt driver?"

Beth raised her eyebrows apologetically as she turned the Jeep into the parking area.

Noticing that Radnor and David hadn't arrived yet, Carla asked, "Did you call Radnor to confirm when he would be here?"

"He said about nine."

"It's five after already. No doubt, David is following him in his vehicle."

"That was the plan. Are you sure you don't want him to know you're here?"

"Yeah, I think so. There's an issue I have to discuss with him that he's unaware of."

"Hmm, care to share?"

In the spirit of their newfound friendship, Carla told her. "University politics. The chancellor said that our former dean, Dr. Cobbett, accepted a position as the principal director of the London Symphony Orchestra. He wasted no time in settling his affairs. He left for his new post during the holiday break, and now we have a vacancy I was hoping to discuss with David."

"What does that mean for him?"

"The chancellor has graciously held out the seat for David. If he'll choose to sit in it. Now that the former dean is gone, David would have free reign to popularize Jim's music."

"What an honor. Do you think he'll accept?"

"I don't know," said Carla, overwhelmed with the feeling of treading new ground. "I'm hoping he understands the gravity of this offer, which is why I'm here in person."

Carla and Beth got out of the vehicle to survey their new surroundings. East of them was the street, the interstate, and then the Schuylkill River. To the west of them, perched on the crest of the knoll beyond the parking lot fence was an old, two-story white square building that looked as though it belonged anywhere but a zoo.

Carla was about to inquire what it was when Beth's cell began to vibrate.

"Sorry," said Beth as she retrieved her phone, "force of habit." Radnor's name was displayed on the screen as she looked at its face. "Hello?"

"Miss Grey, it's Radnor," he said with a hint of agitation. "We must have caught the tail end of the morning commute. We'll get there as soon as we can."

"Where are you now?"

"We just left the 495 and crossed into Pennsylvania. The GPS says we should be there in about twenty-five minutes."

"We're here at the Tiger lot now."

With mischief in his voice, Radnor said, "You are, huh? If you take a look past the fence at the top of the hill, you should see a small building between the trees."

"Uh-huh," she acknowledged.

"That's our destination. Proceed on in, and we'll meet you in front of that building in about thirty minutes. The project coordinator, Martina Neville, is expecting us. Let her know we're running a little late."

Beth agreed and hung up. The two women took the short stroll to the zoo's entrance. Beth surveyed the cartoon-style map of the zoo to locate the building Radnor alluded to. The identifiable block shape in the northeast section of the map was their destination, located just south of the Channel 6 balloon. It was a short walk, so she never looked at the map's legend to identify the building.

Walking by a paddock of okapi, a strange amalgamation of zebra, antelope, and giraffe, the two women were surprised by all the peacocks that openly wandered the pathways alongside their human guests. Making their way past the okapi, Beth and Carla arrived in front of the white block building across from the Small Mammal House.

There it stood, silent among the hedge of trees, a long forgotten fossil marking the passage of time. An integral part of the nation's oldest zoo, the building appeared quite out of place. From a distance, it didn't appear to be anything special. The unusual architecture, white paint, cube design, and location distinguished it from the other buildings and paddocks.

The women circled the immediate grounds, pointing their fingers, offering each other their limited evaluation of what they were looking at. The southwest entrance resembled a colonial residence. It had a single gable on its roof that was situated between two red brick chimneys. Pairs of windows monopolized the second floor, with the exception of a third directly over the main entrance. Windows also skirted the first floor. Between the columned entry and the middle second-floor window was a brass oval relief that was staining the paint below it. Carla thought it might be a family crest, but Beth suspected it was a marker for the Fireman's Association of Philadelphia from the mid-1800s. Regardless, the design was too small, and too far away to make out. Perhaps the woman waiting at the front door could be of some assistance.

Puzzled as to why two women were taking such incredible interest in the building when she was expecting two men and a woman, Miss Martina Neville, approached Beth and Carla.

"Would one of you happen to be Beth Grey?" asked the professionally dressed woman.

"I am," answered Beth. "Dr. Radnor got held up in traffic, but he'll be here. You must be Miss Neville?"

"I am. Dr. Radnor asked me to be your guide today."

While Beth and Martina were getting acquainted, Carla's eyes came to rest on the angled information sign for the building.

It was the last building known to exist that once belonged to the Penn family.

A structure built to John Penn's unique specifications that became part of the fifteen-acre property he purchased in 1783.

It was the house that caused John Penn to board a ship bound for England in 1788 in a luckless bid to get the king to intercede on his behalf, not knowing he would never return to America.

It was the single-person home off the Schuylkill River on the property discussed in that letter to the undisclosed William.

An enigmatic building with a lonely sounding name.

It was called the Solitude.

The three women were finishing up their tour of the second floor when they spied Radnor and David approaching the angled marker for the Solitude. Carla could see the look of utter surprise on David's face as he read the sign that she'd read moments earlier.

The ladies descended the stairs from the second floor so Neville could open the door and invite her male guests inside.

With his checked flannel shirt, khaki dress slacks, and deck shoes, Radnor's attire was a distinct trademark. Though clean-shaven, his long disheveled blond locks gave the impression he was given to erratic behavior. The primly dressed gentleman with the stylish walking stick next to him projected something quite the opposite, yet both men were top-flight experts in their respective fields of endeavor.

"Dr. Radnor, I presume," said Neville with an outstretched hand. "We are pleased to welcome you to the Solitude. I'm Martina Neville." Aiming her practiced salutation skills toward the stylish taller man, she added, "And you must be Dr. David Whealy. It's indeed a pleasure."

"And I, you, Miss Neville," said David as he addressed the attractive, thirty-something young woman. "Thank you for your patience. We—"

He expected to see two women, Beth and Miss Neville. He wasn't expecting a third, but there she was. He nearly lost his professional deportment as he turned a bright shade of pink at the sight of the recognizable figure behind the other two. It was Carla.

Staring at Carla, he finished his last thought. "We're sorry we didn't plan for such heavy commuter traffic or we'd have been here sooner."

"No need to worry. Perhaps we can move into the dining room so we can get comfortable," Neville suggested.

As the other three cut across David, he leaned over to whisper in Carla's ear. "I assume you're going to tell me why you're here?"

A mischievous air colored her deflective response. "San Francisco ran out of chocolate?"

With an expression edging ever closer to that look, David said, "We'll take this up later."

Carla simply nodded. That wasn't the reaction he was expecting from her, but it would have to do until they could resolve the business ahead of them.

The young project coordinator led the entourage beyond the dark green padded door and into the next room. They sat down at the dining table with the lattice-covered secretary behind the ladies and the fireplace behind the men.

Taking her place at the head of the table, Neville presented her spiel on the Solitude House and its builder John Penn. The entertaining meter of her voice reminded Carla of Myung-hee's informational delivery during the Faculty Solo Showdown.

Neville cheerfully engaged her briefing. "When John Penn completed his grand tour of Europe after graduating from Eaton in 1782, he came to Philadelphia to find the stormy political climate against his family exceedingly uncomfortable. Wishing to keep his detractors at a fair distance, he purchased this property away from the political tumult of Philadelphia in 1783 and subsequently built this house. Knowing of the Duke of Württemberg's home in Stuttgart and the apt name he gave his country estate, *La Solitude*, Penn assumed the name for his new home off the Schuylkill. For five years, John Penn lived in this house in relative peace and tranquility, using the time to write his poetry. For reasons known only to Penn, he left America in 1788 never to return.

"Some say he was encouraged to do so through a stipend granted him by the British Parliament as compensation for his American losses. Some say that after Pennsylvania became the next state to ratify the Constitution, he was forced to flee his home and the country."

"Which do you believe happened?" asked David.

"I don't know," responded Neville. "We do know that John Penn spent the balance of his years at his family's estate in England and built a new home for himself called Stoke Park.

"He championed the institution of marriage despite never having been married himself. Four months after his seventy-fourth birthday, on June 21, 1834, he passed away, a wealthy man."

Beth asked, "How did the Solitude become part of the zoo?"

Radnor observed how effortlessly his new protégé asserted herself and was pleased she jumped right into the investigation.

"His brother, Granville, came into possession of it first before it passed to other members of the Penn family," said Neville. "The last descendant of William Penn died in 1869. Since then, it had several private owners before the Zoological Society assumed control of the building." Completing her narration, she asked, "Do any of you have other questions or concerns before you set off on your quest?"

The odd phrase *In my Solitude, the secret shall remain forever* crept back into Radnor's thoughts again. Anxious to get started, he said, "Do you have the plans I asked for?"

She went over to the secretary to retrieve them. Handing them over to Radnor, she said, "We're in the process of restoring most of the second floor right now, so all the antiquities have been temporarily moved. One of the rooms is being used for my office. Unfortunately, all the furniture that populated the second floor were reproductions. We have no original artifacts from Penn's time. The first-floor reconstruction is based on the architectural drawings secured from the national archives in Washington so that's what we're hoping to do upstairs."

"Then there's nothing original from Penn's time on this floor either?" asked Radnor.

"Only the fireplace and the secretary," said Neville.

In a broad sweeping motion, Radnor spread the plans across the table. He affixed his jeweler's monocle over certain areas of the building's overall elevation as he studied with particular interest the dimensions of the walls and the floors. Neville seemed amused at first, not getting what Radnor was up to.

The older man continued his examination of the plans for the next ten minutes before he pointed at a section of the superimposed drawing. "Are you doing anything with the attic?"

"Due to its size, we've decided not to renovate the attic. We only use it to store office supplies and not much else. I can show it to you if you'd like?"

"I see," said Radnor in a disappointed tone. Lured closer by a drawing with dual lines that bisected the square between the floors, he pointed to it. "I noticed that none of these elevations contain markings for the dimensions of this floor. Do you know the actual thickness of these header beams?"

"One of the second-floor planks was rotted and needed replacement. It couldn't be any thicker than ten inches, or else it would come through this ceiling." She pointed to the area over their heads.

He nodded thoughtfully before returning to his analysis of the plans. He pointed to the inner walls this time. "Are these walls the same thickness as the outer ones?"

"No, they're thinner." Identifying the unusual legend on one of the first set of plans, she said, "Here is where they show the difference between inner and outer wall thicknesses."

The legend plainly marked all outer walls as being ten inches thick and the inner ones eight.

Always one to find luck in playing his hunches, Radnor was on to something. He was looking for a hiding place large enough to accommodate the object he was searching for. That's why he asked Neville such odd questions about measurements and dimensions.

Beth seemed to have caught on to her new mentor's approach. His predictable expression confirmed as much. They smiled a mutually understood smile at each other.

He rolled up the Solitude's architectural plans and handed them back to Neville. "I think we can proceed now. Let's start with the attic and work our way down?"

"Sure, this way," Neville said.

Confused by this exchange between Radnor and Neville, Carla turned to David and asked, "Okay, do you understand what just happened?"

"I'm not quite sure, but judging from his line of inquiry, I believe the thing he has us looking for is bigger than a breadbox."

Now it was Carla's turn to give David, that look.

The team of investigators completed their exhaustive search of the entire house and found nothing. Thus, they turned their attention to the last area that could produce results—the basement. Neville was hoping it didn't have to come to this, but she saw no alternative. Grabbing the three available flashlights from her office, she dispersed them to David and Radnor keeping one for herself.

"We're also in the middle of a basement and tunnel restoration. We've scheduled the opening within the next few months," said Neville.

Capitalizing on this brief moment with Anne's successor as Neville led them toward the basement, Radnor approached Beth. "Miss Grey, I'm most impressed with your performance so far. I'm enjoying working with you on this project."

"I appreciate the opportunity," Beth replied. It was only now that she got a good look at Giles Radnor. His frumpy hair and horrendous taste in clothing aside, he wasn't a bad-looking man. In fact, she noted similarities between him and Jim West. It was a characteristic she couldn't put her finger on, but there was something more to Giles Radnor than she even gave Jim credit for. That something was chemistry. But like her newfound friend, Carla, she would have to wait for the business at hand to be concluded before she could delve into that subject. Now that she and Radnor were colleagues and working together, her professional and personal life seemed to be moving in the same stimulating direction.

Checking behind the door and past the left window of the main entrance, they found the access to the basement. From the moment they descended the stairs, its musty atmosphere took on an eerie feeling. The stairs were narrow and partially assembled from red and black brick. A single low-wattage lightbulb above their heads was an ominous warning not to proceed any further. Naturally, they all ignored such prudent advice.

Neville took point, followed by Radnor, Beth, David, and finally Carla.

David reached the bottom as Carla took an additional step in that darkened stairway. As she tried to avoid the low ceiling, Carla turned her ankle. Her loud declaration matched the intensity of the pain that shot up her leg. Caught off balance, she listed forward, arms outstretched as she found David's neck. Wrapping her arms around his broad shoulders broke her fall. The fresh smell of her hair was irresistible as was the softness of her cheek against his. When she tried to stand up, David looked into her eyes and placed one arm around her waist as Radnor came to her aid on the other side.

"Are you all right?" asked David.

"None the worse for wear," she said humorously. "I don't think I sprained it, but it's going to be sore for a while."

Carla stretched her long arms around the two men's shoulders as she transferred her weight.

"Let's bring her upstairs," suggested Neville.

"Nothing doing," said a defiant Carla. "We're down here already! Just put me in that chair over there."

Neville looked to David for assurance that her suggestion was the right one, but all she found in his gray eyes was capitulation. Preferring not to engage in that argument, he suggested they set her down in one of the chairs by the maintenance table.

Once Carla was situated, they surveyed their new surroundings. Feeling the wall with his hand, David found a light switch and turned it on. As he did, a dank basement appeared, but it wasn't at all what Radnor expected to find. It was a patchwork of time periods—some flagstone, some brick and mortar, and some cement. It wasn't consistent, and it wasn't pretty, but it was well on its way to being restored as Neville claimed.

The original work done in the basement was of flagstone and mortar. The subsequent maintenance on the more distressed parts of the wall suffered from shoddy workmanship. The remaining basement walls were older with the side buttressed near the stairs yielding to an apparent seepage problem that was likewise repaired in a slipshod manner.

That's when it hit Beth. "I don't remember seeing a kitchen."

Neville offered up the answer. "A home minus a kitchen was an unfortunate example of the federalist architecture of the period. This particular square building was designed without one because a dependency was built where the Small Mammal House now stands."

Confused, David asked, "If the kitchen dependency was so close to the main house, why did he need a tunnel?"

Neville replied, "So the cooks and servants wouldn't have to traipse through the bitter Pennsylvania winter with their bounty between the dependency and the main house."

As David inquired about why the tunnel was built, Radnor was scanning the walls of the basement comparing them with the plans he read. "Martina, do you know if there are any passageways besides the tunnel?"

"None that we could find. Typical of a hidden doorway feature would be a seam of some kind. We never found such a thing in any part of the house."

Undaunted, Radnor scrolled the flashlight's incandescent beam across the ceiling, the floor and the walls to eliminate that possibility for himself. Satisfied he excluded every corner of the basement from having such a surreptitious entrance, they turned their attention to the tunnel.

It was located behind a hidden door, cleverly disguised as part of the west wall, its handle cloaked behind a small piece of removable flagstone. Pulling the door outward, Neville turned on the switch to the makeshift lighting system that ran the entire length of the tunnel. They were able to see down through its straight, cavernous depth. A series of extension cords strung overhead with maintenance lights dangling precariously every eight to ten feet. They cast a dim light over a gravel-laden dirt floor. The pungent oxygen-starved air took a while to overcome.

Neville led them down the dark, narrow scabbard of evenly distributed red and black bricks cut through over forty feet of earth before it came to an abrupt end.

Both Radnor and David had to sacrifice an inch or two from their respective statures to traverse the tunnel. They used their flashlights to examine the walls and ceiling for any sign of a seam to indicate a hiding place. There appeared to be no break, turn, or doorway in this solid wall of brick and mortar for the tunnel's entire length.

Arriving at a solid wall of dirt where the bricks ended, Neville explained the significance of their current location. "Above us is the

Small Mammal House, where the original kitchen dependency for the Solitude once stood."

Beth asked another question Radnor was thinking of but wasn't fast enough to articulate. "Is this the original tunnel built along with the house or is it part of a renovation?"

"The brick construction is all original," responded Neville. "Using flagstone in the tunnel's construction would have made the structure too weak."

"Oh," said Beth, looking down at her feet and noticing how the dirt floor was bone dry. "The basement's walls were plagued with seepage problems, yet this floor isn't even damp. What could account for this?"

"Although the water table is quite low, this area is part of the Schuylkill River watershed. The damaged corner of the basement that has the greatest seepage problem falls in line with a known underground percolation that takes rainwater to the river. The ground here is too high for such percolation to become a problem."

Beth accepted her explanation with a nod.

Disappointed they found nothing, the entourage turned around to exit the confining space. As they made their way out of the tunnel, David kept his flashlight pointed to the ground so he could watch where he was stepping.

In taking that last step before leaving the tunnel's dirt floor, something didn't feel right to David. He shined the beam on the area, but it was only dirt floor. Stepping back into the tunnel a few steps, he detected a slight difference in gradient and give. The area before the threshold felt different under his foot somehow. It was firmer and flatter.

To satisfy his curiosity, he asked, "Does the foundation extend beyond the basement floor?"

"Not that I'm aware of," Neville volunteered. "As I recall, the plans are quite specific for the house itself. The tunnel may have been an afterthought of the designer since he was unaware of the severity of the Philadelphia winters, but the tunnel was built at the same time as the house."

"Well, the dirt floor inside the threshold feels too hard to be just dirt."

Built so close to the Solitude's foundation, a normal pace would have placed a person's foot firmly in the earth and not over what David stepped on.

Intrigued, Radnor knelt over the section of dirt for a closer inspection, paying no heed to his slacks. "Martina, you wouldn't happen to have a small trowel or shovel, would you?"

"Will this do?" Carla called out from her chair. Locating something suitable from the small maintenance table, she handed it to Radnor. It was a medium-size stiff-bristled brush. It wasn't perfect, but it did the job.

"Thanks, Carla," said Radnor as he went to work on the area. Carla saw the concern for her well-being in David's distressed eyes. Then he smiled at her. She returned it.

Addressing the task at hand, David provided light for Radnor as he swept away the top layer of dirt to define the outline of whatever it was David stepped on. The thin layer of dirt yielded readily to Radnor's careful ministrations to reveal a flat, solid stone. It took up a good portion of the tunnel's thirty-inch width. When Radnor cleaned off the dirt going into the tunnel and he was able to determine the length of the anomalous feature, his excitement went into high gear.

He cleared more dirt away to define the boundary of the object; a smooth slab of some sort. Its dimensions were twenty-three inches by fifteen inches. In flicking some of the particles away from the right side of the stone slab, something else appeared. There were three distinct depressions carved into the stone, but Radnor couldn't see clear enough to make anything of it.

"David, could you shine that light over here?"

Dirt still filled in the lines, but it was apparent something was written there. As each letter was cleared of earth's debris, a recognizable phrase popped out at them. In free-flowing font whose phrase was by now quite familiar to David and his Smithsonian colleague, the Penn family motto was proclaimed. *Dum Clavum Teneam.*

"Could you get me a shovel or trowel?" Radnor asked.

"There's a maintenance locker in the Small Mammal House. I'll check there," said Neville. She disappeared for about ten minutes, coming back with a small drain spade. It was just narrow enough for Radnor to excavate the edges of the crude stone slab.

Radnor and David worked to clear a moat around its outline. They were able to feel the lip of the two-inch thick stone lid from which they might gain some purchase.

"Do you have any leverage on your side?" asked Radnor.

"I have about three-quarter's of an inch of clearance here," answered David.

"Let's try it."

Removing his jacket to give himself greater flexibility, David got back into position on the other side. In a coordinated effort, the men managed to lift the stone lid from its centuries-old resting place. The stone box below it contained a treasure long thought to be lost to the annals of history.

Wrapped in the remnants of what looked to be a well-worn great cloak was a substantial rectangular object. From the small glimpse Radnor had, it was an iron strongbox of particular manufacture.

"Could you give me a hand with this, David?"

With a bit of effort, they lifted the covered object out from its stone-hiding place. Careful not to step into the hole, David strode over it as the two men moved the object near the light emanating from the door at the top of the stairs.

Poor lighting in the basement made a proper inspection of this item impossible, so Radnor suggested they move it upstairs for a better look. David agreed, but he had to help Carla up the stairs first. Once she was situated back at the dining room table, he returned to help Radnor.

They set their new prize down over the fireplace's metal hearth. Pushing aside the loose cloth to expose the object, four pairs of eyes suddenly registered a feeling of satisfaction. The dark lid and its crisscrossing metal strips of bulbous rivets now bathed in sunlight for the first time in nearly 225 years, its lid pierced by a large keyhole at its center.

Neville's four guests looked at each other as if they simultaneously got the punch line of a long-standing joke. One that she remained ignorant of.

Getting back onto his feet and placing his hands on his hips, Radnor said, "Well, there's only one way to find out if we've completed our quest."

Without having to wait for him to ask it, David said, "It's in the car. I'll be right back." They all waited for his return.

♪

Chapter Forty – Four

David turned the corner of the room with valise in tow. The tattered, ancient briefcase with its large buckle was the singular item that detracted from his otherwise high sense of style. But under the circumstances, he didn't mind.

Opening the valise, he dug around for the key they hoped would be reunited with its original box. As much as Radnor wanted to be the one to open it, he wouldn't deprive David of his inheritance. When David produced the key and presented it to him, Radnor said, "No, David. The honor's yours."

During his absence, they had cleared off the dining room table, placed a protective cover over the center, and set the strongbox on top of it. David looked at the key in the palm of his hand before he scanned the faces of those around the table, anxious as he was that this key would open the box in front of them. An artifact that outwardly appeared to be the missing box of Klaus von Richthofen. David felt the weight of history descent upon him.

"Okay, here goes." With that, he took the large key by its bow, tipped the post into the keyhole, and plunged it down until the shouldered collar stopped the key's downward progression. It fit like a glove. All that remained now was for him to turn it. Just as Radnor did with the walking stick's silver ring, David rotated the key clockwise. He felt the bit engage as it turned and the mechanism yielded to the key's gentle force. About a quarter of the way around, they all heard the loud click. He continued the key's momentum around the keyhole until he was able to liberate it from the lid. Looking up at everyone, David removed the key and placed it next to the box. Using both hands, he opened the heavy lid.

Radnor's suspicions were justified when the lid was fully opened and the cloth that covered the locking mechanism was exposed. It was adorned with the crest of King James II.

Sitting next to David when he raised the lid, Carla propped herself up on the arm of the chair to get a better look. "I see something. It looks like a rolled up document!"

Wanting to protect whatever it was, Radnor said, "Allow me." He put on his white inspection gloves before reaching inside to retrieve a large scroll. A loose thin ribbon drooped from the oversized wax seal that held it in place. Rolling it out to its fullest size, he asked, "Beth, could you put on those gloves and hold the upper part of this document for me?"

As Beth did so, Radnor carefully guided his jeweler's monocle over the faded writing to see what he could glean from it.

After a few minutes, Radnor returned to his full height. "Interesting. David, do you know what this is?"

"No, but it looks important."

Beth responded with the answer. "It looks like a land grant."

"Very well done, Miss Grey," said Radnor with a sense of growing pride and confidence in his new colleague. "It's really a Crown grant. Take a look at the signature."

They all leaned over to see the name of the signatory in its large flowery font. Written larger than anything else on the document was the name, James II, king of England. What surprised Radnor more was the date right next to the king's name; it read December 11, 1688.

While Radnor and Beth examined the Crown grant, Carla cased the box again to see what other gems it may have contained. Distinguishing a variance in color, she saw something else lying obliquely at the bottom of the box.

"Beth, do you have any more of those white gloves?" asked Carla. Beth searched her bag and located her last pair. She tossed them across the table to Carla who chose to ignore her sore ankle for the moment. "Thanks."

Now it was her turn to literally unfold a mystery with David at her side. She reached in to secure the item. When they were able to thoroughly examine the familiar-looking document, it brought a smile to David's face. It was the same size and material as his letter fragment. To confirm it, he brought out the fragment from his valise to compare the two. Even the creases where the letter was originally folded was a perfect match. This was the missing evidence he was looking for.

The signed second page confirmed their hypothesis as to which William it was addressed.

> *In deference to you and your wife, Cynthia's infinite kindness in accepting my humble proposal with regard to Robert and the Hundred you now possess, I wish to convey my deepest appreciation on behalf of Robert's late mother, whose life was surrendered on that horrible day in '80 at the exact moment God spared him. I also entrust to you these proofs should challenge be made of you. The first is my signet, which for me, is all but worthless now. The second is a key to a box, found by my father and holds an even greater treasure, but only if the Tories are successful. In the event they are not, keep the key in your possession until such time as it is to your advantage to use it. The box currently rests in the bowels of my Solitude, near the tunnel opening. To protect you from my political adversaries, I wish you to destroy this second page upon your comprehension. I have placed its reproduction inside the box as further proof you had not wrongfully absconded from me that which I have freely given.*
>
> *Know that I consider myself to be your most obedient servant,*

The letter was signed John Penn, seal affixed with the signet and dated December 15, 1787.

Radnor wore out a track into the Persian rug beneath him as he rounded the table, staring at the floor, occasionally scratching his head. He was the picture of absolute concentration. When he completed his internal contemplations, he stopped, folded his arms, and looked at everyone.

"Let's proceed from the beginning based on what we know," said Radnor, breaking the silence. "In 1681, William Penn received a proprietorship of land from Charles II to make good on a debt the king owed his father. A year later, the Duke of York extended his proprietorship to include the three lower counties on the Delaware. This had the effect of irritating Lord Baltimore, who also claimed the three lower counties.

"William Penn sails for England in 1684 to take the matter up with the English monarch to resolve the situation. Before he's able to see the king, Charles II dies, and the Duke of York becomes James II in 1685. The new king's reign is plagued with political intrigue and as a consequence, has no time to address Penn's troubles. In light of this discovery, we can assume Penn received an audience and made his case before James II.

"Based on the date of the document, James II signed this Crown grant on the same day he tossed the king's royal seal into the Thames as he made his escape to France. This action was interpreted by the English Parliament as a willful abdication, setting up the Glorious Revolution of William and Mary.

"We now know the dethroned monarch brought the Richthofen box and the Crown grant with him to France because the detailed inventory conducted after his death listed a physically identical box among his belongings. This fact became lost in the consciousness of history until the missing inventory surfaced in 1848.

"Unable to obtain royal satisfaction for his woes, William Penn engaged the legal machinery of the courts in a failed bid to argue his case. Meanwhile, things were not going so well back in the colonies."

Knowing she had more up-to-date information, Beth asked if she could add to the discussion. Surprised, Radnor yielded the floor to Beth. David and Carla sat absorbing the story they helped to uncover. Neville was trying to keep up with all the names, places, and dates coming at her at light speed.

"That's right," Beth began. "This time, the trouble came from the inhabitants of the lower three counties, as they felt their representatives to Philadelphia were being ignored. Penn came up with a new charter in 1701 granting the lower counties autonomy in three years should they wish it. In 1704, that wish came true with the establishment of an independent legislative assembly in New Castle, Delaware."

"Bravo, Miss Grey," Radnor lauded before taking up his line of reasoning again. "Never able to obtain a decisive proprietorship of the lower counties from the Crown, William Penn dies in 1718, passing the fight off to his sons. A fight the ever-increasing evidence suggests, Thomas Penn assumed.

"With the evidence of the second half of the letter, it is more than plausible Thomas Penn is our mysterious agent who, in 1723, finds the Richthofen box with the James II Crown grant at his French château. It was Thomas Penn who must have approached the Delaware General Assembly with this document so he could force them to do his bidding. He could have taken all of Delaware, but he was only interested in the Lewes Hundred."

Tying the threads together, David said, "That makes sense. With the added weight of the Silas Coates letters from 1724, there could be no question it was Thomas Penn. He must have been the namesake of the so-called Penn Resolution."

Beth then brought up the evidence they gleaned from the Delaware Public Archives. "When the resolution passed the General Assembly, Coates resigned in protest and taxes for the Hundred were suspended."

Neville was beyond clueless now moving her eyes from one speaker to the other in a desperate attempt to follow the line of deductions. Right now, it was Radnor. He nodded his agreement to the irrefutable logic of his fellow researcher's conclusions before taking up the narrative again.

"As long as England was still considered the mother country, Thomas Penn could hold the Crown grant over the heads of the General Assembly and lower the boom on their legislative autonomy anytime he wished.

"Then an event occurs in 1753 which upset the balance; The French and Indian War. By 1763, the adventure had saddled the British Parliament with mounting debt, causing them to institute almost ten years of tax measures aimed squarely at the colonies. The one-sided tyranny of revenue began with the Sugar and Currency Acts of 1764 and ended with the final insult, a tax on tea.

"With the evidence we now have in our hands, we can infer that Thomas Penn, bearing witness to what he saw happening around him, informed his son John of the box containing the Crown grant."

Beth chimed in again. "And of the resolution that gave him the Lewes Hundred."

"That's correct," Radnor said in agreement. "Thomas Penn dies the year before the colonies declare independence and three years later, the Confederation Congress passed the Divestment Act of 1779, stripping the Penn's of their remaining proprietorships.

"As a teenager, John must have felt unable to reveal the true status of the Delmarva Peninsula through the Crown grant, hoping the colonies' impending troubles with England would come to a Tory-favored conclusion."

"So that's why the tax records show revenue once again levied against the Lewes Hundred," said Carla excitedly.

"That's a logical assumption," said Radnor as he continued with his deductions. "The letter confirms its author believed this would happen as well.

"One year after Thomas died, the General Assembly of the lower counties, now called Delaware, declared its separation from England. The Second Continental Congress followed suit three weeks later."

David interjected, "Although it would seem Robert held some importance to John, it never actually says Robert's mother was his wife or that Robert was his son. He never indicated who they were or his relationship to them."

Radnor made note of that revelation as surprise registered on everyone's faces.

David pressed on with his thought. "Sometime after 'that horrible day in '80,' when Robert's mother died, John Penn placed Robert in the custody of William and Cynthia West and gave them the property of Lewes-on-the-water in perpetuity. That same year, William West's name appears on the earliest deed for ownership of Lewes-on-the-water."

Radnor wrapped up his summation with one final thought. "John Penn feared the turnabout in the affairs of the colonies following their victory at Yorktown. Over the next couple of years, he must have realized the mounting determination of these *Americans* to make a solid go of becoming a nation separate from England would render his precious documents useless.

"After he finished the Solitude in 1783, he buries this box containing the documents in the tunnel, hoping one day they'd be useful. However, the signing of the Treaty of Paris ending the Revolutionary War drastically changed his fortunes.

"John Penn became a silent witness to the slow evolution of thirteen separate colonies as they became a nation. The declaration was one thing, but witnessing the fledgling United States come together to draft a more complete constitution in 1787, Penn's hopes were ultimately dashed. He understood that the Crown was powerless to dislodge this new nation from its destiny. Not sure how to proceed in this new environment of unity across these new states, Penn returned to England in 1788 to see if anything could be done about his property. He never returned."

Radnor paused, giving Beth her opportunity. "In 1791, the Sussex County seat moved to Georgetown from Lewes, taking away the coastal town's prestige. Lewes became a historical footnote during the War of 1812. Today, only a place called the cannonball house survives to bear witness to this event.

"After a British Frigate destroyed his home during the bombardment of Lewes, on April 7, 1813, Robert West, we assume to be Robert Penn, hired a privateer named Vernon Tunney, to hunt down and destroy the British frigate that destroyed his home and killed his parents.

"I only managed to find one other historical tidbit attached to the West family and this property," offered Beth. She looked at the faces of the small gathering, appearing to crave more. "It's anti-climactic when you think about it."

That last statement earned a sarcastic grimace from Carla before Beth continued.

"A local Lewes newspaper, *The Breakwater Light*, reported that during the great storm of 1889, West's home suffered significant damage requiring massive reconstruction."

Sensing her conclusion, David added, "Perhaps that's why Jim addressed a home renovation again in 1995. He wanted the home's exterior to match the nearby homes in the development."

"Question," Carla injected, "if James II signed and affixed the Great Seal of the Realm onto the Crown grant before he tossed the seal into the Thames, that would prove the document was valid even if it were the same day he abdicated, wouldn't it?"

"True," suggested Radnor, "but because it *was* the very day he forfeited his throne, the English Parliament could choose not to recognize the document's legitimacy. Either way, it would end up being contested in the courts for years."

Unable to contain her curiosity, Neville said, "But the historical record never showed John Penn ever marrying or ever having a son. We know he died a bachelor even though he was a staunch advocated for marriage."

"Then the question arises, why should a confirmed bachelor seek to encourage others to marry when he failed to take his own advice?" asked David, glancing at Carla, who was sporting a suspicious grin.

"Well," said Radnor, summing up, "despite the historical evidence to the contrary, this letter would suggest John Penn may have had a romantic liaison. Based on the tone of the letter, when Robert's unnamed mother was lost in childbirth, the pain he suffered for her loss must have been great. Unable to keep the child for whatever reason, John secreted Robert into the care of William and Cynthia West and passed onto them the coastal plot of land Thomas Penn was able to wrest from the Delaware General Assembly."

Realizing the implications of this line of deduction, David said with incredulity, "Let me get this straight. If what you're saying is true, then this Robert eventually led to my benefactor?"

"I don't know of his later bloodlines, but all the evidence does seem to point in that direction, yes," Radnor said. "Moreover, had the Crown grant been made public in 1724 rather than used to appropriate the Lewes Hundred, something else would've changed dramatically."

"What's that?" asked David.

"Our national ensign would now bear forty-nine stars instead of fifty."

Panning around the room, David caught sight of Beth's declining head, her chin to her chest. "What's wrong, Beth?"

"Jim never knew any of this. Now he'll never know his true legacy."

"Beth, Jim's canon of music will speak to future generations, which is what I believe he wanted in the first place," said David.

The discussion was broken by the thrum of a vibrating cell phone. This time, it belonged to Martina Neville.

"Excuse me a second." Neville slipped away to the next room.

Still trying to compose herself, Beth asked, "What do we do with these new artifacts?"

Radnor replied, "Under the circumstances, I suggest we coordinate with the Smithsonian, the Philadelphia Zoological Society, and the Kensington Museum. All parties must be made aware of our findings." He looked to David for agreement.

David allowed his eyes to dart over to the key that initiated their odyssey and the rejoined Penn letter splayed out on the table. Returning his gaze to Radnor, he offered a yielding smile. For David, there could be only one answer. Yes.

"Please excuse me," said a harried Martina Neville. "I'm due at a scheduled grant meeting in fifteen minutes."

"Of course," said Radnor. "We'll help you take this box and its contents up to your office so you might properly secure it until we determine its disposition."

"I appreciate that Dr. Radnor," she said. "Dr. Whealy, Miss Grey, Dr. Macklin, it's been a real treat spending the day with you all."

Neville's guests assisted her in putting the basement and dining table back into their original configuration before moving all the items they discovered into her office. They took leave of Miss Neville at the front of the Solitude and made their way back to the parking lot.

It was here the four budding colleagues discovered they shared another trait in common besides a good mystery; hunger.

"Since you all did such a fantastic job, dinner's on me," Radnor offered.

Beth snapped her fingers. "How about a cheesesteak? After all, we are in Philly."

It had been years since Radnor allowed himself the enjoyment of his favorite childhood delicacy, so naturally, he thought it a great idea. Carla shrugged, and David just nodded.

"Great! I know the perfect place," Beth volunteered.

The East Coasters' spirited debate as to which place had the best cheesesteak went on for ten minutes, while the Californians shook their heads, folded their arms, and enjoyed the spectacle.

For most of the trip back to Lewes, the ride was quiet. An exhaustive day of discovery and a satisfying meal took the wind out of their desire for small talk.

They were on the road for twenty minutes before David realized he never did confront Carla as to why she came back to the East Coast.

Keeping his concentration on the road, he asked, "Are you going to answer me?"

Carla continued to stare blankly out the window. "Perhaps if I knew the question."

"Why I should find you here all of a sudden? Not that I'm complaining, but don't you have a department to run?"

"Oh, you didn't stick around long enough to witness the fun we had at your father's expense."

Recoiling at the thought of Carla's imaginative idea of fun, he asked, "What did you do?"

"Remember those calls you missed?"

"Yeah?"

"The department heads and I persuaded Cobbett to cancel his original concert schedule and convinced him that it was in his best interest to invite you back, personally."

"I doubt it was that easy."

"It was a piece of cake. All we did was hold him accountable for the mission statement he himself pronounced when he first came to the university. Then we encouraged him to call you to apologize and to invite you back to assume any position in the music department you wished, including his. If he chose not to do what we asked, we showed him the letter of no confidence signed by all of us, directed to the chancellor and the board. I did all the talking while the others stared daggers at him. Up against such implacable pressure in his own office, he capitulated."

Seeing the truth of such a preposterous scenario reflected in Carla's eyes, he realized she sidestepped the question. "That still doesn't explain why you're here."

Carla's head dropped. "I had a meeting with the chancellor a few days later."

Knowing Carla's legendary temper, her horrified chauffeur asked, "They didn't fire you, did they?"

She let loose with a mighty laugh. "I wouldn't exactly call it a firing."

"What would you call it then?"

"Let's just say I'm now in a position to cancel Cobbett's vision and to replace it with one that aligns with the desires of the faculty and the students."

"How did you manage that?"

"The chancellor told me Cobbett accepted a position with the LSO, cleaned out his desk, and was gone in two days. He didn't even make an attempt to say goodbye, he just left."

"Okay, so who did the chancellor appoint to replace him?"

Carla's unnerving smirk told him everything he needed to know.

"You?! Not that you don't deserve consideration, but the bureaucratic mentality of university brinkmanship being what it is, I would've thought the board to consider Julia or Henry."

Carla chuckled. "Henry is now pestering Peggy as we speak. I told him it was temporary, depending on the outcome of my trip here."

"Ah, so now we come to it. You want me to return to my old position and work for you, is that it?"

"I've been authorized by the chancellor to tell you that the position of music department dean is officially yours." Rubbing her sore ankle, she added, "All you have to do is say yes."

"You could have made that request over the phone," he said with irritation. "That still doesn't explain why you took time off to come here."

"Stop evading the question," said Carla, matching his curt responses with her own. "Now, are you coming back or not?"

Arguing with Carla and her one-track mind was futile. David pursed his lips, giving her the impression he was thinking about it.

"I received an offer from the dean of music at the University of Delaware, but I declined. Told her I was only interested in popularizing West's music. As dean, Dr. Christian said she could allow me the flexibility to do so as professor emeritus."

"What did you tell her?"

"I told her I'd think about it. Meanwhile, they asked permission to copy some of his music so they could premiere it at next year's concert season opener. I'm working with them to make that happen right now."

"That's great, David," she said with disinterest. Trying to find a reasonable compromise in comfort for her sore ankle, she stretched her foot out over the dashboard allowing the material of her pant leg to slide down. Her flawless copper-toned leg now exposed all the way to her thigh, she threw out her trump card. "I'm quite sure Jennifer and Preston, Clayton and Renatta, and the rest of the students you've abandoned would love to hear it."

That did it. Fully aware of how and where to hit David at his most vulnerable spot, she made him cringe. Her words were soft-spoken yet carried a powerful sting.

The idea of returning as dean of music had its appeal, yet he felt obligated to the memory of James Burton West to get his music published, marketed, and performed. He couldn't do that and teach at the same time. David believed his students would forgive him for that.

An uneasy silence returned as David ducked the question and cast a gazing eye toward the side view mirror at Beth's Jeep behind them. Then he looked ahead as he followed Radnor's orange metallic '55 Chevy 3100.

Beth's Jeep quickly passed them on the right as they were approaching the exit ramp for Delaware's Highway 1. Beth turned her head to look at Carla in the passenger seat of David's car. Slowly cruising by, a pleasant smile graced her lips as she waved at her new friend.

That smile reminded Carla of how Jim sketched his friend, Ernie. The kind of reassuring smile that made you feel warm, welcome, and comfortable. Carla returned it along with a gentle wave. Beth and Radnor continued south on I-95 toward Washington.

When they were leaving the restaurant, David noticed Radnor rapidly thumbing his smartphone, no doubt sending his intern another text with more homework for her to do. Her new assignment was to locate any proof that John Penn was ever married or if he ever had children. Now it was up to him and his new hire, Beth to document their adventure and to work out the disposition of their latest discoveries—the Richthofen box and its key, the rejoined Penn letter, the signet ring, and the Crown grant.

Rounding the cloverleaf exit, the two vehicles disappeared from their vision. Merging onto the southbound stretch of road that would take them home, Carla said, "Beth seems to have found a new male companion."

"You mean Radnor?"

"Sure, why not? Didn't you see how smitten he was when she inserted aspects of the storyline with her findings? He didn't seem to mind judging from the look in his eyes."

"I didn't notice."

"I'm not surprised."

The better part of the next hour expended, twilight gave way to evening. The lights of the Lewes area crested over the coastal highway bridge just before the 404/9 intersection. Carla became semiconscious enough to experience the electric tingle of a foot going to sleep.

Peeking through narrow slits, she watched David as he made the turn into Five Points and the road home. The turn caused a jolt of pain to run down the entire side of her leg. Noting the ample space on David's lap, to say nothing of how warm her naked leg would feel there, she preceded to move her tender ankle onto David.

He didn't mind at first until she slouched her body further down on the seat, resting her head on the passenger door. Carla's long hair splayed out across her shoulders and her disheveled pantsuit jacket. The top button of her blouse popped open, increasing the amount of visible cleavage. Ignoring the pant leg material that scrunched into her hip, she slid her foot further up his thigh. Carla mumbled in a half-awake voice, "Ah, that's better."

Surprised at her brazen move, he gave her a quick glance to observe her elongated form. "I'm glad you're comfortable," he said with wry sarcasm. "We're almost home."

Her voice still groggy, she replied, "Good, then you can rub my foot." She gave him a gentle nudge with it as a signal she didn't want him to wait till they got home before he got started.

He reached down and began to rub her sore ankle with his large, powerful hand. His firm but gentle caress moved to her toes, sending a warm rush of relief throughout her entire body. As David's thumb massaged the sole of her foot, the soft smoothness of her skin felt wonderful in his hand. His artful ministrations lasted the remainder of the short trip home.

Once home and parked, he rounded the car to the passenger side to help Carla out.

"How's your ankle?"

"Not bad, but I could use some help into the house," she said, reaching out for David's assistance. She unbuttoned her jacket to keep from ripping it. Supporting her as they went, David and Carla made their way to the front door, her head on his shoulder, her arm around his waist.

Putting the key in the door, he turned it as he turned to Carla. Her deep-charcoal eyes trained on him in a seductive, unrelenting manner. Making their way through the threshold, Carla maneuvered in front of him and tossed both arms around his neck.

Officially out of excuses, he could no longer maintain the superficial barriers he kept between himself and Carla. Beth was no longer a factor. He was no longer Carla's boss. And he still had his home in California, which he didn't wish to part with. The walls he insisted on erecting against such an entanglement collapsed. Walls Carla metaphorically kicked down for good.

The door didn't even have time to close all the way when Carla closed the gap between them with a long, deeply passionate, and all-embracing kiss. Surrendering to an inescapable desire of his own, he returned it.

Married couples would envy what we have!

♪

Chapter Forty – Five

She'd been slogging away at the keyboard all evening trying to hammer out her latest article. Spotlighting UC Davis and their yearlong association with the musical enigma named James Burton West, Ashley Sobon made it her responsibility to keep the public up-to-date on every new piece the university debuted. And the public responded with intense interest.

Completing the season's summary, she printed out her article to give it a proper edit. Errors invariably made their unwelcome appearance on the printed page, mistakes she easily glossed over on the computer screen. Something wasn't quite right. Reading through the article, she attempted to identify the trouble spot.

A Musical Season with James Burton West
By Ashley Sobon

Last Friday night, the UC Davis Symphony Orchestra officially closed out the year's phenomenal concert season with the Ninth Annual Faculty Solo Showdown.

For the second year in a row, the winner was the dean. But this year, the laurels went to the university's new dean, Dr. Carla Macklin, who brought down the house with her poignant debut performance of James Burton West's Symphonic Poem *The Piano's Tears*.

Honorable mentions went to Dr. Julia Winslow for her whimsical interpretation of West's *Caprice for Cello and String Orchestra*, originally written for his son Ethan. And Dr. Antara Singh for her thrilling performance of a piece written for West's younger son, Alexander, a *Violin Concerto in E Minor.*

But the real story is the university's decision to adopt the works of an esoteric composer who managed to remain quite anonymous in this social-media-saturated society we've managed to create. Thankfully, university officials at Davis have assumed sponsorship of this man's work.

Anyone fortunate enough to have heard one of his pieces would agree, the university did a great thing for the average purveyor of orchestral music. The soaring popularity of West's music is remarkable when one considers he was a complete unknown a year ago.

The university credits Dr. David Whealy and Dr. Carla Macklin for their joint discovery and yearlong investigation into the scores this incomparable composer left us.

The orchestra's most devoted fans would remember how they were first introduced to West's music through his *String Quintet.* Two months later at the winter concert series, a fortuitous encore featured his symphonic poem *Hymn* to critical acclaim.

From the outset of the New Year, the music department took a daring chance by scrapping their scheduled concert lineup to showcase West's music exclusively. But the gamble paid off as evident by the packed venues everywhere his music was performed.

At a special concert hosted by the university, the scope of West's compositional prowess and eclectic taste was perfectly captured by the exceptional talent harbored by the UC Davis Symphony Orchestra.

From his quaint, Rossini-like *Overture for Winds* that opened the concert, to his full-on orchestra entr'acte the *Acheronian Overture*, West's music demonstrates a boundless penchant for varying styles. The climax of the evening was his Symphonic Poem *Romanza* with its touching *sotto voce* finale.

The thrilling encore, a spirited fife and drum work with orchestral accompaniment entitled *Patriot's Forge*, received a standing ovation even before the closing chords were sounded.

Several of West's chamber pieces opened the spring concert series this year. Warmly received was a chamber string arrangement of his highly acclaimed *String Quintet in F minor*. The debut of the *Double Reed Sextet*, a wind quintet, and a string quartet, completed the first half of the evening's musical extravaganza.

The second half of the program capped off the series in grand style with another West overture and his only symphony in a major key, the *Symphony No. 3 in D*. The work's brevity notwithstanding, it's destined to become a favorite staple of the repertoire of symphony orchestras across the country.

As we learn more about this devoted husband and father, reluctant composer, and man of letters, we find James Burton West to have been a man in possession of a shy disposition, generous spirit, and a mild nature belying the darker angels of his tortured soul.

According to Dr. Whealy, tragedy left an indelible mark on West throughout his lifetime, which reflected in his work. The music that exuded from his pen, as a result of the loss of his childhood friend and his family, was fueled by and made richer with the power of his anguish.

For nineteen years, James Burton West lived a solitary existence, living only to answer his family's call to compose the music they knew was locked inside of him. And compose he did.

With opus numbers that reached well into the 200s, the concertgoing public will reap the benefits of the fruits of West's compositional genius for years to come.

West's music is not only making a splash on the university circuit, but with major orchestras from around the country.

In an ironic twist, Dr. Whealy's former boss, William Tipton Cobbett III, the current principal director of the London Symphony Orchestra, has requested copies of West's music for an upcoming performance.

Agreeing to stay on as professor emeritus, Dr. Whealy continues to champion West's work here at Davis, but he's also doing so on the East Coast by special arrangement with the University of Delaware.

Faculty Solo Showdown champion and new dean, Dr. Carla Macklin has already chosen her theme for next year's concert schedule. Not surprisingly, along with showcasing women composers throughout history, an ongoing feature of such concerts will be a piece or two by James Burton West.

In the practice hall of the music building, the celebration for another successful year was winding down. As the crowd was thinning out, I had a rare opportunity to depose the new dean about her vision for the music department, her choice of venue for next year's concert schedule, and to broach the subject of James Burton West.

"The faculty's decision to feature West's music rather than continue with the current concert schedule was universal," said Macklin, "It was an easy decision." The dean went on to discuss how her esteemed colleague Dr. Whealy had discovered this man and his work through an unexpected inheritance.

Through their mutual investigation, they learned much about this multifaceted and humble man, but it was the treasure trove of autograph scores, the likes of which would rival the greatest composers, which speaks most directly about the makeup of this enigmatic man.

"When Dr. Whealy asked us to examine these unfamiliar scores, we were astounded. It was as though he discovered the complete works of Johannes Brahms when no one had ever heard of him," Macklin said. "We have an obligation to the public to premiere this vital contribution to the standard repertoire. University officials should be lauded for agreeing with that position."

Macklin was more secretive about her immediate plans. Always on the go, Macklin did admit she was on her way to the airport in the morning. She never indicated where she was going.

If the rumors were true, there's only one place she would be headed.

When she got down to the bottom of her article to read the last sentence and its previous paragraph, she recognized what troubled her. Shaking her head, she rapidly hit Backspace until the offensive idea was removed in its entirety.

Resorting to speculation about someone's personal life in the same article designed to attract readers to another idea smacked of yellow journalism. She could easily maintain such fanciful suppositions on her own, but she wasn't about to put her journalistic reputation on the line for it. It just wasn't the kind of journalism she pursued.

Something more important troubled her. She was unable to penetrate the personality behind the music that was James Burton West. To do that, she needed to interview his discoverer. To do that, she'd have to fly to the other coast, where Dr. Carla Macklin was now, for some reason.

Which brought her back to the original, suggestive topic she'd deleted.

Sobon thought to herself, *What if...*

Chapter Forty – Six

David couldn't have asked for a more perfect summer day as the morning sun warmed his face. The tart scent of salt air filled his nostrils and the light breeze that carried it brushed his cheek. He looked a bit out of character standing there in his khaki shorts, polo shirt, and sneakers.

He had the rods, the tackle, the bait, and two tickets in hand for a day's worth of striper fishing with the charter less than five minutes away from launch. The only thing missing was Carla.

When they left the house for the wharf, she forgot her sunglasses on the kitchen island. She dropped David off to purchase the tickets so they would be ready to board when she got back.

"Hey, are you coming with us or not?" asked the first mate. "We're about ready to cast off."

The sudden appearance of his new vehicle racing into the parking lot settled that question. She rapidly pulled into one of the unmarked dirt parking spots close to the charter's berth. The SUV bleeped as Carla locked it with the electronic key before she ran for the boat.

"Hey, wait up!"

David couldn't suppress his smile as he observed the way she ran up to the dock. She was a siren in motion. Carla's alluring yellow hot pants and matching bikini top were covered with a light black and yellow striped summer blouse. Her long black hair flew effortlessly behind her as she ran, but that's not the part of her anatomy that kept David's undivided attention. Carla's long, well-toned legs were pure poetry as she moved.

Trying not to make it obvious he was staring, he couldn't tear his eyes away as she boarded the vessel. "You certainly cut that close."

"At least I made it," she said giving him a hug. "Now that's more like it."

"More like what?"

"I perceived your handsome gray eyes taking in the wildlife," she said with comedic intent. "Judging from that silly grin, you must've liked what you saw."

Caught staring at her without a compelling alibi, he quietly admitted his indiscretion. "Can you blame me? After all, I believe you half-expected me to notice *the wildlife*."

Carla let a slight giggle escape. "Only because you recently discovered how much I crave your attention."

Taken by her irrepressible personality, David hugged her back, caressed her cheek, and smiled. "You're precious."

Their intimate moment lost when the engine roared to life, the boat initiated its leisurely move starboard-aft away from the dock. Once clear, the captain ordered it ahead toward the Roosevelt Inlet and into Breakwater Harbor.

Moving slowly in the calm of the canal, Carla noticed a large blue heron descending upon one of the pilings. A vanguard of seagulls provided the charter's escort as it lumbered its way through the canal. Standing next to David with her arms still wrapped around him, Carla studied the water. It was decidedly darker and less blue than the Pacific.

"You know, aside from our faculty trip to Catalina, I haven't been out fishing like this since my father took me out to Puget Sound for tuna and steelhead."

"And I'll bet you landed the big ones."

"I sure did. My mom would take our catch of the day and make the best tuna cakes you ever tasted!"

"I'm not partial to tuna cakes myself. Have you ever tried your luck with salmon?"

"When I was little, my dad used to take me to the Skykomish when the salmon were running. We caught our fair share, but he usually got the big ones."

Turning her head to look at David, she donned a thoughtful expression as though she was about to wax philosophic again. David knew something was coming, but he wasn't expecting this.

"I received a text from the university executive board while I went back for my glasses. They wanted you to know they're happy you accepted their emeritus proposal and thanked you again for guest conducting the Faculty Solo Showdown this year."

"It was your doing, you know," he said with a touch of levity. "Using my students as leverage to maneuver me into a position you *knew* I couldn't refuse."

Carla just grinned and gave him a squeeze as she kissed his cheek. "David, your students are the notes of your life. You would've come to the decision on your own anyway. You don't need me to help you make the right choice."

"On that note, I think you're right."

With a chuckle, she said, "Although your wisdom is sketchy at times, it's spot-on today."

David grinned broadly and gave Carla a little squeeze. Still holding her close as the charter made its way beyond the inlet and into the open bay, he said, "Carla, I'm sorry."

"Sorry? For what?"

"I should've opened up about my feelings for you a long time ago. I didn't want to ruin our Thursday evening get-togethers or our friendship. I didn't want to lose that."

"Ah, but this time, it's different."

"You're right, it will be." His thoughts went back to that first kiss and how their relationship blossomed so quickly over the past six months. That's when he turned, cradled her face in both hands, and gave her a passionate kiss.

Married couples would envy what we have!

Carla basked in the new direction their relationship was headed. His gesture of affection was all she needed to confirm that difference. With the pressures of academic leadership off her shoulders, for the time being, her soul felt ecstatic for the first time in months. Being with her man for the summer without the rigors of intense research was going to be a treat, and she was going to make sure they both enjoyed every second of it.

Still clinging to each other, they both watched the shore sink into the distance. She thought of their adventure last year and how well David acquitted himself to it. As she did so, a thought crept back into her mind.

"David, have you ever thought about taking over from where his dad left off?"

The question took him by complete surprise. This was another of Carla's thoughtful subject changers. Most of the time, she did so in a calculating fashion, but he didn't believe she meant to do it now.

"Left off where?"

"Remember when you said your father traced your family's roots back to 1818 before the trail was lost? Why don't you take up the challenge of finding out what became of them?"

"Perhaps."

"You could begin with that early great-great-great-to-the-power-nine Whealy, what's his name? Payton?"

"You remembered."

Giving him the corner lip smirk, she said, "You *were* quite thorough in your description. You could find out if his wife, Diane's singing career ever amounted to anything. Maybe you could find out more about her parents, Richard and Elizabeth Marlow. Were there any buildings Richard created that are still standing? How about that sole Methodist in your family? Do you think you could dig up anything more on Elizabeth? The archives might even have more source material from your father's time. The technology is certainly better?"

"I might have to do that. I could get Beth to help me," he suggested playfully.

Carla wasn't fazed at all by her former rival, especially in light of David's last kiss.

"Why not? In fact, with her connections and resources at the Smithsonian, you might get lucky."

No longer shocked, David offered her a side lip smirk at her gratuitous quip with the not-so-discreet double meaning.

The charter had made it into the gently rolling water of the Delaware Bay, when Carla queried, "What about Payton and Diane's other children? Do you know who they were? If any descendants of the other son or daughter survive today?"

"I don't know why he stopped looking into that side of the family's history, but he did. I suppose I could resurrect his effort if I had the time or the interest to do so."

"Well, you have the time now, don't you? And based on what I've seen you do, I have no doubt that you'll find them if they exist," she said optimistically.

"Isn't it strange how this entire episode began with that lawyer's letter?"

"I don't think a lawyer's letter would have extricated you from your academic obligations." Feigning the pretense of thought, she added, "No, I believe the credit for that goes to James Burton West for his original correspondence."

"Oh, you mean the letter sealed with wax and stamped with that lopsided butterfly?"

"A lopsided what?" Astounded at his inability to see something so painfully obvious, she asked, "Is that what you thought you saw?"

"Sort of, yeah."

Carla borrowed a pen from one of the deck hands and retrieved a napkin from the charter's snack bar. She quickly sketched a respectable likeness of the so-called lopsided butterfly and presented it to David for his inspection.

"Is this a close facsimile?" she asked.

"It looks like it, sure."

"Look at it again and think real hard. What was the name of your benefactor again?"

The comical look on David's face dissolved as the drawing's allusion to a butterfly evaporated and was replaced by a monogram. Finally seeing it, he noticed for the first time the *J* next to the *B*. Then on the bottom he made out a convincingly unmistakable *W.*

Then he gave her…that look.

Epilogue

The day dawned on a pristine Sunday morning in that one stoplight town in southern Delaware. For an entire city block in each direction, the process of renovation was well underway. The town had begun to restore its center to its former colonial glory. Outside the restoration's cordon at the southern end of town were a few restored Victorian homes. Beyond the southernmost home was the empty lot from which a gray squirrel had been shuttling back and forth across the street running his various squirrel errands.

The furtive little guy had been tempting fate all morning. His fluid movements stopped periodically as if playing the child's game of "red light, green light." The erratic motion of his flinching tail, while his body remained motionless, was typical of the species when signaling danger.

Spying a large tomcat out of the corner of its eye, the squirrel expedited his return across the street and into the empty lot that was overgrown with weeds and crabgrass. The lot was surrounded on three sides by a thicket of trees. On the north side was the last Victorian home with a wraparound deck where the tomcat was perched. On the south side was an old two-story cottage so infested with wood rot that a stiff breeze looked capable of blowing the entire structure down to its foundation. Toward the back of the lot was a sparse population of archaic tombstones. Many of them were set off-kilter or faced in odd directions. Some pieces had long since broken off, and the majority of headstones were so badly weathered the writing on them was hardly legible. The lot's general appearance was one of neglect.

Sensing its opportunity, the tomcat bounded off the porch in a frantic effort to chase after the squirrel that had darted into the maze of monuments. The more agile squirrel managed to evade his pursuer by executing a serpentine route through the strange obstacle course to find his refuge behind an ancient marble stone.

The gray rodent never saw the blue and gold history marker as he scurried past. And judging from its current state of disrepair, the human population seemed as ambivalent to its message. The marker was placed to denote the original location of the state's first Methodist church. The old church had long since been torn down and relocated, but its cemetery remained. The sign was partially hidden by foliage, which was indicative of how this cemetery was dismissed from the thoughts of its present-day citizens.

Most of the headstone slabs were about an inch thick and shaped like Halloween mockups with a curved crest and curved lettering to accentuate the name of the person buried there.

This particular white marble headstone, the one the squirrel used as a barrier between himself and the hungry tomcat, was situated in an obscure location not visible from the road but close enough to an oak tree to effect a quick escape.

The only writing plainly visible on it were the years of birth and death, *1803* and *1858* respectively. The numerals for each day had long since eroded to the point of illegibility. The month of birth was entirely obliterated, and the elements so damaged the middle vowel for the month of death, it looked more like a gutted oval. It could've read *Jan* or *Jun*. Spelled out along the curvature of the headstone's crest and still legible by an observer at the proper angle was the name *Elizabeth Marlow.*

As the squirrel zipped past the headstone making a beeline for his favorite tree, it happened to break the oak sapling growing just below and in front of the dates. In doing so, an oval relief was revealed containing a coat of arms presumably belonging to the grave's occupant. The coat of arms sported a knight's helmet facing left with an ornate plume emanating from its top and spreading out to encircle the shield below it. The shield was bisected by a curved line. At each corner atop the shield was a prancing leopard. Centered at the bottom of the shield was a third prancing leopard. The scroll that underscored the shield and plume was just evident, yet the name contained within its thin borders remained quite legible.

It read simply… *West.*

These facts meant nothing to the gray rodent. He didn't concern himself with human trifles scribbled on old stone slabs. He didn't concern himself with the restoration activity up the street either. The only fact that wasn't lost in the mind of the gray squirrel was that he just managed to escape the claws of the tomcat as he darted up the tree. Safe yet again. For the time being.

Author contact information:

Michael DeStefano
c/o Libretti Press
PO Box 413
Ludlow, MA 01056

e-mail: LibrettiPress@yahoo.com

CPSIA information can be obtained
at www.ICGtesting.com
Printed in the USA
FSHW01n1751200618
49502FS

9 781640 826212